THE
PROFILER

Book **One** of the
Munro Family Series

CHRIS TAYLOR

LCT Productions Pty Ltd
18364 Kamilaroi Highway, Narrabri NSW 2390

ISBN. 978-1-925119-01-5

The Profiler is a work of fiction. Names, characters, places, brands, media and incidents either are the product of the author's imagination or are used fictitiously. Any resemblance to actual persons, living or dead, events, or locales, is entirely coincidental.

Published in the United States of America

DEDICATION

This book is dedicated to the late Len Wilde who was my most ardent supporter and to my husband Linden, who has never stopped believing in me.

ACKNOWLEDGMENTS

There are so many people who have helped make this book possible. A world of thanks must go to my friend and fellow author Kylie Griffin, who encouraged me and supported me every step of the way. I would also like to thank Angela Bissell, critique partner extraordinaire, and a girl who loves the Munro family as much as I do.

My editor, Pat Thomas, who is the best editor in the world. She is amazing. To Damon Za for my fantastic cover. My sister, Nicole Guihot, for her excellent editorial comments and suggestions. Nic, I hope you like the final result.

To the fantastic writer organizations such as Romance Writers of Australia, Romance Writers of America and Romance Writers of New Zealand for all the help, support and encouragement they offer new and aspiring writers, including me.

To my readers, thank you for your support and love for the Munro family. Your encouragement and enjoyment make this journey all worthwhile.

And lastly, to my friends and family, especially my husband and children. Thank you for putting up with late dinners and even later conversations as I've emerged day after day from the sometimes scary but always enthralling world I've created on my computer.

A psychopathic killer is stalking the women of Sydney...

Federal Agent Clayton Munro, a criminal profiler with the Australian Federal Police (AFP), has been called upon to assist in hunting down a vicious murderer who is intent upon carving up his victims whilst they're still alive. Guilt-stricken over his wife's suicide, Clayton's forced to set aside his personal issues in order to focus on the case.

Detective Ellie Cooper is also no stranger to heartache. Pregnant and abandoned at the altar by a fiancé intent on pursuing a career with the AFP, her opinion of the elite body of officers is anything but favorable. Angered when her boss orders her to partner with the Fed, she's determined not to cut him any slack.

But women are dying on the streets of western Sydney and the pressure is mounting to find the person responsible.

Will Clayton and Ellie be able to put aside their animosity and work together to catch a killer before it's too late? And what about the special fascination the killer seems to have with Ellie...

THE
PROFILER

PROLOGUE

Bradley Cole smoothed the doll's silky, blond hair with a hand that wasn't quite steady. He loved the fair ones. They were his favorites. They were the ones he tucked in beside him in bed at night. The ones that kept him safe.

Sometimes.

He leaned over and pressed a kiss to the hard, plastic forehead.

The door to his bedroom flew open and slammed against the wall. He cringed at the look on his mother's face. With surreptitious movements, he pushed the doll further under the bedclothes and prayed she wouldn't notice.

"What have you got there, you disgusting little boy? Don't tell me you have one of those filthy dolls in your bed. How many times have I told you boys don't play with dolls? Bradley Cole, you are a naughty, naughty boy."

She stumbled closer, close enough so that he could see the redness that rimmed her eyes. He almost gagged on the stench of alcohol and stale body odor.

Her cheap cotton nightdress flapped around her large frame. She collapsed onto the side of his bed and the steel frame groaned in protest. She reached out and tore off the bedclothes, exposing him to her sharp-eyed gaze.

"What have we here?" she crooned. Her gaze landed on the collection of dolls beside him. Her eyes went wild with excitement.

Terror liquefied his limbs. His stomach clenched.

1

"Well, well, well. You *have* been a naughty boy." Her fist caught him plumb on the cheek. He gasped from the pain. Tears burned his eyes.

"And now we have tears from the sissy boy. A ten-year-old who plays with dolls and cries like a girl. What am I going to do with you?"

She tut-tutted and then hauled herself to her feet. When she turned back to face him, her expression was as icy as her voice.

"Down to the basement. Now."

Bradley froze. He thought fleetingly of making a dash for the phone that sat amidst the clutter on the hall table and then remembered the other times—lots of other times—when he'd dialed the police only to be told not to waste their time and if he made a nuisance of himself again, there'd be consequences.

"I *said*, get up."

She loomed over him. Her fetid breath turned his stomach. Her fist poised for another strike and his fear ratcheted up another notch. Moments later, his bladder gave way.

"You stinking little boy. You're going to pay for that. Do you think I have nothing better to do than to wash your stinking sheets?"

With vicious fingers, she dug into his shoulder and hauled him from the bed. He blinked away the pain, knowing it was nothing to what he'd be forced to endure in the basement.

"Now, get down there like I told you and make it quick. Real quick."

CHAPTER 1

Detective Ellie Cooper climbed out of the unmarked police car and waited for her partner, Luke Baxter, to come around from the passenger side. Drawing her jacket tighter around her slight frame, she tucked an errant strand of chestnut hair behind her ear. The afternoon was cold and dreary, just as it had been the day she'd buried her son. Three years today. It felt like yesterday.

Memories she'd tried hard to hold at bay all day threatened to bring her undone. Familiar pain and anger, combined with deep loss and a yearning for answers surged through her. She compressed her lips against the sudden rush of emotions and made an effort to push the thoughts aside. She was at work. Now wasn't the time to fall apart.

As usual, she took refuge in her job. She flashed her badge at the huddle of fresh-faced, uniformed policemen who stood inside the blue and white, checked crime scene tape that cordoned off part of the scrubby bank of western Sydney's Nepean River. Not far away, photographers and TV crews haggled over positions.

"We're Detectives Cooper and Baxter. Penrith Local Area Command," Ellie said to one of the young officers. "We're here about a head."

The officer nodded and offered his hand. "I'm Constable Jacobs, Richmond Police Station. I took the call from Griffin."

"Griffin?" Ellie asked.

"Yeah, the bloke who found it." His gaze flicked toward

the crowd and his voice turned dry. "And presumably the one who called the media."

"Where is he?"

"I put him in the back of the squad car. I thought he'd gotten enough camera exposure for today."

Luke and Ellie looked toward the police cruiser. The profile of a man seated in the back seat could be seen in the late afternoon light.

"What's his story?" Luke asked.

Jacobs consulted his notebook. "He came down after lunch for a spot of fishing. Apparently, the fish were biting, so he didn't notice the bag right away."

"The bag?" Ellie asked.

"Yeah, the head's wrapped in a trash bag." He glanced at his notebook again. "Anyway, he was here about an hour when he had to take a leak. Walked over there a bit."

Jacobs pointed in the direction of a stand of bottlebrush trees nearby. Their scrubby branches provided effective cover from the road twenty metres away. "That's where he says he found it."

Ellie was relieved the area had been included within the taped barrier and nodded toward the young constable. "Good work on securing the scene, Jacobs."

He flushed. "Thanks, Detective."

She looked at Luke. "Let's go and talk to our fisherman."

"I'll get the camera from the car," he responded. "We need to get a few pictures before we lose the light." He glanced back at Jacobs. "Anyone call the morgue?"

"Yes. I got onto them straight after I called it into the station."

"Good thinking, Constable. Shows initiative," Ellie said. "Why don't you join me while I talk to our witness?"

Eagerness lit up the young constable's eyes. "That would be awesome. I can't wait to apply for the detective's course. I know I've only just come out of the Academy, but it's all I've ever wanted to do and—"

"Jacobs," she interrupted gently, "let's just get on with it, okay?" Ellie hid her amusement. She wasn't *that* old that she

4

couldn't remember feeling exactly the same way.

Even in the fading light, Elle saw the mortification that flooded his expression and felt a twinge of guilt, but they were wasting time, and in homicides, every second counted.

Turning abruptly, she made her way through the tall grass toward the squad car that was parked a short distance away. Jacobs stumbled behind her.

Ducking under the police tape, she came up to the vehicle and rapped her knuckles on the glass.

The man she presumed was Bill Griffin unwound the window and stared up at her with wary blue eyes. His wild gray hair was windblown and in desperate need of a shampoo. Grizzled cheeks covered in a rough beard emphasized the belligerent thrust of his chin. He smelled like fish, river mud and body odor. A damp hessian bag lay on the ground near the car, along with a fishing rod and tackle box.

"Mr Griffin? I'm Detective Cooper." Ellie indicated Jacobs behind her. "I think you've already met Constable Jacobs?"

"Yeah. I already told 'im everythin'."

"Okay, but we've got a head lying in a trash bag over there and so far, you're the only witness."

He shot a furtive glance at the hessian bag and suddenly his reticence made sense.

"I'm not from fisheries," she added. "I couldn't care less whether you have a license, how many fish you have in there or how big they are. That's between you and them. All I'm interested in is how a woman's head came to be lying in a bag under a tree near the river." She gave him a hard look. "You got that?"

Griffin gave a reluctant nod and his gaze slid away. "It's just like I told 'im." He gestured with a dirty finger to where Jacobs stood beside Ellie. "I was doin' a spot of fishin', like I always do. Right 'ere, every Friday. Fish were bitin' good. I'd gone through 'alf me bait already and I'd only been 'ere an hour."

He paused to scratch a scab on his arm. "I 'ad to take a

piss, just like I told the constable. I pulled in me line and left it on the bank with me tackle box. Then I wandered over to them trees over there. That's when I found it." He gave a shudder. "Frightened the shit outta me."

"What made you open the bag?" Ellie asked, pulling out her notebook.

Griffin shrugged and looked away. "I dunno. Just thought I'd take a look."

Ellie knew the area was renowned for break and enters and petty thefts. More than likely, he'd hoped to find something he could sell.

She gave him another hard look. "What did you do then?"

"I picked it up. It was bloody 'eavy. Carried it a ways over there, toward me gear."

"Then you opened it."

The man bristled. "Got curious, that's all. Nothin' wrong with that." He shuddered again. "Wish to Christ I 'adn't. That thing's gonna give me nightmares for months."

"Can you show me exactly where you found it?"

Not giving him time to refuse, she opened the door and waited for him to step out. She followed closely behind as he walked over to the stand of bottlebrush trees. The night was closing in. Light would soon become an issue.

Luke jogged up beside them. Ellie turned to face him.

"We need to get forensics out here with some lights," she said. "It's my guess it's just been dumped here, but you never know what you might find. On more than one occasion, a cigarette butt at the scene's been enough to nail a killer."

Luke issued a brief smile. "Yeah, on *CSI*, at least." His expression turned serious. "I'll give the boss a call. See what he's organized."

Luke pulled out his cell phone. Ellie caught up to the fisherman.

"Just 'ere, it was. Right near the trunk of that one." He pointed to an area at the base of one of the bottlebrushes. There was a faint indentation where the grass had been flattened.

Ellie waited for Luke to finish on the phone before calling out to him.

"Bring your camera over here." She indicated the flattened area. "This is where our fisherman says he found it."

Luke closed the short distance between them and came to a standstill beside the witness. He leveled the man with a hard look.

"When did you call the media?"

Griffin's gaze skittered away and he ducked his head. "It wasn't me that called 'em."

Luke snorted. "Right, they just happened to magically appear." He gave the fisherman a hard look. "You want to hope you don't have anything in that fishing bag of yours that you shouldn't. We might not be from fisheries, but it doesn't mean we don't know where to find them."

The man opened his mouth to protest again and Luke cut him off. "Whether you did or whether you didn't, I don't give a damn. This is our show now. It's a murder investigation and we won't stand for any interference—from you or the media. Got that?"

The man's gaze fell to his feet. He nodded with reluctance.

"Good." Luke handed her the camera and she fired off several shots, taking care to photograph the entire area.

She turned to the fisherman. "We need you to come down to the station so we can take a full statement. Constable Jacobs will bring you in." She turned to the constable who'd come up behind her. "Is that all right with you, Jacobs?"

He nodded emphatically. "Of course, Detective. We'll leave right away."

Ellie nodded her thanks. "We'll be there shortly. Just as soon as forensics arrives and we give them a quick rundown."

Moments later, headlights swept the riverbank. "Looks like them now," she murmured.

———

Ellie pushed away from the bench and moved closer to the stainless steel gurney where Dr Samantha Wolfe, the head of Forensic Pathology in the Westmead Morgue, examined the head of the unknown woman. The doctor's glossy black hair was tucked up in its usual position under a blue surgical hat and although Ellie knew the woman wasn't much older than Ellie, the years spent working with the dead were etched into the lines of fatigue on her face, making her appear older than she was. Even so, Ellie was pleased Samantha had caught the case. The doctor was the best forensic pathologist in Sydney.

"So, what do you think?" Ellie asked, trying hard not to breathe in too deeply of the smell that was unique to the morgue. It was well after nine, and Ellie was feeling the effects of the long day. And it wasn't over yet. She'd told Luke to go home. No sense in both of them hanging around. At least one of them ought to get some sleep.

Samantha peered at her from behind clear plastic safety glasses.

"There's no trauma to the head, as such." The doctor sent her a wry look. "If you don't count the fact that it's been severed from its body."

Ellie smiled reluctantly. There was something very weird about trading jokes while a woman's head lay on a gurney between them.

With gloved hands, Samantha examined the girl's face. "She's definitely Caucasian. I'd hazard a guess she's of European or Mediterranean descent. From the broadness of her features and the olive tones of her skin, even taking into account its deterioration, she's not an English rose."

"How long do you think she's been dead?"

She shrugged. "Hard to put an exact time of death. This time of year, tissue breakdown is slowed down by the cold. We've had some fairly severe frosts over the past few weeks. A bit like being kept in a freezer. If I had to guess, I'd say two, maybe three weeks. She's still in pretty good shape, but as I said, the cold weather would have something to do with that."

With a clank, the doctor dropped a small metal object into an empty kidney dish lined up beside several others on a trolley next to the gurney.

Ellie leaned in closer. "What's that?"

"An earring. There's one in the other ear, too." A few seconds later, another object clattered into the dish. Ellie hunted around for a plastic evidence bag.

"Over near the door." Samantha indicated the rack of shelves on the far side of the room beside the door through which Ellie had entered.

"I'll take these with me," she said scooping them up with gloved fingers and dropping the jewelry carefully into the evidence bag. "They might help us identify her."

"No sign of the rest of her?"

Ellie shook her head. "Not yet." She sighed wearily. "I guess we'll see what tomorrow brings."

"Come and look at this."

The doctor's tone had sharpened. Ellie's heart accelerated. "What is it?"

Samantha was working her way through the woman's honey-blond, matted hair with a pair of tweezers. Bending closer, she extracted a small particle and dropped it into a clean kidney dish.

"I don't know, but her hair's full of it." She continued to part sections of hair, retrieving more and more slivers.

Ellie moved closer and peered into the dish. It was difficult to say what they were. Pinkish-brown in color, the particles were irregular in shape and size, the biggest about half the size of her smallest fingernail.

"I'll send them to the lab." Samantha indicated with her chin toward the other dishes lined up beside the gurney. "Along with those. Hair and tissue samples, blood samples, mouth swabs. Until someone comes forward with an identification, it's the best I can do."

Ellie suppressed a sigh. Someone out there was missing a daughter, a sister—maybe even a mother. "I appreciate your help, Samantha. Any clues on how it was removed?"

The doctor turned the head until it rested on its side. Ellie tried not to look at the single, milky-brown eye as it stared sightlessly up at her. Pointing with her tweezers, Samantha indicated the area where the woman's neck should have been.

"Have a look here. See the striations in the vertebrae? It looks to me like it's been sawn off."

Ellie swallowed and shook her head. "What sort of a monster does something like that?"

"I'm afraid it gets worse." Samantha poked at the ragged, exposed flesh. "There's still blood in this tissue." She raised her head and stared at Ellie. "Have you ever seen a dead heart pump?"

9

CHAPTER 2

"For the love of God, will somebody answer that phone?" The incessant ringing continued behind Ellie. Her fingers clenched around the phone already pressed against her ear and she gritted her teeth. It wasn't the fault of her colleagues that she'd spent the rest of last night drowning memories of her son, Jamie, with a bottle of merlot. To top that off, she now had the unenviable task of identifying a young woman's head.

Luke sidled in from the tea room and propped his hip against her desk, his usual mug of morning coffee in hand. A shock of red hair fell across his eyes as he took a sip. "How did it go last night?"

She grimaced and covered the mouthpiece. "We've got a real sicko on our hands. Samantha's preliminary examination found the head was severed while the girl was still alive."

"Shit! You're kidding?"

"Afraid not. To make it worse, we still don't have an ID. We've joined the queue waiting for lab results. There's a backlog, apparently."

"Of course there is. So, Sam did the autopsy?"

Ellie nodded. "Yeah."

"Lucky break."

"Yeah, let's hope it's not the only one. We haven't got much to go on. A pair of earrings and some weird pink-colored particles found in her hair. Sam thinks the girl could have been dead for up to three weeks."

"Have you sent pictures to the media yet?"

Ellie nodded. "Sam did her best to minimize the shock factor with some strategic drapes, but they were still pretty awful. As much as I want to get her identified, I feel for family members that recognize her. No one should have to see their loved one like that."

Luke's lips compressed.

Ellie did her best to stop her mind from straying to the last moments she'd spent with her son Jamie. She knew exactly what it felt like to identify a loved one in the morgue.

Determinedly pushing the painful memories aside, she concentrated on listening to the elevator music that played monotonously in her ear.

"Who are you waiting on the line for?" Luke asked.

"The Department of Roads and Maritime Services. Thought it would kill some time while I'm waiting. The boss asked me to take a look at a spate of thefts that have cropped up in the Mt Druitt area. I'm trying to get some registration information on a vehicle spotted by one of the victims about the time of the burglary."

Luke shook his head. "You mean the general duties boys haven't already done that? What the hell are they teaching them at the Academy these days? Back in our day—"

"Hey, don't go lumping me in with your vintage. You must have at least a decade on me."

Luke grinned. "Really? And here I just thought you looked good for your age."

Ellie rolled her eyes. "I'm going to pretend you didn't say that, Baxter."

"No offence, Cooper." He sidled closer to her desk. "How old are you, anyway? Or are you one of those girls who can't bear to mention their age?"

Ellie tried for a glare but couldn't quite pull it off. She'd never had an issue with her age. The alternative to no longer having birthdays was pretty grim.

"I'm twenty-seven, if you really want to know."

Luke whistled. "That old?"

She picked up a file and hit him with it.

"Hey! You spilled my coffee."

"Not the least of what you deserve."

"Now, now, Coop. Don't be like that."

Before she could cut him down with a suitably disparaging reply, Detective Superintendent Ben Walker appeared in the doorway of his office, his face grim.

"Luke. Ellie. In here now."

Ellie watched him retreat back into his office. She turned to Luke, her eyebrows raised. Luke shrugged. With a sigh, she replaced the phone in its dock and stood.

"Sounds serious," she murmured.

"Yeah."

"Guess we'd better get in there, then."

"Yeah."

She crossed the squad room floor, wending her way through the clutter of government-issued gray steel-and-laminate desks, Luke close on her heels.

"Shut the door." The curt command came from the direction of the window. Ben Walker stood motionless, his back to them, staring through the glass at the gray, dreary day beyond.

"Is there something wrong, sir?"

"Yes, Detective Cooper. There's something wrong." He leaned over his crowded desk and picked up a piece of paper. "A few moments ago, I took a call from an Evelyn Ward at Cranebrook. Her daughter's missing. No one's seen or heard from the girl since ten last night. The mother called her disappearance in last night and someone downstairs filled in a missing person's report. It's been referred to us because there's still no sign of her."

Ellie frowned. "How old is she?"

"Nineteen."

"*Nineteen?* With all due respect, sir, it's not unusual for nineteen-year-olds to disappear for a day or two. Maybe she's with friends?"

"I know what you're saying, Ellie, but not this girl."

"How can you be so sure? When I was nineteen, there was

more than one occasion when I lost track of time and ended up spending the night at a girlfriend's place. Mom and Dad wouldn't know where I was until I called in the next day."

"What a joy you must have been, Cooper." Luke held his poker face under her narrow-eyed scrutiny.

She punched him in the arm. "Just you wait, Baxter. You, me and the squash courts. Later."

Luke's gaze swept over her petite frame. She barely came up to his shoulder. "You're on," he grinned.

"Cut it out, you two."

Their expressions immediately turned solemn and they murmured apologies.

Ben ran a tired hand through his graying hair. "This is the second girl to go missing in the last few weeks. I've got a bad feeling about this one. I know it hasn't even been twenty-four hours, but the thing is, this girl's never spent a night away from home."

Ellie's eyebrows rose. "How old did you say she was?"

He glared at her. "Nineteen. And yes, she's never been away from home overnight before." His eyes drilled into hers. "She's disabled, Detective. She has Down's syndrome."

Ellie's shoulders slumped and the breath left her body in a rush. "Shit. I'm sorry, sir. I really am. Me and my big mouth. I should learn to close it. How many times—?"

"For fuck's sake, Ellie. Shut up."

Ellie flushed in surprise at Ben's harsh reprimand. "Yeah. Right. I'll stop talking. Right now." She squeezed her eyes shut for a few seconds. When she opened them, Ben regarded her closely, his expression somber.

"I want you and Luke to talk to Mrs Ward. Go and get a few photos of the girl. Talk to the neighbors. Call the TV stations. You know what to do. We need to find this girl. Before another night falls."

"Yes, sir."

"Job's done, sir." Luke gave him a level look. "We'll find her. Don't you worry."

Ben's gaze narrowed. "Yeah, well, just get on with it, okay? Time's of the essence."

They moved toward the door.

"How are things going with the other investigation? Did we get anything from the autopsy?"

Ellie turned back. "It's not good, sir. Samantha Wolfe thinks believes the woman was decapitated before she stopped breathing."

"Jesus."

Ellie remained silent.

"You don't have an ID?"

She shook her head. "Not yet."

"You've got it out to the media?"

She nodded. "Of course."

Ben blew out his breath on a heavy sigh. "I'll get some of the others to go through the missing persons' files. Do we have a time of death, yet?"

"Two or three weeks. That's Samantha's best guess," Ellie replied.

"Well, it's not the Ward girl. But what about the other one? Sally Batten?"

Ellie pursed her lips. "It's possible. I didn't think of her earlier, but she was reported missing a fortnight ago."

"As soon as you've seen the Wards, go and talk to Sally's parents. Show them the head photos. There's no way of knowing if they read the papers. I'm sure the pictures are gruesome, but we don't have a choice. Besides, if it is Sally Batten, they'll have to formally identify her at the morgue and I'm betting the real life version is a hell of a lot worse than the pictures."

Ellie negotiated the right hand turn into Evelyn Ward's street and glanced across at Luke. "What number on Edward Street did you say?"

He consulted the crumpled piece of paper in his hand. "Thirty-six. At least, that's what I think it says." He turned the paper in her direction.

She glanced at it and frowned. "The boss could do with some handwriting practice."

"I guess he had other things on his mind."

"Do you think there's more going on here? I mean, I know this is the second girl to go missing, but it's not that uncommon for teenagers to take off for a while. Especially if things aren't good at home."

"I guess you don't know, then."

"Know what?"

"That's right. I forgot you only transferred in a few months ago."

She waited for him to continue. When he didn't, she sighed and pulled up at the curb outside the red brick house with the number thirty-six painted in black on the neat white picket fence running across the front of the property.

She turned to him expectantly. "So?"

The line spanning the bridge of Luke's nose deepened. He stared out through the windshield. The rain had stopped, but the sky was still heavy with full-bellied clouds.

"The boss' daughter went missing at nineteen, more than ten years ago," he murmured. "She's never been found."

Heat spread across Ellie's cheeks. She thumped the steering wheel. "Shit. I had no idea."

"Yeah, well, he doesn't like to talk about it. She was his only child." He shifted to look at the nondescript brick-and-tile house opposite. "That's why this has probably hit him harder than you'd expect."

Ellie breathed a heavy sigh and shook her head. "Shit."

He grimaced. "Yeah, anyway, let's go and talk to the mother. The sooner we get some pictures out to the media, the sooner we'll find her." He glanced at his watch. "If we're lucky, it might even make the six o'clock news."

Ellie climbed out of the unmarked vehicle and tried to ignore the cold knot of dread in her belly. The girl might have been nineteen, but was likely to have the mentality of a much younger child. Memories of the young son she'd lost stirred at that connection. She tightened her lips and forced

16

them from her mind. Now was not the time. After all, this wasn't about her.

A white metal mailbox overflowing with junk mail—half of it hanging out, wet and neglected—stood near the front gate. No doubt collecting mail was the last thing on their minds. She took a steadying breath and looked across at Luke. "Ready?"

He nodded. "Let's do it."

Ellie hid her reluctance while she accepted the cup of tea and balanced it awkwardly on her knee. She hated tea. Unfortunately, it was all Evelyn Ward had offered and it seemed rude not to accept. The woman had gone to a lot of trouble gathering tea things, including polished silver teaspoons, store-bought fruit cake and matching china. Even the sugar bowl matched, but Ellie didn't fail to notice the way the woman's hands shook as she loaded the items onto the tray.

They were seated on a worn, chintz-covered two-seater sofa in a small but immaculate house. Ellie guessed it was *circa* 1950, but the modern, neutral-colored paintwork was fresh and the place had been decorated with a talented eye.

After pouring the tea, Evelyn Ward took a seat opposite them in the matching armchair. Her cup remained untouched.

"I hope you're not too hot." At their enquiring looks, she shrugged apologetically. "I had to stoke the fire. I just haven't been able to get warm."

Ellie's heart swelled with compassion. Leaning forward, she set her cup and saucer on the cherry wood coffee table and cleared her throat.

"Thanks for the tea, Mrs Ward, but we need to ask you some questions about your daughter. We know you're worried about her. I take it you haven't heard from her?"

The woman shook her head. She stared back at them, her pale eyes swollen and red-rimmed.

"It's just not like her, Detective. I know what you must be thinking... She's nineteen. Of course there's going to be nights when she doesn't come home. But not my Josie." She gave them a hesitant look. "You know she has—?"

"Yes, Detective Superintendent Walker told us." Luke placed his cup on the table and leaned forward. "We need you to tell us about her day yesterday, right up until the time you last saw her."

Tears welled up in Evelyn's eyes. She took a moment to dig around inside the front of her woollen dress and produced a crumpled tissue. Dabbing at the moisture, she then blew her nose. The tissue remained scrunched in her hand.

"I'm sorry, Detective. I just... I'm just so worried about her. I know something dreadful has happened. I just *know* it."

"Mrs Ward." Ellie kept her voice calm. "I know how difficult this is for you, but we need to get as much information as we can if we're going to find her. Now, I think you told Detective Superintendent Walker she was home until about three o'clock when she left for work at the local supermarket. Is that right?"

"Yes, that's right, although she wasn't at home, as such. We went into town together in the morning to get our hair cut."

She touched her head reflexively. "We always go in together. Every six weeks." A thin smile twisted her lips. "She gets hers curled, I get mine straightened."

Ellie returned her smile, hoping to put her at ease. "When you say you went into town, I take it you mean Penrith?"

"Yes. We go to *Hair Affair* in the Westfield Mall."

"How did she seem?" Ellie asked.

Evelyn frowned in concentration. "She seemed just like she always does. Her usual, happy self. She loves going to the hairdresser."

"Did anything happen while you were out?" Luke asked. "Did you run into anyone she knew?"

"No, we didn't run into anyone we knew, but not long after we had lunch, I started feeling unwell. I-I must have eaten something bad. We left soon afterwards and returned home."

"How does Josie normally get to and from work?" Ellie asked.

"I usually drive her."

Ellie consulted her notebook. "I think you told Detective Superintendent Walker your husband Harold dropped Josie off at work yesterday. Is that right?"

"Yes." The woman looked away. Color flushed her cheeks. "I-I had taken quite ill. Since our arrival home, I had spent most of the time in the bathroom. I had a terrible bout of gastric and vomiting. I could barely stand from the cramping. There was no way I was going to be able to drive her there and collect her again. Harold was going to do it, but then he was called to work."

"What does he do?" asked Luke.

"He's a nurse at Westmead Hospital. Someone called in sick. They were already short staffed." She shrugged. "He agreed to go in."

Ellie sat forward in her seat, her notebook open. "Why didn't you call Josie's boss and tell him she couldn't work? I'm sure if you'd explained the situation—"

"I understand what you're saying, Detective and we talked about it. Harold was going to call the store, but Josie begged for us to let her go." Mrs Ward shook her head, tears welling up once again. "She loves that job," she sobbed. "It's her first job. It makes her feel like any other nineteen-year-old."

Ellie gave the woman a few moments to get her emotions back under control. She did her best not to glance at her watch. Time was marching on. They needed to get moving.

"What time did Harold drop Josie at work?" she asked.

"Three o'clock."

"What time did she finish?"

"Ten. That's her usual shift. Three to ten. She mainly packs shelves and does product presentations—things like that."

"Was Harold supposed to collect Josie last night?" Ellie asked.

Evelyn Ward shook her head. "No, his shift wasn't going to finish until eleven. He couldn't possibly be back in time to pick her up. It was one of the other reasons we suggested she stay home last night."

Ellie frowned. "So what arrangements were made to collect Josie from work?"

"Harold had arranged with Josie's supervisor to send her home in a taxi. There's a taxi stand right outside the store."

Ellie scribbled in her notebook. "What's the name of Josie's supervisor?"

"Jason Warner. He's been very good to Josie."

"So, what happened last night?" Luke asked.

The woman clenched her hands again and gave a shaky sigh. "I was still feeling quite unwell, so I hadn't been paying too much attention to the time. When I noticed it was ten thirty and she wasn't home, I started to worry. We only live about seven minutes' drive from the supermarket. She should have been home."

"Did you call the store?" Ellie asked.

"Of course I did, but the phone just rang out. They actually close at ten." Her lips tightened. "I guess there was no one there. I called Harold. He couldn't get away from work. That's when I called the police."

"Have you spoken to anyone at the store today?" Luke asked.

Josie's mother sighed. "Yes, I spoke to Jason. He said he asked one of the other staff, Drew McNeill, to walk with her to the taxi stand. He didn't see her after she clocked off."

"Did he say what time that was?"

"Yes. Right on ten o'clock. It's recorded on her time card."

"The store should have security cameras," Ellie stated. "We might be lucky and catch them leaving the shop. It could give us some idea where she went."

Josie's mother stood abruptly. Hope flared in her eyes. "Well, what are you waiting for? You're wasting time asking me all these questions. My baby's out there somewhere and she's in trouble. Soon it's going to be dark and she's going to spend another night on her own."

Ellie and Luke stood and gathered their things. Ellie looked across at the other woman.

"Mrs Ward, where is your husband now?"

"He's out looking for Josie." She stared down at her hands where they lay twisted together. Her voice dropped even lower. "He's been out searching ever since he arrived home last night. It was his idea for her to catch a cab. H-he's taking it hard." As if a button had been pressed, the woman's face suddenly crumpled. "Oh, my God! Maybe that's it? Maybe there weren't any cabs? Maybe she started walking? Maybe someone came along and took her..."

The woman's thin shoulders hunched forward, quiet sobs wracking her body. Ellie's heart ached. Painful memories of Jamie's death swirled in her head. She fought off the impregnable wall of panic that had become a familiar companion ever since they'd told her about her son. She knew firsthand how useless well-meaning reassurances from strangers were, but offered them anyway.

"Mrs Ward, we don't know anything about what happened, yet. Who knows? She could have met up with a friend after work and gone out."

"No." The denial was swift and strong. "She wouldn't have done that. Not my Josie."

With nothing left to say, Ellie and Luke followed the woman into the entryway. Brightly colored artworks adorned the walls on either side of the foyer. Evelyn caught Ellie looking at them.

"They're Josie's."

"They're very good," Ellie murmured and moved in for a closer look.

Pride flickered in the woman's eyes. "Yes, they are. She's been taking art classes up at the University. The theory is a bit of a struggle for her, but she blows them away with the practical."

"That's the University of Western Sydney, is it?" Luke asked.

21

"Yes, the Penrith campus. She goes there three times a week."

Ellie looked back at Evelyn. "Would you have a recent photograph of Josie? We'll get it out to the media, if that's all right with you? The more people who know about her, the better chance we have of finding her. You never know who might have seen her."

"Yes, yes, of course." She hurried through the doorway and disappeared.

Luke looked at Ellie. "What do you think?"

She frowned. "I think she's legit. She seems genuinely distraught and there doesn't seem to be any reason why the girl wouldn't come home, although I'd like to talk to some of the people she works with, in particular this McNeill fellow. After all, it appears he was the last one to see her."

"Yeah, I think you're right. I wouldn't mind meeting the father, just to get a take on him, but I'm not sensing any undertones here. Seems like a classic missing person's case."

Evelyn came back into the room brandishing a photo and handed it to Ellie. "Here it is. I found it with a few others I've just downloaded and printed."

The picture showed Josie standing in what looked like the sitting room. A glimpse of chintz-covered lounge could be seen in the far left-hand corner. Her plain turquoise uniform fit comfortably over an average-size frame. Medium height. Straight, short, dark brown hair. Guileless chocolate-brown eyes. A warm olive complexion and a smile as big as Mount Everest lit up a small, heart-shaped face.

"She's beautiful," Ellie murmured.

Tears crowded Evelyn's eyes. "Yes, she is." She cleared her throat. "Please bring her home, Detectives. We need to have her home."

Ellie clasped the woman's hand and squeezed, but the words of reassurance wouldn't come. "We'll do our best, Mrs Ward; we'll do our best."

That was all she could manage.

CHAPTER 3

The icy sleet bit into Clayton Munro's cheeks, scorching them with its silent fury. He tugged up the collar of his jacket and tried to ward off the bitter chill. The Woden Cemetery was deserted. Canberra, in July, wasn't the place to be outdoors if you had a choice.

But that was it. He didn't have a choice.

Plenty would disagree with him. After all, she'd been gone nearly three years. More time than some people stayed together. More time than he'd been her husband.

Ancient pine trees stood silent witness, dark and heavy in the winter gloom. He kneeled beside the headstone and stared at the letters carved into the unforgiving stone.

Lisa Anne Munro.
Beloved wife of Clayton
Mother of Olivia
1st March, 1983—2nd September, 2008.
Forever in our hearts.

With an unsteady hand, he reached out and traced her name. Even through the thick leather of his gloves, he was sure he could feel her warmth.

Which was just plain stupid.

He knew that. With his head, he knew that. It was his heart that refused to believe it.

Tears pricked the back of his eyes. He swiped at the moisture with his hand.

For Christ's sake, she was *dead*. When was he going to let go and get on with his life? Wasn't that what everyone kept telling him to do? Even his brother had weighed in the last time, which just went to show that crap about twins being in tune with one another was total bullshit.

And what about Olivia? How was a four-year-old meant to understand why her mother wasn't there to kiss her goodnight? Christ, *he* still struggled with that.

Now he was expected to carry on without her—had even managed to do so. At least, that's what they thought. He couldn't bring himself to tell them it was all a lie.

He was a lie. He hadn't moved on. He couldn't. His life had ended when she'd swallowed the bottle of sleeping pills.

The sound of his phone ringing against his chest snagged his attention. He stood a little stiffly and tried to ignore it. On the fourth ring, he cursed and dragged it out of his pocket. *Why the hell couldn't they just leave him alone?*

"For fuck's sake, Riley, how many times do I have to tell you? I'm not interested. I couldn't care less if she has legs up to her armpits and tits the size of Pamela Anderson's. The answer's *no*."

"Legs up to her armpits? Pamela Anderson? Are you kidding? Even I'd be interested in seeing that."

His heart skipped a beat. The voice was familiar, even though he hadn't heard it in a long time.

"Ben? Is that you? Christ, uh... I thought you were... Never mind. Why the hell are you calling? I haven't heard from you in years."

Ben Walker chuckled. "Sounds like you were expecting someone else, Clay. Is that twin brother of yours still trying to set you up? I thought a man of your advanced years would have settled down long ago."

Clayton's heart pounded. His throat constricted. *Ben didn't know.* He didn't know about Lisa. He snatched a breath of air and fought to answer. "Twenty-eight's not all that advanced, Ben. Besides, it's not a crime to be single."

"Well, you've certainly got that right, but I'm surprised a man of your good looks and charm's still on the market."

Clayton winced. He had to tell him. He owed him that much. "The truth is, Ben, I was married."

"Was? I take it things didn't work out."

Breathing got even more difficult. "Kind of. The thing is, Lisa... She...she died a few years ago."

The line went silent. He braced himself for the usual well-meaning, but ultimately pointless platitudes.

"Clay, I'm so sorry. I had no idea. Why didn't I hear about it?"

Clayton pinched his eyes shut and tried to block the pain. "I don't know, Ben. I thought it would have filtered down to you by now. Maybe everyone thought you knew."

"Well, I'm sorry to hear now. I can't imagine how difficult it's been for you."

Guilt over the manner of Lisa's death assailed him. He remained silent, not even trying to fight it.

Ben cleared his throat. "Listen, the reason I'm calling is to ask for your help. I've got a bit of a situation up here and I could really use your take on it."

Despite the turmoil in his head, Clayton heard the defeat in the voice of the man who'd been his boyhood hero. Pushing his own problems aside, he focused on the conversation.

"What kind of situation?"

Ben appeared in the doorway of his office. "You two, I need to see you. In here. *Now.*"

Luke shot Ellie a questioning look.

"Beats me," she mumbled. She pushed back her chair and headed toward Ben's office, Luke close behind.

"Shut the door behind you, will you?"

Nerves mingled with dread in Ellie's stomach. The last time

they'd been summoned, Josie Ward had gone missing. Was still missing. It had been nearly a fortnight. Evelyn Ward would be out of her mind.

"I know you've been putting in big hours trying to identify the head. I also know you haven't been getting very far. The Missing Persons Unit has come up with nothing so far. We know it can't be Josie Ward and Sally Batten's parents have ruled her out." His gaze narrowed on Ellie's. "Am I correct?"

She nodded and swallowed against the tension that tightened her throat.

"This girl belongs to someone. Every day is another day her family still suffers the pain of not knowing."

The lines of fatigue marking Ben's face deepened. Guilt weighed Ellie down, making it difficult to breathe. It was her investigation but it was going nowhere. Dammit, she was responsible for finding the killer...

Ben turned away and stared out of the window. The pale winter sun shone feebly through the glass, refracting light off several steel-framed photographs that lined the bookcase adjacent. With her newfound knowledge of her boss' tragedy, Ellie scanned the pictures for a glimpse of his long-lost daughter. And found her.

Her heart thudded beneath the cotton drill of her jacket. She swallowed quickly against the surge of emotion and looked away. Another lost child.

Too close to home. Way too close.

"I've decided to bring in some help."

Her gaze swung back to Ben's.

"I know we don't have an ID on Jane Doe, and until we do, we won't know if there's any connection between her and the missing girls, but knowing there's someone out there capable of cutting off a woman's head while she's still breathing chills me to the bone. I've applied to the powers that be for additional resources. They've agreed to pay for the services of an Australian Federal Police criminal profiler."

Ben stared at Ellie and then switched his gaze to Luke, his expression somber. "I think we could use his take on this."

What for? Memories of her ex-fiancée swamped Ellie's

26

mind. Robert Stevens, Federal Agent. The man whose career had meant more to him than his pregnant fiancé. The man who'd decided a wife and child would cramp his style, would hold him back from his dreams of Federal Agent glory. Oh yes, she knew firsthand what Feds were like.

A protest burst from her mouth. "But, sir, I hear what you're saying, but it's only been a fortnight. Surely, we don't need to call in the AFP yet?"

"I understand your reluctance, Ellie, but the trail's going cold. When I get approval to call in specialist services, there's no way in hell I'm going to turn it down."

"But—"

Ben held up his hand. "I know what everyone thinks of the Feds and there are a few who deserve your low opinion, but this guy's different. I promise you. I've known him since he was a kid. Apart from that, he has an enviable solve rate. We couldn't ask for someone better."

Ellie swallowed a sigh of defeat, knowing this was one battle she wasn't going to win. Besides, the extra manpower and a fresh set of eyes and ears could only help their investigation. But did the help have to come from a Fed?

Ben caught her eye, his expression hard. "I expect you to assist Federal Agent Munro in whatever way you can. He's here to help. You'll set aside any ego or misplaced sense of territorialism and get on with finding this killer. Do you understand?"

Ellie lowered her gaze. "Yes, sir."

"Good." His voice was dismissive. His attention turned to the massive pile of paperwork that spilled across his desk. In silence, Luke followed Ellie to the door.

"That goes for you too, Detective Baxter. I won't have an officer under my command treat an investigator who's doing all of us a favor, with anything but courtesy and respect."

"Yes, sir. I understand, sir."

Luke closed the door behind them.

Clayton found the taxi stand outside Sydney's Mascot Airport and joined the queue of travelers waiting for a ride. People were tightening their coats against the cool breeze that drifted in from Port Botany. The temperature had dropped along with the sun, but even the worst of Sydney's winter chill had nothing on Canberra and now he barely felt its effects.

His flight had been uneventful and he'd used the short time in the air to mull over the details of Ben's case. The unidentified head intrigued him, as did the way it had been severed from the girl's body.

He'd only come across one similar case during his career, when a disagreement between a boner from the abattoirs and her unfortunate husband had turned violent. The autopsy had revealed over forty stab wounds, some so vicious they'd severed his spinal cord. The woman had carved up his body with her knife and had then concealed the pieces in garbage bags, disposing of them in various dumpsters around the small country town where she'd lived.

Bridget Bowen was now serving twenty-five years in prison with a non-parole period of fifteen. Although she hadn't used a hacksaw, the level of her savagery had snagged his attention. And even with all her brutality, Bridget Bowen had waited until her husband was dead before cutting him into pieces.

Clayton's lips tightened. It never ceased to shock him, the level of malice one human being could direct toward another. He supposed that was a good thing: He hadn't become so de-sensitized to the frequent horror of his job that he'd lost his ability to care.

He did care...for all of them. Perhaps, too much. Memories of the victims he'd managed to save brought him comfort during the silent, lonely hours before dawn when he'd wake and remember Lisa was gone.

His hand drifted to the wedding band that hung from a chain around his neck and he took comfort from the warm weight of it. He'd taken it off his finger a year ago and only then because he'd wearied of the continual questions it triggered and the inevitable explanations he had to give. Somehow, it had become easier to hide it away from the curious eyes and keep it safe against the haven of his chest. Besides, it was closer to his heart this way.

"You there, you're up next. Bay number two."

Clayton snapped back to the present and focused on the airport security officer who pointed in his direction. Wheeling his suitcase behind him, he made his way toward the next available taxi and opened the front passenger side door.

Eyes so dark they looked black stared back at him, crinkling at the corners when the driver opened his mouth and smiled, flashing a perfect set of sparkling, white teeth. Their brilliance was in such contrast to the scruffy beard that clung to his cheeks that Clayton was momentarily taken aback.

"Where are you off to, mate?" The question was asked around a toothpick the driver held between his lips.

"Penrith Police Station. Can you flip the trunk open, please? I'll throw my bag in the back."

"No problem."

After tossing his suitcase into the trunk, Clayton climbed in beside the driver. The cabbie leaned forward and started the meter before pulling away from the curb.

"Are you a copper, then?"

Clayton shot him a hooded glance. "Something like that."

The man took the hint. Silence fell between them. Clayton looked out the window. Heavy, gray clouds colored the sky and boded well for a wet night. Cars and buses surged around them. It was the start of peak hour, but the driver drove with confidence and admirable skill, weaving in and out of the burgeoning traffic.

Glancing up, Clayton noticed the man's identification. It was a colored photograph, clipped to the rear vision mirror. The face was a little younger and it was clean-shaven, but the dark eyes hadn't changed. Or the smile.

"You've been driving cabs for a while?"

"On and off for years. It's okay. I like to drive around and talk to the passengers, although, most don't want to talk to me." He grinned. "Most people sit in the back, not saying anything. That's city folks for you."

Clayton smiled. "I'm from the country, mate. We don't climb in the back. Not when there's an empty seat in the front. It's just the way it is."

The driver nodded and flashed his teeth. "I spent a bit of time in the country when I was younger. I lived up north, near Maitland. I remember what it's like."

Clayton stuck out his hand. "I'm Clayton Munro."

The driver paused and then briefly returned the handshake. "Lex Wilson."

"Did you drive taxis in Maitland?" Clayton asked.

"Nah, I was just a kid. Moved to the city as soon as I left school."

"Do you still have family there?"

The man's face went blank. "Nope. I met my wife there, but neither of us has been back."

Clayton pondered that. "You must have been together a long time if you met at school?"

"Twenty-five years, we've been together. We met when I was ten."

Clayton shook his head. "Wow, that's fantastic. Got any kids?"

"Two girls. Amy and Anissa. Then there are my dolls, of course."

"Dolls?"

"Yes, I carve them from wood and paint their faces. I even make their clothes. My girls love them and my wife makes good money selling them at the markets."

"I have a daughter, too. I might have to stop by your wife's stall. Is it Paddy's Markets she goes to?" he asked, referring to the iconic markets held every weekend in the city.

"No, the local markets in Penrith. We live out that way."

Clayton smiled. "Well, Lex, you're in luck. By the time you

drop me off, you'll be almost home."

The man smiled back. "I wish. I don't finish for hours yet. It's a late one for me tonight."

Clayton commiserated with him in silence. He'd done his fair share of night shifts.

The streets slid by in the quiet of the oncoming night. Before long, Lex turned the cab into the street that led to the police station and pulled up beside the curb outside the building. Clayton handed him a credit card and moments later, the transaction was completed.

Tugging his bag out of the trunk, Clayton lifted his hand in farewell. "Thanks for the ride, Lex and good luck with your dolls."

A wide, white grin accompanied the slight wave of a hand. The car pulled away and disappeared down the road.

Ellie stared out the window. The sun had long since vanished behind a heavy bank of storm clouds. The squad room door opened on a rush of cold air. She turned as Ben strode across the room and stuck out his hand before enveloping the newcomer in a friendly hug.

"Clayton, you're looking well. It's good to see you again. Thanks for braving the storm and coming up at such short notice. We really appreciate it. Isn't that right ladies and gentlemen?"

Ben swung around and gestured toward the group of officers. Ellie's gaze focused on the stranger who stood just inside the doorway.

Ben stepped forward. "I'd like you all to meet Federal Agent Clayton Munro."

She tried not to stare at the man who watched her with a pair of coolly assessing blue eyes. He looked like Brad Pitt. The younger, clean-cut version. The one that had sent her pulse soaring in *Legends of the Fall* and *Meet Joe Black* and a heap of other movies. She'd seen them all.

Belatedly, she shook his proffered hand, her mouth unable to form anything more than a mumbled greeting. Misinterpreting her reticence, Ben frowned in warning.

"Luke Baxter. Nice to meet you."

Much to Ellie's relief, her boss' attention was distracted by Luke's timely greeting. She snatched a breath. It had been so long since a man had stirred anything inside her, she'd almost convinced herself that her sex drive had died along with Jamie. She forced a couple of surreptitious breaths through her lungs, listening in silence while Ben asked the newcomer about his flight. Talk soon moved to the investigation.

The Fed listened with narrow-eyed concentration. Ellie's gaze wandered over his physique. He looked like he'd come straight from an advertisement for GQ magazine. Despite the fact he'd just stepped off a plane, his navy suit and crisp white shirt were impeccable. A navy, gold and silver striped tie was knotted with precision around a strong tanned neck.

This was not good. She was taking way too much notice of the guy. So what if he was hot? He was a Fed. After her experience with Robert, she'd be stupid to go there again. In an effort to put some distance between them, she strode over to her desk and sat down, concentrating her attention on Ben.

Her boss had moved over to the whiteboard that was fixed to the wall a few feet in front of her. A timeline of the missing girls had been constructed more than a fortnight ago. Josie Ward was last in line.

Ben tapped the whiteboard with the marker in his hand. "Sally Batten's the first one to disappear. Twenty-two years old. She's a student at the University of Western Sydney and attends the Penrith campus. She also works as a part-time shop assistant at the Penrith Westfield shopping complex. Her mother came to the station two weeks before the call came in about Josie Ward. Sally hasn't been seen for a month."

"Does she live at home?" Clayton asked.

"Yeah, we think so," Luke replied. "There's some confusion about that. She was staying on and off at her boyfriend's house in Mt Druitt. That's why her parents didn't call it in right away. They assumed she was with him."

Clayton turned around, his gaze encompassing both Ellie and Luke. "So, does anyone know when she was last seen?"

Ellie filled the uncomfortable silence. "The last time her mother saw her was June nineteenth. We found a couple of friends who were almost certain she'd been to class that day, but then the boyfriend said he hadn't seen her all week."

"Sounds like a caring bloke."

"You've got that right," Luke said. "We went to his apartment about ten in the morning and found him lying on the bathroom floor, covered in his own vomit. Said he'd had a late night. The place stunk of pot."

"Nice. Just the kind of bloke you want your daughter to hang out with."

"Yeah, well Mom and Dad aren't exactly Mr and Mrs Walton," Ellie added. "They live in some shithole at the back of Mt Druitt. Can't say I blame the girl for wanting to get out."

"Sounds like she aimed for the stars." His expression mocked her.

Ellie bristled. "It doesn't make her any less of a victim."

He shrugged. "I didn't say that it did."

"Besides, one of her friends thought they'd broken up. The boyfriend wouldn't confirm the status of their relationship," she clarified.

Baleful blue eyes stared her down. "As I said, sounds like a caring bloke."

Ellie's gaze narrowed on the Fed. She opened her mouth to protest again. Ben cleared his throat, cutting her off.

"Let's continue, shall we? I know it's late and we're all feeling tired, but we need to keep our eye on the ball here." Her boss gave Ellie a fierce frown before turning back to the whiteboard.

"Josie Ward comes in next. Her mother called a fortnight

ago. She's nineteen and lives at home with her parents. She hasn't been seen since July third." He paused. "She's also got Down's syndrome."

Clayton's face sobered. "Christ."

Ben's lips tightened. "Yeah. The general duties boys teamed up with State Emergency Personnel and conducted search parties and door-knocks at the time, but came up with nothing."

"What do we know about her?"

Ben turned to look at Ellie and Luke. Clayton followed suit. Ellie squirmed under his regard. She breathed a silent sigh of relief when Luke answered.

"She was dropped off at work by her father. For various reasons, neither of her parents could collect her that night. She finished work at ten. Her boss arranged for her to catch a cab home."

Ellie recovered her aplomb and took up where Luke left off.

"Unfortunately, the man delegated with the job of seeing her to the taxi stand was Drew McNeill, a twenty-two-year-old co-worker who was more interested in getting home to catch the final half of the football game than he was seeing Josie Ward safely to a taxi. When we spoke to him, he admitted he'd left the store with her and had walked her to the nearby taxi stand, but couldn't remember if there were any cabs waiting and if there were, he couldn't recall any of the cab companies."

She eyed the Fed balefully. "Harold Ward is still beating himself up about it. It was his suggestion that his daughter catch a cab."

The Fed frowned at her. "So no one saw her climb into a cab?"

"No," Ellie replied.

"I take it the girl's father isn't a person of interest?"

Ellie responded again. "That's right. "Apart from the fact he's almost suicidal with guilt over his part in Josie's disappearance, it was impossible for him to be responsible for her abduction. There are several witnesses who said he was at work at Westmead Hospital until eleven that night. Josie disappeared shortly after ten."

The Fed nodded and then turned back to Ben. "What else have we got?"

Ben pursed his lips and referred back to the whiteboard. "The next one we have listed is the head that was found on the banks of the Nepean River. Until we get an ID, we don't know where she fits into our timeline, or even *if*. The forensic pathologist says death occurred up to three weeks before she was found, which means she was killed about five weeks ago. I've put her at the front of the list until we get an ID."

He underlined the name Jane Doe at the front of the timeline and then turned back to face them. "I know I don't need to remind anyone about the savagery of this attack. Identifying this young woman is our top priority." He turned to Clayton. "We've been running her picture in the media for the last couple of weeks. We've had a handful of enquires, but so far, nothing's panned out."

Clayton tapped a finger to his lips, his brow furrowed in thought. "I take it these girls went missing from the same area?"

Ellie answered. "Yes, more or less. They're both from western Sydney and live within a couple mile radius of each other."

"And Sally Batten attends Uni?"

"Actually, Josie Ward's a student, too," Ellie said. "She attends classes at the same campus."

Ben frowned. "Really? I didn't know that."

Ellie shrugged. "Apparently she's been taking some art class a few days a week. Nothing major from what I could gather."

"So," the Fed replied, "has anyone talked to the staff at the university?"

"We've made a start," Ellie replied, "but you're talking about hundreds of people. Faculty members, groundsmen, cleaners, other staff. And that's before we start looking at the students." Her gaze challenged him. "We don't have the unlimited budgets some people do."

He stared back at her, lasering her with his eyes. Heat scorched her neck. She looked away.

Luke broke the tense silence. "We've talked to some of the girls' friends. From what we can gather, neither of them knew each other. Preliminary enquires seem to indicate there's only one faculty member who has a common link to them. Stewart Boston, an art professor. He was Josie's teacher and it looks like Sally Batten was also taking one of his classes."

Ellie returned to the discussion. "The art professor's on a month's leave. He left about a week and a half ago."

Clayton's eyes narrowed. "So, that means he took off shortly after Josie was reported missing. You don't think that's significant?"

He'd addressed her directly, his gaze burning into hers. She held her ground, refusing to be intimidated.

"Possibly. It's too early to tell. Besides, Sally Batten's been missing about a month. And of course, until we've identified Jane Doe, we won't know if there's any connection there."

"But he does work at the University and he just happens to teach two of our missing girls." He drilled her again with his gaze. "And now he's disappeared?"

The sudden tension in the air was palpable. Anger ignited inside her. How dare he come and throw his weight around the minute he arrived? He'd been invited along to help them, not make them feel like incompetent probation officers straight out of the Academy.

Ellie seethed in silence. Ben leveled her with a look of warning and she clamped her mouth shut. The Fed turned back to the whiteboard.

Easing out her breath, she flashed Luke a look of apology. He grimaced and directed his attention back toward Clayton who'd begun to speak again.

"At this stage, it's impossible to tell who we're looking for and whether we're looking for one killer or more. Until we know if the missing girls are, in fact dead, we don't even know if there's a connection between them and the unidentified head."

He spread his arms wide. "I understand your concerns. Anyone prowling the streets of Sydney decapitating women while they're still alive needs to be found, and quickly." He swung around and stared at Ben. "You're right when you say identifying Jane Doe is your number one priority. Once we know who she is, then we can decide if there's a link between her and the missing girls. Until that happens, unfortunately, there's not a lot we can do unless another body turns up."

Ellie grimaced. No one wanted to think about that possibility. But the Fed was right. Until they'd cemented a link between the women, they were stuck in limbo.

"Ben, if you don't mind, I'd like to borrow Jane Doe's file and go through it—get a feel for what's happened so far," Clayton said.

"No problem. Ellie and Luke can give you everything they have."

"Which is blessed little," Ellie mumbled as she gathered up Bill Griffin's statement and the scant forensic reports they'd scraped together so far.

"Where are you staying, Clayton?" Ben asked. "I'll give you a ride."

"Uh, thanks Ben, but I've booked a room in the city. I was going to stay with one of my brothers. Three of them are living in Sydney. I called Tom, but his house is in quarantine. His youngest has the chicken pox. I rang Declan, too—you might remember him?"

Ben nodded. "Yes, he's a bit older than you, isn't he?"

"Yeah, he's three years older. Anyway, he's away on holidays up in Queensland. I didn't even bother to call Brandon. He spends more time overseas on top secret AFP Missions than he does in Sydney." Clayton shrugged. "I decided it was probably easier to stay in a hotel. Besides, I can stay totally focused on the case this way and I'll be free to come and go as I please. I was hoping you'd give me the use of an unmarked squad car."

Color stained Ben's cheeks. "You're forgetting we're State coppers. There's no money for spare vehicles. Ride with Ellie.

She commutes from the city. Besides, she's been on the case since the get-go. She will be able to fill in any gaps."

A surge of alarm burned through her. Sidling up to Ben, she lowered her voice. "Ah, Ben? I was thinking—that is, maybe Luke could—?"

"Luke lives in Cronulla, Ellie. That's hardly practical. He can partner with Cheryl for the next little while." Ben glanced in Luke's direction. "Are you all right with that?"

"Yeah, boss; no worries."

With a muffled groan, Ellie pushed passed him and strode in the direction of the locker room. How the hell had she managed to get herself lumped with another *Fed*?

CHAPTER 4

Ellie took a sip from her double shot espresso and waited for the caffeine to work its magic. It was barely eight thirty and already a headache plagued her. It had started when she'd woken and remembered she'd been partnered with the Fed.

She stifled a groan. It wasn't as if she had anything against him, personally. It wasn't like it was the AFP's fault her ex had turned into a bastard the minute he'd been accepted into its haloed ranks. He'd obviously had the potential to be a loser well before then.

It was just that his weakness hadn't manifested itself until the acceptance papers arrived in the mail. Overnight, he'd morphed into someone she hadn't recognized. The memories still made her angry, although in clearer moments, she grudgingly accepted how lucky she'd been to discover his inherent selfishness well before the wedding march had been played.

Fortunately, she wouldn't have to deal with Clayton for more than the ride to work. Within moments of taking the seat beside her, he'd asked her to drop him off at the Westmead Morgue. He'd then proceeded to stare out the window. They'd spent the rest of the journey in silence. She'd been even more relieved when he'd told her he'd be at the morgue for most of the morning.

The only thing she'd been disgruntled about was that he'd looked good enough to eat in his tailor-made designer suit and crisply knotted tie. He'd offered her a casual wave good-bye with a smile that could have sold toothpaste and her belly had fluttered with nerves. If she was honest with herself, she had to admit it was her reaction to him that had her most out of sorts.

Luke sauntered in from the tea room, his usual brew of coffee in hand. Catching sight of her face, he shook his head. "Not a good way to start the morning, Coop."

Ellie threw him a withering look. "You'd better watch your mouth, Baxter. I'm not in the mood."

"Now, now, Coop. Don't be like that. How could you be out of sorts with the sun barely two hours above the horizon? It's not like you to come to work in a bad mood."

She threw her hands in the air, her frustration evident. "Who knows? Maybe it has something to do with the unsolved cases piling up on my desk. Or the fact that Ben's seen it necessary to bring in outsiders before we've even had a chance to put together something ourselves." Collapsing back into her chair, she blew her breath out in an effort to relieve the tension that had her wound as tight as a guitar string. She looked up as Ben strode in.

"Where's Clayton?" His eyes narrowed on her face. "You did pick him up, didn't you?"

She only just managed to suppress a roll of her eyes. "Of course. I promised you I'd show him the utmost respect, and I am."

"So, where is he?"

"He's at the morgue. He wants to talk to Samantha. Obviously, Luke and I can't be trusted to get it right." She checked her watch. "I'm supposed to be picking him up shortly."

"Don't sound so enthusiastic, Detective." He swung around to face Luke. "How'd you do with the TV stations? Any chance of keeping the story alive for a bit longer?"

He set his mug down on Ellie's desk. She frowned at the wet puddle it formed amongst her mountain of paperwork. Luke continued, oblivious.

"I did manage to get the papers to run it one more time.

They're going to focus on the earrings. It'll come out this afternoon. Let's hope someone recognizes them. At least then we'll have something to go on."

Ben's attention returned to Ellie. "How about the Ward girl? Anything new?"

She squirmed under his regard. "No, sir. Not yet, anyway. We tracked down Josie Ward's supervisor. He's been off sick the last couple of weeks. He showed us a copy of the security tape from her last shift. Unfortunately, there's not much to see once she leaves the store. She heads off in the direction of the taxi stand with Drew McNeill and after that, there's nothing."

"Keep me posted, won't you? Those poor families must be going out of their minds."

Ellie held her breath as he turned abruptly and headed toward his office. With a sigh, she tilted her head up to meet Luke's somber gaze.

"I can't imagine what he's going through."

She suppressed a shiver. "Yeah. There but for the grace of God."

"You got any kids, Coop?"

The question hit her without warning, as if she'd been whacked in the stomach with a baseball. Visions of Jamie flooded her mind, cutting short her air supply. She sucked in her breath and felt the blood drain from her face.

"Cooper, are you all right? Christ, you look awful."

Luke bent over her, his eyes full of concern. Ellie struggled to regain her composure. "I'm fine. I'm fine. I just... You just..." She shook her head. "Forget about it, Baxter. I'm fine. I might just step outside for a bit and clear my head." Her lips twisted. "I'll go and pick up the Fed."

She collected her coat and scarf from the back of her chair and headed toward the locker room to retrieve her handbag. She was almost outside the door when Ben called out to her.

"Ellie, I've just received another call from Jim Whitton."

She frowned, searching her memory and coming up blank.

"The man I told you about a couple of weeks ago. His

41

chest freezer's gone missing. Actually, I should say he's the latest victim. There have been a couple of earlier freezer thefts reported, haven't there?"

"Yes," she replied, relieved to have made the connection at last. "I'm still chasing up a few leads." Tying her red woollen scarf around her neck, she pulled her coat on over her shoulders. "I'm on my way out to collect Federal Agent Munro."

"You need to stop by. Take him with you. Whitton lives in Penrith. Clay will probably want to meet with the girls' families this afternoon, anyway." He handed her a piece of paper. "Here's the address. Take Whitton's statement. Make him feel like someone cares." He grimaced. "And get him to stop phoning me, will you?"

She swallowed a sigh and forced a smile. "No worries, boss."

Ben's expression softened. "I know what you're thinking, Ellie. You're snowed under with more important things right now. We all are. But do me a favor; just go through the motions. Take his statement, make him feel important. You know what to do."

She groaned aloud and shoved the piece of paper into the pocket of her trousers. Pulling her heavy black coat tighter around her, she slung her handbag over her shoulder and headed out the door.

―――――――

From a distance, the red brick-and-tile bungalow reminded Ellie of the Ward house a couple of suburbs across. Similar in age and style, it wasn't until they'd stepped onto the front porch that the similarities came to an abrupt end.

Junk of every shape, size and description filled the small entryway, all the way to the battered front door. Old newspapers, wooden boxes, cardboard and aluminium cans were crammed into every space and crevice. The place looked like a recycling plant.

Clayton gave the front door a dubious knock, its chipped and peeling white paint in keeping with the standard set by the entryway. They were met with silence. Glancing at Ellie, he shrugged and knocked again, this time louder.

"All right, all right. I'm comin'. I'm comin'. Hold ya horses."

The rusted screen door opened with a noisy protest. A middle-aged man with an alarmingly large stomach that protruded over a pair of gabardine work shorts met them at the door. The skinniest legs Ellie had ever seen poked out from underneath. Seemingly oblivious to the cold July temperature, the man looked them over with bright, curious eyes.

"Mr Whitton?" Ellie held out her hand, grimacing inwardly as it was engulfed in a fleshy handshake. "I'm Detective Cooper, and this is Federal Agent Munro. We're from the Penrith Local Area Command. We're here about your freezer."

"Jim." The man grinned, showing an eternity of dental neglect. An odor that almost outdid the stench of the trash wafted toward her. "Call me Jim. Come in. Come in."

She shot Clayton an involuntary look of distaste. He grinned back at her and leaned in close. "Don't worry, Cooper. I've got your back."

Spicy aftershave and warm, male smell assailed her. It was so at odds with the reek of the house, she felt dizzy. With a shake of her head, she forced a light reply. "It's not my back I'm worried about. Who knows what horrors lie inside."

She watched as Jim Whitton disappeared down the hallway and then she took a cautious step inside.

Clayton chuckled low in her ear. "Don't tell me you're scared."

"Yeah, scared of catching some exotic disease no one's ever heard of." She looked around her again. "This place is a health hazard."

With gritted teeth, she continued forward. More garbage filled the front room. A strange odor emanated through a closed door off to her left. She wasn't game to open it.

They continued on through the house. Each room they

passed was progressively smellier and fuller with garbage and other pieces of junk. One room seemed to be filled entirely with old glass bottles. There wasn't a piece of uncluttered furniture in the place.

Jim Whitton waited for them on the back porch that had been enclosed with windows and a door. Surprisingly, compared to the rest of the house, it was only modestly chaotic. An old television sat in a cupboard with both doors missing. A threadbare couch was propped up against the wall with two building bricks replacing an absent leg. A large black cat sat curled upon it, eyeing Ellie and Clayton with suspicion.

"Snowball! Scram!" Whitton shooed away the cat that was very reluctant to move. He pushed at it with his hand. "Let these officers sit down."

"We're fine," Ellie said hurriedly. "We won't take up too much of your time. We're just here to ask you a few questions about the chest freezer you reported stolen."

"Me freezer, yeah. It was right over there. Right near me couch. You can still see where it used to sit."

Her gaze followed in the direction of his grubby finger. She noticed a large, vacant space further along the wall. Dust gathered thickly around it, leaving it conspicuously empty amongst the junk. A rusted upright fridge stood beside it.

She looked around the porch. It was obvious he lived out here. The junk in Jim Whitton's house had forced him outside. All that was missing was a bed. But maybe that's what the couch was for...

Ellie suppressed a shudder as Clayton picked his way through the scattering of debris for a closer look. He gamely squatted near the vacant square. "When did you notice it gone?"

The man scratched a dirty fingernail across his unshaven chin before answering. "Nearly three weeks ago. I'd not long been home from a day at the tip and I came out here for a coldie. Couldn't believe me eyes when I realized it was missin'. I called the local coppers and they told me they'd send someone around, but it's been three weeks and nothin'. Haven't seen hide nor hair of 'em. That's why I kept ringin' the Superintendent. I figured if anyone could get some action happenin' it would be the boss."

Ellie stepped a little closer, mindful of the stench emanating from him. "You work at the garbage depot. Is that what you mean when you say the tip?"

Jim chuckled. "Work? Yeah, I guess you could call it that. I'm a scab, darlin'. I scab from the tip. Where do you think I got all me stuff from? All me little treasures?" His arms spread wide, indicating the house full of junk. "It brings me in a pretty penny from the recyclin' plant."

Clayton coughed loudly behind her. Ellie suppressed a grin. Jim's eyes suddenly narrowed. "You're not gonna turn me in to Centrelink, are you?"

Ellie shook her head. "We're not here for that, but if you're earning additional unclaimed income, perhaps you'd better go and talk to them yourself." Another whiff of the man's odor reached her. Risking a tiny breath of air, she took out her notebook and pen and cleared her throat, suddenly anxious to get this over with.

"Anyway, talking about the freezer. It was a chest freezer, is that right?"

"Yeah, darlin'. Just a plain old Westinghouse. Had it for years. Weren't worth nothin'. But I still want it back. Got nowhere to store me meat or me frozen vegies."

Ellie was surprised he even knew what vegetables were, but remained silent. Clayton picked his way back to them.

"How do you think they got in?" he asked.

Jim's brow creased in confusion. He stared back at Clayton. "Got in? Whatcha mean, got in?"

"I mean, how do you think they broke into your house? Were there any windows broken or a door smashed?"

Jim threw back his head and laughed. "Nah, mate, they didn't break in. They didn't have to. I don't lock nothin' around here. All they had to do was back a pick-up into me driveway and lift it straight off me porch. Me own fuckin' porch. Can you believe it?"

Clayton's jaw tensed and impatience flashed in his eyes.

Ellie knew exactly how he felt. They were wasting time. They should have been over at Evelyn Ward's or Robyn Batten's— asking questions of the people who really did have something to worry about.

She stepped in. "All right, Mr Whitton, we'll see what we can do. It was only meat and frozen vegetables in the freezer, is that right?"

"Yeah, darlin'. That's all I keep in there. And the occasional loaf of bread and a tub or two of marge. But I had at least a month's worth of groceries in there. That's a lot of meat to walk off your porch. I'm on the pension, you know. I really wanna get it back."

"Of course, Mr Whitton. We'll be doing all that we can to find it." Ellie pulled a card out of her wallet and handed it to him. "If you think of anything else, give me a call."

"I surely will, darlin'. I surely will."

Clayton picked his way over to the screen door which led to the back steps. Ellie followed behind him and breathed a sigh of relief that she'd avoided another trip through the house.

She made her way over the grassed area Mr Whitton was sure had provided access for the thieves. The heels of her boots sank into the damp ground. Lifting up the legs of her suit pants, she picked her way carefully through the mud.

Several sets of tire tracks marked the soft dirt. It was obvious he used the driveway, too. After three weeks of use, it was impossible to determine a single set of tire marks among the melee of tracks she saw.

With a sigh of resignation, she headed to the squad car where Clayton waited. When he slid into the passenger seat, she half smiled at him, her guard momentarily lowered. "What the hell did we do to deserve that? He's an absolute loony."

He grinned back at her. "Yeah, but it does look like something's missing. I mean, the only clear space in that entire house is where he says there was a chest freezer." He cocked his head at her. "I'm inclined to believe him."

"I didn't say I didn't believe him," she protested. "In fact, his story's very similar to a couple of other cases I've been working on. In both of those, the freezers were reported missing from the back porch. Both of them are within a few miles of this place." A reluctant smile tugged at her lips. "Someone's obviously got a thing for chest freezers."

"Let's hope we don't find one of our girls in them."

Ellie gave him a disparaging look. "Sounds a bit Hollywood, don't you think?"

"I don't know what to think. But at this stage, nothing can be discounted. Hopefully Josie and Sally will turn up fine and all will be well."

His face looked anything but hopeful. Coldness seeped into her veins. Despite her flippancy, the picture had shifted. The scenery now looked a whole lot more sinister.

The phone in her pocket vibrated against her leg and she pushed the thought aside. Tugging it out, she glanced down and recognized the number.

"It's the boss." She answered the call. "Hey, Ben. What's happening?"

"Ellie, I need you and Clayton to make another house call."

"Sir, we've only just finished with Jim Whitton. We haven't even made it to the Wards' place yet and then we're off to the Battens'. If you can just give us another hour or two—"

"We've had a hit on the head shot. Someone phoned it in about ten minutes ago. Apparently recognized it in the afternoon edition of the paper. I think the close-up of the jewelry did it."

Her heart picked up its pace. "Wow, that's great. Do we have a name?"

"Yeah, the caller says the girl's Angelina Caruso. She's from Mt Druitt. Been missing for just over six weeks."

"Who called it in?"

His voice turned grim. "Her mother."

CHAPTER 5

"Shit, shit, shit." Ellie thumped her fist on the steering wheel and shook her head in frustration. With Evelyn Ward's pain still fresh in her mind, the last place she wanted to be was waiting outside yet another house to confirm the news no parent ever wanted to hear.

Clayton remained silent. He opened the passenger side door and climbed out, his face grave. She was grateful he'd offered to come with her when she broke the news. Fed or no Fed, she welcomed his show of support.

This was the worst part of the job. Swallowing a heavy sigh, she climbed out of the car and joined him on the sidewalk.

The house was an old weatherboard that had seen better days. The lawn had yellowed from the frosts and a lack of water and was half overgrown. Incongruously, bright pots of colorful geraniums lined the concrete walkway, flowering bravely in the crisp winter air.

She climbed the steps with Clayton and looked for a doorbell. There was none. The Fed rapped loudly on the cracked timber beside the rusted screen door that led into the house.

She tensed when footsteps made their way toward them. The silhouette of a woman came into view. Taking a deep breath, she gathered her courage.

"Mrs Caruso?"

The woman peered apprehensively out at them.

"Yes, I'm Jacqueline Caruso. Who wants to know?"

Ellie's lips tightened. There was no easy way to do this.

"Mrs Caruso, I'm Detective Cooper. This is Federal Agent Munro. We're here about Angelina."

The woman's eyes widened and her face paled. With a shaking hand, she pushed a heavy, dark fringe of hair off her forehead and struggled to open the door.

"I-I think you'd better come in."

They stepped into a narrow corridor that ran the length of the house. A tired hall runner in muted colors of navy and red softened their footsteps as they followed Mrs Caruso toward the back of the house.

A modest kitchen opened up at the end of the hall. Like the rest of the house, it was scrupulously clean. The Formica counter-tops sparkled. Not a single cup or dish sat on the dish drainer. The tea towel had been left to hang on the oven door in perfect alignment.

"Can I get you something to drink, Detectives? A cup of tea, perhaps?

Ellie admired her self-control. The woman had to know they weren't there to bring good news. Her restless fingers that played with the ends of the black-and-white checked apron that was tied around her waist, were the only giveaways.

"Thank you," Ellie replied with a quick peek in Clayton's direction, "but we're both fine. Is there somewhere we could sit? We need to talk."

"Of course." The woman touched her head, almost reflexively, patting down a non-existent stray hair. Apart from her bangs, the thick darkness of it was pulled off her face and fixed at the nape of her neck in a tight bun. The look would have been severe on a woman less attractive.

Her olive skin and chocolate-brown eyes hinted at European heritage. Ellie guessed her age to be mid-fifties, but it was tough to tell on a woman time had treated kindly. The dyed hair made it even more difficult.

They followed her out of the kitchen and back down the hallway into a small sitting room. Solid, well-constructed furniture that showed its age filled the room. A small, old-fashioned television sat in a corner unit. Family photographs crowded the mantelpiece above the roaring fire.

Ellie sidled over for a closer look. Her heart clenched as she recognized Angelina Caruso. She caught Clayton's eye and moved her head imperceptibly toward the photographs. His lips tightened.

"Please, Detectives. Take a seat." Jacqueline Caruso's hand shook as she indicated the worn blue two-seater sofa. Orange and yellow cushions nestled in each corner.

Ellie clenched her teeth and perched on the edge of it. Clayton remained standing.

She drew in a deep breath and waited for the woman to seat herself in the matching wing chair.

"Mrs Caruso, I'm afraid we have some bad news."

The woman's hands fluttered nervously. "Are you sure I can't get you anything? A biscuit, perhaps?"

Ellie swallowed against the lump in her throat. "I'm sorry, Mrs Caruso. There just isn't an easy way to tell you this."

A high keening wail erupted from the woman sitting opposite her. She began to rock back and forth on her seat. "Please, not my Angelina. Please, Detective. Please don't tell me you've found my Angelina."

Drawing air into her suddenly depleted lungs, Ellie prayed silently for the right words—and failed. The woman's daughter had been murdered in a horrifyingly gruesome way. Nothing could change that. No words would bring her back.

Without conscious thought, she looked to Clayton for help. His face was somber. He looked as upset as she felt. It had to be done. They needed information and Angelina Caruso's mother might be the only one who could give it to them. A madman had sawn her daughter's head off while she was still breathing...

He had to be stopped.

She leaned forward and captured one of the woman's flailing hands. "Mrs Caruso, we think we've found Angelina."

The woman's eyes turned wild. "Don't you mean to say

you've found her head? Isn't that what you meant to say? I read it in the newspaper. They said they'd found a head. I saw it the other week. The picture looked a little bit like her, but it was hard to tell with all the..." More color leeched from her cheeks. She swallowed and drew in a deep breath. "Today I saw the earrings." A hand fluttered up and touched the plain gold stud in her ear.

"They were my mother's. She gave them to me when I turned sixteen. I gave them to Angelina four years ago. She wore them everywhere."

Her voice broke. Tears of pain pooled in her eyes. "My baby, my poor *baby*." Huge sobs wracked the slim body. She fell forward, her head clutched between her hands.

The sound of the woman's grief almost did Ellie in. Hot tears welled up in her eyes. Her chest tightened with emotion. She was grateful the media hadn't got wind of all the details. At least the woman could be spared that much. For a little while, anyway.

The sobs that came from the woman across from them gradually quieted. Dark, watery, pools of pain flicked to Clayton and then to Ellie. Jacqueline offered a small, self-deprecating smile. Her cheeks flushed, as if she were embarrassed to have given vent to her emotions in front of strangers.

Ellie's admiration for her grew. Hell, if it had been her, she'd have been rolling around on the floor, howling her pain to the world, oblivious to who was watching. In fact, that's exactly what she'd done when they'd told her about Jamie.

Pushing aside the memories, she opened her notebook and cleared her throat. "We have to ask you some questions, Mrs Caruso. We need to know as much as we can about Angelina in the days before her disappearance." She consulted the page in front of her. "You told Detective Superintendent Walker that your daughter has been missing for about six weeks, is that right?"

The woman sniffed quietly. "Yes, it was a Tuesday. May twenty-ninth. She was late coming home from university."

Ellie's heart leaped. Her body stilled. *Angelina Caruso was a student?* She glanced across at Clayton and saw from the taut line of his jaw and his compressed lips that he'd also made the connection.

"Which university did she attend, Mrs Caruso?" Clayton's voice was calm, conversational, despite the turmoil that must be raging inside him, just like it was in Ellie. She held her breath and waited for the answer.

"She's a student at the University of Western Sydney. She's studying physiotherapy at the Penrith campus."

The air whooshed out of Ellie's mouth. Clayton's jaw tensed. His throat moved as he swallowed.

Leaning in closer, she posed another question, her voice pitched low. "Why didn't you report her missing? Six weeks is a long time."

A frown marred the soft, lined skin of the woman in front of them. "What do you mean, why didn't I report her missing? I called the local police station the same night she failed to arrive home."

Ellie caught Clayton's confused gaze and gave a slight shake of her head. Frustration surged through her. Somehow, the report hadn't been entered into the system.

"I'm sorry, Mrs Caruso," Ellie said. "We don't have any record of your call."

Jacqueline Caruso looked bewildered. "I called just after eleven. It was cold and late and I was worried. It's not like Angel to be out so late, especially on a school night." Tears welled in her eyes and she pulled a fine lace handkerchief from the pocket of her slacks. Her cheeks flushed again. She peered at them apologetically. "Please excuse me, Detectives."

Clayton stepped slightly away, giving her some privacy. "No problem, Mrs Caruso. You go right ahead."

Blowing her nose with delicate precision, Angelina's mother took a deep breath and released it slowly. "Her classes usually finish at five on a Tuesday. Sometimes she goes for coffee with friends afterwards, but most of the time she comes straight home. Funds are tight and she was saving for a trip to Europe. My parents still live in Italy," she explained.

"When she wasn't home by eight, I called her cell. It rang out and eventually went to voice mail. I left a message asking her to call me." Her voice caught. "She still hasn't phoned me back."

The woman stared unseeingly across the room. Ellie and Clayton watched and waited in silence. When Jacqueline began again, her voice held a dazed, almost dreamlike quality.

"It was raining. It had only started late that afternoon, but it was really pelting down. I remember hoping Angel had taken an umbrella."

Ellie scribbled in her notebook. "How did she normally get home?"

Jacqueline sighed. "By bus. She can catch one just outside the Uni. It drops her off about a block away."

Clayton's eyes narrowed. "Did she ever catch a taxi home?"

"No. As I said, money's tight. She's been *saving*." Her voice cracked again and she seemed to crumple before them, huge sobs wracking her body. Ellie stared at Clayton, feeling helpless, her own anger at the unknown assailant reflected in his eyes.

Angelina's mother spoke between her sobs, her swollen eyes fixed on Clayton. "W-when can I have her back, Detective? I-I'd like to arrange a proper funeral."

Clayton started in surprise. Ellie knew what he was thinking. They had yet to find the rest of Angelina's remains. He stepped forward and crouched low, near Jacqueline's chair.

"As soon as the forensic pathologist has finished with her, Mrs Caruso. Whilst we appreciate your identification through her earrings, we'll need to make a conclusive finding through DNA. She'll be released to you as soon as they've completed their examination."

"And what happens if you find the rest of her?"

Now it was Ellie's turn to swallow her surprise. Clayton's gaze captured hers and held it for a miniscule moment before his gaze flicked back to Jacqueline's.

"Well, anything else that is found will also be examined at the morgue and afterwards, it will be released to you, along with her—" Clayton broke off, mortification flooding his face.

"Her head." Jacqueline Caruso's lips twisted with bitterness. "That's what you meant to say, wasn't it?"

The flush on his face deepened. He swallowed awkwardly and looked away.

Ellie stepped in to rescue him.

"Yes, that's right." She leaned over and took one of the woman's hands in her own. "We know this is difficult for you, Mrs Caruso. We are so sorry for your loss. We understand what you're going through."

The woman snatched her hand away. Her eyes flared with sudden anger. "How can you understand what I'm going through? Someone's murdered my *baby*!"

Ellie's stomach clenched and she steeled herself against the memories of Jamie that suddenly assailed her. Her vision darkened and she fought against the dizziness that threatened to unseat her.

Clayton shot her a strange look. She heard his voice as if from inside a distant tunnel.

"You're right, Mrs Caruso. We can't hope to know what you're going through. All we can do is promise you we will work night and day to find whoever did this."

Ellie forced oxygen into her constricted lungs and the blackness receded. She gritted her teeth, her eyes fierce as she tried to hold the other woman's tortured gaze.

"We'll find him, Mrs Caruso. I swear to you. We'll find him."

They made their way across the room to the doorway. Clayton turned back. "Mrs Caruso, did Angelina wear any other jewelry?"

Ellie paused and waited for the woman to answer. It came in the form of a jerky nod. "Yes, she loves jewelry. She never went anywhere without at least one or two pieces on. A necklace. Some earrings. She nearly always wears a silver charm bracelet I gave her last year for Christmas. It's one of her favorite pieces."

Clayton's lips compressed and he gave a brief nod. "Thank you, Mrs Caruso. We really appreciate your time."

Ellie followed him out in silence and tried to dispel the harrowing image of a woman that life had just broken into two.

Stewart Boston scratched at his hair and sent a furtive glance over his shoulder to check that no one was watching. He was four suburbs across from where he lived, but it paid to be careful. Cars sped by along the highway adjacent to the strip of shops where the cheap motel was situated. Much to his relief, no one seemed interested in him. His fingers trembled with excitement as he tried to fit the key into the door. On the third attempt, he was in and his belly clenched in anticipation.

Her scent reached him, wafting through the thermostatically controlled warm air to tickle and tease his nostrils. His cock hardened. Blood pounded in his ears, deafening him to everything but the sound of her breathing. His own breath came in short, shallow pants. He approached the bed where she lay spread before him, naked and beautiful. He drank in the sweet sight of her and determined to take her with him when he left for his mini vacation.

"Hello my sweet little cherry blossom. I'm sorry I took so long. I couldn't get away any sooner." He pulled off his suit jacket and tossed it on the back of the single armchair and then tugged at his tie.

Moving closer, he ran a hand that was still not steady down the length of her leg, starting at her hip. She shivered beneath his touch.

He smiled down at her. "We are going to have so, so much fun. I hope you like surprises."

Ellie's fingers worked at the knot of tight muscle in the back of her neck and she stifled a groan of frustration. It had been three days since she'd broken the news to Jacqueline Caruso. With no new leads on the murder, she'd returned to dealing with the pile of other ongoing investigations swamping her desk. The files of the mysterious chest freezer thief were open before her and she skimmed the contents of the initial police report.

The first theft had occurred nearly three months earlier. Ronald Carter of Mt Druitt had called to report a Westinghouse chest freezer stolen off his back porch. The facts were strikingly similar to the one taken from Jim Whitton three weeks ago. And before that, there was one stolen from the Jacksons in Cranebrook. Same *modus operandi*. Same stolen goods. A vehicle had accessed the rear of the property and had stolen the chest freezer from an enclosed back porch.

Ordinarily, such arbitrary crimes would be relegated a lower priority in her work schedule, but Clayton's comment had unsettled her and she was determined to get to the bottom of this so she could discount that gruesome possibility from her list.

Ronald Carter was sure he'd caught a glimpse of a white van as it turned into the back lane from his yard. He'd written down the number plate and that had been included in the report. She'd been trying to track down the owner.

Reaching over, she picked up the telephone and punched in the numbers for the Roads and Maritime Services department. She groaned under her breath when she was immediately placed on hold and wondered how much more time she was going to waste.

Her thoughts drifted to the cute Fed and she groaned again. She shouldn't even be thinking of him like that. So what if he was cute? She'd known cute men before. Nothing changed the fact he was a Fed. She'd best remember that.

After what seemed like an eon, the call went through. With a sigh of relief, she greeted the operator who came on the line and gave him the information she required.

"I'm sorry, Detective. Our computers are down at the moment. I can't access any of our databases."

"Blast. Would you mind checking the details of a license plate for me once you're back online? I'd really appreciate it."

When the operator agreed, Ellie provided him with the plate number. A few moments later, she ended the call and stared at the phone on her desk. She'd been on hold nearly twenty minutes. Didn't these people know how important this information could be to her investigation? Didn't they know she could be that much closer to finding the thief if she knew the identity of the van owner?

With a muffled curse, she picked up her coffee cup and stomped her way to the tea room. She knew she was overreacting. It was just that there was a head without its body sitting in a Sydney morgue and they still didn't have a single clue about where to find the murderer. Or the missing bits.

It was getting her down. Why couldn't they catch a break and *find* him? She'd promised Jacqueline Caruso.

To make matters worse, there was the damnable growing attraction she had toward the Fed who'd invaded her life. No matter how hard she tried to shut him out, he kept intruding on her thoughts, causing her heart to beat just a little bit faster. *What the hell was she going to do about that?*

"God, dammit!" She didn't realize she'd spoken aloud until she saw the Fed in question offer her a crooked smile from where he stood across the room near the coffee machine.

"I know exactly how you feel," he offered. "I went back out to the Nepean River yesterday looking for Bill Griffin. Thought I'd go over his statement again and see if there was anything else he remembered." His lips pursed. "Guess what? No one's seen hide or hair of him for a week. With no fixed abode, who knows how we're going to find him." He shook his head in disgust. "Now, we're down a witness. Our *only* witness."

Ellie growled her frustration. "There must be someone who saw something. How can a living woman have her head sawn off without anyone *hearing* anything?"

Ben strode into the room. His face was deathly pale. Her stomach knotted.

"What is it, sir? What's the matter?"

"Another body's been found. Or, I should say, parts of another body."

"Shit," the Fed murmured behind her.

She knew exactly how he felt.

CHAPTER 6

"This route's becoming awfully familiar." Clayton broke the silence in the car and turned to look at Ellie.

She frowned in response and turned onto the highway that would take them north toward Cranebrook. "Too familiar."

He sighed heavily. "So, what have we got this time?"

"Ben only had scant information. Something about a fisherman hauling in a bag of human body parts out of the river."

He turned to her, shocked. "I was out there yesterday. I didn't see a thing."

"Don't be too hard on yourself, Fed. You're an AFP officer, not Superman."

Hiding his irritation, Clayton turned toward the window. Picking a fight with her would achieve nothing. It was obvious she resented his presence, but earlier, he'd thought they were beginning to move past that. It just went to show he knew zilch. As far as women were concerned, he was totally out of practice. He tried again, straining to keep his tone even.

"Any idea who it is?"

"Nope. No head this time and no torso. Just a couple of legs and arms. Apparently, the fingernails have red polish on them."

"So it could be Angelina Caruso?"

"Seems like it could be. Unless the bastard's carved up another woman. It's anyone's guess where the rest of her is."

Clayton swallowed the bile that rose in his throat. Pressure mounted behind his eyes. Frustration twisted his gut and the weight of responsibility was like a cement pylon across his shoulders. He'd been in Sydney an entire week and was no closer to discovering the identity of the killer than when he'd arrived. He believed they were looking for someone who appeared perfectly ordinary. Someone everyone saw, yet nobody noticed.

Which left him with a million different possibilities.

He'd spent the majority of the week interviewing friends of the missing girls, teachers, administration staff. Hell, he'd even interviewed the cleaners. And for all his efforts, he'd come up with nothing.

He pressed his eyes shut with the heel of his hands and took a deep breath, trying to curb the irritation that knotted inside him. When he groaned and opened his eyes Ellie was looking at him, questions filling her curious green eyes. The same green eyes that had kept him sleepless since he'd arrived.

He frowned. His attraction for her had blindsided him from their very first meeting. She didn't even come up to his shoulder, but the fire in her eyes and her scintillating aura of defiance and determination had captivated his attention.

She was obviously unhappy about his presence, but he'd expected that. He'd yet to walk into a squad room full of State police officers and be welcomed with open arms. They might be all batting for the same team, but most State officers thought less of the AFP—they were to be tolerated and only if absolutely necessary.

It had a lot to do with the fact the AFP declared themselves an elite force, the crème de la crème of policing. He was the first to concede this notion engendered a fair amount of arrogance and conceit among some of its members and there were a number of federal officers who openly considered their State counterparts the poor relations.

He'd never thought of them like that. It was the State police who did the grunt work—the real detective work, as far as he was concerned. The day-to-day grind of keeping the streets safe. Putting their bodies and lives on the line to make sure it was so. And thank God they did. He couldn't imagine the chaos if the State lawmen decided to hang up their boots for a day or two.

Clay's gaze flicked back to Ellie. A few strands of her glossy, chestnut-colored hair had defied the short, straight bob and curled around her ear like a lover's finger. Teasing, tempting, tantalizing. He itched to touch it. To touch her. Swearing under his breath, he turned back toward the window and gazed unseeingly at the passing traffic.

"What's the matter, Fed? You look like someone's just stolen your last all-day sucker."

He choked. A kaleidoscope of images of Ellie with her mouth open, her tongue tasting, tumbled through his mind. He tried and failed to keep the heat from spreading to his face. The fabric of his suit pants grew tight and he squirmed. It was an immediate and entirely unwelcome response, and one he had absolutely no control over. He clung to visions of his wife Lisa, with her soft-brown eyes and silky blond hair, in an effort to dislodge the dangerously erotic thoughts that threatened his sanity. Guilt settled like concrete in the pit of his belly.

For Christ's sake, what the hell had come over him? Lisa had been gone for nearly three years and he'd barely had a passing thought about another woman. He sure as hell hadn't wanted to sleep with any of them. Damned if he knew what it was about this pint-sized spitfire that suddenly had him responding in a way he thought had died along with his wife?

How could he even be thinking about another woman? He'd promised himself to Lisa—his heart, his mind, his soul. Forever and ever. Amen.

Somehow, that message was getting lost between his heart and his head—or more precisely, his groin, and he wasn't happy about that. Worse still, he didn't have a clue what to do about it.

Despite his best intentions, Clayton's gaze slid back toward her. Small hands and slim fingers, with neat, unvarnished nails, gripped the steering wheel with confidence as she manoeuvred in and out of the heavy midday traffic. Her delicate wrists were just visible beneath a white tailored blouse and smart navy jacket. She'd tossed her heavy, woollen cloak and scarf into the back seat as she'd climbed into the vehicle.

His gaze dropped lower and wandered across her chest. He was disappointed to find most of it concealed beneath the jacket, although he recalled an earlier time in the heated squad room when she'd discarded it. Unbuttoned at the throat, her sheer blouse had allowed him a glimpse of pale skin. The generous swell of cleavage had done nothing to cool his interest.

Swallowing an impatient groan, he dragged his gaze away and stared back out the window. *Christ, what was he doing?* He'd only just gone through all of this and here he was, ogling her again? What was he? A randy teenager? She deserved better. Lisa deserved better.

And what about Olivia? He had a daughter to consider.

"I think this is it." Ellie's voice interrupted him as she pulled the car over to the side and stopped in front of a vacant lot. Police vehicles and unmarked cars cluttered the area as personnel from various police and forensic departments swarmed around.

Clayton opened the door and climbed out. He waited as Ellie retrieved her scarf and coat and tugged them on. He caught a glimpse of her chest as her blouse stretched tight and was annoyed by his body's immediate reaction.

She looked up. "Did you bring a coat?"

He shook his head, unable to meet her eyes. The air was crisp and the light wind had a bite to it, but for someone used to living a couple of hours' drive from the snowfields, this Sydney winter barely registered.

She shrugged. "Might as well go and see what all the fuss is about."

"Detective Cooper, what a pleasure to see you again."

A curly haired surfer type with bulging forearms and keen gray eyes sidled up to Ellie and gave her a friendly nudge. *Too friendly.*

Clayton tensed. He shouldered his way forward and inserted himself between them. Thrusting his hand out, he forced the other man to acknowledge him.

"Federal Agent Munro," Clayton stated.

"Detective Jake Lyon. Forensics." He eyed Clayton with obvious distrust and tried to crush his hand in a meaty grip. Clayton held his gaze, refusing to flinch. A knowing smirk tugged at the other man's lips and he grudgingly surrendered Clayton's hand.

Ellie appeared oblivious to the exchange. She was all business as she turned to Jake. "What have we got?"

Putting aside his display of macho prowess, Jake's face turned serious. "I've never seen anything like it, Coop. It's probably best I show you."

He headed toward the group of technicians and local police who were busy securing the scene and pushed his way through. Clayton and Ellie followed after him.

"A local fisherman got it caught in his line and hauled it in. He was fishing from the shore. Lucky for us, the killer used half a dozen heavy-duty bags to wrap them in or the hook would have broken through and let go." He flicked his gaze to Ellie's. "We might never have found her."

Clayton spied the black plastic garbage bags where they lay torn and open on the ground. Tugging on a pair of latex gloves from his jacket pocket, he squatted and opened them wider.

The stench of rotten flesh hit him like a physical blow and he turned his head away, scrambling to control his stomach. It was lucky he hadn't had lunch.

Squeezing a tiny breath through his mouth, he forced his head back around. There was no way he was going to disgrace himself while Jake "the bodybuilder" Lyon looked on. He caught another glimpse of the greenish-black, swollen flesh and bones that filled the bag.

"Shit." The muttered curse fell from his lips. They'd been in the water awhile. The decay was advanced. The pieces were barely recognizable as human body parts. He caught a flash of red nail polish on the grotesque fingers and his stomach clenched again.

He stood and met Ellie's eyes, his lips pursed grimly. "It's not good."

She held his gaze. He could see the resolve in her eyes as she psyched herself up to look inside the bag. His admiration for her grew. Stepping away to give her room, he waited as she moved forward and squatted near the gruesome discovery.

He could tell the exact moment she spied the rotting remains. Her whole body tensed and she swallowed a little convulsively against the putrid stench. He knew how difficult it was for her to overcome the instinctive need to retch. He'd fought against the same urge himself. Like any normal person would.

His eyes narrowed and determination hardened into resolve. He'd been brought in to unravel this. And he would. Before any more women were mutilated. The weight of responsibility settled on his shoulders and this time he welcomed the feeling. It's what he did best. Putting together intricate details of a perpetrator until a picture emerged of a killer they could identify—killer that would strike again if he could. There was nothing surer.

He looked over to where Ellie stood speaking with some of the other officers. As if sensing his interest, she glanced up. She held his gaze for long moments, her green eyes fierce, before turning away again.

His gut knotted in response and he gritted his teeth. Being busy was good. Finding a killer was good. It helped to keep other unwelcome and distracting thoughts about Ellie from his head. She sidled up close beside him and his breath shortened. He tried not to inhale her vanilla-sweet scent.

"The morgue guys are here." She nodded toward the bag on the ground a short distance away. "They're taking it in. I told them we'd tag along."

His gaze bounced off her. "Good. Let's do it. We need to get her identified."

Clayton and Ellie strode into the cool, fluorescent-lit environs of the Westmead Morgue just as Dr Samantha Wolfe reached for a surgical mask. The black trash bags lay open on a stainless steel gurney not far away. It was late afternoon, but the place still looked lively. Three other pathologists worked on bodies stretched out on nearby gurneys. Every now and then the sound of a Stryker saw squealing through bone interrupted the almost-surreal serenity of the large room.

Clayton suppressed a shudder. Christ, he didn't know how the hell people worked in a place like this. The smell alone was enough for him.

Spying the two of them from across the room, Samantha signaled a greeting.

"Detective Cooper, I see you've drawn the short straw again."

Ellie's lips compressed into a semblance of a smile. "I guess you could say that." She glanced toward Clayton. "I think you've already met Federal Agent Munro."

Well-shaped eyebrows rose above the green surgical mask. Brown eyes, alive with mischief, raked over him. "The profiler from the AFP, right? We met the other week."

Clayton nodded a brief acknowledgement. Ellie took off her jacket, draping it over the back of a chair near the doorway they'd just entered. Opening a cupboard nearby, she pulled out a plastic apron and a mask and tugged them on. Turning back to the doctor, she indicated the garbage bags.

"We're hoping these belong to Angelina Caruso. If they don't..." Her voice drifted off.

With eyes that had seen the worst man had to offer, Samantha's gaze rested briefly on Ellie and then moved over to Clayton. "It means one of two things. Either there are two sick bastards out there carving up women or it's another victim of the same sick bastard." Her gaze narrowed in contemplation and her tone challenged him. "I take it that's why they've called in the Feds."

He kept his expression neutral. "I'm here to help."

Her lips smacked with appreciation. "Hmm, love 'em or hate 'em, they sure make 'em cute down there."

Heat flooded his face. Irritation and embarrassment surged through him. He risked a sideways glance and was disconcertingly pleased to see Ellie's cheeks were also flushed with embarrassment. She suddenly seemed awfully interested in the array of protective gowns, hats, gloves and shoe coverings filling the cupboard that remained open beside her.

His irritation at the doctor's inappropriate comment subsided in the face of Ellie's obvious discomfort. A tingle of delight and something that felt very like anticipation ran through him.

So, she wasn't as unaware of him as she'd let on. That was an interesting development and one he shelved away for further contemplation when the time was right. When guilt wasn't filling every one of his pores and Lisa's beloved face wasn't materializing before him.

He gave an impatient shake of his head. Lisa had been his world and he'd failed her. Whatever he was feeling for the fiery detective was purely physical—a male's spontaneous reaction to a beautiful woman. Nothing more. He'd best remind his libido of that sometime in the near future. The way his heart kept skipping a beat whenever she came near was becoming damned annoying.

Ellie peeked in the Fed's direction. The embarrassment that had clouded his features a few minutes earlier had subsided and had been replaced with a grim determination. She watched him as, with impatient tugs, he pulled protective clothing over his suit. She could only guess at what had soured his mood.

Samantha's reference to his looks had hit a nerve. Either that or he was completely unaware of his own physical beauty and had his thoughts totally immersed in the case.

She gave a mental shrug and finished tying the plastic apron around her waist. She didn't know much about him— hell, she didn't know anything about him. Apart from the fact that he was drop-dead gorgeous and was an old friend of her boss.

Oh, and of course...that he was a Fed. She couldn't forget that.

"I found this in the bag when I emptied it out onto the gurney." Samantha held up a bloodied gold chain with a small round stone pendant hanging from it. Ellie moved closer.

"I'll DNA the blood on it, but it's my guess it belongs to the victim," Sam added.

Clayton shifted closer and made his way around the opposite side of the steel table. His eyes were like flint as they stared at the mess of decomposed body parts spread out in front of him. "What kind of a sick bastard does this?"

The words were thrown out in a snarl. Ellie felt the heat of his anger as it swirled across the gurney, enveloping her. Her gaze locked onto his and she almost gasped at the fury she saw in them.

Not that she blamed him. She felt exactly the same way. Her gut tightened as she took in the display before her. The girl's arms and legs lay in a bloated, brackish-green heap. Samantha had arranged the pieces in their anatomical position. The open wounds at the juncture of two of the girl's limbs were dark with congealed blood. The sight of it didn't bode well for the manner of her death.

Ellie swallowed the bile that rose up in her throat and turned away. Clayton was right. How could one human being do this to another? Not even animals carved their prey up in such a sadistic way.

Samantha bent over the table, closely examining the severed limbs. "It looks like saw striations through the bones. I can't say for sure until I check them under the microscope, but it looks like the same kind of saw that was used in the last case."

Turning back to the gurney, Ellie willed the nausea to settle. She snatched small breaths of air through her surgical mask and tried to keep her mind focused on the job. Clayton looked across at her, concern now clouding his eyes.

Answering his unasked question with a grim nod of reassurance, she forced herself closer to the woman who lay in pieces on the table. A glint of something metallic caught her eye.

Reaching out with gloved fingers, she lifted one of the woman's arms. Around her left wrist, a heavy silver charm bracelet swung slightly with the movement. The bracelet was dark with what looked like blood and debris, but was still intact.

Clayton saw it simultaneously. His gaze clashed with hers. Ellie's hand shook as she lowered the arm back to the gurney. Clayton moved closer. His aftershave tickled her nostrils and smelled so good she immediately felt ashamed for even thinking of something so normal while she stood over the battered remains of the daughter of Jacqueline Caruso.

"It's her," Clayton murmured.

Ellie nodded. "Yes, I think so."

His eyes darkened and he moved to stand beside her. His sleeve brushed up against her arm. "Are you all right?"

She drew in a steadying breath. "Yes."

"Look at her hands. She put up a fight."

Ellie looked. Angelina's fingernails were long and neatly shaped. On her left hand, bright red paint had chipped off in pieces and one nail had broken off in a jagged line. Ellie peered closer and could see dirt and other matter backed up underneath them.

Samantha's expression was sober. "I'll take scrapings from under her nails and let you know what we find."

"Let's hope it's something useful," Ellie managed.

"The other hand doesn't look quite as traumatized," Clayton said. He held the girl's wrist and turned over her right hand. The nails and crimson polish were intact. Only a shadow of some material could be seen beneath them.

He met Ellie's curious gaze. "I'd say she's left-handed."

She looked away and cleared her throat against the sudden wave of emotion that threatened to undo her. All she could think of was how she was going to break the news to Jacqueline Caruso.

"I'm taking it you know who she is?" Samantha asked.

Ellie nodded. "We think it's Angelina Caruso. Her head was brought in a few weeks ago. The jewelry matches."

The doctor gave a brief, grim nod. "At least that means only one woman suffered the horror of being carved up alive. I guess we can be thankful for that." She picked up a tool from the stainless steel tray beside her and bent over what remained of Angelina. "I'll let you know what we get back from the lab. Let's hope there are some skins cells under those nails."

Ellie threw her a grateful smile. "Thanks, Samantha. We'd really appreciate that."

"I'll give you a call when I know something."

Stepping away from the table, Ellie peeled off her gloves and other protective gear and threw them in the garbage bin and watched Clayton do the same.

"Let's go," she murmured.

He opened the door and waited for her to precede him. She caught his heavy sigh on the air behind her and knew exactly how he felt.

CHAPTER 7

Clayton took a healthy mouthful from the icy bottle of beer and stretched out in the large beige armchair he'd moved close to the sliding glass door leading onto the balcony of his hotel room. The door was half open, allowing the crisp winter air to drift in around him.

The night sky had settled in and lights from a thousand or more office windows twinkled back at him. His gaze shifted to the myriad of blue and red and yellow neon advertising signs glowing off the tops of many of the skyscrapers. Earth Hour in Sydney would be surreal. With all the lights switched off, the night would be black enough to see the stars.

It was something he missed about Canberra. He'd been in Sydney almost a month and he'd yet to catch a glimpse of a single star. Too much artificial light, he guessed and too many tall buildings blocking the view.

Nevertheless, it was still an exciting place to be. Most of Canberra's streets quieted down after six, but Sydney lay awake for hours, with people passing in the street below him, cars and buses and taxis, horns blowing and the occasional shout. There was something so alive about it. Despite the fact he was a country boy, he could definitely see its appeal.

He concentrated on the noise from the street, fifteen stories below him. His lips turned up into a wry grin. Already, it had become a faint murmur, a background noise that barely disturbed the weariness of his thoughts. He took another swig from his beer and relished the malty taste on his lips.

DNA tests had confirmed their suspicions. He'd gone with Ellie to see Jacqueline Caruso. The memory of the woman's face, crumpling with grief and devastation would stay with him forever. Even though she'd known her daughter was dead, to have it hammered home all over again by two police officers coming to confirm they'd found some more of her must have been unbearable.

His jaw tightened. Frustration surged through him. They needed a breakthrough. Something, anything that would bring them closer to capturing Angelina's killer.

It would be days, weeks even before the lab would have results on the material under her nails and even longer to identify the killer's DNA—if they were lucky enough to find any, and if they did, that it matched someone in the database.

Panic nipped at his gut. He tamped it down. Now wasn't the time to lose control. What he needed was a cool, calm head. To do what he did best. To put the pieces they did know into an organized framework and slowly but surely build a picture of the killer.

A pile of old case files lay spread across his bed. He'd requested them from the records department, had specifically asked for cases involving violent assaults and homicides that featured female victims. Though he'd spent the best part of the evening making notes on them he was still not completely convinced he was on the right track.

Then there was the art professor. Stewart Boston was definitely still on his radar. Now that they'd established both of the missing girls and Angelina had attended the university, interviewing the professor had taken on a greater urgency. What was more, the man fit the evolving profile.

He was a person people would trust—especially his students. A man who wouldn't look out of place on the campus or on a suburban street. A man Josie Ward would have willingly accepted a ride from.

After numerous frustrating manpower hours trying to track

Boston down, they'd at last discovered he'd left the country for Fiji. According to his flight details, he was due to touch back down in Sydney in two days. Clayton chafed at the delay, but knew he had no choice but to wait it out.

The plan was to follow the man home from the airport in the hope that if he were involved, he'd lead them somewhere significant. It wasn't uncommon for a psychopath to return often to the scene of his crimes. Even if it didn't work out that way, they'd ambush him anyway. A surprise interrogation was far more effective than one when the interviewee had a chance to prepare. Clayton relished the idea of confronting the professor. When they'd put the plan together, he'd insisted he would ride with Ellie when it was conducted.

Unbidden, images of Ellie swam before him. Her spicy, vanilla perfume teased his nostrils. Her hazel-green eyes, alight with intelligence and good humor seemed to mock him at the same time her generous lips curved into an inviting smile.

His body tightened in response, even though he knew this attraction was crazy. Who was he kidding? She'd never looked at him invitingly. Besides, he was still in love with Lisa. His wife. The love of his life.

Wasn't he?

Of course he was. With an impatient shake of his head, he pulled himself upright and stood. Finishing the last of his beer, he dropped the empty bottle into the trash can near the sink and went to his briefcase lying where he'd left it on the table. He reached for the photo album that went everywhere with him.

The worn, black leather showed signs of age, but it was something he'd never part with. It had been a graduation gift from his wife. Given to him three days after their first anniversary.

They'd always planned to wait until after they'd finished university to get married, but Mother Nature had other plans. Well, that and Lisa's forgetting to take the pill when they went away together for the summer break.

They'd gotten married right away, of course. Not out of any sense of duty, although he'd certainly felt that. But it was Lisa, his Lisa. The girl he'd loved and adored since the first moment he'd caught sight of her across the loud and noisy university courtyard during orientation week.

So what if they were only twenty-two? So what if things were happening a little ahead of time? They'd only had a year left of their studies. They'd already decided to get married straight after graduation.

She was going to be a teacher. She loved everything about kids. She used to giggle and wink at him and say she couldn't wait to have a tribe of her own.

He was studying forensic science. With his father a District Court Judge and all four of his brothers in the police force, the law was in his blood.

Clayton took a seat at the small round table in the far corner of the room and opened the leather-bound album. His heart tripped over like it always did when he saw the photo.

With tender fingers, he caressed the white parchment of the funeral card, touching the soft features of his first-born child, forever captured on its cover.

Dominic Clayton Munro
21st October, 2006—23rd October, 2006

He'd lived for two days. Two whole days. Born early at twenty-three weeks and weighing just four hundred and fifty grams, the doctors had told them there was little hope.

Still, he'd sat by his son's high-tech hospital crib and had watched and prayed for every second of those forty-eight hours. He'd seen the tubes and electrical devices and monitors and equipment of every description going into and out of his son's tiny body and still he'd prayed he would make it.

But he hadn't.

Lisa had been inconsolable. Clayton had felt the loss like a physical blow, but he'd buried his pain, along with his son, and had helped his wife look forward to the future. Less than a year later, they'd had Olivia.

Olivia. The thought of his precocious four-year-old brought a smile to his lips. He checked his watch and closed the album with a sigh. Olivia would be going to bed soon and he still hadn't called her.

Pulling his laptop toward him, he connected to Skype and saw that she was already online. With a click of the mouse, the call went through. Anticipation built as he saw a fuzzy image of her face materialize on the screen before him. His heart lightened.

"Hey, baby, how was preschool? Are you being good for Grandma?"

Rick Shadlow drew a tortured breath deep into his lungs and wished he was dead. Curled up in a ball on the cold tiles of the filthy bathroom in his apartment, he hugged himself and willed the pain away.

She was gone. And it was all his fault. He should never have said the things he did. He should never have sent her away. They'd had fights before, but not like this. Never like this.

A low keening wail started from the pit of his belly, his muscles cramping and twisting and flinching as the howl made its way up his windpipe and out through his clenched teeth. The pain in it hurt his ears and his hands came up around his head in an effort to block out the noise.

"Sally...Sally...Sally... Why?"

He'd loved her with everything that he was. He'd have given her the world. He hadn't meant what he'd said. He hadn't meant any of it.

But now she'd disappeared. The cops had been there. They'd told him so.

He howled again and swiped at the snot hanging from his nose. Tears had soaked into his T-shirt, turning the dirt that streaked it a muddy gray. His hair hung lank and unwashed around his ears. He couldn't remember the last time he'd showered. Not since Sally had gone, that was for sure.

Taking another deep breath, he pulled himself into a sitting position and reached for the bag of white powder that sat on the lid of the toilet. He picked up the belt and tightened it around his arm with a hand that shook. It took him four attempts to make his lighter work, but finally, he held the bluish-orange flame to the blackened, old teaspoon.

With the fingers of one hand, he drew the drug up into his last syringe, careful to drain every last drop. Crazed with need, he sank the sharp tip into his vein and pushed the dispenser home.

Relief surged through him. Oblivion was only seconds away.

Ellie strode into the squad room and came to a halt in front of Clayton. He glanced up from the file spread across his desk.

Her normally arrow-straight hair looked mussed and untidy as it curled riotously around her face. She grabbed at the wayward strands and tucked them impatiently behind her ears, a frown marring the smooth skin of her forehead.

He busied himself shuffling papers around on his desk while he brought his traitorous pulse rate under control. She leaned toward him, peering at the file opened on his desk.

"What have you got there?" she asked.

"Good morning to you, too, Detective Cooper." He leaned back in his chair and stacked his hands behind his head. The movement took him further away from her and he sighed under his breath, unsure if he felt disappointment or relief.

She blushed and glanced down at her feet. "Yeah, well, good morning, Fed."

He let that go. "It's the old file on Wayne Peterson. I'm sure you remember him? He got released about three months ago."

Her eyes widened. "You think that piece of scum could be responsible for our girls?"

Shaking his head, he ran a frustrated hand through his hair. "Who knows? Maybe. It's just something I'm looking into. After all, the bastard's just done ten years for violent assault and rape—perhaps he's upped the ante?"

"Yeah, well they usually learn how to hone their skills inside, don't they? Not many, the likes of Collins, come out better off." She propped her hip on his desk. "What made you finger him? I thought you liked the professor?"

"Yeah, I did. I still do, but I'm just canvassing all angles. I think it's worth checking Peterson out." With a grimace, he leaned over and picked up the file. "Where do you want me to start?" He flipped over the first couple of pages and began reading.

"First arrest, twelve years old. Stealing women's underwear off clotheslines." He looked up at her. Ellie raised an eyebrow. He shrugged unapologetically. "I got hold of his juvie record."

"What else?"

"Next arrest was when he was fourteen. A bit more serious that time. Caught setting fire to a neighbor's cat. He was let off with a good behaviour bond. A string of arrests for assault—all before he turned sixteen. He finally landed in juvie just before his seventeenth birthday. He put a bloke in hospital for a month after a fight over a girl. Seems like he wasn't happy with the way the victim looked at her."

Ellie's lips thinned. "And the rest of it, as they say, is history."

"You got it in one." He consulted the file again. "Got into drugs while he was in detention—just grass, by the look of it, but by the time he'd hit the big time, he was hooked on some pretty heavy stuff."

With a sound of disgust, he closed the file and threw it onto his desk. "At least, that's what his barrister tried to argue at his trial for the rape of that nineteen-year-old. The one he tied up and raped so many times she nearly bled out internally."

Ellie's eyes darkened with anger. "Let me guess. Now he's out on the streets again?"

"Yep. He was let out of Long Bay in April. Out on parole and free to come and go as he pleases. The address he gave to his parole officer is in Penrith. That's what got my antennae up."

A frown creased her forehead as she picked up the file and opened it. "Is that where he's from?"

"Somewhere around there. I think his parents lived at Cranebrook. Seems like they disowned him years ago."

"They should have drowned him at birth and done us all a favor."

"You won't get any arguments from me, babe."

She tensed and her eyes widened on his momentarily before she looked away. A faint blush stole into her cheeks.

His heart accelerated and he cleared his throat, casting around for something to say. "Are you up for paying Peterson a visit this afternoon?"

Suddenly, she turned on him. "I want to hear your take on all this. After all, that's what you're here for, isn't it? To give us some idea about who this monster is?"

Her cheeks were flushed and her breath came fast. Clayton looked away and gave her time to compose herself.

"I take it you don't think Peterson could have done it?" he murmured.

Frustration rolled off her in waves. "How the hell do *I* know? You're the expert. That's why they pay you the big bucks."

Clayton forced himself to remain calm. The tone of his voice belied his inner turmoil when he said, "You're right. And I wouldn't want you to think you're not getting your money's worth."

He ignored the narrowing of her eyes and the glare she shot his way. She was gorgeous when she was all fired up. Hell, she was gorgeous anytime.

"Does Peterson fit the profile?"

"Yes."

Temper flared in her eyes. "So, you've put something together and haven't even bothered sharing it with the rest of us."

Anger seared through him at her inference. "You think I care more about my ego than I do about putting away an animal that doesn't even deserve to share the oxygen on this planet? Is that what you're trying to say?"

She had the grace to look embarrassed and lowered her eyes to concentrate on the stapler that sat on the end of his desk. "I'm sorry; I was out of line," she mumbled.

Clayton tugged loose his tie, frustration making his fingers clumsy. "The truth is, I have prepared a profile—well, a rough one, anyway. I haven't shared it with anyone because I only put it together late last night. You've only just arrived for the day. I thought you'd be upset if I started without you."

Her cheeks flushed crimson. A spurt of satisfaction pulsed through him, but he didn't persist. Instead, he continued with his explanation.

"While I chewed my way through Chinese take-away left over from the night before, I decided to pull any file relating to ex-cons with similar MOs. I didn't find an exact match, but there were three I found that were pretty interesting."

"Three?" She sounded surprised. "But you only said—"

"Yeah, I know. Peterson was one. Then there's a bloke by the name of Bobby Cutmore who's been in and out of the slammer for years for rape and some pretty violent assaults. The third one's a serial rapist by the name of Duncan Brown."

"But you don't think either of them did this?"

He shook his head. Seeing she was about to argue, he cut her off. "They're both in the big house."

Ellie deflated. "How long?"

He picked up two other files from a crowded corner of his desk. Opening the first one, he flipped over a few pages and read aloud.

"Duncan was put away a couple of years ago for a particularly vicious rape. He still has three years to run on his sentence." He opened the second file. "Cutmore's due for release next month."

A sigh escaped her lips. Okay, Peterson it is." She leaned back against his desk and crossed her arms over her chest. "Tell me about your profile."

He opened his eyes wide. "What, without the others? Ben's on the phone and Luke's gone out for coffee. You really want me to start before they get back? Because that would be kind of rude, you know."

Ellie grinned. "Okay, okay. I get it, but I still don't care. I want to hear it. Now."

Clayton's lips twitched and he made a production of pushing back his chair and sighing before he stood and wove his way through the clutter of largely vacant desks to the whiteboard that retained the information Ben had written on it nearly a month ago.

Picking up a marker, he spoke, making notes as he went. "Okay, based on what we know, here's what I think. We're looking for a white male, somewhere between twenty-five and forty. Not too young—a young guy might not appear trustworthy enough for a young girl to climb into their car—but maybe even a bit older. He's someone so ordinary, nobody even notices him. I also think it's safe to assume the guy's a local to the Penrith area. It's his territory. He's familiar enough with the area that he feels comfortable. So comfortable, he can pick up young women off the street and make them disappear and nobody even notices."

He paced around the cluttered confines of the squad room. "He's invisible to most of us. He goes about his daily excursions without raising the least suspicion. He's someone any one of us could pass by on the street and not even notice. He's someone Josie Ward would trust."

Ellie shuddered. Images of a smiling Ted Bundy flitted through her mind. Dread prickled her scalp. "So, he's like a cop or someone like that?"

"Yeah, possibly. Although Josie Ward went missing fairly late at night. It would be unusual to see a copper on his own doing a patrol that late. They're usually out in pairs. It would be a risky move for him. People would probably remember something like that."

Her frown was fierce. "That's if Josie's one of his victims. We don't know that yet."

Clayton opened his mouth to protest, but she cut him off with a wave of her hand.

"Okay, okay; what else?"

He let that pass. It was true, they didn't have proof Josie was a victim of their killer, but in his gut he knew things weren't looking good for her.

He turned back to the whiteboard. "Well, we know he likes to use a saw. So some kind of handyman—a builder or a carpenter—or even just someone who likes to play with timber in his spare time."

"Gee, that really narrows it down."

Her voice was as dry as over-cooked steak. Clayton ignored it and continued to write points on the whiteboard. "If we work on the theory that the missing girls are connected to Angelina's killer, he's either unemployed or has flexible working hours. He might even be a shift-worker." He turned around and held her gaze. "There doesn't seem to be a consistent time when any of the girls disappeared."

He ticked them off on his fingers. "Josie Ward was after ten at night. Angelina Caruso we're not exactly sure, but my guess is late afternoon or early evening. Her last class finished at five. No one saw her after that. For Sally Batten, it's also unclear, but I'd back the girlfriends who thought they saw her at class, to the dope-smoking boyfriend who wasn't sure when she'd last been home. One thing we do know is that they all disappeared on weekdays. Which means he's either at work on the weekends or he's tied up with his own life, then."

"What do you mean?"

"Well, he could have a family of his own. Don't forget, this guy appears to the rest of the world as just another average citizen. Maybe he leaves town on the weekends and goes to his holiday house. A lot of psychopaths lead typically normal lives during their downtime." He grimaced, his frustration evident. "Who knows? Despite what you see on TV, there's still a lot of guesswork involved."

"The art professor definitely ticks some of the boxes," Ellie said. We'll have to get a copy of his timetable. Find out when he has free time. I'd also like to know where he lives."

Clayton nodded thoughtfully. "Yeah, at the moment, he's up there with Wayne Peterson and I can't wait for him to step off that plane. But there are still a vast number of other possibilities. Even a taxi driver could fit the profile. Flexible working hours, unobtrusive, generally trusted at face value."

"Except none of our girls caught a cab."

"As far as we know... Josie Ward was supposed to catch one," he added.

Ellie opened her mouth to protest and he held up his hand, knowing what she was about to say. He gritted his teeth against another surge of frustration at how little he had to go on to develop the profile that could make all the difference.

He drew in a deep lungful of air and blew it out slowly through his lips. Ellie walked over and took the whiteboard marker out of his hand.

"Okay, let's assume our girls are connected. One thing I definitely agree with is that he lives around here." She drew a red circle around the suburbs of Greater Western Sydney displayed on an enlarged map taped to the whiteboard. They included Penrith, Cranebrook, Mt Druitt, Auburn, Fairfield and Blacktown.

He stared at the black dots representing each girl's last known location. On the same map, within easy driving distance of one another, two blue dots had been added to represent the places they'd found the body parts. It was clear it was the killer's hunting ground.

She turned to face him. "So, the question is, has he left any calling cards?"

"Have you heard anything from the lab?"

She shook her head. "Not yet, but I'm hopeful we'll get something. There was a lot of matter underneath Angelina's fingernails. Having her limbs sealed in the plastic bags helped to preserve some of the evidence, even if it did spend time in the water."

"You never know your luck."

Ben appeared in the doorway of his office. "Ellie, I've just had Jim Whitton on the phone. I thought you told him to call you direct?" Without giving her a chance to respond, Ben continued, "Anyway, he wants to know how you're going with his missing freezer." Spying Clayton, he strode toward them. "How's it going? Any leads?"

"Not really," Clayton replied, "but I found out Wayne Peterson has been back on the streets since April. Apparently, he's living in the Penrith area. I thought Ellie and I might go out and pay him a visit."

Ben's lips twisted. "Peterson. He's a nasty piece of work. I can't believe he's been let out." He glanced across at Ellie. "You got anything else?"

"No, sir. We're still waiting to hear back from the lab."

Ben sighed, his expression grim. "All right, well I guess that means you two are heading back out."

Clayton's voice lowered. "Right you are. I'm just in the mood to go visiting."

CHAPTER 8

Ellie deftly negotiated the early morning traffic and threw a glance at Clayton. "Did you talk to the parole officer?"

"Yep. Some guy over in the Penrith office. Sounded overworked and underpaid, like most of the poor bastards. The name Wayne Peterson barely registered with him."

She frowned. "I thought you said he was released three months ago?"

"That's right." His mouth was set in a grim line as he turned to look at her, his eyes speaking volumes.

"I take it Peterson hasn't been reporting like he's supposed to."

"Right again, Detective. You're pretty good at this."

Shaking her head in disgust at the system, she checked her rear view mirror and changed lanes. "So when was the last time he saw his PO?"

He sent her a dry look. "Take a guess."

Her eyes widened in disbelief. "You don't mean to tell me he's *never* shown up?"

"Not quite. He reported in during the week he was released. Gave the PO the Penrith address. After that, nothing."

"And the PO didn't report the breach? What the hell's he doing? Does he have any idea who Peterson is? Did he even bother to have a look at that fifteen-page record of his?"

Clayton threw his hands up in surrender. "Hey, I'm hearing you. Don't shoot the messenger. I'm on your side, remember."

The pent-up air in Ellie's lungs deflated. Banging her fist against the steering wheel, she gave vent to her frustration by cursing aloud.

They rode in silence for a few moments before he spoke again.

"I made some calls and had a couple of uniforms go over to his digs about twenty minutes ago. Apparently, they saw him through a window. Let's hope he hasn't caught wind of us and done a disappearing act."

Ellie's gut tightened. Cold, hard anger swirled inside her. The killer, whoever he was, had proven himself capable of unspeakable violence. She'd do whatever it took to find him and lock him away forever. Preferably down a very deep, dark hole.

Her lips compressed. Too bad that wasn't an option.

Clayton shifted in his seat and looked at her as she turned into Peterson's street. "Okay," he said. "Here's how we're going to handle it. You wait in the car while I work out if he's still in there. When I give you the nod, you come out."

"Yeah, like that's going to happen. Listen here, big shot. You're riding with *me*, remember? For all I know, you've spent most of your time behind a desk. I mean, have you even been out in the field before?"

Not waiting for his reply, she continued, steel in her voice. "We're going to do this *my* way or not at all. This is *my* turf, remember? If anyone's going to be sitting in the car, it'll be you. You got that?"

He held up his hands. "Okay, okay. I've got it. God help us if I tread on your turf."

Unamused, she kept her face forward and cruised to a stop a few houses down from the one they sought. The street was quiet, with only the occasional passing car interrupting the lazy silence of the morning. The skeletons of well-established Chinese elm trees, winter bare, lined both sides of the nature strip. Most of the yards were fenced with cheap wire and weathered wood palings once painted white. Overgrown lawn reached through the gaps, beckoning to the sidewalk.

Clayton's voice was a low murmur. "There's a car parked on the nature strip outside his house. Call the plates in so we can check who it's registered to."

Ellie squinted through the glare of the sun and took note of the details. Within minutes, the dispatcher returned with the information. The white 1982 model Falcon was registered to Arthur Jones. She hung up the handpiece and turned to him, a question in her eyes.

"A former cell mate of Peterson," Clayton supplied. "They were in Long Bay together a few years back. As they say, birds of a feather."

"I didn't find mention of Jones in Peterson's file."

"That's because it isn't in there." With a shrug, he turned to face the windscreen. "I made a few calls. Tracked down some of the officers in charge of Peterson's later arrests. Let's just say, most of them take a special interest in knowing who he associates with and where this bastard is."

Her lips twisted in derision. "Too bad the members of the parole board didn't see it that way."

"Yep. You've got that right. The hardest part is knowing there's not a damn thing we can do about it. Until the powers that be see fit to increase the funding for parole officers, there are going to be more and more of them failing to keep proper tabs on their clients."

Drawing oxygen deep into her lungs, Ellie held onto it for as long as she could. With a long sigh, she let the air slip through her parted lips. She turned to him. "You ready?"

A feral gleam of anticipation lit up his baby blues. "Bring it on."

———

"Open up! Police!" Ellie banged on the door again. Clayton covered her back, every nerve in his body on edge.

Adrenaline surged through him. He instinctively went for the gun at his hip and cursed silently when he realized he didn't have one. As much as he loved what he did as a profiler, it was times like this he remembered just how much he missed being in the thick of it.

Ellie shot him a quick look over her shoulder, her service revolver drawn. He signaled with his hand to go in. Peterson was already in breach of his parole. They wouldn't be breaking any laws by entering uninvited.

She turned the door handle then shook her head. It was locked. He nudged her aside and braced his shoulder against the weathered timber door. Taking a breath, he pushed hard.

The hinges squeaked in protest and he felt the wood give a couple of inches. Another shove and it gave way altogether. He collected himself and peered into the gloom. Ellie closed in behind him.

In the dim light, they discovered they were in a small lounge room. Two filthy couches stood against the walls. One sagged so low, part of it scraped the dirty floor. The other one was in a similar state of disrepair. Gaping tears in the cushions exposed pale gashes of foam. The smell of unwashed bodies, sweat and rotting food was overwhelming. The room was cold, silent and empty.

Moving on noiseless feet down a worn, carpeted hallway, Clayton signaled to Ellie that he was going to check out the room that opened to his left. She acknowledged him and continued past, her gun still drawn and at the ready.

As his eyes adjusted to yet another darkened room, he realized it, too, was empty. A noise coming from the direction Ellie had taken suddenly registered in the stillness.

A yelp of surprise.

Then the sound of flesh upon flesh and a moan of pain. He tore down the hall and came upon them.

Peterson lay face down on the scraped linoleum floor of the kitchen. Ellie leaned over him, her knee pressed against his back. The click of handcuffs was loud in the now-silent room.

Clayton came to a halt. "Looks like you've got everything under control."

For a pint-sized woman who looked like she weighed less than a hundred pounds, wringing wet, she sure knew how to handle herself. Although Peterson wasn't a big man, he outweighed her by at least half.

One single bloodshot eye stared at him balefully. "Fuckin' coppers. What the fuck do you want?"

Clayton *tsked tsked*. "Now, now, now. That's no way to speak in front of a lady. She deserves a little more respect." He stepped forward and pressed his boot deliberately against the man's neck. Peterson tried to twist his head away, his single eye now glaring at him with murderous intent.

Clayton increased the pressure, resisting the urge to slam his fist into the malevolent face as memories of the man's criminal history flooded back to him.

As if sensing how close he was to losing control, Ellie intervened. Standing, she rolled Peterson over and out from underneath Clayton's boot.

"We're just here to ask you a few questions." She eyed the lowlife. "We can do it the easy way or the hard way. You pick."

"You've already got me in fuckin' handcuffs."

Clayton stepped forward again, his fists clenched at his sides. "Hey, watch your mouth, buster. I'm not going to warn you again."

Ellie laid a restraining hand on Clayton's arm. "Who's living here with you, Wayne? You've got a pretty tidy setup here." Her gaze slid over the overflowing trash can and the sink full of dirty dishes. A dozen or more empty beer bottles stood haphazardly around the kitchen, along with a couple of half-empty cans of baked beans and a loaf of bread which spilled out across the cracked Formica counter. A grimy toaster stood in the corner.

Peterson grunted in response. Clayton gave him a none-too-gentle shove with his boot. "What was that, you grub? I'm afraid we didn't hear you."

Another grunt followed by a wad of spit that landed just shy of Clayton's shiny black boots.

Clayton's eyes narrowed. "Now you've really pissed me off." He bent down and heaved the man to his feet. Momentum dragged him forward. He pushed Peterson against the nearest wall.

"I thought I told you to mind your manners, dirt bag," he snarled. With a hefty thrust of his arm, Peterson' head hit the wall behind him.

"Munro, let it go."

Ellie's low voice slowly penetrated the fog of anger that enveloped him. Now he remembered why he'd opted for a desk job. He didn't have to put up with scum like Peterson.

Releasing the man's filthy flannel shirt, he stepped away. The smug look on Peterson' face was nearly enough for Clayton to have another go. But that's exactly what the little worm wanted. He could see it in his eyes.

Turning his back on him, Clayton went to lean against the open doorway that led back down the hall and tried to get his anger back under control.

"Right. Now, Wayne, let's try that again." Ellie was all brisk efficiency as she pulled a notebook and pen out of her jacket pocket. "We know this house belongs to Arthur. Where is he?" Her eyes drilled into Peterson' whose jaw jutted out at a belligerent angle.

"How the fuck would I know? I'm not his fuckin' mother."

Clayton tensed and pushed away from the wall. The look he gave Peterson was deadly. "I thought we'd already been over this, scumbag? Perhaps you need another reminder?"

He stepped closer, his eyes narrowed menacingly. Ellie moved between them.

"You haven't been checking in with your parole officer, Wayne," she said. "That's very naughty of you. And you're fraternizing with a known criminal. That's also a no-no. You know we could arrest you right now and throw you back in the slammer. Now, how about you try being nice to us for a change. Answer our questions and then we'll be on our way." She spread her arms wide in a magnanimous gesture.

"It's really quite simple."

The parolee eyed her distrustfully. "What kinda questions? I ain't done nothin'."

"Well, we're real glad to hear that, Wayne. It'd be a real shame for you to have to go back to the big house after only a few months. It's nice being on the outside, isn't it?"

With a non-committal shrug, the man's gaze dropped to the floor.

Clayton strode over to him and pulled up a couple of paces away. His sheer size alone must have felt intimidating to the much smaller man. Just as he meant it to. "Where were you on May twenty-ninth?"

Peterson looked at him blankly and didn't respond.

"How about July third? Come on, dirt bag, it was only a month ago. Where were you?"

Peterson shrugged again and looked even more confused. "How the fu—" He glanced toward Ellie and wisely tried again.

"How the hell would I know?" I wouldn't even know what day it is today, let alone what I was doing a month ago."

Clayton's face was now only inches away. The man's stench clogged his nostrils. "Well you'd better start thinking, buster, because we've got a bunch of young girls missing and one of them has turned up dead. We have you in our sights, scumbag. We know how much you like young girls."

Panic flared in Peterson's eyes. His gaze sought Ellie's. "It wasn't me! I dunno what you're talkin' about. You can't go pinnin' anything on me!"

Clayton glared at him, unmoved. "We're waiting on some DNA evidence from the lab. If it comes back as yours, we'll be back; you understand? And you'd better pack a decent supply of toothbrushes this time around. You won't be going anywhere for a long, long time."

Peterson struggled against the handcuffs. His eyes darted nervously around the room. "You can't do this to me! I dunno nothin' about no missin' girls. I swear!"

"Tell it to the judge, dirt bag." Clayton turned away and propped himself up against the doorway. Ellie stepped forward and unlocked the handcuffs.

Clayton's gaze remained narrowed on Peterson, pinning him where he stood, silently daring him to try something. It would give him immense satisfaction to see the worm back behind bars, where he belonged.

As if sensing the razor-edge hold Clayton had on his self-control, the man wisely chose not to move. Clayton screwed up his nose as another whiff of putrid body odor reached his nostrils.

"You might consider having a shower now and then, Peterson. You're on the outside, now. Or are you worried Arthur might take advantage of you?"

Peterson's face flared crimson and anger sparked in the bloodshot eyes. Clayton turned away. "Come on, Ellie. Let's get out of here."

Ellie unlocked the car and looked across at Clayton. "So, what do you think?"

He shook his head. "I don't know. He seemed a bit too out of it to be our man. I actually believed him when he said he didn't know what day it was. He looks like he's been on a bender for weeks."

He opened the car door and slid into the passenger seat, feeling grim. "Our guy's way too organized. And much more discreet. The way Peterson looks, not to mention the way he smells, there's no way he'd go unnoticed—and I can't see any of our girls going anywhere near him. At least, not without a struggle. And so far, no one's seen or heard anything. Besides, I'm certain we're looking for someone ordinary. I hate to say it, but I don't think he's our man."

"Well, I guess we'll know when the lab gets the results from Angelina Caruso. At least, we *hope* it's DNA evidence they find. You shouldn't have told Peterson we had it when we don't know that for sure."

Clayton flushed, but remained defiant. "That low-life

woman hater doesn't deserve procedural fairness."

"That may be so, but it doesn't mean—"

He lifted his hands up in surrender. "Okay, okay. I get your drift. I let him get under my skin. I shouldn't have."

"No, you shouldn't have."

A grin tugged at his lips. For all the money in the world, he wouldn't feel sorry for scum like Peterson. His eyes lit on her face. "So, sue me."

She returned his grin reluctantly. "You're incorrigible."

His smile widened. "Maybe so, but you like that in a man."

She laughed out loud. "And here I thought I'd totally misjudged you as the arrogant, egotistical Fed I'd pegged you for the minute I laid eyes on you."

"Funny, my first glimpse of you made me feel like I'd been run over by a Mack truck."

The air was suddenly charged with emotion. Neither of them dared to breathe. Her fingers tightened on the steering wheel. The pulse in her neck beat a frantic rhythm.

For a whole, long minute neither of them said a thing. Clayton was the first to break the taut silence.

"Look, I'm sorry. I shouldn't have said that. It was out of line and I have no idea where it came from. I don't even know what I was thinking. I—"

She turned away. "It's okay, really. It's okay."

"But—"

The buzz of her phone silenced him and he turned to contemplate the view outside the window while she answered the call.

"Hi, Ben. What's up?"

Although Clayton tried not to listen, it was impossible not to hear Ellie's sudden intake of breath. He turned reflexively and caught the tension in her body. Her mouth went tight while she listened.

Clayton's gut clenched. Christ, not another body.

Ellie ended the call and his heart sank at the sad resignation reflected in the shadowy depths of her eyes.

"That was Ben." Her lips thinned into a grim line. "He thinks someone's found Josie Ward."

CHAPTER 9

Even from a distance, Luke Baxter's face looked grave. Ellie and Clayton made their way across the vacant lot on the outskirts of Penrith Lakes. The grass was winter dry, long and unkempt. Graffiti stained the sides of the forest-green colorbond fence that bordered the property. A new subdivision of recently completed rendered-brick houses in varying shades of gray and charcoal stood less than fifty yards away from where the body had been found. The area was now cordoned off by blue and white crime scene tape.

The light had already started to fade when Ellie reached the circle of uniforms. She greeted Luke with a brief hug. "Hey, partner. How are you holding up?" Her eyes searched his, knowing the pain in their light blue depths was reflected in her own.

Luke shrugged and looked away. "You know."

"Yeah." She cleared her throat. "It was good of you to come."

He shrugged again and glanced toward Clayton, who stood off to one side. "I was at the station when Ben took the call. He's taking it pretty hard, too."

"I bet," she murmured.

Clayton moved closer. "Has her family been told?"

Luke shook his head. "No, not yet. I wanted to—see her first. You know, so I could tell her mother she...she hadn't suffered."

Somebody had covered her with a blanket. The kind you might have on the back seat of a car. Bending down, Clayton peeled it back and revealed what was barely recognizable as Josie's face. The girl's sightless eyes stared back at him, her once-innocent features now frozen in a death mask of horror.

He dropped the blanket back into place and stood. "How did she die?"

Luke cleared his throat. "Strangulation, we think. The decay's too advanced to show bruising, but there are no other signs of violence—apart from her arms."

Ellie frowned at him. "Her arms?"

He swallowed. "Yeah. She's ah... She's missing both arms."

"Christ." Clayton shook his head. "What the hell are we dealing with?"

"She's still wearing her uniform. No overt signs of sexual assault," Luke added. "I guess we can be grateful for that."

Ellie remained silent. They all knew the degree of decomposition made it impossible to tell whether she'd been raped. She looked up as a white van with the Westmead Morgue insignia painted in stark black across its sides came to a halt a short distance away.

"The morgue's here," she murmured.

They waited in silence as an unfamiliar forensic pathologist climbed out of the van, accompanied by two orderlies.

Ellie frowned as they approached. "Where's Samantha?"

The FP stuck out his hand and she shook it. "Jack Simmons. You must be Ellie Cooper. Sam's been held up with another case. She asked me to come out here and collect this one." He looked at the body that lay on the cold, bare ground.

Ellie watched as they slid Josie Ward into a black body bag and loaded her onto a gurney. Dread built inside her at the thought of telling Evelyn Ward.

Knowing it had to be done, she closed her eyes briefly

and gathered her courage. She looked across at Luke. "I'll go and see her mother."

Clayton stepped closer. "I'll go with you."

"Actually, you know, I think I'd rather tell her myself," Luke interrupted. "Evelyn and I have been talking a bit on the phone. I want to offer to be there when she formally identifies Josie."

Ellie looked at him, surprised. He shrugged uncomfortably.

"She called the station one day to see if we'd heard anything. The call was put through to me. It kind of became a regular thing. She's been calling every few days since Josie disappeared."

"Luke, I had no idea. That was very kind of you."

He shrugged again and looked down at the ground. "What could I do? I couldn't even imagine what she must have been going through, not knowing if her daughter was alive or dead." He met her gaze. "It was the least I could do."

"Well, I still think it's a pretty wonderful thing you did. I'm sure it's given her great comfort to be able to talk to someone about it."

Luke's face turned grim. "Fat lot of good it did."

Clayton laid a hand on the other man's arm, his eyes fierce. "We'll find him, Luke. You make sure you tell her; we're going to find him."

The sound of the van's rear doors closing snagged Ellie's attention. She lifted her gaze to Clayton's.

"We might tag along to the morgue then. Someone needs to be at the autopsy." She looked back at Luke. "If that's all right with you?"

"Yeah, go. I'll ask one of the others to ride along with me."

"Okay, then." She glanced at Clayton. "We'd better get going."

Striding back in the direction of her car, she turned to look over her shoulder. Luke still hadn't moved. "I'll see you back at the station," she called out to him. "Good luck."

"Yeah, thanks," he muttered. "I'll need it."

———————————

"Well, if it isn't Sydney's hardest-working detective and her pin-up boy from the south." Samantha Wolfe's eyes were alight with mischief as she looked at them from behind the green surgical mask.

Ellie acknowledged her in silence. Someone who voluntarily chose to work among the dead was entitled to any kind of sense of humor they could hold onto.

She sure as hell couldn't have done it. It was bad enough on days like this, when she had to go to the morgue while working on a case. And she wasn't even the one picking up the scalpel.

Unlike their previous visit, the gurney where the now-naked body of Josie Ward lay was the only one occupied. The morgue was silent save for the occasional noises made by Samantha as she performed the post-mortem.

Donning a plastic gown and tucking her short hair under a protective cap, Ellie pulled on a pair of latex gloves and moved closer to the stainless steel table.

Samantha had already made the Y incision and was in the process of dissecting and weighing the girl's organs. Clayton stepped forward, similarly attired in protective plastic. "What have you found?"

"Not much, yet. Heart, liver and lungs are all within normal limits. No stab wounds, bullet wounds or any other signs of violence. Apart from the severed limbs, of course, but that's not what killed her."

His eyes were intent on her face. "So what do you think she died from?"

"I had her x-rayed when she was brought in. There's a tiny bone at the base of her tongue that's been snapped clean through. It's called the hyoid bone. A fracture usually indicates strangulation." She glanced back at the body. "The decomposition's too far advanced to see bruises or other marks around the neck, but it looks to me like that's what happened to this one."

Ellie tried to block out the images. "What about the arms? What can you tell us about them?"

Samantha walked around to Josie's left side. She turned the body and adjusted the light until the blackened wound at the girl's shoulder could be clearly seen. Picking up a pair of tweezers, she leaned closer and pulled out various small pieces of vegetable matter. "It's pretty dirty. There's a large abrasion on her back where her skin's been scraped away and there's a ton of debris and other garbage in this wound. It's the same on the other side."

She lifted her gaze. "It looks like the killer had hold of her by the ankles and dragged her along on her back for a distance after she died. You'll see there's a substantial amount of debris and other rubbish also caught in her hair and another large abrasion on the back of her head."

Ellie's gaze moved to the young girl's once-shiny brown hair. It was shorter and a little curlier than she remembered from the photos Evelyn Ward had given her, but then she recalled the woman had told them they'd both been to the hairdresser the day Josie disappeared.

She leaned closer to examine the material in the girl's hair. "What do you think that is?" she murmured to Clayton, pointing to a tiny, curling sliver of debris caught amongst the strands.

He bent closer, his head only inches from hers. With a gloved finger, he touched the flake of material.

"Looks like a fine wood shaving. It's pale and fine, so something like pine, perhaps. Maybe she collected it along the way?"

Her gaze moved over the girl's head. When she looked closer, she could see more tiny slivers of wood shavings, some bigger than others, but all similar in color and shape and all caught in Josie's hair.

She met his eyes. "Either that or she's been on the floor of a carpenter's workshop."

Samantha sidled over for a look. "Whatever it is, there's a fair amount of it. I'll put it under the microscope, see what we can find out about it. Come and have a look at the shoulder wounds. I've flushed them out."

Ellie straightened and moved further down the table until she stood close to Clayton where he'd stopped near Josie's hips. Samantha tilted the body onto its side again so they both had a better view.

She pointed with the tip of her scalpel to the wound at the girl's left shoulder, which was now clean and free of debris.

"If you have a look here, you can see clear striations from the teeth of a saw. It's the same on the right. And both bones are still full of blood."

Ellie's heart sank. "You mean...?"

The doctor nodded, her expression grim. "Her heart was still beating when the arms were severed."

"Christ, not again," Clayton muttered, stepping back and running a hand through his hair.

Ellie swallowed against the bile that rose in her throat and tried not to imagine the horrors Josie Ward had endured in the moments before her death. She prayed the girl's family never found out.

Her eyes burned into Samantha's. "Do we know if it's the same one?"

"The same saw you mean?"

"Yes, if it's the same one used on Angelina Caruso."

"I'll have to make up some slides and compare them microscopically, but I'm hoping there aren't two madmen out there cutting limbs off women while they're still breathing."

Clayton pulled viciously at the expensive tie around his neck in an effort to loosen it as he paced back and forth across the room. Ellie could see he was struggling to keep his anger under control.

He swung around and pinned Samantha with eyes that were dark with emotion. "How soon can we have the results?"

"The slides can be prepared overnight. The wood shavings might take a little longer to identify."

Impatience and irritation flared in the blue depths. "What about the material found under Angelina's fingernails? Do you have any results back from that?"

Her brow creased in a frown. "Not yet. We had to outsource it. Our budget's tight and—"

"We need those results." His tone brooked no argument.

"I'll chase it up."

"Yesterday isn't soon enough." He turned and strode out of the room.

The sun's orange-red glow had completely disappeared over the horizon and the night's winter chill had set in when Ellie caught up with Clayton outside the morgue. The tension in his body was still evident as he leaned against the squad car and waited for her. Despite the dimness, designer sunglasses shaded his eyes from her view.

"It's not her fault, you know." She frowned at him as she unlocked the car with the remote and climbed in.

A moment later, he slid in beside her, pulled off his shades and sighed. "I know. I guess I should go back in there and apologize. It's just that I feel so responsible. And at the moment, I've been about as useful as tits on a bull."

His eyes were bleak when he turned to her. "I'm being paid the big bucks, as you so eloquently put it, to find this monster. All I've managed to do since I got here is to count the bodies."

His frustration and feelings of inadequacy became almost a tangible presence between them. A wave of sympathy washed over her. She wondered briefly about his past. Had someone he'd loved met with a violent end? Was that the driving force behind him?

He interrupted her musings with a hard stare. "Don't go feeling sorry for me, Ellie. That's not what I need. Chew me out, tell me what an incompetent, ineffectual, over-paid bastard I am, but don't feel sorry for me."

Her eyes narrowed on his face. "All right, but remember, you asked for it. "You're one of the most incompetent, ineffectual, inadequate, completely over-paid, arrogant, egotistical *Feds* I've ever met."

A reluctant grin tugged at his lips. "You don't hold back, do you?"

She offered an unrepentant shrug. "Why should I? You've been here nearly a month and as you just admitted, all you've really done is help with the body count."

She turned on the ignition and put the car into gear, checking her mirrors before pulling out into the heavy, peak-hour traffic. Flicking him a glance, she continued.

"You offered a reasonable possibility in the guise of Wayne Peterson, but after ten minutes with him, even I could tell he wasn't our man. Stewart Boston's still at the top of your list and by this time tomorrow, maybe we'll have all the answers we need."

She drew in a breath. "In the meantime, I don't want to hear you bemoaning the fact that you've ridden in on your white charger and in all the time you've been here, you still haven't managed to solve the mystery or win the girl."

His gaze slid over her in a slow inspection, paying extra attention to her heaving chest. The heat rose in Ellie's cheeks. "Um, that was meant in the metaphoric sense, not the literal one."

His grin was lascivious. "I know what you meant."

She turned away and kept her concentration firmly on the road in front of her. She needed something to keep herself occupied. If the conversation continued in its current vein, things could turn dangerous. She had no arsenal against those emotion-filled eyes. Not to mention the broad shoulders, narrow hips and impressively taut butt.

Oh, yes. Even through his tailored suit pants, she'd noticed his butt.

"What do you say we go and grab a bite to eat? It's been a long time since that bagel and coffee I had for breakfast."

She shot him a look of disbelief. "Breakfast?"

He grimaced. "Yeah, I got busy reviewing the case material and forgot about lunch. Then with the house call we made and the call out..." He shrugged.

She mulled over his suggestion, buying some time by concentrating on the passing traffic around them. Sharing a meal with him was probably not the wisest thing she could do right now. Her hormones were reminding her it had been way too long since she'd been in the company of an attractive man and everyone knew it was suicide to get involved with a work colleague.

Was she really contemplating an on-the-job fling? Because of course, that's all that it would be. He lived in Canberra. It would never work. It couldn't work. And yet...

"It's just dinner, Ellie."

Fire seared her cheeks. She bit her lip, grateful that the night had settled in enough to conceal her burning face. For goodness sake, what was she? A teenager?

"I know that," she managed. "I was thinking about the case."

"Liar." His voice was soft, caressing in the darkness.

She stole a peek and fell into the teasing light of his blue eyes. Her heart picked up its rhythm and suddenly oxygen was in short supply.

He was so close.

Too close.

Not close enough.

"Okay, let's do it."

His eyebrows rose and she blushed again.

"W-what I mean is, let's have dinner. We've got to eat, right? We might as well do it together and we can go over things for tomorrow. Boston lands a little after ten in the morning. It wouldn't hurt to review our game plan."

Clayton nodded, his eyes glinting in the streetlights as they passed.

"Sure. Good." His lips turned up into a cheeky grin. "Your place, or mine?"

Keeping her gaze fixed firmly on the road in front of her, she found herself stumbling on a reply.

"I-I really need to go home and take a shower. After all that's gone on today, I couldn't bear the thought of eating in these clothes." She took in the wrinkled suit and blouse.

"They still look pretty good to me, but I know what you mean." He checked his watch. "How about we meet in the city about seven thirty? That's not too far away from your place, is it?"

"No, I've got a unit over at Darling Harbour. I'll catch a cab."

His eyebrows rose again. "Darling Harbour? That's pretty swish."

"Early inheritance."

He whistled in appreciation. "Sounds like my kind of family."

She laughed as images of her mother and father came to mind. Having made a fortune on the stock exchange in the nineties, her parents had cashed in well before the crash in 2008. They owned a luxurious apartment overlooking the harbor at Point Piper, among several other lucrative investments and had felt the need to share their good fortune with their only child.

Ellie had never bothered arguing with them. Not that she'd ever been spoilt in the traditional sense. As a child, she'd been raised to be thankful for all that she had and to give generously to those less fortunate.

And it just went to show, all the money in the world didn't shield you from heartache and tragedy. She felt a pang of loss at the thought of Jamie.

"Hey." Clayton's voice was soft and apologetic. "I'm sorry if I offended you. I was trying to be funny."

She forced a wobbly smile. "No offence taken. And it was kind of funny."

A look of mock-hurt contorted his features. "Only kind of?"

She chuckled. "Okay, it was pretty funny." She spared him a wry look. "My father would have found it hysterical."

"Sounds like we'd get on famously." He grinned and her heart did a somersault.

Get a grip, Cooper. You're not sixteen.

She negotiated a lane change and continued to silently castigate herself. Once again, he seemed to read her mind and diverted her feverish thoughts with another question.

"So, this is your town. Where should we go to eat?"

CHAPTER 10

The iconic shape of Centrepoint Tower loomed over the city skyline, illuminated by golden lights. Clayton had met her in a cab outside her apartment. Upon Ellie's request, the cab driver had dropped them off at the entrance to the Pitt Street Mall. Her heart beat with anticipation as they drew closer. She'd called and made a reservation the minute she'd dropped Clayton off at his hotel.

He was a visitor to the city she loved and she wanted to take him somewhere special. She had to remind herself it was not a date, but nevertheless, she wanted to surprise him and let him see the city of her birth at its glittering best.

Besides, after all that had happened with their case and the little or no progress they'd made, she was in the mood to drown the mounting frustration with a good merlot.

Knowing how difficult it was to get a reservation at the revolving restaurant, she'd been relieved and excited when the maître d' informed her of a cancellation and accepted her last-minute booking.

It was still early evening, and although the winter air was crisp, small pockets of people wandered through the mall window shopping, talking, laughing. A few late-working business professionals strode past hurriedly with smart briefcases in tow, looking as if their thoughts were on making the next train.

Ellie eyed Clayton with appreciation. He wore a crisp

white dinner shirt and tailored black suit pants. A matching jacket hung from his fingers. For the first time since she'd met him, he was without a tie and the top few buttons of his shirt had been left undone, giving her a tantalizing glimpse of smooth, male skin.

There was something about a well-dressed man that did it for her. With his tousled, shower-damp hair and deep-blue eyes with their hint of sadness, he couldn't have looked any sexier.

And the feeling seemed to be mutual, if the admiration warming his gaze was anything to go by. Heat crept into her cheeks every time his gaze swept over her simple but stylish black crepe dress. Its low-cut neckline emphasized the fullness of her breasts and the cinched-in waist held by a jewelled butterfly brooch at her hip accentuated her curves.

Becoming flustered by his thorough perusal, her three-inch heels caught on a crack in the pavement and she stumbled. His arm shot out and grabbed her elbow, preventing her from taking a fall.

"Careful, partner. You might do some damage. I'd hate to see you break a leg and leave me with all the driving. I've kind of gotten used to being chauffeured."

Her face flamed and she looked away. His fingers were warm on her arm. It seemed every nerve ending was acutely aware of the feel of his skin on hers.

She gritted her teeth. *For Christ's sake, Cooper, get a grip. It's his fingers. Just his fingers.*

Those fingers tightened when she surreptitiously tried to pull her arm away. Knowing to tug any harder would only draw attention, she tried to act as nonchalant as he was.

They passed under a streetlight and she caught the reflection off a heavy chain that hung around his neck. A gold ring rested against his chest. It looked like a wedding ring, but he'd said nothing about a wife. And it wasn't on his finger.

She shelved her curiosity, determined to enjoy the evening. Surely, if he was married, he would have said so. He seemed way too honorable to be the cheating type.

"So, where are we eating?" he asked, glancing around him with an air of casual interest.

With the pressure of his hand burning her skin, Ellie suddenly regretted her impulse to take him to Centrepoint Tower. The place was way too formal, way too expensive, way too intimate to take a work colleague.

She shuffled through her mind with increasing panic for somewhere else to go. There was no decent restaurant in the city where they could expect to get a table without a reservation this late in the evening. Dressed as they were, it would be ludicrous to suggest fish and chips down at Circular Quay.

With a sigh, she muttered, "The Centrepoint Tower Restaurant." The traffic lights changed just as she said it and cars accelerated forward. Clayton bent his head toward her, his face almost level with hers.

"Sorry, I missed that."

She caught a whiff of his expensive-smelling cologne and tried to remember what they'd been talking about. God, she really needed to get out more. If the mere whiff of a man's aftershave had her mind turning to mush, what hope was there for her?

As they came upon the entry to the Tower, she answered his question. With a raised eyebrow and a smile tugging at her lips, she indicated the bank of elevators that would take them up to the restaurant. "We're going up there."

He frowned and his face lost all color. She was immediately concerned. "Are you okay? You don't look so good."

His throat worked. He swallowed. A deep red stain rose up from his neck and stole across his sculpted cheekbones. He wouldn't meet her eyes.

"Clayton? Are you all right?" She grabbed his arms and gave him a little shake, her concern now bordering on panic.

He shrugged and met her eyes. "I'm scared of heights."

Her mouth fell open in surprise. "You're scared of heights?" She shook her head in disbelief allowing her gaze to travel down the long, lean length of him. His sheer size had made her feel instantly safe and protected, as if nothing could ever faze him. And yet, this giant of a man had just admitted he was afraid of heights.

A chuckle escaped her and then another. Without meaning to, full-blown laughter overtook her until tears of amusement filled her eyes. His frown was fierce enough to scare a small child. He stood his ground in silence as she tried to contain her mirth.

"I'm sorry; I'm sorry." She swiped at the tears in her eyes and struggled to compose herself. "It's just that, you look so—"

He shook his head. His lips were pressed together.

"I know what you're going to say. But it doesn't make any difference. I'm scared of heights." He shrugged again. "Always have been."

Clearing her throat of residual laughter, she took hold of his arm and led him with confidence toward the lifts. Her nervousness had disappeared. All of a sudden, it felt easy. So easy. Like she was out with an old friend. A friend who happened to look like he'd come from a *Vogue* photo shoot and who had the ability to make her heart jump somersaults with his smile—who said they couldn't work through that?

The elevator doors opened and she felt the tension in Clayton's arm. She peered up at him and saw his lips were pressed tightly together. He wasn't kidding. He really did have a thing about heights.

"Look, if you'd rather we go somewhere else, I'm sure we'll find another place—somewhere on the ground floor, perhaps?" She gave him an encouraging smile.

He looked down at her, determination in his eyes. "No, this is fine. I'd love to have dinner in Centrepoint Tower." A grin tilted his lips. "It's something I've always wanted to do."

She grinned back at him. "Liar."

He smiled and her heart flipped over. "Okay, well maybe it isn't at the very top of my list, but it's definitely up there."

She shook her head. "Not."

"It's only more than one thousand feet off the ground and one of the tallest buildings in the southern hemisphere. I'm sure you're aware of that?" The tautness around his mouth relaxed slightly and his eyes glinted in amusement.

"Really? Wow, that is high," she replied and then shot him a cheeky look. "You still game?"

He drew in a deep breath, expanding his already-broad chest to an even more impressive width. "Bring it on, partner."

The elevator doors slid open and they stepped out onto a parquet floor, so shiny she could almost see their reflections. Hundreds of wine bottles, ensconced behind a wall of glass, bordered the entryway, golden light reflecting off their polished necks. Soft music emanated from some as-yet-unseen source. A maître d' dressed in formal evening wear stood behind a polished wooden lectern and greeted them as they entered the restaurant.

"Good evening, sir. Good evening, madam. Do you have a reservation?"

"Yes. It's in the name of Cooper," Ellie replied.

The man ran his finger down a list of entries on the page before him. "Ah. Yes, here it is. A table for two. If you'll just follow me..."

Ellie peeked at Clayton. A little color had returned to his cheeks, but his mouth still looked tense. She looked back at the maître d'.

"We might go and have a drink at the bar, first, if that's all right?"

"Of course. Just let me know when you're ready to be seated."

She steered Clayton toward the bar with a solicitous hand at his elbow. He pulled away.

"I'm not an invalid, you know."

She grinned at his scowl. "Oh, I don't know, you're looking pretty unsteady to me."

113

He tried to maintain his frown. "This is all your fault, Cooper."

Her eyes opened wide in mock surprise. "My fault? How was I to know you were afraid of heights? A big strapping man like you? You must be at least six two, maybe even six three? And those big, strong shoulders—"

He growled a warning. "Ellie..."

She grinned unrepentantly. "Just kidding."

Sliding onto a chocolate-leather barstool, she turned to survey the rows of sparkling crystal glasses and colorful bottles of liqueurs that lined the back wall of the bar. The soft ambient lighting of the restaurant reflected back at her, throwing off shards of light that looked like little shooting stars.

Clayton slid onto an adjacent stool, the tension easing from his mouth. He turned to look at her. "What's your poison?"

"I'll have a margarita, thanks."

The barman appeared and Clayton ordered her drink and then asked for a scotch.

Ellie looked along the illuminated tortoise-shell bar. It seemed to stretch for miles, all golden and shimmery. With the room slowly revolving, it felt like she was suspended in air.

Clayton reluctantly raised his gaze toward the city skyline, visible in every direction. They were high enough to see the stars. "It really is one hell of a view."

She grinned cheekily. "Breathtaking, even. It takes seventy minutes for us to complete a full revolution. On a clear day, you can see almost as far as the Blue Mountains."

He took a cautious peek at the panoramic view, visible even through the glass shelving behind the bar.

"Glad you came?" she asked softly.

His gaze slid over her, leaving a trail of fire. It paused at her breasts. Her pulse skipped into overtime and butterflies filled her stomach.

His eyes met hers. The blue of his irises had turned dark cobalt. "There's nowhere else I'd rather be."

Ellie stared at him and swallowed; the nerves which had

returned from nowhere suddenly threatening to cut off her oxygen supply. Her chest was tight and she was sure he could hear her frantic heart battering against her ribcage.

She ignored his response in an effort to play it cool. The barman assisted by returning with their drinks. Glad for the excuse to break eye contact, she reached for her handbag.

Clayton stilled her with a hand on her arm. "Please, let me."

Excruciatingly aware of the warmth of his skin on hers, the nerves that had filled her throat now jangled with increasing urgency in her belly.

Unable to help herself, her eyes met his again. Their knowing depths sparkled with good humor, along with some residual tension.

He gave her a sardonic look and raised his glass. "What shall we toast to?"

She shook her head slightly to clear it and picked up her margarita. Out of habit, her tongue snuck out and licked at the salt that rimmed the glass. She leaned across to clink her glass with his, pleased to see her hand remained steady.

"To new friends."

His eyes held hers while he sipped his scotch. Her heart rate ratcheted up another notch. She took a healthy swallow of her drink.

"Friends." He rolled the word around in his mouth, as if sampling it. "I guess that's as good a place as any to start."

"Better than being enemies," she quipped, taking another mouthful. Already, she could feel the tequila working its magic on her nerve endings, dulling their response to his nearness.

His answering smile was slow and sexy. His gaze strayed to her cleavage once again and he replied in a low drawl. "You can say that again. If you'd had your way, I'd have dropped dead in the squad room that first night."

The memory assailed her. Heat seared her cheeks. She looked away, grateful for the dim lighting.

"So, was it me in particular, or Feds in general, that had you all steamed up?"

Ellie closed her eyes, mortified. No amount of subtle lighting would save her this time. He grinned, his eyes alight with good humor.

She gritted her teeth, determined not to let him know how embarrassed she was.

"You're speaking in the past tense, Fed. Who says I still don't wish you would disappear and go back to where you came from?"

His darkening gaze came to rest on her lips. "I say."

His low, husky voice washed over her and she shivered. Her nipples tightened in response. Panic flared inside her and she gulped down the rest of her drink.

He was a Fed. A good-looking, charming, arrogant, very good-looking, smug, annoying, exceptionally good-looking Fed. What was she doing here with him?

Hadn't she learned from her experience with Robert? Hadn't he also been a good-looking, charming, arrogant— all right, not nearly as good-looking—Fed? And hadn't he walked away, leaving her broken-hearted, with barely a fare thee well?

Of all the men in the world, why did she have to hook up with another one? She blushed as the thought sunk in. She wasn't *hooking up* with him. It was just dinner. Not even a date. Just two work colleagues who happened to be together at dinner time.

A simple sharing of a meal, that was all. So what if she'd spent nearly every second since dropping him off at his hotel trying to decide what to wear? So what if she'd sprayed her very best Dior perfume on her neck, across her wrists and then touched it to the back of her knees? So what if she'd made the extra effort to apply eye shadow, blusher and mascara in addition to her usual slash of deep plum lipstick? That didn't turn this into something it wasn't. *Did it?*

A tiny sigh escaped her and she signaled to the barman for a refill. She could still taste the tart and spicy bite of the tequila, lime and Cointreau on her tongue. It had slid down her throat all too easily.

Clayton raised his eyebrow and a grin tugged at his lips.

"You might want to take it easy, partner. You haven't had anything to eat, yet. A pint-sized thing like you won't take long to get sloshed."

Her tongue darted out to lick a grain of salt from her lips. She held his gaze and watched, transfixed as his eyes darkened like waves at midnight.

"Maybe that wouldn't be such a bad thing. It's been a real shit of a month."

The barman returned and placed another margarita in front of her. She picked it up and took another healthy swallow. A pleasant buzz built inside her head. The Fed was looking tastier by the minute. Even the eyebrow he raised again when she finished her drink a few moments later looked sexy.

With concentrated precision, she placed her empty glass back on the bar, pleased to see it remained upright. She turned to him and smiled. "I love margaritas."

His gaze moved over her, soft and intimate as a caress. He leaned close and braced her shoulders with his hands. His lips brushed her ear and she shivered with awareness.

"I'm going to see about our table. You need to get some food into your belly."

A protest tried its hardest to be heard, but the best she could do was a little squeak as he stood and cautiously made his way back to the maître d'. Ellie drew in a lungful of oxygen and did her best to forget how it felt to have him so close his breath tickled her ear.

The barman approached and took her empty glass. "Would you like another, madam?"

Mm, would she like another?

It was true, she'd barely eaten all day and the alcohol was going straight to her head, but her limbs felt deliciously weak and the nerves that had twisted her inside and out had completely disappeared.

She was having dinner with the most gorgeous man she'd ever laid eyes on and all of a sudden, she couldn't think of a single reason why she shouldn't.

"Yes please." She gave him a warm smile. "Another one is exactly what I need."

———————————

Clayton waited for the maître d' to finish with the couple in front of him and tried to stem his impatience. He stepped forward as soon as the way was clear.

"Ah, I was just wondering if you could show us to our table? We'd like to eat now."

The man looked up and smiled. "Of course. If you'll follow me."

"Hold on a second. I need to get my—"

"Wife, of course." The man glanced toward Ellie where she sat at the bar. "Please, take all the time you need."

Clayton stumbled and turned on his heel. Heat inched up his neck. His *wife*? Ellie wasn't his wife. Why hadn't he corrected the man?

She wasn't anything like his wife. His wife was cool and blond and passive. Ellie was none of those things. She couldn't be more different from Lisa if she'd tried.

But she wasn't trying. She was his work colleague. His partner for the short time he was in Sydney. A friend; that's what she'd called him. And yet, she'd blushed when he'd gotten too close and had flirted with him with her eyes. At least, it felt like flirting. It had been so long for him, he was now beginning to wonder.

She was well into her third margarita when he reached her. He watched her lift the glass with a hand that wasn't quite steady. A reluctant grin tugged at his lips. If she wasn't careful, she wouldn't last until dinner.

"Hey." He spoke softly, so as not to startle her. She jumped anyway and almost toppled off the stool.

Her dress rode high, exposing an expanse of shapely, nylon-coated thigh to his appreciative gaze. She tugged it down, blushing furiously.

"Where did you go? I thought you'd disappeared." She gave him a wry smile and shrugged lopsidedly. "Story of my life."

Tenderness welled up inside him. The feeling was so foreign and strange, it took him a moment to recognize it. He gazed down at the top of her head with its freshly straightened hair and almost forgot about his fear of heights. She wasn't his wife, but she was someone he cared about. More than he wanted to admit.

He tilted her chin up with his finger. "Our table's ready, partner."

"Table. Right. Ready." She grinned up at him. "Okay, let's do it."

She stood and wobbled on her ridiculously high black sandals. He stepped forward and slid his arm around her tiny waist, drawing her in firmly against him and steered her toward the waiting maître d'.

The man nodded knowingly and concealed a grin. "Please, follow me," he murmured.

It felt weird walking across a room that was moving. Clayton had almost managed to forget how far off the ground they were until he looked up and saw the lights of the city spread before them.

Without warning, Ellie grabbed him by the arm. "There's something wrong, Munro. We're going round in circles. I think I need to sit."

He stifled a grin. "It's okay, Ellie. We *are* going around in circles. We're at the Centrepoint Tower Restaurant. One full revolution in seventy minutes, remember? You're the one who brought us here."

She looked up at him with wide, wondering eyes, a quizzical expression on her face. "Right. Yes, of course. It's all good then."

This time the grin escaped. "

"Yes, sweetheart, it's all good." He caught her wide smile and felt something give in his heart. Helping her into the chair the maître d' had pulled out for her, he settled her comfortably at the table. She stared at the silverware, a slight frown marring her features.

He felt a stab of concern. "Are you sure you want to stay for dinner? Because I can take you home in a cab, if you'd rather."

"No way. I'm starving. What's on the menu?" She picked up the elegant, gold-embossed menu from where it lay on the table beside her. Clayton stifled another grin when she peered at the pages in consternation.

"Need some help?"

She shook her head and then winced. "No, no. I thought for a minute the menu was turning in circles, too." She let out a wicked laugh that went straight through him. Her gaze fell on the half-empty glass of scotch he'd carried with him to the table and then back to her empty cocktail glass. She looked up at him and grinned. "I think I need another drink."

He grinned back at her. "You know, partner, I think you're right." He signaled to the waiter who glided over to their table. "Could we have a large carafe of iced water, please?"

"Of course, sir. Right away." He glided away and Ellie frowned.

"Iced water?"

"Yes, Ellie. Iced water. Believe me, you'll thank me in the morning."

She tilted her head to one side and rested her chin on her palm, her elbow propped on the table. "That tequila's gone straight to my head."

"I take it you're not a seasoned drinker?"

"You can say that again. A glass or two of wine every now and then just about pulls me up."

He indicated the empty cocktail glass. "So what prompted the margaritas?"

Ellie ducked her head. "I guess I felt the need to unwind. It's been a pretty stressful few weeks."

Clayton nodded. "You won't get any argument from me."

Ellie sighed into her hand and then peered at him from beneath her thick lashes. "You're awfully cute, Munro."

His heart hitched. "Thank you, Ellie. You're pretty cute yourself."

She blushed and looked away. The waiter appeared and filled their water glasses. Clayton picked up the menu and scanned it quickly.

"What would you like to eat, Ellie? How about a steak with garden vegetables?"

"Sounds great. I could eat a horse."

"How do you like it?"

"Medium rare."

"A woman after my own heart." He looked up at the waiter and gave him their order.

"So, you and the boss go way back?"

He started in surprise. "Yes, I've known him most of my life. He was the Local Area Commander in my hometown. As a teenager, I was a bit of a handful. There's plenty to distract you when you think you're eight foot high and bulletproof." He smiled in reminiscence. "Dad was a District Court Judge and didn't look kindly on misbehavior. He took me down to the PCYC and introduced me to Ben. He was the youth officer there at the time."

Clayton picked up his glass of iced water and brought it to his lips. "I guess he hoped it would keep me occupied and off the streets."

Ellie's gaze slid over him. "You, a wild child? I don't believe it."

"Ask Ben." He flashed her a grin. "Better still, don't."

"So, he's the reason you became a copper?"

He thought for a while and then replied. "I'm not sure it was the only reason—I have law enforcement in my DNA—but he certainly left a lasting impression."

She regarded him again from behind the curtain of her lashes. "You're awfully cute, Munro. Did I tell you that already?"

CHAPTER 11

The early morning sun shone determinably through the squad room windows, banishing the storm clouds that hung around the day before. Shards of light bounced off the cream walls and largely unoccupied metal furniture. Clayton strode in and Ellie kept her head down, pretending to be absorbed in the file that lay open on her desk. It was barely eight and her pounding head reminded her of her overindulgence the night before.

Fleeting memories of their night out flitted through her consciousness and the heat in her face intensified. What the hell must he think of her? The end of the night was a blur, but she did recall leaning very close to him in the taxi on their way home—and had she actually told him he was *cute*?

With a moan of disgust, she inched her head upward, wanting to sneak a peek so she could discover his whereabouts. A pair of perfectly pressed charcoal gray suit pants filled her vision, inches away from her desk.

Her cheeks burned hotter, but she had no choice but to continue her upward journey. Bright, cobalt eyes regarded her with amusement.

"I'm pleased to see you survived the night. No ill effects, I hope?" He flashed a wide, white grin.

Flustered, she looked away and busied herself with the paperwork on her desk, doing her best to ignore him. "I'm fine, thanks. Perfectly fine."

A few moments later, she peeked beneath her lashes. He

was still there. Still grinning. *God, why didn't he just leave?*

"Can I get you a cup of coffee? I'm on my way into the tea room."

"No, no. I'm fine," she managed to croak before burying herself back in her paperwork, hoping he'd take the hint.

He didn't.

Instead, he propped himself up on the corner of her desk. Swallowing a sigh, she filled her lungs with air and steeled herself.

Her eyes met his. She swallowed again. He looked good enough to eat. Her gaze wandered across his shoulders. His dark suit contrasted nicely with yet another crisp shirt, this one in a soft, pale blue that brought out the sapphire in his eyes. A Ralph Lauren tie patterned with navy and red stripes provided just the right amount of color.

In contrast, she felt tired and disheveled. After sleeping past her alarm, she hadn't had time to wash and straighten her hair. It now hung in messy, tangled waves around her face and would annoy her for the rest of the day.

Not only that, she was wearing yesterday's suit. In her excitement to get ready for last night's date, she'd forgotten to pick up her dry cleaning. She groaned under her breath, grateful that at least her underwear was clean.

Date.

Had she really just thought that? It wasn't a date. Hell, she could barely remember some of it.

A familiar pair of black stilettos landed on her desk. She looked up, startled.

Clayton shrugged. "You left them in the taxi."

She was mortified. Not only had she imbibed more than enough, she'd also felt comfortable enough to kick off her shoes. *God, what else had she done?*

Another moan escaped her. Fire exploded across her cheeks. She looked around in desperation for somewhere to hide. Clayton chuckled.

"It's nothing to be embarrassed about, Ellie. We've all been there. A few too many drinks, a few loose inhibitions..."

Ellie dropped her head to her desk, willing the floor to

open up and swallow her. Why wouldn't he just go away? Why was he torturing her like this?

Her temper flared. Why *was* he torturing her like this?

"So, what's with the ring around your neck?" As soon as the words hurtled out of her mouth she regretted them. His face turned to granite, the sparkle of humor that had been there moments before, vanished. She kept her gaze on the desk in front of her and willed him to walk away, no longer wanting him to reply.

"It's my wedding ring."

Pain sheared through her at his words. Questions burned in her mouth, but she refused to give them voice. Let him explain if he wanted to. It was none of her business.

He had a wife. He was married.

"Ellie, look at me." It was a heartfelt plea and one she was powerless to resist. She looked up. His eyes were dark with emotion.

"Her name was Lisa. She died almost three years ago."

Self-loathing surged through her veins. His wife was dead. And she'd been about to accuse him of all sorts of things. She should have known he had more integrity than that.

She did know.

She'd been by his side for nearly a month. Despite the strains of the job, she'd seen how sensitive he was to the families of their victims, how empathetic he'd been to their suffering and how determined he was to give them justice. He was a Fed, but he was nothing like Robert.

"Talk to me, Ellie," he said softly.

She closed her eyes and then opened them again and braved a glance in his direction. The emotion in his eyes tugged at her heart. "Clayton, I'm... I'm sorry. I didn't know—"

"Ellie. Clayton. I'm glad you're here." Ben strode up to them looking grim, a sheaf of papers in his hand. "These have just come in from the lab. It's the forensic results on the girls we've found." His voice was cautiously excited. "This might be the break we need."

Clayton straightened, instantly alert. "What have you got?"

Ellie leaned forward in her seat, her animosity forgotten. She waited for Ben to speak.

He shuffled through the papers in his hand. "Looks like we've got some DNA from underneath Angelina Caruso's fingernails. The lab guys found skin cells." He looked up, his face stark. "She obviously put up a fight."

Referring to the notes, he continued. "Those strange particles you saw in Angelina's hair have been identified as paint chips. They've been traced back to a Dulux brand called Coconut Ice. It's a paint usually applied to wood and other similar surfaces."

His gaze flicked from Clayton to Ellie. "Unfortunately, as I've just discovered, it's a fairly common brand that's sold in almost any hardware store."

Ellie released the breath she'd been holding and leaned back in her chair. Disappointment surged through her.

"So, the paint chips are going to be next to useless. It will be impossible to track down every can of Coconut Ice sold in the last few months. Besides, the paint could have been stored in his back shed for months, years even."

Ben sighed. "I know what you're saying, Ellie, and I agree. Tracking down the paint sale's going to be impossible. But about the storing for years... It's interesting to note that particular brand of paint is new—it's only been on the market for about six months."

"Oh, well, that certainly narrows it down."

"There's no need for sarcasm, Detective Cooper. We're all feeling the strain here."

She blushed under his quiet reprimand, made even worse with Clayton standing a few feet away, listening to every word. She mumbled an apology.

Clayton crossed his arms over his chest. "What about the DNA evidence? Have we got a match on that?"

Ben grimaced. "No, at least, not yet. We've only just started running it through our database. Of course, it's only going to find a hit if our perpetrator's already in there." He shrugged. "But, you never know. We could get lucky. It's unlikely this is the first time he's crossed the line."

"Any news on the wood shavings found in Josie Ward's hair?" Ellie asked.

Ben turned over a couple of pages and scanned the contents. "Looks like it's *radiata* pine. A soft wood that's popular with handymen and hobbyists." He looked up and held her gaze. "Again, it's available in most good hardware stores. But what's really interesting is the same kind of shavings were also found underneath Angelina Caruso's fingernails."

Ellie let out a sigh of relief. "Oh, thank God for that. I know I shouldn't say that, but at least we know there isn't another madman out there doing this."

"I agree," Clayton said. "What about the saw marks?"

A bleak smile thinned Ben's lips. "Yeah, that's probably some of the better news. The saw striations left on the bones of both girls are a match. They were definitely made by the same saw. Samantha Wolfe tells me a saw's teeth pattern is unique to the particular saw. A bit like a person's fingerprints. If we find the saw, we'll likely find the killer. According to the lab results, it's a stainless steel hacksaw."

He acknowledged Ellie's raised eyebrow with a nod and added, "There were microscopic pieces of stainless steel in the wounds. Apparently, it's not uncommon for a saw to leave bits of itself behind, particularly if you're sawing through tough material."

"Like bone," Clayton muttered, his face dark.

Ben's eyes were brutal as they stared back at him. "Yes, like bone."

Ellie broke the tense silence by clearing her throat. "I take it the DNA didn't match Wayne Peterson?"

"No. We'd have arrested him by now if it had."

A thought suddenly occurred to her. "What about the trash bags? Did they have any luck with them?"

Ben flipped through the pages of the report. Ellie looked at Clayton from beneath her lashes. His shoulders were slumped and his head was down. He stared at the floor. She felt the same weight of responsibility and disappointment.

"It doesn't look like there's anything here about trash

bags." Ben pierced her with a look. "Were they both wrapped in trash bags?"

She inclined her head. "Angelina was. Both her head and her limbs. The bags looked like they'd come from the same source, too. At least, to the naked eye. Black, heavy quality." She winced. "Probably available from every shop and supermarket in Sydney."

"I can't find anything in here about trash bags."

Passing Clayton the lab papers, Ben continued. "I suggest you get onto the lab and find out about them. At the very least, they should be checked for fingerprints. You never know. It might give us a lead and at the moment, that's something we're preciously short of."

"Sure, boss. No problem."

Ben strode toward his office and Ellie looked up at Clayton. "So, what do you think? Got any new brainwaves about who the hell we're looking for?"

"He likes to shop for bargains at Bunning's Warehouse?"

Her answering frown was fierce. "It's not a laughing matter, Munro."

"I'm not suggesting it is. But you've got to admit, I'm probably right. All the evidence we've found so far could be purchased from a Bunning's. Or a Home Depot. Or any other hardware store, if it came to that. I bet there's at least a dozen of them out here."

So what do you propose we do? As far as I know, those shops don't have individual customer databases and we don't have a clue who we're looking for."

"It could narrow down his location, though. Most people shop at their local stores. It would be unusual for him to travel to a distant suburb to buy his hardware. Whether he bought it especially for his little games or had them in his back shed, they had to have been purchased from somewhere."

She groaned aloud, searching for elusive connections. Frustration gnawed at her. "I wonder if that's significant, or are we just clutching at straws?"

Clayton looked down at her, understanding reflected in

his eyes. "I know what you're saying, but I think we need to consider everything, no matter how desperate it makes us feel. The fact that the paint hit the shelves not long before Angelina disappeared seems to be a coincidence."

His expression changed to one of grim determination. "But I don't believe in coincidences. Not when they're teamed up with dead bodies."

Ellie sighed and glanced at her watch. "We'd better get moving if we're going to meet the professor's plane. I called the airline a little while ago. They're expecting it to land on time."

"Let's get to it then. Now that we have found foreign DNA on one of our victims, I won't need much of an excuse to demand a sample from Mr Boston."

––––––––––

Clayton scanned the throng of passengers pouring out through the arrivals gate at Sydney's Mascot Airport and looked for Stewart Boston. A picture of the professor had been supplied to them by the university. He could have picked him up at the airport, but he was hoping Boston might lead them to the place where he'd taken the girls. According to the forensic reports, Josie Ward hadn't been killed where she'd been found. He had to have some hidey-hole where he carried out his savagery—*if* he had carried out the savagery. That was yet to be decided.

Clayton glanced over at Ellie where she stood a few feet away. She wore a fitted skirt that ended just above her knees and conformed to the roundness of her butt. Slim, shapely legs were encased in black nylon stockings ending in ankle-length leather boots with chunky two-inch heels. She casually strode back and forth amongst the people who waited for the arrivals. His eyes tracked the gentle movement of her butt. When he realized what he was doing, he dragged his gaze away.

"Get a grip, Munro," he muttered under his breath,

forgetting for a moment that his words had been captured by the microphone pinned discreetly to the lapel of his jacket.

Ellie half-turned and frowned at him, but otherwise remained silent. Clayton refocused his attention on the arriving passengers.

"There he is." Ellie's words sounded through Clayton's earpiece. He looked toward the arrivals gate and spied the man who'd just appeared in the entryway.

She was right. It was Stewart Boston. He wore a loose flowered shirt and a pair of dark board shorts. On his feet were some leather flip-flops. Wispy blond hair hung around his face. He didn't look like a man who'd left murder and mayhem behind him, but Clayton had learned long ago how deceiving looks could be.

The man turned to a young woman who walked a few feet behind him. She had a knapsack slung over one shoulder and leaned toward him as he spoke. They were too far away to hear what was said. A short time later, the woman headed toward the exit and Boston turned toward the luggage carousels.

Clayton wondered whether the woman was significant or if she was merely another passenger. Their plan only allowed for the following of one of them. Without evidence to the contrary, he had no reason to suspect the woman had anything to do with Stewart Boston or the investigation.

He glanced over at Ellie. "He's heading toward the baggage claim."

She shot him a quick look. "You tail him. I'll go and get the car. Let me know which direction he takes out of the airport."

Clayton grimaced. Their plan was to follow Boston, regardless of his mode of departure. If he took a train or the bus, Clayton would board with him. If he left in his own transport, or had a friend collect him, Ellie would follow in the car. Either way, they hoped to keep him within sight until he arrived at his destination.

"I'll call you as soon as I know where he's going."

Ellie nodded and walked away. Clayton followed their target, making sure to keep a discreet distance behind him. It was easy enough to do. At that time of the morning, the airport swarmed with travelers.

He watched while Boston collected two suitcases off the carousel and then turned toward the exit. Staying back, Clayton spoke into his microphone.

"He's heading for the exit, so the train's out. It's either the bus, a taxi or a private vehicle."

"Gotcha. I'm parked in the drop-off zone outside of the Qantas Terminal. Let me know as soon as you know."

"Copy that." Clayton followed Boston out of the exit and into the crisp winter morning. The sun shone wanly through the scattering of clouds. A light breeze blew in from Botany Bay and ruffled his hair. People drew their coats around them, but Clayton barely felt its effects.

Boston joined the queue of travelers who waited for a taxi. Clayton hung back and spoke once again to Ellie.

"It looks like he's catching a cab. Move the car up a bit closer so I can climb in as soon as we know for sure. There's so much traffic, it will be easy to lose him."

"Will do," came the quick reply.

The line for the taxis crawled forward. Boston looked vaguely restless, but that could have been simply because of his wait for a cab. Clayton remembered when he'd flown in a month ago. He'd been lucky then to obtain a cab so quickly.

The security guard pointed to Boston. "You're up next. Bay number five."

The professor hauled his suitcases toward the vacant cab. Clayton waited until the driver popped the trunk and Boston tossed his cases in the back before striding away in the direction where Ellie had parked.

"Okay, it looks like he's taking a cab. It's a black and white Holden Commodore Sydney Taxi Cab, registration TC 1829. I just saw him load his suitcases into the trunk."

"Where are you?"

"Right here." Clayton opened the passenger side door

and climbed in. Ellie looked at him, her face tense.

"He's just pulled out. Up there."

Ellie accelerated and joined the line of traffic heading out of the airport. Boston's taxi was two cars in front of them. Clayton drew in a deep breath and released it slowly. The first part of the plan had been a success.

"Do we have Boston's residential address?" Ellie asked.

"Yep. He lives about a block away from the Penrith campus."

"So he's certainly within our killer's perimeter."

"Yep."

Ellie glanced at him, her eyes alight with excitement. "This could be it, then."

Clayton couldn't help the surge of anticipation, but tried to remain cautious. "Could be."

"Let's hope he puts up a fight. I'm spoiling for an excuse to play dirty."

Clayton grinned and looked up and down the pint-sized length of her. She looked tough enough to fight a bantam. "Lucky you have me along, then. There's nothing I enjoy more than playing dirty."

Her cheeks turned scarlet, and she grinned back at him. His heart did a somersault. His body hardened with need. Christ, he could barely think when she smiled at him like that. It wasn't good. It wasn't good at all. With a gargantuan effort, he focused his attention back on the road.

"Boston doesn't look like the type a young girl would be taken in by," Ellie commented. "I mean, he's got to be in his fifties and that balding hair and beer belly's not the most attractive attribute. He looks sleazy, more than anything."

"Maybe it's all in his manner. Maybe he has the knack of charming girls into his room or wherever it is he takes them? Don't forget Ted Bundy could charm the pants off anyone. Even law enforcement officers were taken in by him."

Ellie shot him a wry look. "Somehow, I don't think you'll fall into that category."

A shaft of pleasure surged through him at her compliment. He grinned.

"Are you actually acknowledging my skills, Detective Cooper? Because that's what it sounded like. You know how they pay me the big bucks... I just want to make sure you get your money's worth."

"Humph," Ellie snorted, her eyes alight with mischief. "Don't worry about me getting my money's worth. It's our erstwhile and completely unsuspecting taxpayers I'm concerned about."

"Well, worry no more. I've been looking forward to chatting to Professor Boston for weeks. Leave him to me."

"Not on your life, sweet cheeks."

Clayton grinned. A warm glow started low in his belly and gradually spread upwards. Suddenly, the day seemed even brighter.

Professor Stewart Boston climbed out of the cab and retrieved his suitcases from the trunk. Ellie and Clayton watched from their hiding spot nearby. They'd followed the cab until it came to a halt outside the university's Penrith campus and now held their breath as they waited for Boston's next move.

His residence was nearly a block away. It was unlikely he was headed there on foot, lugging two suitcases. The more likely option was that he was going to the office he had on campus.

It was nearly lunch time and the place was crowded with students as they moved between lessons. The professor started up the flight of steps that presumably led to his office.

Ellie shot a look at Clayton. He stared back at her and then nodded. With excitement surging through her, she opened the car door and took off after Boston, Clayton close on her heels.

They caught him at the top of the stairs, just as he was inserting his key into the door to his office.

"Professor Boston? I'm Detective Cooper. This is Federal Agent Munro. We'd like to have a talk to you."

The professor paled beneath his tan. "F-federal Agent? I-I haven't done anything wrong. W-why would you want to talk to me?"

Ellie narrowed her eyes at him. "You tell us."

Boston's gaze darted from Ellie to Clayton and back again. "C-can we at least do this in my office?"

"Of course," Ellie replied. "After you."

Stepping back, she gave the man time to turn the key and edge into his office. Dumping his suitcases by the door, he headed straight for the solitary desk that filled most of the room and seated himself behind it. Perspiration gathered on his lip and he swiped at it with a hand that was less than steady.

Ellie stared at him and his fingers twitched around a pile of papers on his desk. She took one of the chairs that stood opposite and made a show of pulling out her notebook. Clayton remained standing.

"So, Professor Boston, we'd like to talk to you about a couple of your students." Ellie's gaze bored into his, but the Professor's opaque eyes darted away and a shaky hand reached up and brushed a hank of long, pale hair off his face, exposing small patches of scaly, pink scalp.

She couldn't tell if his hair was gray or dirty blond, or a mixture of both, but the grooves and crevices lining his forehead seemed to indicate he was a man long since removed from his prime. Her earlier assessment of his age as a man in his mid-fifties seemed to be accurate.

"W-what is it you'd like to know, Detective? I've been away for a while and I'm still catching up on the paperwork." His thin shoulders hunched forward and he waved a limp hand in the direction of his desk.

Clayton braced his hands on the laminate and leaned forward, his face inches from the professor's. "Josie Ward."

The man shivered under the menace of Clayton's stare. Sweat popped out on his brow and his eyelids took on a life of their own as he blinked in rapid succession.

"She was one of your students," Ellie added.

The professor found his voice. "Yes, yes. I know who you mean. Josie. Lovely girl. Very sweet. And so talented. That's one of her paintings over there. She gave it to me for my birthday."

Ellie and Clayton turned to look at the wall he'd indicated. A large canvas displaying an abstract array of bright colors dominated the space. Ellie wasn't an artist and didn't have a creative bone in her body, but even she felt the uplifting of her spirits as she gazed upon the artwork.

Clayton's expression remained grim. "You must be pretty close to her if she's giving you birthday presents."

"Yes, Detective. We are. Josie is special. Very special."

Anger darkened Clayton's eyes and his mouth tightened. "And now she's lying in a freezer in the morgue."

A howl of pain escaped the professor's slack lips and he lowered his chin until it almost rested on his chest. His head moved from side to side. The howling continued.

Ellie's heart pounded. Was this it? Was he about to confess? Was he their killer? He was creepy enough. She'd been on edge from the moment he'd opened his door. Something about the way his gaze had slid over her from top to bottom, surreptitiously leering at her cleavage had made her skin crawl.

He made her skin crawl.

She glanced at Clayton, who'd gone still. Watching. Waiting. Harsh emotions chased themselves across the chiseled planes of his face.

Professor Boston lifted his head and stared at her. "Sh-she's dead? H-how?"

"You tell us," Clayton growled.

Confusion flooded his face. "Y-you can't think I had anything to do with it? I could never hurt Josie. I swear. It wasn't me."

"What about Sally Batten?" Clayton demanded, looking unconvinced.

Bewilderment clouded the pale eyes. "Sally?"

"Yes, Sally Batten," Ellie replied, her eyes narrowed. "She's another student of yours. Studying the Impressionists. She takes classes with you on Tuesdays and Fridays."

A little smile tugged at the corners of his lips. "Ah, yes. Sally. Poor, Sally. So much determination, so little talent." He lifted his gaze to Ellie's and shrugged. "There's nothing I can do to change that."

Anger surged through her at his nonchalance. She caught Clayton's fierce frown seconds before he exploded.

"She's been missing for nearly eight weeks. Surely you must have noticed?"

The professor frowned and tilted his head to the side. "Eight weeks? Has it been that long? Yes, I guess you're right. It probably has. I've been away, you see. I've lost track of time."

"Conveniently away, as far as I'm concerned," Clayton replied, his tone cold steel.

The professor's voice trembled when he spoke, but he didn't look away. "You can't honestly think *I* have anything to do with it? Those girls must have classes with a number of teachers."

Clayton leaned forward again, his eyes narrowed on the professor's face. "Unlucky for you, Professor. You were the only teacher Josie Ward had. At the very least, I'm thinking you're our prime suspect for her murder."

What little color Stewart Boston had in his cheeks drained out of his face and his mouth dropped open in shock.

"M-murder? But that's obscene. I-I couldn't murder anyone."

"If I listened to protestations of innocence every time I made an arrest, the jails would be empty," Clayton stated, pushing away from the desk.

Ellie sat forward in her chair. "Where do you live, Professor?"

He blinked rapidly. She could almost see him trying to re-align his thought processes. "Live?"

"Yes, like when you go home at night. Where do you live?"

"W-why is that important? I-I have a very ill wife. She's

dying. I-I wouldn't want you disturbing her."

The nervousness was back. Ellie's instincts went on alert.

"Just give her your address, asshole." Clayton was back looming over the desk, all menacing blond intimidation.

Professor Boston tugged at his hair and licked his lips. His gaze bounced off the surfaces around the room.

"Um, er…"

Clayton gave him a hard stare and perspiration returned to the man's forehead, the fine sheen of it reflecting pale light from the only window.

"I-I live in Penrith. South Creek Road."

"That's not far from the Nepean River, is it?" Ellie asked, her eyes narrowed.

"No, not far. I-I like to go fishing there. It's a lovely spot."

She caught Clayton's gaze and could tell from the look on his face that he'd also made the connection. Anticipation knotted in her gut.

"How well do you know Angelina Caruso? She's a physiotherapist student here," Ellie added.

A frown deepened the lines across the professor's forehead. "Angelina Caruso? I'm not sure that I know that name."

"When did you last see Sally?" Clayton demanded.

The professor shook his head. "I-I'm not sure about that, either. I've been away. I can't remember. I'd have to check my class roll. I-I can get back to you about that if you like."

"You do that," Ellie replied. "I want to hear from you before the day's over."

"In the meantime," Clayton said, sauntering toward the back of the office, "you can start explaining this sculpture collection."

The professor looked puzzled. Ellie walked over to the wood and glass cabinet that hung on the back wall of the office. Clayton pulled open one of its doors and Ellie's chest constricted.

Inside were more than a dozen wooden sculptures carved from a pale-colored wood. Adrenaline surged through her and her heart rate spiked. Her gaze locked with Clayton's.

As a single unit, they turned to face the professor.

"Tell us about the sculptures, Professor," Ellie demanded, striding back to the desk.

Boston continued to look confused. "Th-the sculptures? Th-they're mine."

"Where did you get them from?" Clayton asked, also crowding the desk.

"W-what do you mean? I-I made them."

Ellie was flooded with a surge of adrenaline. So much fit. It was all circumstantial, but there was too much of it to ignore. They had to take him in. She glanced across at Clayton, who nodded.

"Professor Boston, we'd like you to accompany us to the station to answer a few more questions about the murder of Josie Ward."

The professor's eyes widened in fear and he stood and backed up against the wall.

"No, no, you've got it all wrong. You don't understand."

"Tell it to your lawyer," Clayton growled and led him out of the office. "Let's go, Professor. It's time we got better acquainted."

CHAPTER 12

Clayton stared at the papers on his desk and frowned. He'd spent the last few hours interrogating the professor and although the man had finally cracked and blubbered about trading grades for sex with some of his students, he'd refused to admit he'd had anything to do with the disappearance of Sally Batten or the murders of Angelina Caruso and Josie Ward.

And there was something else that kept niggling him. Stewart Boston didn't fit the profile. He was too old. His university file had stated his age as fifty-five. Fifteen years older than the outer limit of Clayton's profile. Not that it was impossible, but he didn't know of a single instance of an apprehended serial killer who'd been in his fifties.

His disquiet sat heavily on his shoulders. Ellie was convinced they had their killer. And he couldn't blame her. The evidence against the professor, although purely circumstantial, was building up.

According to the class roll, Sally Batten had attended his art class on the day she'd disappeared. Then there were the sculptures. Boston had admitted he carved them from *radiata* pine, the same kind of timber they'd found in Josie Ward's hair and under Angelina Caruso's fingernails. A crew had been sent out to the professor's house with a search warrant and even though they had yet to report anything untoward, it was always possible something incriminating would be discovered. Boston had been reluctant to supply them with his address details, after all.

But still, Clayton wasn't convinced. Something about the professor bugged him.

With a heavy sigh, he opened Boston's file and skimmed over its contents. The man had been employed at the university for more than two decades and although there were a couple of brief mentions of possible unsavory behaviour toward some of the female students, nothing had been proved and the complaints appeared to have been shelved.

Flipping over another page, Clayton came upon the professor's medical records. Scanning the paragraphs, his gaze caught on a phrase. His breath came faster and his pulse thudded in his ears. He reached over and picked up the phone and punched in the number for the morgue.

Minutes later, he pushed back his chair and yelled for Ellie, urgency roughening his voice.

She appeared in the doorway of the tea room and frowned. "What is it?"

"It's not him."

She shook her head. "What do you mean, it's not him?"

"It's not Boston."

"How can you be so sure?" she protested. "He had access to our girls. He's someone they would trust and the carvings—"

"It's not him."

"But—"

"He has *alopecia areata*."

She looked at him blankly.

"So?"

"It's an autoimmune disease where the white blood cells attack the cells that contain hair follicles. No one really knows what causes it, but one of the side effects is hair shedding. Regularly. I phoned Samantha. There was no hair found on either of the bodies. He couldn't have done what he did to them and not have left some of his hair behind."

"But what if he'd washed them—?" Her protest was weaker.

"They were covered in blood and other detritus, remember?" He pursed his lips. "He didn't wash them."

Ellie's shoulders slumped. Clayton knew how she felt. He put an arm around her and gave her a comforting squeeze. "I know."

"I was so sure..."

"He was a good fit in a lot of respects, despite the fact everything we had was circumstantial. We'll send his DNA sample to the lab anyway, just to be sure, but I think we have to accept he's not our man." Grim determination surged through him. "We have to keep looking."

————————

The sun had barely poked its head above the horizon to announce the beginning of another day when Clayton picked up the phone and dialed his twin's number. He could have called Tom or even Declan for advice. After all, both of them had years of experience in law enforcement, but there was nothing like shooting the breeze with his twin. So much more got said without either of them saying anything. It had always been that way.

Catching a glimpse of gold and orange and pink through the window near his desk, Clayton took a moment to appreciate the beauty of the dawn as it filtered slowly across the sky. Riley answered the phone, interrupting his reverie.

"Clay, do you have any idea what time it is?"

"Mate, how's it going? I'm glad to know I'm not the only one up at this ungodly hour."

"Who said I was up?" Riley grumbled.

Clayton chuckled. Unable to sleep and with too many unanswered questions whirling around inside his head, he'd decided to go into work early. The squad room would be at its quietest and he'd spend some time figuring out what the hell he was missing. He'd stared at the files for more than an hour and had little to show for it other than his continued certainty they were looking at the wrong man.

"I assume this early morning wake-up call means you've gotten over your little spat about Denise?" Riley said over a yawn.

Clayton grimaced, recalling their last conversation. It felt like a lifetime ago. Despite the love and affection he had for his brother, it irritated him no end that his twin was forever trying to force eligible women on him. As if he couldn't find one on his own. As if he was even interested.

"As a matter of fact, I haven't, but I have better things to do than argue with you over whether I should be racing some strange and unsuspecting woman down the aisle, especially when that advice comes from one who also happens to be footloose and fancy free. When you decide to saddle yourself with a wife, then I might have cause to listen to you when you offer advice on women."

Riley laughed. "Okay, okay. I hear you. No more matchmaking. Why are you calling, anyway?"

Clayton's thoughts turned somber. "I'm in the middle of a scary one, mate."

Immediately, sensing his change of mood, Riley's voice became businesslike. Clayton could almost picture him pulling his six-two frame into an upright position and tugging a notepad and pen off his bedside table.

"What's going on?"

With a heavy sigh, he gave his brother a summary of the events that had kept him sleepless for the best part of a month, including the fact the killer amputated his victims while they were still breathing.

"We're hitting a brick wall, mate. No hard evidence to tie to anyone. The only DNA we've managed to find hasn't matched anyone in our database or the suspects we've interviewed. No hair, no blood, no semen. The only thing we have are some wood shavings and a pile of pink paint chips. It's frustrating the hell out of me."

"Sounds like he's pretty careful, which usually means he's done it many times before. That level of care takes a hell of a lot of planning. How's he overpowering them?"

Clayton sighed again. "We haven't figured that one out yet. One girl was found in pieces. The other one was intact, apart from her arms. The coroner ruled death by strangulation, which still doesn't tell us how he gets them off the street and into his car."

Clayton issued a groan of frustration. "We're going round and round in circles, mate. We had two suspects, but one of them doesn't match the DNA profile and the second one's been eliminated for other reasons."

"All right, let's talk about what you do know. You said all the girls went missing on weekdays; is that right?"

"Yeah, they did, although until we find Sally Batten, we can't say for sure she's related. The only link we have is the professor at the university and, pending DNA results to confirm what we already know, he's no longer a suspect."

"But you think this other girl's connected?"

"Yeah, I do. I don't have any proof other than what my gut's telling me, but I think she's another one of his victims."

"Okay, so for the purposes of the argument, let's count her in. So, they all disappeared through the week. To me, he either works on weekends, or else he fits it in around his job, which means he has a job that's pretty flexible."

"Yeah," Clayton replied, "I'm thinking shift work. He's obviously freer during the week. He either works weekends or does something else that takes him out of town. There's got to be a reason why no one's disappeared then."

"Yeah, that makes sense. And I think he has his own vehicle and probably his own house."

Clayton thought for a moment. "You're right. He must take them somewhere. Neither of them was killed where they were found. So he does the deed in one location and when he's finished, he dumps them."

"I think that puts paid to my part-time weekend-work theory. Unless he lives with his parents, in this day and age, it's almost impossible to have a house and car without a full-time job, even if he's renting."

"Yeah, you're right. We need to start looking at people who earn a reasonable living, who have access to a vehicle, who possibly do shift work because two of our girls disappeared early in the afternoon and the other one went missing later in the evening."

"A courier would be a good fit," Riley suggested. "Especially one with a van. He's got a ready-made hiding spot."

Clayton frowned. "But why would a university student get into a courier's van?"

The door to the squad room opened. Clayton glanced up and caught sight of Ellie. She nodded a brief hello and headed for her desk. Riley spoke again and Clayton forced himself to concentrate on the conversation.

"Maybe he says he has a parcel for them?" Riley suggested. "Who knows? He's obviously got some line worked out—one that works."

"Yeah, yeah you're right. It bears further consideration, that's for sure. I raised the idea with Ellie about a taxi driver a few weeks ago, although as far as we know, only one of our girls may have caught a cab."

Clayton cursed himself when Riley pounced.

"Ellie? That's a nice name. She working with you, is she?"

"Yes, Riley," he forced through gritted teeth. "I guess it's a nice name and yes, she's one of the detectives working the case with me."

"Mm, I see... Is she hot?"

He grimaced and struggled to banish images of Ellie smiling, frowning, thinking, teasing. He peeked over at her. She had her head lowered, already engrossed in the files on her desk. Dammit, he didn't need this kind of distraction or these questions. He had a murderer to find.

He lowered his voice. "Let it go, Riley. I've already told you, I'm not interested."

His brother's voice was unapologetic. "Hey, you know best, Clay. Whatever you say. By the way, I was talking to one of the boys about you the other night."

The casual tone immediately set him on edge. He braced himself as Riley continued.

"Yeah, Max. He's a young constable from Sydney. Keen as mustard. Says he's got a friend in Balmain—Dianne. He says you ought to look her up. She's twenty-five, blond, filled out in all the right places—"

"Riley." Clayton's warning came out through tightly clenched teeth.

"Seeing you're in Sydney for a while—"

"Riley, butt out. Did you not hear a word I said? I'm not interested. When are you going to get it?" Anger flared into life. Heat flooded his cheeks. "I had a wife, remember? A perfect wife. A perfectly beautiful wife. It wasn't her fault she couldn't cope. Just imagine what it would be like burying the woman you loved three years after your wedding. Would you be happy to have me shoving potential brides in your face?"

The silence on the other end of the phone was deafening. He felt a twinge of guilt. His brother meant well. All of his family did. It was just that he didn't want to be someone's pet project. He was fine just the way he was. He had his daughter. He had everything he needed.

Ellie's wide green eyes surfaced in his memory. The way she'd looked at him a few nights ago, tipsy, completely guileless as she'd leaned into him in the back seat of the taxi. Her softness and warmth pressed up against him had felt so good. Too good.

With a snort of impatience, he pushed the memory aside and forced himself to apologize. "I'm sorry, Riley. I shouldn't have said that. I was a bastard. You didn't deserve it."

"No, mate. I'm the one who's sorry. I guess I just hate seeing you so unhappy. I know what you had with Lisa, but mate, she's gone and she's never coming back. You're too young to spend the rest of your life shut off from love."

Clayton's lips tugged upward into a soft, sad smile. "Yeah, I know. But that's just the way it is. None of us get to write the script, mate."

This time it was Riley who let out a heavy sigh. "You've got that right. And it bloody sucks."

"You said it, bro." He struggled against the sadness that threatened to overwhelm him. Now wasn't the time or the place. He was at work, for Christ's sake.

He sat up straighter at his desk and cleared his throat. "Anyway, thanks for your help. Riles. I really appreciate it."

"No worries, anytime. You take care, okay? Good luck with the case, and give Olivia a big hug and a kiss from her favorite uncle."

"Yeah, I will."

Clayton leaned across to hang up the telephone receiver and Ellie quickly averted her gaze. The last thing she wanted was for him to catch her looking at him. She was too far away to hear his conversation, but she wondered who or what had put the sadness in his eyes. She snuck another peek at him and watched as he sat for a few moments, deep in thought, staring blindly at the scatter of paperwork on his gray steel desk.

He hadn't mentioned his wife, his *dead* wife, or their dinner date again. Not *date*, she corrected, tamping down on her irritation. Why did her stupid mind insist on referring to it as a date? He'd asked her to share a meal with him. He was a stranger to Sydney. Dinner with a work colleague naturally won out over a solo meal of Chinese take-away in a hotel room.

If it had been a female colleague who'd suggested it, or even another male one, she wouldn't have given it another thought. People went out to dinner all the time. It didn't mean anything. It was only dinner.

It was just that he didn't feel like just a work colleague. And it hadn't felt like just dinner. It was scaring the hell out of her.

Ever since her messy breakup with Robert, she'd sworn never to mix business with pleasure again. It made things too awkward when the pleasure went south, as it inevitably did. She was lucky in a way that Robert had literally gone south to Canberra, to further his career as a member of the

Australian Federal Police. Otherwise, she might have been the one to put in for a transfer.

At least that was one thing she didn't have to worry about with this Fed. He was only here for the short term. Once his job was finished, he'd ride off into the sunset, never to be seen or heard from again.

Which was fine. Exactly how she preferred it, in fact. It actually made it easier to decide whether she wanted to take things any further.

Take things any further? Was she totally out of her mind? It just went to show how far her normally sensible thinking had gone to the dogs since a killer was let loose on the city and a way too good-looking Fed had landed on her doorstep.

The whole squad was on edge. It had been a fortnight since they'd found Josie Ward. Every time the phone rang, she expected it to be another gruesome discovery. Sally Batten was still unaccounted for. And they were the ones they knew about.

With a sigh, she flipped open Ronald Carter's file. She'd been doing her best to work on his missing freezer. She'd come in early to try and give it some attention. With the onset of the murders, the stolen freezers had been put on the back burner.

At least she'd made progress there. His chest freezer was still missing, but the license plate number had finally come back, ascribed to a woman by the name of Michelle Wilson. The address on her driver's license was in Cranebrook.

It was certainly the right location and it was probably worth looking into. Although, why a woman in her mid-thirties would be driving around stealing old chest freezers off back porches was baffling.

There was always the chance Ronald took down the plate number wrong. Even one digit would make a world of difference. It had happened before.

Anyway, she'd have to check it out, just to make sure. Besides, it would give her something to tell Jim Whitton when he made his weekly call. She'd never have guessed an old Westinghouse freezer would mean so much. She was beginning to suspect it wasn't the freezer at all. Maybe he just craved the contact.

She lifted her gaze off the paper and glanced casually in Clayton's direction. Her heart jumped. The momentary sadness had vanished and his eyes now burned into hers with fierce determination.

She snatched a breath. The oxygen in the room seemed to have evaporated. He stood and came toward her. A staccato rhythm pounded against her ribs.

Get a grip, Cooper. What are you? A teenager? He's a guy. Just a guy. So what if you've been having hot fantasies about him? He doesn't know that. You're a professional, for goodness sake. Just nod and get on with it.

Right. Just nod.

She nodded.

And get on with it.

She got on with it. "Any luck with the—?"

"I just came to check if you—"

They spoke simultaneously and then looked awkwardly away. Heat stole into her cheeks. God, now she couldn't even string a few words together. How the hell did he manage to turn her into a nervous and jittery idiot with his mere presence? This was her territory. Her domain. He was the interloper.

So why the hell didn't it feel that way?

She gritted her teeth and forced her gaze upwards. "You first," she said, proud of her nonchalant tone.

He flashed a wry grin. "Sorry, I came over to check if you'd heard anything more from the lab? Have they run those tests on the trash bags?"

She took a surreptitious mouthful of air and released it slowly, busying herself with the mess of papers on her desk. "No, um. I mean, yes, they've run the tests, but I'm still waiting to hear if they found anything."

She risked another glance at him. He was standing way too close, with his way-too-taut butt casually propped against her desk. Another pair of perfectly pressed pants filled her vision. It was kind of irritating how neat and in control he always looked. Even his dark red tie sat in a perfectly knotted position around his neck.

She got a whiff of his spicy aftershave and briefly closed her eyes at the memories it evoked. His arm, strong and muscular around her as she'd leaned into him on the back seat of the taxi, her mind spinning and whirling from one thought to another, until everything had swirled together in a mad kaleidoscope of colors, sounds and images.

And then she'd needed air. Had begun to crave oxygen like a woman possessed. She knew if she hadn't managed to drag it into her lungs when she had, she'd have disgraced herself in the taxi.

As if he'd sensed her predicament, Clayton had leaned over and tapped the plexiglass partition dividing them from the driver, asking him to stop.

Within moments, she'd been bent over at the waist on the sidewalk, dragging crisp, night air into her lungs in an effort to settle her tequila-soaked belly.

And he hadn't said a word. Not one. Except to ask if she was all right and if she needed him to do anything, get anything.

They'd been almost at her apartment. She remembered they'd walked the rest of the way. Well, he'd walked. She'd stumbled along beside him, not even aware she'd lost her sandals, grateful for his supporting arm around her waist.

And then he'd bid her goodnight.

In the moonlight, or maybe it was the glow from nearby buildings—she couldn't quite remember—his hair had shone golden. He'd looked like an angel. Every feature, every pore alight, as if touched by the hand of God. His eyes had stared down at her with concern and just a hint of laughter. Amusement that he hadn't given reign to. Then, or now.

But that didn't mean he wouldn't. He was probably waiting for the perfect time to embarrass her. To make the most of her humiliation. Especially after her dig about his wedding ring. How the hell was she to know his wife had died?

A twinge of guilt at her bitchy thought tightened her belly.

She prayed he'd move away and leave her in peace.

She should have known better. Warm, masculine fingers reached over and tilted her chin up until their eyes met.

"Ellie, I—"

"Clayton, Ellie. Good, you're both here."

Catching sight of Ben's drawn and pale face over Clayton's shoulder, her heart leaped into her throat.

The warmth of Clayton's hand dropped away. His voice was infuriatingly calm. "What is it Ben?"

"I've just received a report of a child missing. Down near the lake. A two-year-old boy. They think he may have been kidnapped."

Ellie's world spun. A noise reverberated in her ears, echoing inside her head. Her vision blurred and narrowed and she collapsed back against her chair.

Gulping in air, she squeezed her eyes shut and then opened them again, blinking rapidly as she tried to concentrate on what Ben was saying.

"Three squad cars have already been dispatched. I've also called the local State Emergency Service and they're going to get a band of volunteers together to form a search party."

"W-wh...?" She cleared her throat and avoided Clayton's curious stare. "Where are the parents?"

"The boy's mother was jogging with her son near the lake. He was in a stroller. She went to throw some rubbish in a bin about fifteen yards away. When she turned back, the boy and the pram were nowhere in sight. She searched the area and then called 000. I need you to go down and talk to her. See if you can calm her down. She's already way past hysterical."

CHAPTER 13

Ellie manoeuvred the squad car in and out of the early morning peak-hour traffic and tried to keep from thinking about the scene that would confront her in the next few minutes. She glanced at the man who sat beside her. "Thanks for coming along," she murmured.

Clayton shot her a look full of concern, searching her features with eyes that were dark with shadows.

"Are you all right? You seem a bit...disorientated."

Ellie bit her lip and forced a tight smile. "No, I'm fine. It's just that it's...you know...a two-year-old." She dragged in a ragged breath. "It's always tougher when a kid's involved."

"They may find him yet. He won't be the first toddler to have wandered off."

"But he was strapped into a stroller."

Clayton shrugged. "Sometimes they get them open. It does happen. One day you don't think they have a clue how to work all those clips and the next, you see them undo it. Just like that, you realize they can."

"So, what are you suggesting? That he's wandered into the lake? Like that's a more comforting scenario."

Clayton remained silent and turned to stare out the window. Ellie felt a twinge of guilt for her bitchiness, but couldn't ignore the panic she was barley managing to keep under control.

Her jaw clenched. It wasn't Jamie. It wasn't anything like Jamie. The fact that it was a two-year-old boy was the only thing they had in common. And like Clayton said, there was still hope he'd turn up unharmed. Not every child that went missing was returned to his mother in a box.

A swarm of orange-overalled State emergency personnel crowded the stretch of parkland that lay adjacent to the Penrith Lakes. The sun glinted with diamond-bright sparkles over the still water. The pretty, late-winter morning was at odds with the grim features of the uniformed police officers and the SES volunteers who waited anxiously for instructions.

Ellie parked the squad car and climbed out. Not waiting for Clayton, she strode across the grassy embankment and zeroed in on the officer in charge.

"Williams. What's the story?"

The officer gave Ellie a grim nod of recognition. "Detective Cooper, we're in the process of forming a search party. Zack Clements. Two years old. Last seen by his mother about twenty minutes ago. He was strapped into his stroller when she went to deposit some litter in the trash bin over there."

Ellie's gaze followed the officer's arm as he pointed toward a wheelie bin that stood a short distance away.

"She left the stroller here, on the walking track. When she turned back, both Zack and the stroller were gone."

Clayton strode up and stopped beside her, offering his hand to Williams.

"Federal Agent Clayton Munro. I'm helping out. Was there anyone else in the vicinity?"

Williams looked him up and down and then glanced at Ellie, a question in his eyes. Ellie gave a brief nod, impatient to get things moving. The officer turned back to Clayton.

"Not as far as we know. Millie Clements doesn't recall seeing anyone around, but she was pretty engrossed in her jogging and was listening to music on her iPod."

"Where is she?" Ellie asked quietly.

Williams indicated with his chin. "Over there. I've tried to find out a phone number for her husband or at least a friend, but she's almost beyond stringing a sensible sentence together at the moment."

Ellie looked across at the young woman who stood several yards away, wringing her hands and walking around as if in a daze. She wore jogging sweats that aligned themselves closely to her tall, athletic body. Her white-blond hair was pulled back tightly into a ponytail that bobbed innocently with her movements, at odds with the grim scene unfolding around her.

Barely sparing Clayton a glance, Ellie walked over to the distraught mother. Taking a few deep breaths, she did her best to slow the hammering of her heart.

"Mrs Clements?"

The woman looked at Ellie with terror in her eyes. Ellie's stomach knotted. She swallowed hard and fought off the memories of another time, another child.

"I'm Detective Ellie Cooper. I need to ask you some questions."

The woman nodded disjointedly and made an effort to stand still, hugging herself with her arms.

"Please, Detective; please find him. Please find my baby."

"We're doing the best we can, Mrs Clements. We're putting together a team to search the edge of the lake and we'll speak to anyone who was here at the time Zack went missing. I understand you told Sergeant Peters you didn't notice anyone around at the time, but sometimes we don't see what's right in front of us."

The woman nodded rapidly. "Yes, yes, you're right. That's what I told him. I was—I was jogging, just like I always do. Every morning. With Zack. He was in the stroller, strapped in, as always. He loves to come with me. He loves the birds. He loves the water."

Her voice cracked on the last word and Ellie's heart twisted. She wished she had words of comfort to offer her, but she knew nothing would alleviate the fear that ravaged the woman's face. Only the discovery of her son, alive and well, would do that and Ellie knew better than to make rash promises.

"Has Zack ever unstrapped himself before?"

"No, never. He's only *two*."

"Yes, I know. And so far, there's no sign of the stroller, so we're working on the theory someone has taken both of them."

The woman emitted a wail of anguish that pierced Ellie's heart. She stood helplessly by while Millie Clements struggled to come to terms with the possibility she'd just suggested.

"Who would take him? Who would take my *baby*?"

"We don't know, Mrs Clements. But we're going to do our best to find out."

"Hey! Over here! I've found something!"

The shout sounded from close to the edge of the lake. Ellie looked up and saw a crowd of officers and SES personnel move as one toward the area from where the shout had originated.

Blood pounded in her ears. She strained to see past the group of people. An orange-clad SES volunteer was bent over in the water, reaching toward something. A gasp went up through the throng. A flash of red. A wheel. Two.

It was the stroller.

"Someone call an ambulance! He's still inside!"

Ellie didn't know who'd shouted, but the words reverberated in her ears, her mind, her heart. She turned toward Millie Clements with leaden feet.

All color had leached from the woman's face. Her mouth opened and closed. She fought for breath. Her gaze moved wildly from the lake to Ellie and back again.

And then she screamed.

And screamed.

And screamed.

Hours later, back in the squad room, Ellie could still hear

the woman's desolate cries of devastation in her ears. Her hands shook as she tried to complete the paperwork. She'd tried and failed three times to open the computer database. Her chest was tight and her breathing still hadn't regained its rhythm.

She risked a glance in Clayton's direction and immediately wished she hadn't. He sat at the desk across the room, but his gaze remained steady on hers, concern and curiosity warring in their depths as he stared solemnly back at her.

They'd returned to the station in silence. No words could come close to explaining the tragedy they'd witnessed and neither of them had tried—for which Ellie had been eminently grateful. She'd been beyond words, anyway. Was still finding it difficult to accept what had happened and she couldn't string a coherent thought together.

No matter how hard she tried, images of Jamie kept surfacing, suffocating her. The crushed pram. The look on the face of his day care attendant. The paramedics. The screaming...

Ellie's screaming.

Perspiration gathered on her upper lip. She swiped it away and tried once again to focus on the task in front of her.

"How are you holding up?"

The words were uttered softly, gently and they nearly did her in. He'd closed the distance between them and now stood before her, his face grave with concern.

She fought against the urge to collapse in a mangled mess of emotion and cry her heart out. It's what she felt like doing. But she hadn't come this far to fall apart in front of an almost-stranger. Steel straightened her spine and toughened her emotions.

"I'm fine."

Clayton's gaze didn't waver. She forced herself not to look away.

"You're not fine. No one would be fine after witnessing something like that. I'm sure as hell not." He leaned forward and put his hands flat on her desk. "You're allowed to be upset, Ellie. You're allowed to be angry. You're allowed to rant and rave at the injustice of life. It's what I feel like doing."

"So, go ahead," she offered as nonchalantly as she could manage, her gaze skittering away at last. "Do what you have to do."

His face darkened and his eyes turned stormy. "Do you have kids, Ellie?"

Panic seized her throat, her stomach, her limbs. She coughed and choked and spluttered and gasped for air. Her arms flailed helplessly. Clayton looked alarmed.

"Christ, are you all right? Ellie? What can I do?"

He came around her side of the desk and thumped her between her shoulder blades. She yelped and gasped and he thumped again.

"Stop," she wheezed. "I'm fine. I'm fine. Just..." She looked up at him and got caught in the warmth and concern that filled his eyes. How good would it feel to lean on someone, even for just a little while? To share the burden, the pain she carried around with her every waking moment.

Then he blinked and the moment was gone.

Ellie cleared her throat and looked down at the papers that crowded her desk. She moved files and hunted for a pen, picking up one thing after another, her movements stiff and jerky until they became frantic.

Clayton frowned. "Ellie, talk to me. Please. You're having a delayed reaction to a very traumatic event. I know. I was there, too. You need to talk about it, make some sense of it. That's the only way to deal with it."

Anger, white hot and lightning fast rushed through her veins. What the hell did he know about dealing with trauma? Okay, so he'd lost his wife. Big deal. It didn't come close to the loss of a child.

"What the hell would you know about it, Fed? Okay, you buried your wife way too young. Commiserations for your loss. But that woman just lost her *baby*, her two-year-old. He never got to go to school, learn to drive, fall in love. She's never going to have those memories. Her last memory of her son is going to be watching his lifeless, blue body as they pulled him from his stroller. She turned her back on her baby to answer a phone call and forgot to set the brakes. A simple mistake that she'll live with for the rest of her life. Don't tell me you know how to deal with this kind of thing. You don't have a *clue*."

The spiteful words fell out of her mouth before she could stop them. She was shouting before she finished. Her face burned with anger and the effort it took her not to fall apart. Her breath came in harsh gasps and she knew she had to get out of there before she lost control altogether.

Clayton's face closed. His lips pressed together in a tight, white line. He'd stood in silence and taken the brunt of her tirade without flinching, but his visage now looked as if it had been carved in stone. Pain had flashed briefly behind the shadowed depths of his eyes, but he'd concealed it almost as quickly as it had appeared and Ellie wondered if she'd imagined it.

Guilt, swift and accusatory, seared through her. It wasn't his fault. He didn't know about Jamie. He didn't have a clue. And that's exactly the way it was going to stay.

Taking a deep, shuddering breath, Ellie pushed back her chair and stood. Avoiding his gaze, she strode toward the locker room to fetch her coat. She needed some air.

Clayton stared after Ellie, his thoughts in turmoil. He was still reeling from her attack, trying to make sense of it, trying to justify it.

The death of the toddler was a shock to them all. As a father, he'd never get used to seeing the life of a child cut so horrendously, tragically short. It sliced to the heart of him and made him fearful and grateful for his own daughter all at the same time.

He pulled out his phone and dialed his mother-in-law's

number. He had to speak to Olivia. He needed to hear her voice.

"Hi, Janet. How are you? How's Olivia?"

"Clayton, how are you? Is everything all right? You don't normally call this time of day."

He swallowed and took a breath. "I know. I just... Everything's fine. I just wanted to say hi to Olivia."

"Well, that's nice honey, but she's at pre-school. She won't be home until after three o'clock."

Clayton glanced at his watch and cursed under his breath. Of course, she was at school. It was barely eleven. "I'm sorry, Janet. I guess I just lost track of time. It feels like I've been up here forever."

"How are things going? I've been following the stories on the news. Dreadful, just dreadful. I hope you're getting enough rest."

Her voice was soft, caring and he was grateful she didn't bombard him with questions about the case. He'd always gotten on well with Lisa's parents and his career wouldn't be what it was today if Janet and Bob hadn't been willing to step in and look after Olivia when his job called him away—which happened more often than he liked.

"I'm fine," he said and willed away the headache that had made itself known behind his eyes. "Things are hectic, you know, but I'm fine. It's nothing I can't handle."

"We worry about you, Clayton. The things we've been hearing on the news—it sounds scary. We both know how serious you take your job. You're not responsible for this madman, you know."

Clayton closed his eyes, grimacing as he rubbed at the spot across his forehead where the headache had become more persistent. "I know, Janet. I know and I appreciate your saying so. But I'm here to find him. People are relying on me. That's why I'm here. To find him."

Janet sighed on the other end of the phone, but remained silent. Clayton was grateful she didn't try and argue with him. She knew better than that.

"Anyway," he added with forced cheerfulness. "Say hello

to Olivia for me when she gets home. Tell her I'll Skype her tonight."

"Of course, Clayton. You take care, you hear?"

"Yes, Janet. And thanks. I'll talk to you soon."

Clayton ended the call and slipped the phone back into his shirt pocket. Taking a deep breath, he squared his shoulders and headed toward his desk. He needed to go over everything again. Every scrap of evidence they had. There wasn't much, and he had to do it.

The pressure of responsibility sat surely and squarely on his shoulders, no matter what Janet said. He'd been called in to put together a profile of the monster they hunted—a profile that would lead to the killer's exposure. So far, he'd failed everyone.

He glanced across at Ellie's still-vacant desk and his thoughts went back to the anger and desolation that had suffused her features just before she'd stormed out. That had to be more than just a reaction to the child's death.

She was a professional, a cop of some years' experience. As tragic as the toddler's drowning had been, it hadn't warranted the utter devastation he'd caught in her unguarded eyes.

It had been personal. Way too personal. And he had no chance in hell of prying it out of her.

The door to the squad room swung open and Clayton looked up in surprise as Ellie walked back in, her face unreadable. She tugged off her coat and headed for the locker room.

———————

Ellie closed the bathroom door behind her. Catching a glimpse of herself in the tarnished mirror that hung above the solitary sink, she sighed and ran her fingers through her windblown hair in a vain attempt to regain some semblance of order. The riotous curls defied her, springing back as quickly as she could smooth them down.

With a sigh, she gave up. Turning on the tap, she bent over the sink and splashed cool water onto her face before patting it dry with paper towel. She stared at her reflection in the mirror and cringed.

Her eyes were huge in her pale face. Pain stared back at her, dark...fathomless. Memories buffeted her consciousness, but she refused to give them access. She was at work, surrounded by colleagues—people who didn't know about her son. She couldn't afford to break down, to give the memories free reign. If she did, she'd splinter into a thousand pieces and she'd never be able to put them back together again.

If her colleagues found out she'd be an object of pity, of whispered conversations, of sick curiosity. Not again. She couldn't go through that again.

Determination surged through her and she riffled in her handbag for a brush. With vicious strokes, she dragged the bristles through her hair, unwilling to stop until it had been returned to an almost-normal state. A quick slash of rouge across both cheeks added vital color. She finished with her usual plum-colored lipstick.

Stepping back, she surveyed the results and decided she'd pass muster from the casual observer. Only people who knew her well would see the shadows of darkness beneath her veneer.

It would have to do.

Tossing her handbag back into her locker, she shut the door and made her way back to the squad room. Her gaze glanced off Clayton. He sat at his desk, surrounded by paperwork, a frown darkening his features.

She owed him an apology.

Taking a deep breath, she stopped beside his desk and waited for him to look up. When he did, she almost reeled back from the anger in his eyes.

Misunderstanding its cause, she stumbled over her words. "Clayton, I'm... I'm sorry. I was such a bitch. I-I don't know why I yelled at you like that. It wasn't your fault. I know that." She shook her head. "I'm so sorry."

The anger in his gaze slowly faded and his shoulders slumped on a heavy sigh.

"It's all right, Ellie. I'm not mad at you. I wish you'd tell me what happened to make you so upset, but it's not you I'm angry at. It's me."

She gaped in surprise. "You? Why would you be mad at yourself? I was the one behaving like an immature brat. You were only trying to be nice. You're always trying to be nice." She shrugged. "It irks me sometimes."

A tiny grin tugged at the corner of his bottom lip.

Her heart leaped in response.

"Really? Why would being nice irk you?"

"I don't know. As I said, I can be a bitch. It's not you; it's me. And don't go trying to change the subject. You haven't answered my question. Why would you be mad at yourself, Clayton?"

Shadows flitted across the blue of his irises, deepening them to cobalt.

"I was brought up here to find a killer and I haven't. He's still on the loose. Will probably strike again. May have already struck again. And what have I done to stop him? Nothing. Zilch. Zero. If any other women lose their lives to this maniac, it will be on my head."

"No!" The word was wrenched from her with a surge of anger. "Don't be ridiculous. How could you even think such a thing? We're a team. You're part of a *team*. No one expects you to solve this on your own. Not a single person on this taskforce expects that of you. Don't you dare go putting that kind of pressure on yourself. How can you hope to function with a clear head when you're filling it with that kind of bullshit?"

Her breath came fast. Her cheeks were hot. She looked at Clayton and saw the tiny grin had morphed into a full-blown smile and gratitude and a flash of admiration had already replaced the shadows.

"You sure do have a way with words, Ellie. I'll give you that."

She returned his grin. "So, are we friends again?"

He stared at her. His gaze wandered over her face and then lower, to pause on her bottom lip. When he met her gaze again, his eyes had darkened with unfathomable emotion. "It's a start."

Ellie blushed from the intensity in his eyes. Her mouth went dry and all of a sudden, she couldn't think of a single thing to say.

"I—um…"

"Clayton, Ellie. I'm glad you're both here. I just got off the phone to Samantha Wolfe. She called as soon as she heard. The lab… They've found some fingerprints."

Ellie raised her voice so that Clayton could hear her over the chatter of nearby patrons who were also enjoying an after-work drink at the Hilton's Marble Bar in the heart of Sydney.

"After all the excitement, I didn't even find out where the fingerprints were found?" she said and leaned over to take a sip of her iced water.

Clayton smiled and nodded toward her glass. "Glad to see you don't always hit the hard stuff."

Heat stole up her cheeks. She offered an embarrassed grin. "Every time I think of that night, I cringe."

"Don't." His voice lowered. "I had a good time. It was nice to know you felt comfortable enough to let your guard down."

His gaze filled with warmth and she looked away. A pulse throbbed in her neck and the room suddenly felt overheated.

After driving into the city from Penrith, she'd pulled up outside his hotel, fully intending to wish him a quick farewell and then head to her unit in Darling Harbour. Her only thought had been to kick off her heels, open a bottle of merlot and put the day behind her, but he'd turned to her as soon as she'd pulled up at the curb and had issued the invitation.

Despite some reservations, she'd eventually succumbed to the pleading in his eyes and had agreed to go with him for a drink—a celebratory drink after their first real break in the case. With criminals being fingerprinted for eons, there was a much higher likelihood they'd find a match than with the relatively recent DNA database.

Notwithstanding the shitty start to the day, they'd managed to end it on a high. An almost perfect set of fingerprints. She should have felt elated. She would have felt elated, if she wasn't so damn nervous.

He cleared his throat. "To answer your question, it was the good old trash bag. The one they found part of Angelina Caruso wrapped in." He grimaced. "The one they overlooked."

"Better late than never, I guess."

He shrugged in response and took a sip of his drink. She leaned back into the cedar-colored, studded-leather booth and concentrated on soaking up the ambience of the dimly lit bar located in the basement of one of Sydney's oldest hotels.

She'd suggested the bar because it was a place that never failed to relax her. Discreet lighting glowed dully off the dark mahogany wall paneling, encompassing them in a quiet intimacy. The bar's elegant furnishings, soft, easy listening music and air of sophistication made it popular with older professionals.

She much preferred it to the noisy city bars downtown that overflowed with loud bands and raucous young people who, in her eyes, looked barely legal.

She frowned. God, she must be getting old. If she'd started thinking of anyone over the age of eighteen as young and was avoiding the crowds and loud music she'd once embraced wholeheartedly, it wouldn't be long and she'd be applying for the pension.

She gave a quick shake of her head. *Get over it, Cooper. Stop feeling sorry for yourself.*

Yeah, it had been a shit of a day. Shit of a month, really. Thank God it was nearly over. For the past three years, she'd struggled through the month of July. It was the month when she had to suffer through the anniversary of Jamie's death and now a madman had chosen the western suburbs as his playing field.

But, although she wouldn't have believed it three years ago, the pain from her son's memory had eased infinitesimally. She grimaced. Well, until the discovery of the toddler in Penrith Lakes, which had brought the horror of it back in clanging, banging Technicolor.

But they'd just gotten their first real break on the case and now she was sitting in a booth across from the hottest guy she'd ever known, with nothing but a tiny wooden table between them.

She casually lifted her glass and let her gaze wander over him. Using the straw, she took a sip of water and then sat the glass back down on the table. Despite the fact that he'd been at work all day, his shirt remained blindingly white and unrumpled. A perfectly knotted maroon and gray tie lay straight against the broad expanse of his chest.

He'd shrugged off his dark navy suit jacket as they'd walked in and had hung it over the back of a nearby chair before taking a seat across from her. A sexy, five-o'clock shadow darkened the chiseled line of his jaw.

Realizing she'd been staring, Ellie turned her head abruptly and took another sip of the icy cold water. The straw gurgled loudly and she blushed. Clayton grinned, his straight, even teeth showing white in the dimness.

"Would you like another? I'm pretty sure they're still making it."

Her blush deepened and she was once again thankful for the discreet lighting. Ignoring his quip, she took refuge in the case.

"When will we know if we get a hit?"

His eyes were full of knowing, but he didn't pursue it. Instead, he sat forward and took another sip of his scotch.

"Sometime tonight, with a bit of luck." He swirled the ice in his glass. "Let's hope they come up with a name."

Her lips tightened in response as her thoughts returned to the DNA they'd recovered from Angelina Caruso, and hadn't matched. "Yeah, that would be a good start."

He finished his drink and sat the glass on the table. The silence between them lengthened. She felt the warmth of his gaze upon her and her heart picked up its pace.

"Tell me about yourself, Ellie."

The invitation was murmured softly, politely. A request, not a demand.

Still, she froze. Her past was her past. She didn't share it with anyone. That's how it had always been. That's how she wanted it.

Wasn't it?

Then why did she suddenly feel an almost overwhelming urge to confide in him? To finally let someone else know about her pain?

She moved her empty glass aimlessly back and forth across the table in front of her, staring blindly at the wet circle of condensation as it stretched and lengthened. His gaze continued to probe, gentle but insistent.

Her tongue darted out to swipe at the moisture on her lip. A strand of hair had worked its way loose from the short ponytail she'd scraped together in the bathroom at work. She pushed it back behind her ear. She searched for courage and came up empty. Sighing inwardly, she feigned a smile as cowardice won out.

"Hey, nothing much to tell. I was born in Sydney. Royal North Shore Hospital, to be precise. My parents have a unit in the eastern suburbs at Point Piper. They retired a couple of years ago. They're determined to visit as many cities across the world as they can." She shrugged. "Last time I heard, they were in France."

He leaned forward in his seat and rested his chin on his hands. His gaze encouraged her to continue. "What about brothers and sisters?"

A wave of repressed longing surged through her and she shook her head. "Nope, just me."

His eyes widened in surprise. He leaned back against his chair. "Really? Wow, I always wondered what that would feel like."

"I gather you have some?"

A wide grin followed. "Some? Yeah, I guess you could say that. How's six sound?"

"*Six?*"

"Yep, four brothers and two sisters."

She shook her head in amazement. "Wow, that must be fantastic?"

"Which could only be said by someone who's an only child." His voice was dry, but his eyes glinted with amusement.

"Hey," she shrugged a little self-consciously. "I had to make mine up. There was my big brother Marcus and my little sister Daisy." She grinned. "Don't get me wrong. They were pretty good to have around. They never told me what to do; they never got me into trouble and I always got to be the princess."

Sadness pricked at her eyes and she looked away. "But that's not to say I didn't always want a real one."

"They're not all they're cut out to be, believe me. Not when there's that many of them."

Ellie braced her elbows on the table and rested her head in her hands.

"I bet you had the best time growing up."

Clayton picked up his glass and tilted it to his mouth. The ice in his drink clinked. For a few moments, the only sound was the crunching of the ice between his teeth as he chewed.

Then he smiled. "Yeah, I guess I did. You never really appreciate things when you're a kid. Hey, there are times even now when I wish they'd learn to mind their own business."

"That's not something I've ever had any experience with." Her thoughts strayed to her parents and her gaze fell away. Through all of the turmoil and pain she'd experienced, first with Robert and then with Jamie, they'd never done more than offer to listen, and even then, they'd insisted it was only if she felt like talking.

She didn't know whether she liked it that way, or not.

Maybe if they'd been more forceful, more persistent, she'd have opened up a lot sooner and learned to let out her pain instead of bottling it up inside.

———————

Clayton caught the brief flash of pain in her luminous eyes before it was concealed behind a curtain of dark lashes and wondered at it. He couldn't imagine what it must have felt like growing up alone.

He thought of his twin and their recent telephone conversation. It was one of many similar conversations he'd endured from one or another of his siblings since Lisa's death.

Granted, no one had said anything for the first couple of years. But lately, it seemed as if everyone managed to slip it into their conversation.

He frowned, irritation surging through him. It wasn't as if he'd locked himself in a monastery, for Christ's sake. He still dated occasionally. He'd asked Ellie out, hadn't he? So what if she was a work colleague. It still counted, didn't it?

His gaze rested on the woman opposite him. Ellie. Beautiful, feisty, tiny Ellie. Christ, he'd probably crush her if he took her in his arms.

He couldn't believe he'd actually thought about it. Was still thinking about it. He'd worked with attractive women before. What was so special about this one?

His gaze wandered over her soft, full lips now coated in a plum-colored gloss. She must have re-touched her makeup before they'd left the station. He caught a glimpse of creamy flesh peeking out from the open neck of her tailored blouse—the deep shadow between her breasts intrigued him. The smell of her vanilla-scented perfume enticed his nostrils and all of a sudden, his head was full of her.

The night they'd gone out to dinner she'd nearly blown his mind with her sexy, curve-hugging dress. It was the first time he'd seen her wear one. The image of her crowded his dreams. He hadn't managed a decent night's sleep since. Morning would find the crisp hotel sheets tangled around him, his hand working his erection as he wondered what it would feel like to touch her.

His cock hardened in reaction to those memories and he frowned again, shaking his head and muttering condemnations under his breath. This was getting ridiculous.

"Hey, it can't be that bad."

Her gentle murmur penetrated his thoughts and he looked up. Wide green eyes were soft on his face.

"Sorry." He grimaced and looked away, grateful for the protection of the table that hid the evidence of his desire.

"Tell me about them."

He blew out a breath and raised his glass, forgetting for a moment that it was empty. His mind scrambled to pick up the threads of their conversation.

"My family? You want to know about my family?"

"Absolutely. I'm sure there must be plenty of stories to tell about four brothers and two sisters."

He grimaced again, but it reluctantly fell away into a grin. "You don't know what you've let yourself in for."

She sat forward and her knees brushed his under the table. He ignored the heat that flared back to life in his groin and signaled the waiter.

"If we're going to do this, I suggest we gird ourselves with another drink." He gestured toward her empty water glass. "You might like to order something a little stronger than that."

Her lips widened into a grin. "That bad, huh?"

He cocked an eyebrow, doing his best to act casual, despite the acceleration of his pulse.

"Oh, yeah. In fact, I'd probably make it a double."

She laughed out loud and the sound of it went straight through him. His cock hardened almost painfully at the sheer sexiness of the sound. She may have looked delicate, but there was nothing slight about her throaty mirth.

The waiter appeared a few moments later, a notepad and pen in hand. Ellie ordered a glass of merlot and another scotch for him and then smiled her thanks. The young boy blushed and stammered. Clayton knew exactly how he felt. He couldn't seem to get his fill of her. She intrigued him, engaged him, made him laugh. And she made his heart beat faster.

Which was a first. A first since Lisa.

"So, where do you fit in the family?" she asked when the boy had left with their order.

He drew in a deep breath. "Are you sure you're ready for this? Because, for someone who's never had a sibling, it's going to sound completely crazy." He tugged at his tie and loosened the knot. "Hell, what am I saying? My family *is* completely crazy."

Her eyes were fixed on his face. "And yet you love them." It was a quiet statement of fact.

He turned serious. "Yes, you're right. I do. For all their faults and failings, I'd do anything for them—as they would for me."

"It must be nice to know they have your back."

"Yeah, I guess it is. Even my sisters—who whinge and bitch about me all the time and always side with each other against the boys—even they would be there for me if I needed them. I couldn't think of life without them. All of them."

Ellie sighed wistfully. "It sounds like you have an interesting family. You're very lucky, even if they're not perfect."

"Yes, I am." He stared at her, trying to delve into the shadows that had deepened her eyes to emerald. Reaching over, he covered her hand with his and took a deep breath. "Tell me about Jamie."

———————

Ellie gasped, snatching her hand away. Shock and anger surged through her. He *knew*.

"You *bastard*. How dare you pry into my personal life? You have no right! We *work* together, Munro. Nothing more. I don't know what impression you got the other night, but I sure as hell—"

"Calm down, Ellie. You're overreacting." His gaze held hers. "I like you. I want to get to know you. That's all."

"That's *all*? How can you say that?" She pushed back from the table and began a feverish hunt for the handbag she'd stowed on the floor near her feet.

"Please don't leave, Ellie. What do you want me to say? I'm sorry. I didn't realize you couldn't talk about it."

She sat up abruptly, almost banging her head on the table in her haste and glared at him. "Upset? You call this upset? I'm not upset, Munro. I'm *furious*."

Aware of the curious gazes of several nearby patrons, she forced herself to lower her voice. Her teeth clenched with the effort.

"How would you like it if I'd pried into *your* past? Discovered things you didn't want anyone to know? Did you run a check on me through the database?"

He frowned and shook his head. "Of course not. I just... I Googled you, that's all." He shut his eyes briefly. "I'm sorry. I screwed up. I should have minded my own business. It's just that...earlier today... I tried, Ellie... I tried to get you to talk to me. You were hurting over that young boy. I could tell it was more than just the tragic waste of a young life. It was personal. The pain in your eyes... Ellie, I..."

His cheeks flushed crimson and he looked away. As if coming to a decision, he squared his shoulders and turned back to face her, his eyes intent on her face.

"I like you, Ellie. I *really* like you. I haven't felt this way since my wife died and it scares the hell out of me."

Her heart pounded and her chest felt tight. Time suspended. Emotion darkened the blue of his eyes to deep cobalt. He leaned closer and the spicy scent of his cologne filled her nostrils.

A long moment passed. She was the first to look away.

"That's a low blow, Munro. I don't care how much you like me; it doesn't justify snooping into my business without my knowledge or consent. If I wanted you to know anything about me, I'd have told you." The anger inside her settled into a slow, cold burn. "Didn't that ever occur to you?"

He flushed again and avoided her eyes. "Of course it did. But you didn't seem too forthcoming in that department." He shrugged apologetically. "I thought I'd do a little research."

Her anger stormed back to life. "*Research?*"

His lips twisted in a grimace. "I'm not explaining this very well. I'm sorry. I had no idea you'd react with so much hostility. It's a matter of public record, after all. All I did was skim over a few newspaper reports. I'm sure you must know it was in all the major papers."

Her groan didn't begin to do justice to the anguish that tightened her chest until she could barely breathe. She closed her eyes and buried her face in her hands. Images of Jamie and the headlines from one newspaper after another raced through her mind in a kaleidoscope of black-and-white words and pictures. She'd committed every article to memory.

Of course, she knew it would come out eventually. She was grateful the latest anniversary of his death had passed without notice. Last year, she hadn't been so lucky.

Memories of being holed up in her apartment with the blinds drawn, fielding calls from the media on her answering machine flashed through her mind.

It still didn't excuse what he'd done. No matter that a few moments ago she'd been considering unloading on him. That was different. That was her choice. By Googling her in the name of research, he'd invaded her privacy and taken the decision from her. He now knew everything about her, right down to the one detail she'd managed to keep hidden from everyone at the station.

She knew the newspapers hadn't spared her. The press had relished the fact she was a single mother and a police officer who'd been on duty the afternoon her son had been killed. And when she'd attended the scene of the accident, oblivious to the fact her son was involved...

It was a moment she'd never forget. Couldn't forget.

The overwhelming panic that had assailed her as she'd recognized Jamie's daycare attendant sitting on the sidewalk, wailing. The navy-blue Peg-Perego pram, almost unrecognisable as a bent and twisted pile of metal, the heart-wrenchingly familiar blue-and-white puppy dog blanket still hanging out of the side of it.

And Jamie. Her young, innocent son... A mass of broken bones and ruptured organs. By the time she got there, the paramedics had already covered his tiny body with a sheet.

She'd put in for a transfer straight after the funeral. She couldn't bear the looks of pity leveled at her way by her well-meaning colleagues.

Three transfers later and she ended up at the Penrith LAC. Despite the long commute from Darling Harbor, it had provided her with a haven where she'd been able to lick her wounds in private and heal without well-meaning interference from others. Enough time had passed that it was no longer breaking news and if anyone at the station did know, they'd kept it to themselves.

Everyone else had respected her privacy. Why the hell hadn't *he*?

She glared at his guilt-ridden features. Whatever she may have felt for him was now consumed by cold, hard fury. "Keep your apologies, Munro. I don't want them. We're work colleagues, nothing more. As soon as we nail this nutcase, you'll skip off to wherever you came from and your life will continue as normal."

Pain and disappointment threatened to overwhelm her. Hot tears burned behind her eyelids. She blinked hard and took a great, gulping breath, refusing to allow them to fall. She would *not* let him see her fall apart.

He looked stricken. "Ellie, I didn't—"

"Shut up, Munro. Just shut *up*." Blindly, she fumbled again for her handbag and stood, narrowly avoiding the waiter as he approached with their drinks.

"And you can find someone else to chauffeur your smug Fed ass around. I've had enough." She turned and stumbled up the stairs toward the exit without a backward glance.

CHAPTER 14

S hit, shit, shit.

Clayton stared after her retreating back with a sinking feeling of dread. Talk about a monumental stuff-up. How the hell was he supposed to know she was going to react like that?

It's not like he'd done anything illegal. Hell, in his family, everyone stuck their nose in where it wasn't wanted. It was a sign they cared. Even on those occasions when he was pissed off because it was his business they were poking into, he always knew they had his best interests at heart.

He picked up the glass of scotch from where the waiter had cautiously left it on the table and took a healthy swallow. Frustration prickled his scalp. He should have just kept his mouth shut. Especially after she'd told him she was an only child. She wouldn't be used to the interference a sway of siblings had on your life. It was even worse when they were concerned for you. As he was for Ellie now.

After discovering the story about her son, his concern for her and her recent experience with Zach Clements had only deepened. He'd wanted to take her into his arms and tell her it would be all right. That he'd look after her and make sure nothing bad ever happened to her again. He'd wanted to whisper words of comfort against the softness of her hair and hold her until the desolation in her eyes faded away.

But he'd been unable to do any of those things. They'd been at work, for one. More importantly, they were work

173

colleagues. He wasn't her husband; he wasn't even her boyfriend. He had no right to hold her, to comfort her, no matter how much he wanted to.

He dragged his fingers through his hair and did his best to ignore his underlying fear. He refused to acknowledge the possibility that she'd never forgive him. Tugging his cell phone out of his pocket, he dialed his twin's number. He needed help. Riley knew him better than anyone.

He took another fortifying gulp from his glass and listened to it ring out, praying Riley would answer.

———————

Hours later, Ellie still fumed as she paced the length of her small but cozy two-bedroom apartment.

She'd been so wired when she'd turned the key in her lock that she hadn't even taken time out to eat. A half-empty bottle of merlot sat on the kitchen bench. She stared at it as her hands clenched and unclenched at her sides.

The more she thought about it, the angrier she got. Not even her *family* pried into her private life like that. In fact, she wouldn't have believed any sane, normal person would do such a thing. She'd never dream of invading someone's privacy that way.

But he had. *Googling* her, for God's sake! It was just so...so...*crude*.

With a groan of irritation, she picked up her empty wine glass and refilled it before striding into the living room. She hadn't yet drawn the curtains and the city lights, with their fluorescent blues and reds and yellows, reflected a colorful display off the water.

It was a view she normally savored. Her third-floor unit had an unobstructed view of Darling Harbor. On a fine day, the water shone blue and crystal clear, reflecting a million diamonds as it bathed in the sun's rays.

At this time of night, the noise from the street below was a muted hum and mid-week pedestrian traffic was minimal.

She drew in a deep breath and let it out on a heartfelt sigh and collapsed onto the white leather three-seater. Leaving the lights off, she tucked her feet up underneath her and took refuge in the burnt-orange scatter cushions. She pushed one under her head and grasped another one tightly to her chest.

When she'd bought it, her mother had taken one look at the couch and had shaken her head in disapproval.

"White is so impractical, Ellie. How are you going to keep it clean? No one in their right mind buys a white couch with a toddler in the house."

But Ellie wouldn't be dissuaded. She didn't care how many hours she'd spend wiping sticky handprints off it. She loved it.

Three months after she'd bought it, Jamie was killed. There were no more sticky handprints to worry about after that.

Long-held-back tears burned her eyes. He'd been gone three years and on days like this it felt like yesterday. The agonizing shock. The paralyzing horror. The utter disbelief as what happened sank in.

Pent-up grief gripped her in a vicelike hold and she shuddered. Wine spilled over her fingers, cold and wet and sticky. With a shaking hand, she placed the glass on the low table beside the couch and finally gave herself permission to grieve.

She curled up in a fetal position and let the sobs come. With her knees digging into the cushion pressed against her chest, she gripped her legs tightly and gave vent to the pain.

It took her awhile to realize the high keening cries reverberating in her ears were coming from her. The tears continued to fall. She swiped at the snot that ran down her face—her nose was so blocked, she could barely breathe. She snatched gulps of air through her mouth.

The tightness in her chest and the thumping in her head eventually forced her to take deeper breaths, to cram more oxygen into her constricted lungs. After a few moments, she sat up and reached for the box of tissues she kept on the carved wooden coffee table in front of her.

She blew her nose noisily—once, twice, three times—and wiped the moisture from her cheeks. She shuddered again, but this time in relief of a sort. It had been a long time since she'd let herself cry over her son. Too long.

She knew a good deal of her anger at Clayton arose from the memories his prying had thrust upon her. Memories she'd tried hard to ignore and control as yet another anniversary of her son's death came and went.

And she hadn't even called Eva. It was downright unfair, but the last time she'd spoken to his daycare attendant the woman had sobbed uncontrollably for the entire conversation. It was tough enough holding herself together. She wasn't up to being anyone else's emotional support.

With another heavy sigh, Ellie picked up her almost-empty wine glass and drained it. Her belly gurgled loudly and she remembered she hadn't eaten since breakfast.

Swinging her legs over the side of the couch, she dropped the crumpled cushion and eased herself upright. She filled her lungs with a long, steadying breath. Another shudder ran through her as she released it, but it was a shudder of relief and finality.

In stockinged feet, she padded into the kitchen and flicked on the electric jug where it stood on the counter near the sink and gathered the makings of a cup of coffee.

Opening the fridge, she took out a container of left-over Chinese take-away and put it in the microwave. It was far from ideal, particularly given the grueling hours she'd been putting her body through, but it would do for tonight.

She actually enjoyed cooking most of the time. She loved poring over recipe books, shopping for ingredients, putting it all together and sampling the final product. It was relaxing—therapeutic even.

She grimaced. She couldn't remember the last time she'd prepared a proper meal. Probably around the time Josie Ward disappeared.

Frustration surged through her. What were they missing? Would the fingerprints tell them anything? She'd begun to dread the sound of the phone ringing.

As if she'd conjured it up, her cell phone hummed. It was still in her handbag on the table in the hallway where she'd tossed it when she'd stormed inside. For a moment, she was tempted to ignore it.

But it was almost ten o'clock. Too late for a social call. Which meant it could only be work.

With a sigh of resignation, she took the few steps out of the kitchen and into the hallway, pulling the phone out of her bag. She checked the caller ID.

Clayton.

Her pulse skipped a beat, even as her anger renewed itself. He was calling to apologize. She was sure of it. He was that kind of guy. Polite and courteous, to a fault. At least, most of the time.

She wasn't ready to talk to him. She knew that much. Tired and drained and achy from her crying jag, she couldn't deal with the day anymore. Not even for one minute.

Silencing the call, she turned the phone off and padded back to the kitchen. After pouring the boiling water over the coffee already in her cup, she added sugar and took a sip, sighing as the caffeine filtered through her system.

With mug in hand, she switched off the light in the kitchen and made her way down the hallway to her bedroom, guided only by memory and moonlight.

Clayton strode into the squad room and Ellie kept her head down. She wasn't ready to talk to him. The fact that Ben had informed her the moment she'd arrived for duty that they hadn't gotten a hit on the fingerprints had further soured her mood. She was thankful he hadn't asked her where the Fed was. Still peeved, she'd left Clayton to find his own way to the station.

She'd checked her phone when she'd crawled out of bed, but he hadn't left a message. It was probably just as well. Then she'd have to acknowledge he'd rung. For now, she'd do her best to ignore him. As much as anyone could ignore a six-foot-plus wall of muscle whose impeccably dressed body was now planted firmly in front of her desk.

She swallowed a groan and studiously continued writing in the file before her, paying no heed to the pulse that beat a frantic rhythm in her neck.

"So, you're just going to ignore me. Is that it?"

His voice was loud enough to cause curious gazes to turn their way. She blushed and damned him silently to hell. Why couldn't he leave her alone?

"I'm not going away until you look at me, Ellie."

She cringed inwardly at the determination in his voice. She should have known he wouldn't give up easily. Despite their lack of progress, his dogged persistence with the case was proof of that. But did he really have to turn it on her?

He cleared his throat noisily. "I'm sorry for going behind your back. I should have just asked you. I know that now, but as much as I'd like to, I can't take it back."

He hesitated and she willed herself to keep writing.

"All I'm asking is that you forgive me."

Her eyes snapped up to meet his. "Why should I?"

He shrugged and she almost softened. He looked so lost and helpless. He looked completely unsure of himself. A state she'd never seen him in.

"I just thought you might... We might—"

"Clayton. Good, you're here." Ben strode across the squad room, his expression grave.

A tightness gripped her throat. She'd seen that look before. "What is it, boss?"

Ben gazed down at her, a frown creasing his deeply lined forehead. "A couple of hikers have come across a body in bushland. It looks like it's Sally Batten."

Ellie deftly manoeuvred the squad car in and out of the

early morning traffic, scowled in ferocious concentration. Her protest that Clayton catch a ride with someone else had fallen on deaf ears and he now sat rigidly in the seat beside her.

They hadn't spoken since Ben had given them the news. Even now, she studiously avoided the weight of his stare. Her jaw clenched when he broke the tense silence, his voice low.

"You don't have a monopoly on grief, Ellie."

Anger steamed to the surface. Hot. Immediate. Choking. Her eyes narrowed on his face. She fought for control.

"Oh, like you know what you're talking about. How many children have *you* buried?"

He hesitated and she thought she caught a flash of pain in his eyes. When he replied, his gaze stayed fixed on a point outside the window and his voice was thick with emotion.

"None."

"I know you lost your wife...."

"Yes, and it felt as if my world ended the day I buried her." His voice seethed with quiet pain.

She gritted her teeth. Okay, so maybe he did know something about it. But a spouse hardly counted against a child. Anyone would agree with that.

Clayton's face darkened with fury and disbelief when she said as much.

"You've never been in love before, have you Ellie?" He didn't wait for her to reply. "You've never known what it's like to love someone so much you want to breathe in the very air they breathe out, just so you can keep a part of them inside you. You've never known what it's like to want someone so much you feel like you'll die if you can't be near them, touch them, hold them."

She shivered at the raw passion in his voice and the pain that lingered in his eyes and felt a stab of envy for the woman who'd invoked such a reaction. Then she shook her head, appalled.

For God's sake, she was feeling jealous of a dead woman. How low could she go?

Still, she couldn't help the wistful thought that maybe one day someone would feel that way about her. His gaze was still fixed upon her. She turned away.

"What? Nothing to say, Cooper?" His voice dripped sarcasm. "That's funny; you've never been short of words before."

Ellie pressed her lips tightly together and turned left off the main road. They bounced along a rough dirt track in taut silence. Spying vehicles up ahead, she sighed inwardly in relief. Avoiding his gaze, she murmured, "Looks like we're here."

Tall gum trees stood in a thick line bordering both sides of a narrow, sandy track. It wasn't yet mid-morning, and the sun was only a lukewarm presence in the sky. The smell of eucalyptus and lemon scented the still air. Clayton breathed in deeply, appreciating the smell of the bush despite the reason that had brought them there.

A small group of bystanders and a larger contingent of uniformed police officers crowded the scene. Crime scene tape had been strung up around the trunks of the huge gums in a rough rectangle around the body.

Ellie walked ahead of him, picking her way through low bushes, long grass and other shrubbery before ducking under the tape.

"Hey, Jake. Good to see you again." Ellie gave the forensics officer a bright smile.

Clayton's jaw tightened. *Great. The good-looking beefcake was back. Just what he needed.*

"You too, Ellie." Jake gave her a slow onceover that set Clayton's teeth on edge. "Looking good, as always."

"We have to stop meeting like this," she replied with a quick smile. "Surely we can think of somewhere better?"

"Yeah, a drink down near the Quay sounds like a much better idea. Mid-afternoon would be good, when the sun's got some heat in it. These early winter starts are a bitch."

With a snort of impatience, Clayton strode forward and planted himself between them. Nodding toward the body that lay on the ground covered by a blue tarpaulin, he did his best to ignore the smell that emanated from it and shot Jake a narrowed look.

"What have you got?"

Jake's eyes widened knowingly. A sardonic grin tugged at his lips, but he remained silent and turned toward the corpse.

"The ID in the handbag we found lying a few feet from the body says it's Sally Batten. Twenty-two years old, she's been missing a couple of months."

Clayton's eyes drilled into his. "You're sure it's Sally?"

Tension sizzled between them.

"Well, Federal Agent Munro, we haven't carried out DNA tests yet, but there are some definite similarities to her license photo. She was half-buried under leaf matter and of course, the cold temperatures have helped slow down the decomposition. Even though there's a fair amount of it, I'd hazard a reasonable guess we're talking about the same person."

Ellie stepped forward, effectively placing herself between the two men. "Who found her?"

Jake flicked his head in the direction of a young couple who were huddled together a short distance away with a uniformed officer who looked like he was still taking notes.

Clayton took them in at a glance. Early twenties, fit-looking. The male with longish brown hair and a light fuzz on his chin had his arm around the girl. Her blond head was buried against his chest, her arms tight around his waist. His gaze returned to the forensics officer.

"Hikers," Jake continued. "Out bushwalking early this morning. Stumbled across her."

Stepping closer to the bundle covered by the tarpaulin, Clayton kneeled on the damp ground and lifted the stiff plastic away from what remained of Sally Batten.

The smell hit him even harder. Rank. Rotten. Putrid. Sweet.

His nostrils and stomach rebelled and he stood and moved a couple of feet away, trying not to gag. He caught a glimpse of a smirk lining the beefcake's face and tensed.

Turning slightly away, he fumbled in the back pocket of his suit pants and pulled out a pair of latex gloves, pretending that getting the gloves was his intent all along.

Ellie squatted beside the body. With gloved hands, she tugged at the trash bags that partly covered the remains. "Phew, she's in a bad way."

Clayton moved up beside her and hunkered down as close as his stomach would allow. He'd never been fond of fieldwork. There was a reason why he'd found a home behind a desk.

Taking hold of the tarpaulin, he hauled it and the trash bags further out of the way until what remained of Sally Batten was revealed.

She was dressed in what had once been a long-sleeved, white T-shirt. It had been ripped away at her right shoulder, exposing one side of her chest. Dark stains that looked like blood covered most of her shirt.

Pulling the covering down lower, Clayton tensed, his gaze shooting to Ellie's. Her face reflected his sudden anger. Not only was Sally naked from the waist down, she was missing both legs.

He shook his head in bleak despair at the savagery of the monster they hunted.

A torso, two arms and now two legs. Christ, the bastard was collecting body parts. *What the hell were they dealing with?*

A hot ball of anger and dread lodged in his gut. It was something out of a horror movie. Things like this didn't happen in real life. It was unthinkable. It was beyond comprehension. Yet, it was happening.

"No legs," Ellie murmured, her lips compressed into a thin line.

His gaze swept over the rest of the body. Everything else seemed to be intact. Her arms and hands were relatively clean. He leaned forward and examined the area where her legs used to be. The underside of her torso was caked in mud and black debris clung to the open wounds.

He met her gaze. "She wasn't attacked here. There's a copious amount of blood on her shirt, but barely anything on the ground beneath her. And there's mud all over her back."

He pointed to her arms. "There's no mud on her hands. I'd say she's been dragged along the ground by her arms for some distance. And not long after it rained, from the amount of mud that's on the bottom of her."

He took in the slight form of Sally Batten and frowned. "The monster we're hunting isn't large. In fact, I'd put him somewhere around one hundred and twenty or thirty pounds. Sally wasn't a big woman and yet he had to drag what's left of her to get her here. A larger man would have simply carried her."

"We're lucky she was protected by the bushland. With the rain we've had since she went missing, a lot of our evidence would have been washed away," Ellie said.

Clayton nodded. "We need to get her to the morgue and see if they can give us a time of death." He motioned with his head in Jake's direction. "That's if you can drag yourself away from your boyfriend."

She followed his gaze. Jake wandered around the crime scene taking photos. A smile tugged at her lips.

Her gaze eventually came back to his, amusement sparkling in their green depths. He tensed, not at all in the mood to be played with.

"I'm sure Michael will have something to say about that."

He stared at her blankly. "Michael?"

Her grin widened. "Yeah, Michael. Jake's partner."

Heat flared up Clayton's neck and he looked away in confusion. "But, what about...? He asked you out—I heard him."

She laughed and shook her head. "He wasn't asking me out, you idiot. He was mucking around. Stirring me up." She looked at him from underneath her lashes. "Sounds like he stirred *you* up."

Clayton clamped his lips shut as his embarrassment deepened. She was right. He was an idiot. If she hadn't been involved, he probably would have noticed straight away.

"You two seen enough?"

He looked up to see Jake looming above them. Standing slowly, he peeled the latex off his hands and wadded them into a ball. "Have you taken photos of the body, yet?"

"Done before you got here. I'll email them to you when I get back to the station."

"Sure," Clayton replied. "Send them to Ellie's address. I don't have access to a secure server here."

Jake's eyes taunted him. "What, you couldn't get clearance, Fed?"

If Ellie hadn't told him Jake played for the other team, Clayton would have been ready to take the man's head off. Now, he just smiled and shrugged. "Something like that."

Jake's eyes widened in surprise and then comprehension. He looked across at Ellie. "I guess I'll see you round, sweet cheeks."

"Yeah. Thanks, Jake. You take care."

"You too, Coop."

"As much as I like to ogle your eye-candy, Detective Cooper, this is getting beyond a joke."

Ellie strode into the sadly familiar environs of Samantha Wolfe's workplace with Clayton close behind her.

"You're not telling me anything I don't already know, Sam." She closed her eyes briefly and shook her head. "Let's hope this is the last of them."

The doctor frowned, concern filling her world-weary face. Her eyes turned serious. "Are you any closer to finding him?"

Ellie's shoulders slumped. "No. We're not."

Clayton moved toward the stainless steel gurney where the remains of who they believed to be Sally Batten had been laid out. His face was hard and closed.

Samantha gazed after him. "I won't ask how the profiling's going, then."

He didn't so much as glance in the doctor's direction. Ellie suppressed a sigh, knowing how personally he took their lack of progress.

She understood how he felt. She was part of the taskforce. She'd lost count of how many nights she'd lain awake tossing and turning with frustration over their inability to come up with something. Anything. It gnawed at her insides.

She'd even given up straightening her hair. The extra twenty minutes it took every morning seemed an abominable waste of time when there was a killer on the loose.

The strain of the fifteen-hour days she'd been putting in was starting to tell. Apart from her wild and unkempt hair, her nails hadn't seen a file for weeks and were now chipped and dry. She couldn't remember when she'd last slept the night through. Insomnia had become her friend.

Not that the Fed seemed to be suffering. At least, he didn't appear to be on the outside. Despite their early morning trek through the bush, his suit pants looked as crisp as ever.

His eyes, although ringed with fatigue, still burned with grim determination, as if he'd never let the killer get the better of him. She sighed, hoping that was true.

"So, we've got a young adult female. Judging from the width of her pelvis, I'd say somewhere between the age of sixteen and twenty-five."

Samantha turned the torso over and inspected it closely. "No obvious signs of violence. No punctures or bullet wounds." She ran her hand over some small lacerations. "Looks like she's been gnawed on by an animal—a dog or a fox, most likely, judging by the teeth and claw marks. It looks like it had only just started in on her. I wonder what disturbed it?"

Ellie grimaced and tamped down her impatience. She couldn't care less about the dog or the fox—or whatever had decided to sample the contents of the bag. It had nothing to do with the investigation and she didn't give a damn. Precious seconds were ticking by.

Clayton cleared his throat and pinned the pathologist with his gaze. "How did she die, Dr Wolfe?"

Moving further down the table, Samantha bent low over Sally's neck and examined it closely. "Probably strangulation, like the last one. It's a bit difficult to tell because any bruising has been camouflaged by the decomposition, but an x-ray will tell us if there are any broken bones."

She looked up at them over her protective mask and clear, plastic glasses. "Bones in the neck don't always break, but there's a fair chance in most strangulation cases. And of course, there's also the blood loss. He's severed two arteries cutting off her legs. That's enough, in itself to cause her death." Samantha looked down at the remains. "Any idea who she is?"

Ellie looked at Clayton and sighed. She cleared her throat and looked back at the doctor. "We think it's Sally Batten. DNA will tell us for sure. We have samples that can be used for comparison back at the station."

Clayton pushed forward. "What about her legs? Can you tell us anything about how they were removed?"

Dread settled in Ellie's belly at what Clayton hadn't said. She couldn't prevent the thought forming. *Was Sally alive when they'd been removed, like the others?*

The pathologist moved lower. Bending over the girl's torso, she examined the place where her right leg used to be. After a few moments, she straightened and turned to them, her face grim.

"It's like the others. Saw marks across the bone and blood in the tissue. I'll have to check under the microscope, but I'm guessing it's a hacksaw. A microscopic comparison will tell us if it's the same one used on the others."

Clayton stared at the girl's remains, his eyes blue steel. "Let's see if the bastard left behind a calling card. I want every surface, every nook, every cranny, every fingernail examined and everything and I mean *everything* bagged and sent to the lab."

With a curt nod, he strode across the room toward the exit. "And make sure the trash bags aren't forgotten this time," he threw over his shoulder. Yanking off his gown and gloves, he tossed them into the waste disposal before disappearing through the doorway.

Samantha eyed Ellie for a moment with baleful eyes. "He might be cute, but he could do with some work on his manners."

"You bring out the worst in him, Samantha. Besides, he's under a lot of pressure. We all are."

Stepping away from the gurney and its sad offering, Ellie pulled off her protective gear and tossed them into the bin.

"Well, at least he's easy on the eye. I hope you find some time to have a bit of fun with him. You know what they say about all work and no play..."

Ellie ducked her head in an effort to hide her blush. "Call me when you get the lab results."

Samantha shot her a knowing look. Ellie turned and bolted for the door.

Ellie couldn't get the pathologist's words out of her mind as she waited for Clayton outside the station. He'd gone inside to collect the address of Sally Batten's parents and thoughts of him kept playing through her head.

His blue eyes, sparkling with good humor, shadowed with anger, burning with determination. Smiling, frowning, laughing, arguing, thinking, teasing, plotting, joking. He was all she could think about.

Which wasn't good. It wasn't good at all.

She barely knew him. So what if her gut told her she could trust him? She'd proved in the past she couldn't rely on that.

Take Robert. Her heart had come alive the moment she'd laid eyes on him at the Academy. By the end of their first night of training, she'd known he was the man she would marry. Twelve months later, he'd abandoned her and their unborn child at the altar.

So much for gut instincts.

But there was something about the Fed that drew her in a different way. Maybe it was the hint of vulnerability she saw in his eyes in unguarded moments. Or the shadow of sadness that sometimes passed over his face, like that morning when he'd been on the phone.

And then there was his kindness and compassion when he'd spoken to the families of some of the victims. Surely, she couldn't be wrong about that?

With a groan of frustration, she pushed the thoughts aside. There was a maniac terrorizing the young women of western Sydney. She didn't have time for anything else, no matter how tempting.

The station door swung open. The Fed strode toward her and her pulse took a crazy leap. She watched him surreptitiously from underneath her lashes. So much for the pep talk. Her libido thought she had all the time in the world.

CHAPTER 15

He stared at the television screen and felt the excitement curl deep inside his gut. It blossomed into heat and spread throughout his body. His fingertips tingled and he was momentarily lightheaded from the surge of emotion.

The pictures flashing across the screen showed a swarm of police surrounding the wooded bushland where he'd dumped her. Sally Batten. That's what they said. He was surprised it had taken them so long to find her.

It hadn't taken them anywhere near as long to find Angelina. Images of the girl flooded his thoughts. She'd been nothing like Sally, but Angelina was special because she was the one who'd started it. It was Angelina who had given him the idea. It was almost as if she'd whispered it to him through the window of his car. From the moment he'd seen her, he'd known what he had to do.

He'd spied her at the bus stop outside the university and immediately fell in love with her tall, slender body and long, golden-brown hair. He loved all of them, but the ones that looked like Rapunzel held a special place in his heart and even though her hair was darker than what he normally preferred, she'd been perfect in every other way.

He'd always been in love with Rapunzel. Even when his mother had destroyed every doll she could find, he'd managed to save Rapunzel. He could still remember with a clarity that surprised him, how he'd pressed his lips against her long blond hair and had taken comfort in the painted blue eyes that had peered up at him with sympathy and understanding. Rapunzel knew what it was like to be imprisoned. She knew exactly how it felt to be controlled by a woman who wanted him dead. They had so much in common that way.

And she brought him comfort, like the soft, silky underpants and the sweet-smelling dresses he'd stolen off the neighbors' clotheslines. Nothing made him feel more whole than when he slid the apparel over his skinny, boy's body and felt them envelop him in their warmth and acceptance.

He only wished he'd been more careful. If he had, his mother would never have found out, would never have screamed vitriol at him with disgust and hatred burning in her eyes...would never have hunted down every doll and piece of stolen clothing in the house and destroyed them.

Not that it had made a difference. It didn't make him stop. Yes, he'd cried tears of anger and wished her dead. But he didn't stop. He couldn't. All it did was to teach him how crucial it was to be more careful. A lot more careful. It was a lesson he hadn't forgotten.

Chapter 16

Ellie pulled the unmarked car over to the curb and parked outside the house where Sally Batten had lived with her parents. The garden was dry and overgrown. The lawn was yellowed. Her stomach churned with dread. The sad display was surrounded by a dilapidated picket fence that may have once been white. It looked as tired and neglected as the last time she'd been there with Luke. It felt like a lifetime ago.

"This sure as hell doesn't get any easier," she murmured.

Clayton looked just as tense as she felt. "You're right about that."

They'd barely spoken on their way to the Battens' Mt Druitt address. Thoughts of the body they'd left in the morgue not long ago and the parents they were about to visit had filled her mind. She still hadn't found the right words. Two months ago, their daughter had been studying to be a dietician at the local University. She had a boyfriend and a part time job. She was just another young woman getting on with her life. Now she was dead.

Taking a deep breath, she filled her lungs to capacity, holding it for as long as she could—a technique she'd used countless times to help her calm down. Carbon dioxide escaped her lips in infinitesimal amounts until there was nothing left.

All she felt was lightheaded.

She grimaced. So much for relaxation techniques...

Clayton studied her with a quizzical expression, one eyebrow cocked. "You ready?"

Eyeing him solemnly, she snatched another breath of air. "I guess so."

———————

George Batten opened the door and introduced himself before they had a chance to knock.

"I seen you sittin' out there for the last little while. You had that look about you. Figured you'd be comin' in."

His grizzled face was covered in white whiskers that matched the color of his hair. Bleary, red-rimmed eyes and dirty, loose overalls contributed to his generally unkempt appearance. Ellie put him somewhere in his mid-fifties.

She held out her hand. "Mr Batten, I'm Detective Cooper. We met a few weeks ago." She indicated Clayton with a bob of her head. "And this is Federal Agent Munro. I'm afraid we're here about your daughter."

George Batten seemed to deflate before their eyes. The bulky form that had filled the doorway only moments before, now somehow seemed smaller as fear and uncertainty darkened his bloodshot eyes.

His voice was rough with emotion as he ushered them inside. "I shoulda' known that was what you were here for. Tell me, Detectives." His eyes pleaded with Ellie's. "Is she still alive?"

Dread pooled in the pit of her stomach. She glanced at Clayton and saw from the tension around his mouth that he was equally affected. She took a sharp breath, needing to get it over with.

"I'm sorry, Mr Batten. Some hikers found a body in bushland a few hours ago. We'll need to confirm her identification by DNA, but we think it's Sally."

A low moan escaped him. He shook his head back and forth. "No, no, no! I can't tell Robyn. I can't! I can't tell her, Detectives. Sally's her baby. It's gonna kill her."

"We need to speak with both of you, Mr Batten," Clayton interjected quietly. "It's important. If we're going to have any chance of finding out who did this to her, it's imperative we get as much information from you as possible."

The calm timbre of his voice seemed to register and the man made a visible effort to pull himself together. Though George's lips still trembled with emotion, he drew in a deep breath and let it out on a heavy sigh.

"Of course, Detective. I understand. If you'll just excuse me a minute, I'd... I'd like to talk to me wife."

Ellie leaned back against the cold red brick wall of the house and sighed. No matter how many times she did it, it never got any easier. She cringed when she heard the loud keening cry of a female from somewhere inside the building. The tightness in her chest was suffocating and she fought to keep her breathing even.

Clayton's grim face swirled in front of her. His eyes softened as if he realized how close she was to losing it.

"Keep your chin up, Cooper. I know you can do it. Besides, it's the least we can do for them. And for Sally."

She gulped in some much-needed oxygen, conveying her gratitude with her eyes. Reaching out, she touched the back of his hand with her fingertips. "Thanks. I needed that."

She watched, mesmerized, as his eyes darkened with emotion. It took him a moment to reply.

"No problem, partner."

A minute passed. Then two. It felt like a lifetime.

Then Clayton cleared his throat. "I...uh... I guess we'd better get in there."

She snatched her hand away, unaware until that moment that they'd still had contact. Heat flared across her cheeks and she looked away, flustered. "Yes, yes, of course." We-we should go in now."

He held the squeaky screen door open for her. Cautiously, she made her way down the darkened hallway toward the sound of quiet sobbing.

Robyn Batten was enormous. She lay spread-eagled in a recliner armchair, with much of her body hanging out over both sides. A huge floral nightgown enveloped her, stretched taut across her massive breasts.

Her eyes looked oddly tiny in the soft, fleshy face. They peered at Ellie in pain and anguish.

A large-screen plasma TV took up most of one wall. State-of-the-art surround sound speakers were set up around the room. A Saturday morning sports commentary show filled the screen, its volume muted.

The room was cozy with a fire burning low in the fireplace on the far side of the room, incongruous with the thick air of devastation. Although it was almost too warm, Robyn Batten had at least three woollen blankets draped over her knees.

The woman brought her enormous arms up to her face and scrubbed at her eyes with her hands. The flesh on her bare arms flapped with her effort. Ellie tried not to stare.

She turned away, refusing to catch Clayton's eye. She was having a difficult enough time holding it together as it was. The woman was a heart attack waiting to happen. Thank God her husband had broken the news first.

Ellie forced herself closer and spoke to the woman in the chair. "Mrs Batten, we're so terribly sorry for your loss. If there's anything we can do—"

A huge shudder passed through her massive frame. A moan of pure agony rumbled out of the woman's belly as her grief renewed itself.

"I want my baby back. I want my baby back." She gulped and sobbed and wobbled. Tears flowed from her tiny eyes and down her cheeks before disappearing into the folds of her neck.

Ellie watched, helpless and transfixed. George Batten stood off to one side, seemingly at a loss as he struggled with his own grief. She swallowed a sigh of relief when Clayton stepped forward.

Kneeling close to the woman's chair, he clasped one of her fleshy hands. Understanding and compassion filled his eyes.

"Mrs Batten, we're going to do everything we can to find the man responsible for Sally's death. But we need your help. We need you to tell us everything you can remember about the day she disappeared."

His eyes stayed fixed on her face. "It's very important, Mrs Batten. Do you think you can help us?"

The woman drew in another shuddering breath, but continued to hold his gaze. Clayton waited her out. A few moments later, the wailing quietened to a gentle sobbing.

Ellie knew how important it was to speak to her. The majority of mothers knew more about their teenage daughters than their fathers did. It was a fact of life.

As the sobs eased to an occasional sniffle, Clayton gave the fleshy hand another squeeze.

"Mrs Batten, I understand you've already spoken to my colleague here when you filed the missing person's report, but I need you to tell me again. Can you tell me about Sally's movements the last day you saw her? I think it was about June nineteenth, a couple of days before you contacted the police. Is that right?"

Robyn Batten hunted down the neck of her nightdress with her hand. Pulling out a tissue, she blew her nose noisily.

"Yes, that's right. Tuesday, June nineteenth. The day's remained scorched in my memory for the last two months."

Clayton's voice remained calm and low. "What can you remember from that day?"

A huge sigh sent mountains of flesh rippling beneath her clothes. Her eyes closed and her head dropped forward. More chins than Ellie cared to count rested heavily on the woman's chest. It was a few moments before she spoke.

"My baby went to university like she usually does. She's studying to be a dietician, you know." For a moment, pride found a home on the woman's face and then memory reasserted itself and the pain returned. Her eyes fluttered open. It was terrible to watch the light fade as the reality hit her again and her gaze turned bleak.

"She...she also works as a shop assistant at Target in the Westfield Mall at Penrith. A part-time job."

"How did she get to Uni?" Clayton asked.

Robyn paused to wipe her nose. "She usually catches the

train." Her gaze flicked to Ellie and back to Clayton. "We don't live far from the station. An easy ten-minute walk."

Ellie kept her gaze planted firmly on the notebook opened in her hand.

As if reading her mind, Robyn sighed. "Not that I've ever done it, but that's what Sally said."

"You said 'usually,' Mrs Batten. Did she catch the train on the day she went missing?" Clayton asked.

The woman shook her head. "No, she didn't. It was raining, you see. Pouring, actually. I could hear it pelting down on the roof." She looked across the room to her husband who listened in silence. "George was at work. He starts early." Her gaze came back to Clayton's. "I gave her some money to catch a cab."

"Did Sally know a girl by the name of Josie Ward?" Clayton asked. "She was a young girl with Down's syndrome. She was studying art at the university."

Robyn Batten shook her head. "Not that I remember."

"What about Angelina Caruso?"

Again, the woman shook her head.

Clayton posed another question. "Did Sally work that Tuesday after class?"

"Yes, I spoke to her at lunchtime, during her break. She told me she'd be going there. She sounded fine, although I remember I could barely hear her over the rain. It was really coming down."

"So, you called her on her cell phone?" Ellie asked.

"Yes, she always has it with her, although she usually switches it off while she's in class."

Ellie filled the taut silence with another question. "Mrs Batten, what time did Sally finish?"

Her voice, now dull with pain, came out in a low monotone. "Her shift finished at five thirty. When she wasn't home by eight, I called her. It went straight through to voicemail." She shrugged, setting off another avalanche of movement. "I thought she might have gone over to Rick's place."

Clayton spoke up. "Who's Rick?"

"Her boyfriend." George Batten's voice shook with anger and disgust.

Ellie lifted her head in surprise and stared at him. He hadn't spoken since they'd entered. She suddenly recalled the dingy flat she'd gone to with Luke all those weeks ago when the call about the missing girl had first been made. *Rick Shadlow.*

"I take it you and Rick didn't get on?" she asked, now directing her attention to the man on the other side of the room.

His lips twisted into a sneer. "That's puttin' it politely. He's a scumbag. A loser. A low-life crim. I dunno what she sees in him." His gaze was defiant as it met hers. "We raised her better than that."

"I'm sure you did, Mr Batten. Tell me," Ellie added, "what is it that you don't like about him?"

George's face twisted in disgust. "Everythin'. He's twenty-five and I don't think he's ever held down a job in his life. Apart from sellin' drugs. He's a dope-head. He even tried to push some onto Robyn when he found out how much pain she gets in her legs."

Ellie and Clayton exchanged a glance. "Did Sally ever do drugs?" Clayton asked.

Robyn shook her head vehemently. "Of course not! Sally hated anything to do with drugs."

"Why do you think she liked Rick?" Ellie asked. "She obviously knew of his drug usage. What kept her with him?"

He snorted in disgust. "Oh, I know what kept her there. He's a pretty boy, isn't he, Robyn? She's always sayin' how he looks just like that kid off that *Twilight* shit. What's his name...?"

"Rob Patterson?" Ellie supplied.

"Yeah, Rob Patterson. That's the one."

"I seem to recall one of Sally's girlfriends told us she thought they'd broken up. Did Sally mention anything to either of you?" Ellie asked.

Robyn Batten look bewildered and her husband just

shook his head. "Sally never said anythin' to us. She would have known how pleased I'd be."

"How did they meet? He's a few years older than Sally. I take it they didn't go to school together?" Clayton asked.

George looked over at him. "No, they didn't know each other from school. He was too old for her. We tried to tell her that. She wasn't havin' none of it. They met at the local TAFE college. Sally was doing a woodworkin' course a couple of nights a week. She was really lovin' it."

His lips twisted in disgust. "That's where she met him. He was doin' the same course. Only thing I ever saw him put his hand to. Besides the drug dealin'."

Ellie sucked in a breath. It felt like she'd been punched in the gut. Her gaze clashed with Clayton's and she could see he'd also made the connection. She tried to get her heartbeat under control and strove for a casual tone.

"So, Rick was learning about woodworking, too?"

"Yeah, I guess that's why he was there. His old man's a pretty good machinist. He's got a shop a few miles away, over in Pemberton. He sure as hell must be disappointed in how that kid's turned out."

"He was pretty good with his hands though, George," Robyn sighed. "He gave Sally some really beautiful things he'd made out of wood."

A pulse pounded in the side of Ellie's neck. Her voice came out strangled. "Really? Do you think you could show us some of them?"

Robyn fluttered her hands helplessly. "I'm sure George can find them. Sally kept them in her room near her bed. Said she wanted to keep them close."

Ellie turned to George. "Would you mind?"

A disgruntled *humph* was her only answer, but he grudgingly lumbered forward and left the room, returning a short while later with a handful of carved, wooden ornaments.

Turning them over slowly in her hands, Ellie marveled at their detail. A tiny horse with each hair of its mane painstakingly defined. A dolphin so life-like, she could almost see it leaping out of the water. A starfish. A mermaid. A heart. One thing Robyn said was definitely right. The pieces were truly beautiful.

She handed them over to Clayton, knowing their significance was not lost on him. He looked at them for a few moments before turning to encompass both of the Battens.

"We'd like to keep these, if we may. They might be of some use to us finding out what happened to Sally."

Robyn struggled against the chair, moving her bulk into a more comfortable position as she peered up at him.

"You don't think Rick had anything to do with it, do you? For all his failings..." She stared defiantly at her husband. "That boy really loved her."

Ellie looked down at her notebook. "Mrs Batten, you said you called Rick when you couldn't reach Sally. Did you end up speaking with him?"

Her eyes clouded over. "Yes, he told me he hadn't seen her for almost a week. They'd had a fight and she hadn't called him."

Ellie exchanged another look with Clayton. So, they could have broken up after all, just like the friend had said. Her pulse continued to pick up its pace. It could be the break they were waiting for. They had to find Rick Shadlow.

Clayton stood and stretched to his full height. Ellie didn't know how he'd managed to stay squatting for so long. She mused about the strength of his thigh muscles.

Refusing to allow her thoughts to wander anywhere down that path, she favored the Battens with a slight smile, mindful of their grief, but unable to completely contain her excitement.

"Thank you so much for talking with us. We know how tough it is for you and we really appreciate it." She offered her hand to both of them.

Clayton did the same before turning to usher her toward the door. As they reached the doorway, he turned and posed a final question.

"Mrs Batten, do you know if anyone saw Sally leaving work that afternoon?"

"Yes, Colleen Mayger, a girl she works with, said she saw her getting into a cab." She shrugged. "It was still raining."

Ellie was already on the phone by the time Clayton made it to the car. She paced up and down the sidewalk. He could feel the excitement pulsing off her in waves.

"Yeah, Rick Shadlow, the boyfriend we checked out when Sally went missing. He lives in that dump on the southern side of Mt Druitt. Can't tell you his date of birth, but he's around twenty-five. There's a chance he's got a record. Can you run a check for me?"

She paused, listening to someone on the other end of the line. He waited in silence at the curb. The car was still locked and Ellie had the keys.

"Thanks, Luke. Fantastic. I know I don't have to tell you I need them, like, yesterday." She grinned into the phone. "Yeah, yeah, yeah. We'll see. Talk to you soon." Ending the call, she turned triumphant eyes up to Clayton.

"This is it; I know it. Luke's going to run a check on Shadlow. Just because we didn't get a hit on his DNA or fingerprints, doesn't mean we don't have something on him."

A reluctant smile tugged at his lips. "Take it easy, Ellie. We don't have much to go on yet."

Her eyes widened in protest. "Hey, you heard what they said. He's a loser, a dope-pusher. Probably been in trouble before. I remember now the place he lived in reeked of grass. Luke and I called on him weeks ago, when Sally was first reported missing," she offered by way of explanation. Her eyes gleamed. "We have the breakup—"

"Alleged breakup. I'd like to reinterview Shadlow myself, get my own take on him—"

"And then there are the wood carvings."

His hand tightened on the smooth pieces of wood he still carried. As she unlocked the car, he climbed in and pulled an evidence bag out of the glove box. Dropping the pieces into it, he closed the seal, scribbled the time and date on it and reached over to place it on the backseat before turning to face her.

"I know what you're saying. But we need to take it slowly. We haven't determined that he has any connection with either Josie Ward or Angelina Caruso. Besides, he's not really the kind of guy who fits the profile. He—"

Her eyes flashed with sudden fury. "Oh, so just because you're feeling inadequate and superfluous, you're telling me I'm barking up the wrong tree? Is that it?" Without waiting for him to reply, she jerked the car into gear and pulled out onto the road.

"You know, the first minute I met you, I knew you were a stuck-up, arrogant, know-it-all Fed. You're all the same. Every one of you. For a while there, I thought maybe I'd misjudged you. But I should have trusted my instincts."

She flicked him a look full of scorn. Her color was high. A pulse beat frantically in her neck. She took a corner at break-neck speed. He gripped the armrest.

"Ellie, be reasonable. All I said was—"

"*Reasonable?* You've done nothing but hold me back since you got here. I've spent countless hours with you, chauffeuring you around while we wasted precious time on your *hunches* and now when we have our first real lead, you're telling me to take it easy?"

She glared at him. Her eyes sparked green fire. A car slowed to turn in front of them and she braked heavily.

"For Christ's sake, Ellie—either pull over or keep your eyes on the road. You might be harboring a death wish, but that doesn't mean I am."

Her eyes narrowed dangerously. "What the hell is that supposed to mean?"

He groaned and ran his hand through his hair. "For Christ's sake... Just forget it, okay?"

"No, I damn well won't forget it! This has obviously got

something to do with Jamie—who you would never have even known about if you hadn't pried into my personal life by Googling me on the Internet."

"What the hell is wrong with you? We've been over this. I told you why I did it. I care about you... I care a lot."

Her mouth clamped shut. She stared hard at the road. "Yeah, well tell someone who cares back because I sure as hell don't."

He turned away and stared out the window. He refused to keep arguing with her. So much for following Riley's advice; an apology was the last thing on his mind now. After speaking with his brother, he'd felt guilty enough about his actions to call Ellie, then and there and offer up a heartfelt apology. When she hadn't answered, he'd been determined to do it the next morning. In person. It was probably better that way, anyway. But Ben had come in with the news about Sally and he hadn't had a chance.

Now she wouldn't be able to torture one out of him. His caution about Rick Shadlow had nothing to do with arrogance. He'd been a profiler for a long time. The description given to him by the Battens just didn't fit. A typical psychopath rarely formed emotional attachments and when they did, it was for appearances' sake only. According to Robyn Batten, Shadlow loved Sally. Clayton would have thought that if anyone could spot fake affections, it would be the girl's mother.

And then there were the carved animals. Ellie was excited about them, but he'd looked at them closely. They'd been painstakingly and intricately created, with every minute detail carefully and lovingly added. He could almost feel the love when he'd held them in his palm. That was something else that didn't sit well with the psychopath theory.

The ringing of Ellie's phone interrupted his train of thought. She pressed the hands-free button to answer it.

"Baxter, that was quick. What have you got?"

"Well, you're right about one thing; he's got a record."

"Whoopee. That'll give us just about everything we need.

I wonder why his prints didn't show up when they ran the comparisons? We'll need to run them again. I bet—"

"He's not your guy."

"What do you mean, he's not my guy? You couldn't have run checks on him that quickly."

"No, of course I haven't. But I checked the dates."

She groaned in frustration. "What dates? What the hell are you talking about?"

"The dates of the disappearances. Well, the last two, anyway. According to the timeline, Sally Batten disappeared on June nineteen and Josie Ward on July third."

She drummed the steering wheel. "Yeah, that's right. They went missing fourteen days apart."

"Well, that's the thing. It couldn't have been Shadlow."

"Why the hell not? For God's sake, Baxter. Spit it out!"

"He was locked up for possession on June twenty-eight. It must have been soon after we paid him a visit. He didn't make bail. He's sitting on remand in Long Bay."

"Fuck." Ellie ended the call with a vicious stab at the phone.

Clayton kept his gaze averted. "You can say that again."

"Fuck, fuck and double-fuck." She banged her fist on the steering wheel and then turned to glare at him. "Don't say another word."

He sighed and shifted to stare out the window at the passing traffic. It wasn't even lunchtime, but already he'd had enough of the day. He was just as disappointed as Ellie that their lead had fizzled out. Apart from the taxi lead, which certainly warranted further exploration, they were back to square one.

"Don't think I'm apologizing Fed, because I meant every word I said."

He turned to look at her, his gaze flicking over the rigid set of her jaw. "I guess that makes us even, then."

They rode in tense silence all the way back to the city.

"Drop me off at the hotel. I've got a few things to do."

"Aye, aye, Captain," she muttered caustically underneath her breath.

He laughed in genuine amusement when she screeched to a halt outside his building.

"Thanks for the ride."

She left him standing in a cloud of smoke.

CHAPTER 17

Michelle Wilson smiled at the young couple that stopped beside her stall. A young girl about the age of her youngest daughter clutched the hand of the gentleman and smiled shyly back at her.

"Can I have a look at your dolls?" the child whispered.

Michelle smiled again. "Of course." She leaned across and lifted one of them out of the display box. "This one has pretty blond hair, just like you."

The little girl took the doll carefully, her eyes wide with delight. "She's beautiful."

The girl turned to the woman who stood beside her. "Look, Mommy. She's got a real dress and shoes and she even has nail polish."

The girl's mother smiled indulgently down at the child. "You're right, Jasmine. They are beautiful." She lifted her gaze to Michelle's. "The craftsmanship is incredible. Do you make them?"

Michelle flushed with pleasure. "No, not me. My husband. He's the one who likes to potter around in the shed."

"Well, he's very talented. You must be very proud of him."

Jasmine stood entranced by the doll, stroking the doll's hair and face with awestruck fingers. The man next to her reached for his wallet. "How much are they?"

"Forty dollars," Michelle replied. "Each doll is unique. My husband never makes two the same."

"In that case," the man replied, "they are a real bargain.

And I agree with my wife. The quality is exceptional."

Michelle smiled and nodded. "Thank you. I will be sure to tell my husband."

Pocketing the bills given to her by the man, she watched them walk away, hand in hand, and sighed. For a moment, she longed for things to be different. Even though her husband had a job that brought in a steady income and her daughters went to good schools and she lived in a nice house on a nice street in a nice neighbourhood, she still wished things were different.

She'd known since she was a child that her husband wasn't like the other boys. Even though they were only ten when they met, it was obvious to Michelle he was different.

The nuns and brothers to whom the government had entrusted their care also knew. Not a day went by in the orphanage when they weren't punishing him for it. She could never understand it. So what if he liked to play with dolls? So what if he preferred to wear underwear that had been allocated to the girls? It wasn't what the other boys did, but what did it really matter?

There had been many a time when she'd intervened and had sided with him against the others when a fight had erupted. More and more, it had seemed her husband had been in the middle of it. She hadn't cared. She couldn't stand to sit by and watch someone smaller and weaker get bullied for being different.

She was different, too. With her white-blond hair that fell below her knees, and her skin so pale it almost looked translucent, she'd also suffered more than her fair share of harsh taunts. She'd often cried herself to sleep at night, with her head pressed tightly against the hard, calico pillowcase and wished with increasing desperation to be more like the others—the children with their plain brown hair and ordinary skin tone. She didn't even know where her coloring had come from. The orphanage was the only home she could remember.

Michelle sighed again, knowing to dwell upon the past was an exercise in futility. It didn't change anything. Besides, there was much to be grateful for. Business at the markets had been brisk, as usual. It was only mid-morning, but already she'd sold more than half of her stock. The fact that her husband had been spending increasingly more time in his shed with his dolls and less time with his real life family wasn't really an issue. *Was it?*

He'd been more withdrawn than usual the last few months, but she'd put it down to the pressures of his job. He'd been doing permanent night shifts since June and found it very hard to sleep during the day. She guessed it had something to do with his life at the orphanage when they'd been severely beaten if they'd been found anywhere near the dormitory during the daylight hours.

Still, she worried about him. She wished she could let it go, but she couldn't.

As much as Clayton tried to switch it off, his brain kept returning to the puzzle. Spread out across his freshly made hotel bed were the files of each of the girls. He'd been at it all afternoon and even after he'd gone out for a solitary dinner of fish and chips down at Circular Quay, his mind had refused to let it go. His latest argument with Ellie had also kept him tense.

He'd walked to the Quay from his hotel. He'd hoped the cool August night and the sights and sounds of one of Sydney's famous landmarks would soothe the jumble and confusion of his thoughts. He'd passed groups of tourists and locals enjoying a night out at the numerous restaurants that lined the promenade. Their bright holiday clothing and happy, carefree conversations distracted him momentarily, but not for long. Even the sound of the water lapping against the pier had failed to relax him.

Eventually, he'd called it quits and had made his way back up the hill to his hotel.

Now, he looked at the dates again.

Angelina Caruso was the first to disappear on May twenty-ninth. They now knew Sally Batten was the next to go missing on June nineteenth. A Tuesday, so her mother had said. Two weeks later, Josie Ward disappeared.

Something clicked in Clayton's brain and he checked the files again. May twenty-ninth was a Tuesday. So was July third, the day Josie disappeared.

He had to tell Ellie.

Okay, it could probably wait until morning, but he wanted to hear her voice. Clayton's heart thudded. *There, he'd admitted it. He was falling for her. Hard and fast.* He checked his watch. It was nearly ten. Late, but surely not too late.

He scrolled through his call log and then paused. What if she was still mad? What if she didn't answer, like last night? He didn't want to sit on this until morning. He could always call Ben, but this gave Clayton the excuse he'd been looking for to go and see her.

Picking up his jacket from the back of a chair, he shrugged it on, grabbed her card with the address and sat down to pull on his boots. Running his hand quickly through his hair and smoothing it down as best as he could, he grabbed his wallet and room key card off the table and headed out the door.

Ellie sighed and let the day's frustrations seep out into the hot, soapy bath water. She couldn't believe the day she'd had. Thank God it was over. She cringed as she thought of the way she'd attacked the Fed. Okay, so he was a little conceited, but he definitely hadn't deserved the heated spray she'd given him.

Though she'd arrived home as mad as hell, another hour of pacing and cursing and a healthy glass of merlot she'd barely tasted, had cooled her temper enough to think. She owed him an apology. Another one.

It would be so much easier if he didn't rankle her like he did. The way he'd taken it upon himself to stick his nose into her private life had left her fuming and even though he'd apologized, she was sure he still didn't really appreciate how much it had upset her. She wasn't used to people prying into her life without her knowledge. It wasn't something she'd ever experienced.

Reaching for her razor and the new bar of orange and frangipani-scented soap, she stuck one leg out of the water and lathered it. She'd been so busy the last few weeks, she hadn't had a spare minute to indulge herself. The long, long workdays had, more often than not, extended into the night. She'd been lucky to manage a light meal, a quick shower and bed.

She observed the length of the hair on her soapy leg. A wry grin tugged at her lips. Lucky it was winter. It didn't matter so much when she wore trousers every day. And even the few times she'd worn a skirt, the state of the hair on her legs was concealed beneath stockings or tights.

She finished running the razor along the length of her first leg and switched over. Giving it the same treatment, she rinsed off the soap and stood. Lifting her arms, she grimaced and padded across the bathroom to the shower. Taking the razor and soap in with her, she lathered and shaved under her arms, then reached for the shampoo.

Knowing it would leave her hair curling riotously and totally out of control—but wanting to feel clean all over—she scrubbed it and then applied conditioner. Rinsing out, she reveled in the luxuriant warmth and steam of the shower.

After long minutes, she turned the faucets off and squeezed the water out of her hair. Opening the clear glass door, she stepped out of the shower and onto the fluffy, white bathmat. Her mother had voiced an opinion about that, too. So what if it wasn't quite so white and fluffy now? It was what she'd wanted at the time. That should have been all that mattered.

After giving her hair a brisk rub, she wrapped a bath sheet

around her body. With a sigh of satisfaction, she switched off the light in the bathroom and padded down the carpeted hallway to the kitchen. A glance at the clock on the wall near the sink told her it was just after ten. Time for a hot cup of coffee before bed.

The water had nearly boiled when her front door buzzer sounded. Frowning, she stepped into the hallway and pressed the intercom.

"Who is it?"

There was a moment of silence before Clayton's deep, familiar voice filled the air.

"It's me. Clayton. I just...I've been going over the files. I think I've found something. Um, I mean... I just wanted to... Christ, I'm sorry. This was a stupid idea. I'm sorry, Ellie. It can wait until morning. I'll see you tomorrow."

Although her heart had started pounding the second she'd heard him speak, she knew it wasn't wise to invite him in. She'd already cursed him to hell for prying into her private life. It would be more than hypocritical to ask him into her apartment. It was as private as it got—her sanctuary from the rest of the world. The last thing she wanted was to have him invading it.

"Why don't you come on up and tell me about it?" The words were out of her mouth before she could stop them. She suddenly realized what she'd said. Nerves came to life in her belly. Depressing the button with fingers that were slightly shaky, she added, "Um, give me a few minutes. I just stepped out of the shower."

The outer door to the apartment block clicked open and Clayton took the stairs two at a time. His head was full of images of Ellie warm and wet and soapy. Christ, why did she have to go and tell him that? Now he could barely remember the reason he'd come.

Something to do with a break in the case. Yeah, that was

it. Tuesdays. It had something to do with Tuesdays. He shook his head in disgust. He was bullshitting himself. He wanted to see her. Simple.

Drawing in some deep breaths, he paused on the landing between floors in an effort to get his heart rate back to normal. In. Out. In. Out. His stamina had slipped. He hadn't had his usual workout since he'd arrived in Sydney. Even still, a few flights of stairs shouldn't have done him in. He refused to acknowledge being out of breath had anything to do with the woman who was even now waiting for him on the other side of her door.

Despite his best efforts, his heart continued to pound and his chest felt tight. He felt like a teenager on his first date. Which was just ridiculous. He'd turned twenty-eight on his last birthday and this was definitely not a date. It was a work meeting. Nothing more. No different to when they'd brainstormed in the squad room.

Except his palms hadn't felt sweaty then. And his heart hadn't thumped so loudly. And Ellie hadn't just left a hot, steamy shower.

"Christ, just get on with it," he muttered testily under his breath. She was just a woman. He'd worked with plenty of them. It was only that none of them had made him feel the way she did.

He hurried up the last few stairs. She was probably wondering what the hell was taking him so long. Steeling himself with another deep breath, he knocked decisively on her door.

Thirty seconds later, it opened. She stood on the other side, dressed in jeans and a dark red sweater that complemented her light coloring. Her face was free from makeup and her still-damp hair sprang out in wild disarray.

She smelled of citrus and vanilla and something else. She smelled delicious. She smiled at him and his heart did a backflip, refusing to behave itself, despite his pep talk.

"Come in."

Opening the door wide, she gestured for him to enter. There was a small living room to his left, straight off the hall.

He stepped past her and moved into the room. She closed and locked the door behind him.

Even though it was late, she hadn't yet drawn the curtains and his gaze swept over the view of the city skyline visible through the sliding glass doors that led out onto a balcony.

"Nice view."

She came into the room and stopped a few feet away. "It is, isn't it? Thanks to Mom and Dad's early succession planning. I'm a lucky girl."

An electric log fire glowed warmly from the middle of one wall. Soft orange and yellow light bounced off the tasteful Australian landscapes that hung near the window on the opposite side. A white leather couch decorated with bright red and orange cushions dominated the rest of the room.

"It's a great spot." He eyed her with curiosity. "But a fair commute to Penrith."

She acknowledged the tacit quest for information with a slight tug of her lips. "I'm sorry for snapping at you earlier. I was out of line. You're working harder than any of us to solve this. If there's something you want to know about me, just say it, okay?"

Heat crept beneath the collar of his polo shirt and he was glad the only light in the room came from the fire. Struggling for something to say, he wished he could remember Riley's words of wisdom about the sensitivity some people had toward sharing personal information.

Of course, he could understand it. He knew exactly how it felt to have people coming forward—some of them almost strangers—expressing concern and sympathy, watching him with pity, understanding, compassion and just plain old curiosity. Lisa had been gone three years, but still he remembered.

He'd known why they were curious. For most, it was simply because they cared, and there was nothing wrong with that, even if it had made him uncomfortable.

He gazed at Ellie in the dimness and his heart clenched. Her eyes were wide and uncertain and despite her obvious effort to look calm and collected, the anxious fluttering of

212

her hands and the way her gaze kept skittering away from him told him differently. It increased his confidence to realize he wasn't the only one feeling nervous.

She cleared her throat. "Can I get you something to drink?"

"Sure, what are you having?"

"I...ah... I just boiled the water. I was about to have a cup of coffee, but I can get you something stronger, if you like."

"No, coffee's fine." He grinned at her. "I thought I was the only one who drank coffee right before bedtime."

Her gaze slid away again at the mention of bedtime. She ducked her head. "The kitchen's through this way. We can talk while I make it."

He stared at her in silence, distracted by the way her sweater seemed to mold itself to her breasts. He was almost certain she wasn't wearing a bra.

A tiny frown appeared between her eyes. "Clayton?"

"Sure, sounds good," he managed and followed her out of the room.

She'd already spooned ground coffee beans into a stainless steel coffee pot when he wandered into the kitchen. Like the living room, it was small, but cozy. A worn pine table and two blue, painted wooden chairs stood against the wall near the door.

His gaze drifted across the row of small china knickknacks that lined the window sill. An array of photos of people he presumed to be her friends were plastered symmetrically across the fridge, held by colorful magnets.

She had her back to him and he took a few moments to admire the tidy view. Apart from the clingy dress she'd worn the night they'd gone out to dinner, he'd only ever seen her in smart but somber-looking business suits. And mostly trouser suits, at that.

A couple of times, she'd come to work in a short, straight skirt that had fallen just above her knee and he'd been able to admire a very fine set of legs—at least, as much of them as he'd been able to see. But the faded blue Levis she had on tonight really did her justice. Her small round butt was lovingly cupped by the denim and his hands yearned to touch her.

Dropping his gaze lower, he smiled in surprise. She was barefoot. He hadn't noticed it before. No wonder she'd seemed even smaller when she'd opened the door. Although she usually favored a sensible court shoe over a stiletto, he'd never seen her without some sort of a heel.

It somehow made everything seem more intimate. The last barefooted woman he'd shared a room with had been his wife. His *late* wife.

Riley and the rest of his family were right. He needed to push the guilt aside and start living in the present. The loss of Lisa was still sharp and real, but she wasn't here. And she never would be again. It was Ellie his body burned for now. It was Ellie's image that woke him as he lay panting and sweaty amongst the twisted sheets. The thought of letting the memory of his wife recede scared the hell out of him, but maybe it was time?

Ellie turned to face him, holding a steaming coffee mug in her hand. She smiled shyly and his pulse accelerated.

"Black, right?"

His eyebrows flew up in surprise. "What gave me away?"

"I've shared the tea room with you, remember?"

He grinned back at her, willing the nerves away. "I'm flattered you noticed."

"Ha, don't feel too special. I'm a detective. I notice everything."

"Touché."

He reached out and took the hot cup out of her hand and their fingers touched. He heard her slight intake of breath and did his best to get his own heart rate back under control. An awkward silence fell between them. They both looked away.

"How about we—?"

"Why don't you—?"

They spoke in a jumble. A bark of nervous laughter escaped him as Ellie turned away and busied herself at the sink.

Clayton bit his lip. Christ, being here was *so* not a good idea. What the hell had he been thinking? He cleared his throat and tried again.

"How about we retire to the couch and talk there while I enjoy your million dollar view?"

"Good idea." She picked up her mug and he stepped politely aside as she led the way out of the room.

"Even better," she threw over her shoulder, "we could sit out on the balcony. The air's a bit crisp, but with that southern blood of yours, I'm sure you'll be able to handle it."

He stopped dead in the living room. Unaware of his sudden consternation, Ellie slid open the glass doors.

"Um, actually... If you don't mind, I'd rather sit in here."

She turned in momentary surprise before comprehension filled her eyes.

"Oh, God, that's right. I'm sorry. I should have remembered. Especially after that night at Centrepoint. It was thoughtless of me. I don't know how you managed to cope. You even ate most of your meal. At least, I think you did. Are you sure—?"

His heart soared at her nervousness. "Ellie."

Her jaw snapped shut and he tried to conceal a grin. She looked away, embarrassed. Tenderness welled up inside him. He could almost hear the ice cracking from around his heart.

He gestured in the direction of the couch. "Let's sit in here. I've always wondered what it would feel like to sit on a genuine white leather couch."

"Really?"

"No, not really." He grinned. "But I was still pretty young when my daughter was born. My career hadn't gotten to the point where I could shop for furniture like this. Besides, my wife would never have brought anything white into our house. She was far too practical for that."

Her eyes widened in surprise as she sat down on the three-seater a few feet away. "You have a daughter? That's wonderful. I had no idea."

His cheeks burned with embarrassment. Of course she

wouldn't. He was the only one insensitive enough to use Google to pry into his co-worker's private life.

"Yeah, Olivia," he mumbled. "She's four."

As if sensing his discomfort, she leaned closer. "Clayton, I didn't mean that how it sounded. I wasn't referring to your Google search. I was merely expressing surprise."

He grimaced. "Yeah, it's okay. I'm glad you brought it up, anyway. I wanted to tell you again how sorry I am for invading your privacy. I honestly had no idea you'd find it so disturbing and I'm mortified that you did." He held her gaze, hoping she could see how sincere he felt. "Will you please forgive me?"

Her eyes stayed somber for long moments and his heart sank. Christ, she was never going to get over it. He was going to lose a chance with the only woman who'd sparked his interest since his wife had died. And all because of some stupid Google search. He closed his eyes briefly at the enormity of it, dismayed by the wave of disappointment that washed over him.

And then her voice reached him, soft and uncertain.

"It's okay, Munro. Don't sweat it. I over-reacted. It was a big deal for me, but then, I have…issues." She looked away and cleared her throat.

"Jamie died in early July. I'd suffered through another anniversary of his death right before you arrived in Sydney. My parents called from Florence to check that I was okay. I thought I'd managed to cope with the memories reasonably well until the incident with the little boy, Zach Clements. It was too close to home. It brought everything back: the darkness, the despair, the absolute desolation that only losing a child can bring. I should have kept up with my therapy, but I couldn't. I didn't want to keep talking about it. All it seemed to do was keep the whole terrible time in my head, where I didn't want it to be. I wanted to shut myself off from it, away from the guilt and the pain and the utter devastation of knowing that there was nothing I could have done to save him and there was nothing I could do to bring him back."

She lifted her gaze to his. He was stricken at the sadness in their emerald depths.

"You probably did me a favor. You forced me out of hiding."

"Christ, Ellie. I'm so sorry. I had no right. I, of all people, know everyone grieves in their own way. It wasn't my place to force you into something you weren't ready for."

Her lips tightened. Tears glinted in her eyes. Her voice dropped to a husky whisper.

"But was I ever going to be ready? Maybe I needed to be pushed? Maybe you did me a favor? You forced me out of hiding."

Without warning, huge tears spilled over and ran down her cheeks, silvery trails in the dim light. Clayton's chest tightened on a surge of emotion.

Unable to sit idly by and watch her cry, he scooted closer and drew her into his arms. She shuddered and buried her face against his chest. They sat in silence while he held her. Quiet tears soaked into the front of his shirt.

After a few moments, she pulled away and leaned over to tug some tissues out of a box on the coffee table. She swiped at her eyes.

"I'm sorry. I didn't mean to do that. I guess I'm feeling a little vulnerable tonight."

His heart filled with tenderness and he drew her back to his side. She snuggled her head close against his chest and breathed in deeply. They sat in companionable silence. He stroked the velvety-softness of her cheek over and over with the back of his fingers...

His heart rate accelerated. She felt so good against him. So warm. So right.

Images of Lisa swam before his eyes. Momentary guilt weighed him down. He pushed it aside with a surge of irritation. He was with Ellie. Beautiful, warm, giving Ellie. He wanted her. What was wrong with that?

Nothing. Everything. Uncertainty, desire and anger churned up inside him. Determinedly pushing them all aside, he tilted her chin upward with his fingers and leaned in closer. Slowly, slowly, he touched her lips with his.

Soft. Moist. Warm. Comforting. And the faintest taste of coffee. It lasted less than half a minute, but it seemed like a lifetime. She was the first woman he'd kissed since Lisa. He couldn't believe how good it felt.

He pulled back slowly.

Her eyes, wide and full of wonder, never strayed from his face. Unable to resist, he kissed her again.

This time, as if given permission, the passion that had been smouldering deep inside him burst free. He reached around and cupped the back of her head in his hand to hold it still while his lips devoured hers.

His tongue swept into her mouth and took all she was willing to give and more. Heat exploded through him and centred in his groin. He was rock-hard and on fire.

Her arms twined around his neck and drew him even closer. He heard a moan and wasn't sure which one of them it came from—and didn't care.

Releasing her head, his fingers moved of their own accord and trailed down her neck and then lower. Soft and unbound, he filled his hands with her sweater-clad breasts while his lips continued their onslaught.

The scent of her perfume filled his nostrils. She smelled nothing like Lisa. She felt nothing like Lisa. She wasn't Lisa. She was Ellie and she felt so damned right it scared him.

Breathing hard, he pulled back and hugged her close to his chest. He rested his chin on her head and fought to regain control. It was madness. It was insane. It was unavoidable and he knew he had to taste her again.

He lowered his head and swept her tight against him. He kissed her with all the longing that had been building up inside him from the moment he'd spied her across the floor in the squad room. She met his passion without hesitation and he reveled in the heat and softness that was her.

Long moments later, he loosened his arms around her. She pulled away slightly and stared up at him, her eyes full of light and shadow, passion and uncertainty.

Her voice was a husky whisper. "If there's one thing you do know how to do, Fed, it's kiss."

He ducked his head in embarrassment, feeling unaccountably shy.

"Surely you've heard that on more than one occasion?"

He blushed and couldn't meet her eyes. Christ, where was his confidence when he needed it? He felt like a tongue-tied schoolboy about to go all the way for the first time.

Her grin slowly faded as she realized just how uncomfortable he was. "Hey, I meant it as a compliment. You are an incredible kisser. Not that I've had loads of experience," she added hurriedly, "but I do know a good kisser when he comes along."

She offered him another grin. He did a weak imitation of returning it. Leaning forward on the couch, he rested his hands on his thighs and stared straight ahead. A sigh escaped his lips. He spoke quietly into the near darkness.

"I met Lisa my first week of college. By the second week, we were dating." He shrugged. "I was eighteen."

Comprehension dawned on her face. "You mean, you've never... You haven't...? There hasn't...?"

He sighed again and sunk back against the couch. Reaching over, he took her hand and entwined her fingers with his. "No, there hasn't. Well, not really. There were a couple of times I got to second base in high school, but that didn't compare to how it was with Lisa. We were adults for one, and we were in love. It made such a difference."

She frowned and he could have kicked himself. Why the hell was he talking about his wife—even a dead one—with a woman he'd just been making out with? Any idiot knew that wasn't a good idea.

But what else was he supposed to do? She'd asked him the question. He wasn't going to lie to her. Besides, she knew he'd been married.

"What was she like?"

He turned to face her and shook his head. "Ellie, we don't have to do this."

"No, I want to hear about her. She was obviously an important part of your life." Her hand tightened in his. "Your face softens every time you mention her."

His eyes closed and he drew in a deep lungful of air. Exhaling it slowly, his gaze sought hers in the dimness. "You're a remarkable woman, Ellie Cooper."

"I was thinking the same thing about you. The way you look, the way you sound when you talk about her..." She shook her head. "I hope I find someone who feels as strongly about me one day."

"You say it as though I'm still in love with her."

"Aren't you?"

He pulled his hand out of hers. Guilt, sharp and oppressive, weighed heavily inside him. His memories of Lisa had grown hazy. It had been happening for weeks. Little things. Like how she'd looked when she smiled. And frowned. The smell of her perfume. The sound of her laughter. They had all started to fade.

Panic tightened in his chest. What if one day he couldn't remember her at all? What if she disappeared from his memory like an old, familiar song he hadn't heard in quite awhile?

Ellie's voice came to him in quiet reassurance. "It's okay, Clayton. It's okay. It makes me realize how special you are when you're still in love with your wife who's been dead for... How many years ago did she die?"

"Three." He nearly choked on the word and cleared his throat. "She died nearly three years ago."

Ellie shook her head. "Wow."

"Yeah, wow," he replied quietly. Taking a deep breath, he released it on another sigh. With a fierceness that surprised him, he caught and held her gaze. "She was all I'd ever wanted. I thought I'd spend the rest of my life with her. And then...and then, she left us."

"How did she die?"

Pain and guilt warred in his gut. He clenched his teeth and closed his eyes. Drawing in a deep breath, he opened them again and found Ellie's wide with compassion.

"She committed suicide."

Ellie gasped and her mouth went slack with shock. Clayton looked away, unable to bear the thought of seeing judgement in her eyes.

"How?" The question came softly and without inflection. He glanced up, relieved to find her expression filled with nothing but concern.

"She overdosed. Undiagnosed post-natal depression. That's what the doctors told me afterward. After it was too late." He stood and paced the small confines of the living room, unable to sit still a second longer.

"I should have seen it, Ellie. I should have realized. She was my *wife*, goddammit. I was meant to protect her, to look out for her. In sickness and in health. That's what I'd promised. And I failed her. I didn't see it. Her pain was right before my eyes and I didn't see it."

Ellie stood, too, shaking her head. "No, Clayton. That's not fair. I'm sure you weren't the only person in her life. And she was the one who made the decision. No one else. Don't do this to yourself."

He wanted to throw her quiet words off, along with the balm they offered to his battered spirit. It wasn't the first time he'd heard them. His family, even Lisa's parents had made similar pleas.

He'd refused to listen, hadn't wanted to. For nearly three years, he'd embraced the pain and the guilt, had even welcomed it as a way to atone for the loss of his wife. But somehow, with Ellie, it was different. He wanted to believe the words now. He wanted to be free of the guilt that had weighed him down for so long.

He reached out and took Ellie's hand. Holding it tightly in his, he led her back to the couch and sat. His eyes burned into hers, suddenly wanting her to understand.

"Ever since I met you, I've struggled. It used to be so easy to accept my responsibility for Lisa's death, to accept the blackness of my guilt as good and proper punishment for my failure to see the signs and protect her. I'm a profiler, for God's sake. I should have noticed."

He dragged in a breath and continued. "I haven't slept well since the funeral. Most nights, I wake and remember and then I can't fall back to sleep. But ever since I met you, things have been different. I'm still waking up in the middle of the night, but Lisa isn't the woman foremost on my mind. She isn't the woman I've lain awake this past month fantasizing about, wanting to taste all over with my lips. She isn't the woman I've yearned to feel writhing beneath me. And I don't know what to do about it."

Ellie flushed, but her gaze remained steady on his.

Clayton implored her. "I've never met anyone like you. You're smart and funny and persistent and annoying."

"Don't forget cantankerous, rude, bitchy and stubborn."

He smiled. "Thoughtful, kind, honest and beautiful. You're all I've been able to think about since I arrived." His voice lowered to a whisper. "You're the first woman since Lisa who's made me feel alive." He drew her closer. "It scares the hell out of me, but I can't do anything to stop it. Dammit, Ellie, I'm falling in love with you."

CHAPTER 18

Ellie's mouth fell open in surprise. It was the last thing she'd expected him to say. With her mind whirling in confusion, she tried to process his words.

Without warning, he put his arm around her and hauled her closer until she was almost in his lap. She squirmed, but his arm only tightened around her.

"You're over-thinking this, Ellie. It's not that complicated. I loved my wife very much, but it's only since meeting you that I've realized the guilt had taken over and that's what's been tying me to Lisa, to her memory. And it's not fair, to her or to me. What we had was wonderful, all I ever dreamed, but she opted out and I have to live with that."

His eyes remained somber on hers. "After she died, I never thought I'd meet another woman who'd do it for me like she did. It's been three years and no one's even come close." He picked up her hand and held it tightly. "And then you came along, and it's different—yet so good."

He lifted her hand and pressed a kiss to her knuckles. "Beautiful. Sexy. Smart. Sassy. Somehow, with your entrancing smile and caustic tongue, you've managed to captivate me." He shook his head and his lips tugged upward. "You're all I can think about. There's a crazed killer on the loose and you're the one constantly on my mind."

He drew her even closer until their faces were only inches apart. He traced his fingertip softly across her lips. Ellie drew in a sharp breath and her heart rate increased its pace. She watched in fascination as his desire-filled gaze followed the progress of his finger.

"You've made me feel alive again, Ellie. It sounds like a cliché, but it's like I've woken up from a long, deep sleep. All of a sudden, I feel like a man, with all the wants and needs and desires of a man. And I'm starved for the taste of you."

His mouth came down on hers, crushing his final words against her lips. Warm and passionate, his tongue pressed with hot persistence until she opened her mouth for him.

He groaned at her capitulation and drew her flush against him. His mouth continued to ravage hers. His breathing rasped against her ears and her heart thudded.

Her limbs were heavy and disjointed. She was powerless to move away from him. Not that she wanted to. She'd been attracted to him right from the start, even if she hadn't been prepared to admit it. His warm lips moved lower and nibbled at the skin of her neck and she sighed.

"You taste so good," he murmured. "So soft. So beautiful. So sweet. I'm never going to get enough."

His words sent a surge of excitement arcing through her, leaving her breasts tingling for his touch. Her nipples hardened beneath her sweater. Need pooled between her legs and she tightened her arms about him. He dragged his head up for another soul-wrenching kiss.

His lips were magic. Enough for her to forget everything but him. The coffee lay cold and abandoned on the side table. A biting wind nipped in through the opened doors and she was oblivious to all of that.

Sensation continued to build between her thighs and a mewling sound of need escaped her lips. Her clit tingled and throbbed and she almost sighed in relief when his palms cupped her breasts through her sweater and fondled them.

His fingers scraped over her aroused nipples and she moaned again. She ached to feel his hand on her bare skin and pulled away. She lifted her sweater over her head in one swift motion.

She wasn't wearing a bra. Or knickers. There hadn't been time. She'd barely had time to toss the towel on her bed and pull on a pair of jeans before he was there. She'd grabbed the sweater off the back of the chair in the living room and had hurriedly pulled it on as she'd rushed to open the door.

Now it lay discarded on the floor somewhere. It didn't matter where. All that mattered was the feel of his hands on her heated skin.

His mouth closed over one of her nipples and she gasped and pressed against him. It had been so long since she'd been with a man. Too long. Her body was ready to explode.

But it wasn't just her lack of sex that caused her to burn and tremble and shudder with every caress. It was *him*. *Clayton*. The man she'd had a crush on ever since he'd touched down in her life. A co-worker. A Fed. The type of man she swore she'd never date again.

Not that this was dating. This was sex. This was lust. This was two consenting adults sating their physical needs. It was as simple as that. Oh, he may have gone all romantic and mentioned the 'L' word, but she knew better than to pay heed to that.

The man was still in love with his dead wife, for God's sake. He'd known Ellie for a bit over a month. It couldn't be love.

It was two people admitting to an attraction and acting on it to their mutual advantage. It had been quite awhile for her between lovers and apparently, even longer for him. Surely they could enjoy each other for the moment and take what each of them was more than willing to give?

A mind-blowing orgasm beat a drink after work any day. She knew what she'd rather have. And by the feel of the solid hardness against her butt, he would be only too happy to oblige her.

And mind-blowing it would be, if the quality of his kiss was anything to go by.

His tongue stole into her ear and she shivered. Her nipples puckered in response. His hand brushed across them again, teasing them into hard little nubs. She grabbed his head in both hands and dragged it upward.

"Kiss me, Clayton."

His eyes darkened with emotion and his lips came down once again to claim hers. Hot and possessive, they roamed over her mouth before his tongue plunged inside. Heart pounding, she clung to him, reveling in the excitement that was building deep inside her. She squirmed in his arms, wanting to be closer to his hardness. Her clit pulsed with need.

"I want you inside me." Her whispered words elicited a groan from deep inside him. Releasing her mouth, he pushed her back gently against the cushions, his gaze sliding from her face to wander and pause at her naked breasts.

"Christ, you're so beautiful. More than I imagined." His fingers traced lightly across her heated flesh. She moved restlessly, needing to feel his weight upon her. Wanting him to hurry.

"Easy, now, sweetheart. We've got all night." He bent low and circled her nipple with his tongue. The heat of it against her cool skin seared her. She gasped and pressed up into his mouth.

"Clayton." It was a moan of want, of need, of impatience.

He chuckled and moved slightly away. His hands found the top of her jeans. With agile fingers, he undid the button and slid the zipper down. Lifting her hips, she wriggled on the couch while he tugged them off her and tossed them onto the floor.

She lay naked beneath his heated gaze. His gaze moved over her like a warm caress. Need settled wet and hot between her thighs. She reached for him.

Pulling his shirt off over his head, he made quick work of his boots and jeans. She watched in fascination at the play of taut muscle across his chest and abdomen.

Just as she'd imagined. The Fed had a body to die for.

Her fingers tingled at the thought of touching him. He shucked off his underwear and stood almost shyly in the dim light of the room and let her look her fill.

She took her time. He was all perfectly proportioned

muscle, with not a skerrick of excess fat. An impressively broad pair of shoulders tapered into narrow hips. His cock stood thick and tall and ready. Her clit hummed in expectation.

He moved closer and the light from the fire glanced off the wedding band that hung around his neck. Ellie swallowed and looked past it to the wide expanse of golden chest.

His skin was pale, not bronzed, but he was from Canberra and it was the middle of winter. He'd hardly be sporting a tan. He was still beautiful.

And that was the only way she could describe him. Beautiful. She'd never seen such male perfection. Apart from in movies. And that's what he looked like. A movie star. She suddenly felt unaccountably shy and uncertain. She half sat up and drew her knees to her chest.

He was beside her in an instant. Concern furrowed his forehead.

"Ellie, what's wrong? What did I do? I'm sorry, if you'd rather I closed the curtains... I just want to look at you, that's all. But—"

She shook her head and smiled softly. "No, it's nothing. And I don't mind the light." Her voice dropped to a shy whisper. "I want to look at you, too."

She drew her knees down and reached for him again.

He needed no further encouragement and settled himself on top of her. She felt the pressure of his erection against her womanhood and sighed when desire re-ignited inside her.

It had been so long since she'd been with a man. But this wasn't just any man. This was Clayton and so far, being with him was better than anything she'd imagined or experienced. The Fed who she'd been determined to dislike, but who'd managed to overturn her pre-conceived character flaws at every turn... He was charming and kind, smart and funny. And okay, he was drop-dead gorgeous. He was nothing like Robert.

So, he was still in love with his dead wife. She could live with that. It just went to show how deeply he loved and how loyal he was. She had to admire that.

His forehead rested on hers. His lips hovered inches from her mouth.

"You're thinking too much again, Ellie. I can feel the heat coming off your forehead."

She grinned wickedly, hoping to distract him. "Maybe, I'm thinking about how good it will feel when I finally have you inside me... Thick and hard and hot. I have to tell you, I'm suitably impressed with your offering."

He growled low in his throat. Arms taut with muscle slid underneath her and held her close as his mouth took possession of hers.

Heat flared between them. His arms tightened around her and Ellie's pulse picked up its rhythm. His bare chest scraped across her already sensitized nipples and she arched up against him. His cock pressed against her clit. She moaned, filling with need.

He moved his hips against her. Her legs fell open in unspoken invitation. He groaned and settled himself between her thighs, his solid hardness pressed against her entrance.

A sudden thought intruded. She broke off his kiss with a gasp.

"What about a condom? Do you have one?"

––––––––––––––––

Clayton tensed and then collapsed against her, breathing heavily. A few moments later, realization dawned. Anger stirred to life inside him. Coldness filled the pit of his belly. He lifted his head and looked at her.

"A condom? Why the hell would I have a condom? I didn't actually come over here to seduce you, Ellie. "Is that what you think? That I *planned* this?"

"No, no. Of course not." A blush stained her cheeks and she wouldn't meet his eyes. He pushed away and sat on the edge of the couch, his breath still coming in short gasps.

Reaching down, he picked up his jeans and stood to pull them on.

She watched him in silence, her knees drawn up to her chest, her arms draped protectively around them. Her eyes were huge and solemn.

"Please sit down, Clayton. Whatever you're thinking, I can tell you, you're way off base. I don't think you planned to end up on my couch. The only reason I asked was because I'm..." Her cheeks stained a darker color in the dim light. She stared at the floor.

He shook his head, totally bewildered. Almost defiantly, she looked up and met his eyes. "I'm not using any contraception, okay? I know that probably makes me sound like an idiot. A single twenty-seven-year-old, passably attractive woman just winging it, but the truth is—"

She paused again and looked away. He could see she was struggling with what she wanted to say.

His anger softened. "What is it, Ellie? What are you trying to tell me?"

Filling her lungs with a deep intake of air, she let it out slowly and met his gaze again. "The truth is, there hasn't been a need for contraception. I haven't had sex since Jamie died."

His heart swelled with tenderness at the embarrassment on her face. He came over and sat down close beside her. Tugging her resisting form toward him, he enfolded her in his arms. Her head fell onto his chest and she let out a quiet sigh of relief.

He bent his head and kissed the top of hers. Her silky hair smelled good. "Tell me about Jamie," he murmured against it.

She was silent for so long, he didn't think she was going to answer. He swallowed his disappointment.

But then she spoke. Softly, haltingly, as if the words still had the power to wound.

"It happened just over three years ago. An accident. A hit-and-run. They've never found the person involved. But it gets worse. There were no brake marks at the scene." Her eyes, dark with anguish, locked on his. "Somebody didn't even try *not* to kill my baby. Worse, they might have hit him intentionally."

"Christ," he muttered, tightening his arms around her. "I had no idea. When I found out about it on line, I only read the newspaper reports written the day after it happened. The police were still making their enquires. I didn't realize no one was charged."

Her lips trembled. "Nope. Not one single suspect was even interviewed. Even though it happened in the middle of the afternoon on a busy city street, nobody saw a thing. Even his daycare attendant couldn't help. She was hurt, too. Not critically," she added, "but enough broken bones and a concussion to see her hospitalized for a couple of months. She was lucky."

Clayton enfolded her in a hard embrace, wanting to take away her pain. Knowing he couldn't.

A shudder went through her. The quiet sob pierced his heart.

"He was my baby, Clayton. My little boy. He was only two. His coffin was so tiny. It shouldn't have happened. Not to him. Not to my baby. Why couldn't it have been *me*?"

The anguished question let loose a torrent of emotion.

Tears spilled over. More sobs wracked her body. Clayton felt her pain as his own and held her, whispering quiet words of love and comfort against her sweet-smelling hair while she cried and cried and cried.

It was a long time later when she lifted her head and offered him a wet, wobbly smile.

"I'm sorry. I seem to be awfully good at blubbering all over you. First your shirt, and now your chest."

She reached for a tissue and with gentle strokes, wiped the dampness off his skin. He tensed when she unintentionally caressed his nipple. His body came to instant attention. It didn't take her long to notice.

Her eyes widened and she looked up at him. He held her gaze, hoping she could see in them how much she meant to him, how much he wanted her. Her hand stole up and touched his lips with her fingertips, feather soft and fleeting. He sucked in his breath as his heart hammered in his chest.

His eyes never left her face.

She reached up and pulled his head down to hers. As their lips met, heat exploded in his belly. Within minutes, his cock was rock hard, pressing with increasing urgency against his jeans.

Breathless, he broke off the kiss and gasped for air. Taking her face in his hands, he stared down at her and tried to get his breathing under control.

"We don't have to do this, Ellie. I don't have a condom and—"

"It's all right. I remembered I have some in the bathroom cabinet. A friend of mine gave them to me over a year ago." She offered him a wry grin. "I think she was trying to tell me it was time." Her eyes burned into his. "I'll be back in a minute."

He frowned at her, still uncertain. "Don't feel you have to—I mean, are you sure?"

"I want you, Clayton. I need you. I need you inside me, filling me. I've been so empty."

She pulled his head down to hers again and kissed him long and hard. "I've never been surer."

A few minutes later, Ellie returned from the bathroom with a handful of foil packets.

Clayton grinned. "Wow, that's what I call a hint."

Heat spread across Ellie's cheeks, but she opened her hand and offered him the contents. With a growl from deep in his throat, he took them from her and stood. Within seconds, his jeans once again lay discarded on the carpet. He followed her back down on the narrow couch. He tried to manoeuvre his long frame over hers.

"How about we head for the bedroom?" she suggested.

Needing no further encouragement, he scooped her up in his arms, collected the condoms and strode out of the room.

"Second on the right," she murmured, turning her head to press butterfly kisses over his chest. "Mm, you taste so good."

Desire blazed through him. He tightened his hold and lengthened his stride. Less than a minute later, he laid her on top of the queen-sized bed that took up most of the small room.

A lamp on a low wooden table beside the bed had been left on and bathed her skin in a soft, yellow glow. Her hair had dried into a wild tangle of caramel-colored curls that moved with a life of their own. She smiled a little self-consciously up at him. He'd never seen her look more beautiful.

Joining her on the bed, he took her in his arms and reveled in the feeling of her naked warmth against him. Her generous breasts pressed against his chest and her satiny-smooth legs entwined with his.

He kissed her with all the passion that had been building since the first moment he'd seen her. His mouth moved lower, down her sternum and sideways, to capture one of her hard, rosy nipples.

She gasped. He tugged it into his mouth and began to suckle. Her hands gripped his hair, pulling at it almost painfully while he continued his onslaught.

"Clayton, stop," she panted. "It's too much."

"It's never too much," he murmured against her heated skin and he made his way over to the other one.

Taking the nub into his mouth, he laved it with the same attention, swirling his tongue around the puckered peak before suckling at her breast like a baby.

She moved restlessly beneath him. "I need you inside me, Clayton. I need you, *now*."

She didn't have to ask him twice. He reached for a condom where he'd left them on the bedside table and sheathed himself. Positioning himself above her, he nudged open her thighs with his knee and pressed his engorged cock against her warm opening.

She was wet. So wet. He pressed a little harder and the head of his cock slipped inside her. His heart pumped. It was agony. It was ecstasy. The muscles throughout his body screamed for release.

She lifted her hips impatiently and he couldn't resist any longer. With a guttural sound from deep inside him, he plunged all the way into her snug wetness.

So tight. So warm. So moist. So right.

He was home.

"Christ," he moaned, beyond words.

Her arms tightened around him as he moved inside her. Slowly at first, his breathing quickened, along with his pace. Her breath came out interspersed with little moans and breathy pants as she drew closer to orgasm.

"Yes, Clayton. Oh, yes. That's it. Don't stop. Please, don't stop."

He couldn't stop if she'd begged him to. His thrusts became harder, faster. Her legs tightened around his hips, pulling him even closer. He knew he couldn't last much longer.

"Oh, oh, Clayton. *Yes!*"

She shuddered beneath him, pulsing around his cock. His control snapped.

He plunged into her slick wetness time after time, faster and faster. She moved beneath him, thrusting her hips up to meet his demands. Her arms tightened around him as she urged him on.

His cock swelled even further and moments later, his release exploded through him. Time stood still. A groan of heart-felt relief escaped his tightly compressed lips.

With his breath coming in harsh gasps, he collapsed against her. His heart pounded against the wall of his chest and he struggled to slow it down. Her arms remained around him, holding him close. He shifted his weight so that she no longer bore the brunt of it, taking care to ensure they were still joined.

Possessiveness surged through him. His arms tightened around her and pulled her even closer. The guilt that had been his constant companion eased.

He loved her.

It was true.

She was his.

CHAPTER 19

The sound of Ellie's cell phone woke her. Pale shards of light filtered through the open curtains. She struggled to orientate herself and turned and saw Clayton, still asleep beside her. The blanket had slipped around his hips and his bare, broad chest filled her vision.

Memories of their night together bombarded her. She blushed, recalling her wantonness, her eagerness to have him inside her. Oh, but she felt so wonderful. So sated. So relaxed. Sex had never been so good.

The persistent ringing intruded once again and she scrambled out of bed and hurried into the kitchen where she'd left her phone. It stopped just as she reached it. A few moments later, it beeped to tell her there was a new message. Putting it up to her ear, she waited for the message bank to connect.

A movement out of the corner of her eye snagged her attention. She turned and spied Clayton, wearing nothing but a pair of striped cotton boxers and a wide grin, lounging against the doorframe of the kitchen. He gave her a slow and thorough once-over and his eyes sparkled with appreciation.

Heat burned through her. In her haste to get to the phone, she'd left the room without a stitch on. Her gaze swept frantically across the countertops. There was nothing but the tea towel that would provide any coverage and even it wasn't really up to the job.

Squaring her shoulders, she kept her back to him and concentrated fiercely on her voice message. It wasn't as if he hadn't already seen her naked. But somehow, being naked during a passionate lovemaking session wasn't quite the same as standing stark-bollocky in the kitchen with the morning sun streaming through the window.

He chuckled behind her and she immediately had thoughts of killing him slowly and painfully. His warm arms came around her and drew her back against his chest, eliciting a gasp of surprise. His hands found her breasts and kneaded their fullness. She tried again to concentrate on her message.

It was from Ben. They'd tracked down the witness who had seen Sally Batten get into the cab. She'd given them the name of the cab company. With another gasp, this time one of excitement, Ellie pulled out of Clayton's arms and moved away.

He saw the look on her face. "What is it?"

Momentarily forgetting about her state of undress, she grinned with excitement.

"We've got a witness who's given us the cab company Sally Batten rode home with. This could be it, Munro." With trembling fingers, she dialed Ben's number.

"Have they—?"

She held up her hand as the call connected. "Boss, I just got your message. What can you tell me?"

Ben sighed on the other end of the phone. "Colleen Mayger just called. She's working an early shift. Luke and Cheryl spoke to her late yesterday about Sally."

"You said she's identified the cab company."

"Yeah, she remembered this morning. It was an Orange Cab. They work mainly in the western suburbs."

"Did she get a look at the driver? We might be able to interview him and find out where he dropped her off."

"Sort of. Male, dark haired, dark beard. Slight build. Maybe fortyish. This kid's only nineteen, so we've got to assume the age could be anywhere from about thirty on. Anyone over twenty-five looks old to a teenager."

Ellie's excitement continued to build. She grinned even wider into the phone. "Yeah, I know what you mean."

"Anyway, I've got some people contacting the Orange Cab Company to check their records about drivers working during that time."

"We may even be able to narrow it down further," she added. "Sally was picked up outside the Westfield Mall. It was raining all day. There must have been a pile of cabs there. Someone might remember her."

"Yeah, we'll put the word out. I've already faxed a picture of Sally to the cab company's head office. They're going to circulate it around the staff. We're also waiting on Colleen to come into the station and work with us in putting together a composite of the driver."

"Sounds good." She tried to keep the excitement out of her voice. "This might be the break we're after."

"Yeah. It can't come soon enough," Ben replied, his tone somber.

"I'll see you at the office shortly," glancing over her shoulder at Clayton.

"Yeah, no worries. Listen, get onto Clayton and fill him in, will you? It'll save me another call. The phones are going off in here like you wouldn't believe. I'll see you shortly."

Ellie ended the call and whooped as she turned to Clayton.

"We might be close to identifying the cab driver who picked up Sally. Ben's got people doing the leg-work with the cab company as we speak." Unable to contain her excitement, she leaped forward and threw herself against him. "This is it; I know it!"

His arms tightened around her and drew her close. She'd forgotten she was naked until she came in contact with his warm, hard chest. With a sigh of defeat, she melted into his embrace and savored the feeling of skin on skin. For about three seconds.

Pulling away, she strode out into the hallway and headed toward the bedroom. "I'm going to take a shower," she threw over her shoulder. "I'll fill you in on the way to the station."

"So, I take it this means you're going to continue to chauffeur me around, after all?"

She turned and caught his lazy smile. He gave her another slow once-over.

What the hell. She'd just had the most amazing sex of her life. He was entitled to a little look. She sucked in her belly and thrust out her chest. His eyes darkened with desire. He reached her in three long strides.

His lips were liquid fire as they moved over hers. His tongue, warm and demanding, thrust its way inside her mouth and tasted her.

She shuddered when his hand cupped her bare bottom and pulled her into him, holding her still against the long, hard length of him. His erection pressed itself against the softness of her belly. Warmth spread through her and her clit tingled.

She pulled away, gasping. "Clayton, we can't do this now. We have to get to work. I just told Ben..."

He silenced her with another mind-blowing kiss. Her limbs were weightless and she was grateful for the support of his strong, muscular body.

"Work can wait. You just told me he's already got a team of people canvassing the cab company." He pressed his cock against her, moving her hips across its hard length with unmistakable intent. "This can't. Besides, I won't take long."

He picked her up and strode into the bedroom. Depositing her none too gently on the unmade bed, he shucked off his boxers and joined her, pressing his body against the length of hers.

Grasping her head in his hands, his lips devoured hers. She dragged air into her lungs each time his onslaught receded, trying desperately to regain a modicum of control over her pounding heart.

He released her head and moved his mouth lower to graze over the stiff peaks of her breasts. He nipped at the sensitive tips and she gasped. His voice was a low, panting murmur. "You like that, don't you?"

All she could do was moan.

He shifted his weight until he towered above her, taut muscles bulging as his arms strained with the effort. He reached over and tore open another condom. His cock, huge and erect, brushed her stomach and she shivered with need. Moisture pooled between her legs and her clit pulsed a 'yes.'

Bending low, he captured her mouth with his, fusing them together. At the same time, his cock plunged inside her.

She tore her mouth away, gasping from the impact. He rose above her, all beautiful, hard male flesh...and plunged into her again.

With her legs tight around his hips, she urged him on with little moans of desire and jumbled words of encouragement. Hot, desperate need exploded inside her. She kept time with his increasingly frantic thrusts.

His face went still and she knew he was close.

Pulling him down on top of her, she held him tight against her, while he continued to pound into her. His breath rasped in her ear and she reveled in the sound as her own climax beckoned.

"Oh, Christ, Ellie. You're so wet. You're so tight. I'm gonna come. Christ, I'm gonna come."

He thrust into her, feverish with passion and the need for release. She locked her arms around his neck and took his mouth in hers. He pulsed inside her.

It was enough to tip her over the edge. Moving her hips restlessly beneath him, she concentrated on the feel of his thick cock still buried deep inside her. Sensing her urgency, he lifted his head and flicked at her erect nipples with his warm, wet tongue.

He took one into his mouth and suckled. She gasped. Sparks of desire shot through her, inflaming the fire that burned between her legs. Thrusting her hips upward, she let her passion spill over, shouting in relief as she orgasmed.

As her breathing returned to normal, she looked at the clock on her bedside table and shook her head in disbelief. Fast and furious, it had been all over for both of them in less than four minutes.

As if reading her mind, Clayton raised himself up on his elbows and grinned down at her.

"See, I told you it wouldn't take long."

Fifteen minutes later, after dropping Clayton off at his hotel to shower and change, she picked up a couple of jumbo-sized black coffees at a drive-through and waited in the car outside his building.

She took a sip of the hot, restorative brew. As the caffeine began to work its magic, she breathed a grateful sigh of relief. She didn't know how much sleep they'd gotten, but her eyes were like sandpaper and her muscles hurt in places she didn't know existed.

Still, it had been worth every minute: the tired eyes, the sore muscles. She'd never been loved with such thoroughness and expertise as she had with the Fed. She felt good. She felt *really* good. Almost boneless... And she owed it all to him.

As if she'd conjured him up, he came jogging out of the hotel looking like he'd stepped out of the pages of GQ.

The tailored white shirt and dark-maroon-and-white striped tie complimented the charcoal-gray suit and topped off the overall picture of a man who was comfortable in his own skin and confident of his appeal.

He flashed her a grin. All white teeth and shadowed cheeks. He hadn't taken the time to shave. Still, he looked hot.

Heat crept into her cheeks and she looked away, grateful for the sunglasses that shaded her eyes from his way-too-observant gaze. She didn't know why she suddenly felt shy—after all, the man had seen her naked and touched her in places no man had for a long time, but she couldn't deny it.

Despite their night and morning of shared passion, she felt awkward and unsure.

Oh, he'd spoken words of love, but everyone knew they

meant nothing. It was just what guys did, wasn't it? He'd probably already forgotten.

The passenger-side door opened. Spicy cologne and the aroma of warm male assaulted her nostrils and she braced herself against it. God, he smelled good. It evoked images of naked skin and sensual lips, firm planes and tight buttocks.

She closed her eyes against those thoughts and shook her head. This was ridiculous. She was a grown woman. A woman of some experience. She wasn't a dreamy-eyed, naïve virgin romanticizing over her first time. *Christ, Cooper. Get a grip.*

"Thanks for the coffee. It smells great."

So do you, she almost added before clamping her mouth shut. *What the hell was she doing?* They were on their way to work.

That's what they were. Work colleagues. Why the hell hadn't she remembered that last night, before she let her much-neglected libido dictate the terms?

With a little sigh, she flipped on her indicator and headed out into the traffic.

"What's the matter, Ellie?" His voice, soft and full of concern, almost did her in.

She cleared her throat and concentrated on the road in front of her. "Nothing. Nothing's wrong. Just tired, I guess."

A frown creased his forehead. His eyes were concealed behind dark Ray Bans, but she felt them upon her as she turned her attention back to the road.

"Look, I know this is a bit awkward, but it doesn't have to be. I don't regret one instant of our time together. In fact, I can't wait until we—"

"Please, let's not talk about it," she interrupted as panic started to set in.

He cursed and took off his sunglasses. His eyes bored into hers. "Ellie, we did nothing wrong. It was great. It was wonderful. You made me feel alive."

"Can we please just not talk about this right now? I'm really not ready to do this." Her hands tightened on the steering wheel. "Let's just say it was nice for both of us and leave it at that, okay?"

"*Nice?*" Clayton's jaw tightened and a pulse beat in his neck. "Is that how you're describing it?"

Ellie swallowed against the full-blown panic that threatened to take over. She didn't know why she was anxious, but there it was. Could it be she didn't want him to renew his declarations of love in the cold, harsh light of day when there were a lot fewer reasons to hide under? After all, he now knew about Jamie and somewhere along the way she'd come to accept he was nothing like her ex.

Maybe she felt she didn't deserve it? Didn't deserve to be happy? She made an impatient noise deep in her throat. *What was this psycho-babble bullshit?* She'd been to enough shrinks to know it was exactly the sort of crap they'd come out with.

Last night had nothing to do with Jamie. It was just sex. Wild, uninhibited, mind-blowing, soul-satisfying sex. Good for the body. Good for the soul. Nothing more, nothing less.

That was why she was irritated with Clayton for trying to make it into something it wasn't.

"Ellie, talk to me." His voice, low, commanding, caring, sent a shard of pain straight to her heart. How could she talk to him? How could she tell him how *damaged* she was? She couldn't fall in love. She had no capacity to love left inside her. That had all been taken away the day she'd buried her son.

She skimmed a glance in his direction. He deserved more. Much more. He was good and kind and generous. He had a heart as big as an elephant. He deserved a woman who was whole.

Besides, he didn't love *her*. He couldn't love her. It was obvious—he was still in love with his wife.

She cleared her throat, determined to put it all behind her. "I've been thinking about the taxi thing."

He sighed, disappointment filling his eyes.

Gritting her teeth, she ploughed ahead. "Sally Batten caught a cab home, right?" He grudgingly offered a nod of agreement.

"Josie Ward was also going to catch a cab home.

Angelina was on her way home. Now, I know we've been told that she usually caught the bus, but what if she didn't?" She turned to him as the thought began to take hold. "What if she *didn't?*"

Clayton's head spun and he struggled to keep up with the change in conversation. His mind had been crowded with images of them together, skin on skin, heart to heart and all Ellie wanted to do was pretend it didn't happen.

It was like asking him to fly to the moon. It had been the most fantastic night of his life and she was asking him to forget about it.

It wasn't going to happen, but now wasn't the time to argue his point. For whatever reason, she was determined to make light of it and for the moment, he had to be satisfied with that. There was still a killer on the loose and it was his job to find him.

Swallowing another sigh, he focused his attention on the conversation. "You've got a point. It's definitely worth considering. We know it was raining when Josie and Sally disappeared."

"And Angelina," Ellie added, her voice indicating her growing excitement. "At least, it was that morning. Her mother told us that. If it was still raining when she left the university, it's feasible she caught a cab home."

He picked up on her excitement. "A cab driver fits the profile. They're mobile, trustworthy and invisible. We pass by them every day and never even notice. If you needed one, you wouldn't hesitate to flag it down and jump into the back of the first one that stopped."

"Or the front. Some people ride in the front, you know."

"Of course. I always ride in the front." A synapse connected in his brain and his pulse leaped. "I bet that's how he does it."

Ellie frowned. "Does what?"

Sitting up straighter in his seat, he took a healthy swig of his coffee. "Okay, let's just assume our guy's a taxi driver. Most people get in the back, right?"

She nodded.

"So, how does he overpower them? They were all fit and healthy young women. I don't think this guy is large, so how come they don't get away? What does he do to immobilize them?"

"Maybe he waits until he picks up a passenger that sits in the front?" Ellie said. "Or what if the back door wouldn't open and it was raining? They'd probably jump in the front. It would be pretty easy to pull a gun or even a knife on someone sitting a foot away from you."

"You're right. None of them were shot, but that doesn't mean he hasn't used a gun to threaten them. All he needs is to frighten them enough to get them to do as he says."

She nodded again. "He's already gotten them into his car. It's not too much of a stretch to imagine he intimidates them first by taking them somewhere different from where they've asked to go. Short of pulling open the door and taking their chances by leaping out of the moving vehicle, what choice do they have but to go along with it? By the time he pulls the weapon, they're already feeling vulnerable."

"Okay, so let's look harder at the cab companies. We know Sally caught an Orange Cab. It's as good a place as any to start. The girls were all picked up around the Penrith area. We can go through the driver records and see which ones tend to cover that strip. That should help narrow it down a little bit. And then of course, there's the Tuesday thing."

A frown creased her forehead and she shot him another quick look. "What Tuesday thing?"

He shut his eyes briefly, remembering he hadn't told her. Then he remembered *why* he hadn't told her. With clenched teeth, he forced those images out of his mind and turned to her.

"The girls all went missing on Tuesdays. I'm not sure why I

didn't see it before, but I worked it out last night." He flushed and looked away. "It's what I came over to tell you."

Silence met his revelation. He snuck a peek in her direction. She looked bewildered and then bemused. A grin tugged at her lips.

"So, you really didn't come over to seduce me?"

He groaned. "I thought we'd already been over this. I told you last night—"

Her face softened. "I know."

The heat in his cheeks intensified. He cursed the sunglasses she'd replaced over her eyes, concealing them from him. He needed to see her, dammit. He needed to see what she was thinking.

"So, we've got Tuesdays; we've got taxis. We've also got DNA and fingerprint evidence. More than we've had since the start of all this." Her eyebrows rose as another thought occurred to her. "Maybe we could ask our list of drivers to volunteer to give samples?"

He grimaced. "That would certainly be the quickest way to eliminate potential suspects, but I'm not liking your chances of men lining up to volunteer their DNA."

"Well, if they've got nothing to hide, they should be happy to do anything they can to hasten the investigation. I know if it was me, I'd be lining up in a flash."

"Unfortunately Ellie, not everyone is as civic_minded as you."

"Still, it's worth a shot. And you never know, our guy might just be silly enough to fall for it."

"Yeah, except for the fact that he's been ultra-meticulous at his crime scenes. If it wasn't for the fingerprints on that plastic bag and the skin cells under Angelina's fingernails, we'd have next to nothing and even that evidence has led nowhere."

"You're right. But it's worth a shot. I think we're definitely onto something with these taxis." She smiled and his heart lightened.

Maybe she just wasn't a morning person?

He could live with that.

CHAPTER 20

"**R**iley! What the hell are you doing here?" Clayton stopped in mid-stride as he entered the main door of the station, Ellie right on his heels. His brother vacated the olive-green, molded plastic chair he'd been seated in and made his way toward them.

"Hey, little brother." Riley leaned close and gave him a friendly punch on the arm. "Just thought I'd drop by and say hello."

Conscious of Ellie standing behind him, he flushed and looked away. His feelings for her were still so new, he wasn't ready to share them with anyone, including his family. *Especially* his family. He swallowed a groan when she stepped forward and offered her hand.

"Ellie Cooper, nice to meet you."

Riley eyed her curiously and returned her handshake. "Riley Munro. I'm Clayton's older brother."

"Yeah, by about three minutes," Clayton snorted.

"Three minutes? You mean, you're *twins*?" Ellie looked back and forth between them, confusion clouding her features.

"Yeah, fraternal twins," Riley agreed easily. "As you can see, I was the one who got all the looks."

Her gaze traveled over his bronzed skin. Closely cropped, black curly hair emphasized the piercing greenness of his eyes. A broad nose and well-formed lips hinted at an Aboriginal heritage. She shook her head, still staring in confusion.

Taking pity on her, Clayton explained. "Mom's white, with English blood running through her veins right back to the days of the convicts. Dad's an Aboriginal. Some of us took after Mom. Riley here looks a lot like Dad." He shrugged, hoping she'd understand.

"Wow, that's amazing." She still sounded dazed. "Didn't you say there were six of you?"

"Seven, actually. Five boys and two girls," Riley replied, his mouth stretching into a grin that revealed straight, white teeth.

She looked over at Clayton, who was doing his best to ignore the conversation as he moved his weight from one foot to the other. He just wanted to get her away from his brother and his much-too observant eyes. He should have known it wouldn't be easy.

She angled closer to Clayton, her curious gaze now coming to rest on his face. "So where do you fit into the line-up?"

Clayton snorted. Impatience surged through him. The longer they lingered, the greater the chance Riley would sense a closeness between them that was far more than what was necessary between partners. And his twin would know. He'd been a cop as long as Clayton. But with Ellie's bright, questioning gaze still upon him, he had no choice but to reply.

"Fifth," he muttered, groaning inwardly, catching the speculative gleam in his twin's eyes when he looked from one to the other.

"So, Ellie, how long have you been working with my brother? He's not a bad sort, is he? If you're in the market, that is."

Clayton shot him a murderous look. Ellie appeared not to notice as she laughed good-naturedly.

"Yeah, he's not a bad sort. Once you get over a few minor character flaws." Her eyes softened on his face and his heart thudded. He felt Riley's gaze upon them, but was powerless to drag his eyes away from her.

"*Ah hm.*" Riley cleared his throat, breaking the spell.

Clayton flushed again and refused to meet his twin's eyes. In growing desperation, he cast around for an excuse to leave.

"We've got to get upstairs, mate. We think we might have just caught a break in the case we've been working on."

He took Ellie by the elbow and steered her away from his brother.

"No worries, Clay. I'm in town a few nights. I'm staying with Declan. Give me a call when you get free. We might all meet up for dinner."

"Yeah, sounds good," he threw over his shoulder and hurried them toward the stairs and away from Riley's knowing gaze.

"I can't believe you have a twin!" Her eyes gleamed in amusement as they climbed the stairs.

He frowned and pushed open the door to the detective's room that was alive with activity. "He lives up north, in the country. I don't know what's brought him down to Sydney. He hates the city."

"Maybe he's come to visit you. I take it you're pretty close? Most twins are."

"Yeah, I guess so," Clayton mumbled, swallowing a sigh of gratitude as Ben strode toward them.

"Clayton, Ellie. Here's what we've got." He handed them a computer printout containing a list of names. "These are the guys who cover the Penrith area for the Orange Cab Company. I've highlighted the ones who were on duty during the times our girls went missing."

He pointed with his finger at the page Clayton had taken from him. "Of course, we don't know for sure what time Angelina disappeared, but I had the cab company put anyone who was rostered on during the twelve-hours either side of the approximate time of disappearance. We're going with the theory they all went missing on a Tuesday and we'd rather have too many than not enough."

"Absolutely," Clayton agreed, scanning the list. Nothing jumped out at him. He looked up at Ben. "Have you run this through the data base?"

"Cheryl and Luke are working on it. So far, nothing much

has come of it. A couple have had minor scuffles with the police. No arrests. Certainly nothing to spark our interest."

Ellie took the page from him and skimmed it. She frowned and bit her lip in concentration. Clayton tore his gaze away and fixed his gaze on Ben.

"I'm liking the sound of a cab driver more and more. It certainly fits the profile." He moved away and paced the room as he relayed their latest brainstorming to Ben. When he finished, Clayton was breathing a little faster. His gaze remained fixed on Ben's face.

"He's a cab driver, Ben. We're looking for a cab driver. I *know* it."

Ben's expression turned grim. He quirked an eyebrow at Clayton. "You still think our guy lives nearby?"

"Absolutely. The girls went missing within a couple mile radius. One after another in a fairly short time period." His eyes narrowed. "He's working from home."

Ben clapped his hands. "All right everybody, listen up. I want every available body on this one. We know our guy works for the Orange Cab Company. His name must be on that list. There are about a hundred names on it. At least half of them live in the area we're interested in. I want you to split the list between all of you and start door knocking. Make sure you have pictures of the missing girls. Ask some questions. Look for the body type. See if you get a reaction. Someone must know something."

Ellie's gaze returned to the piece of paper in her hands. "Wilson," she mused. "Why does that name sound familiar?"

Clayton frowned. "Wilson. You're right. I've heard that name before, too." He walked closer and peered at the paper over her shoulder. "The address matches up to the area we're interested in. But then, so do a lot of them."

"Yeah, I guess so. And hey, it's a fairly common name out here."

Clayton's phone rang. He pulled it out of his jacket pocket and checked the caller ID. Apprehension filled him when he recognized the number. He shot her an apologetic look. "I need to take this. It's my mother-in-law. She's looking after Olivia."

He turned away abruptly and pressed the answer button. Tension set his jaw. She never called him during working hours. "Janet, what's the matter?"

"Oh, Clayton, I'm sorry to call you while you're working, but it's Olivia."

"Olivia? What happened? Is she all right?"

"Yes. No. I mean, she's okay, but she's had an accident at pre-school. She's fallen off the flying fox and broken her arm."

"The flying fox? What the hell would she be doing on a flying fox?"

"I know. That's what I thought when the pre-school called to tell me. Apparently, it's part of the playground equipment."

His lips compressed. "How bad is it?"

"Pretty bad, I think. It's been broken in a couple of places. They're talking about taking her to surgery to reset it."

"Christ." Fear and anxiety coursed through him. His little girl was in pain and probably scared out of her mind. He had to be there for her. His mind raced and he cursed aloud. "I'm going to call the airlines and get the next flight to Canberra. Hopefully I'll be there in a couple of hours. When did they say they're going to operate?"

Janet sighed. "Well, they haven't yet. We're still in the emergency department of Woden Hospital. She's had the x-rays done, but we're waiting for a consult from the orthopaedic specialist. It was an intern that told me he thought they'd have to operate."

"Tell her I'll be there soon."

"All right, Clayton. I will. And thank you. I feel so terrible."

He heard the tremor in her voice and knew she was struggling to keep her own fears at bay.

"It's okay, Janet. It wasn't your fault. I'm glad she's with you. I'll see you soon." He ended the call and immediately dialed the airlines, cursing again as he was placed in a queue. After what seemed an eternity, he managed to secure a flight that departed in just under an hour.

Striding over to where Ellie now sat at her desk, he

propped his hip against the government-issued steel and sighed.

"I have to fly to Canberra. My daughter's broken her arm pretty badly. They're talking surgery."

Concern and tenderness beamed up at him. His heart clenched with emotion.

"Oh, no! Clayton, go. Don't worry about us." She swept an arm around the room crowded with officers who leaned over desks or hunched in front of computers. "We've got it under control. As Ben says, there must be at least fifty or sixty names to get through. This isn't going to get solved in the next twenty-four hours. We're probably going to be at it for days. There's no telling how many of them will be home when we call."

She gave him another encouraging smile. "Go; your daughter needs you."

He breathed a grateful sigh of relief, wanting so much to drag her into his arms, but knowing she probably wouldn't welcome it in front of the curious eyes of her co-workers.

He settled for a lingering look, hoping to convey with his gaze what he felt. "Thanks, Ellie. I really appreciate it. I hate to run out on you like this, but I'll be back as soon as I can. Maybe even tonight, if I can."

He checked his watch. "I'll be in Canberra by eleven. Depending what happens, I might make it back on a late flight."

"Hey, don't stress it, Fed. I'm sure we can handle things here while you're gone. Go, do what you have to do. And when you're ready, come back and help us nail this bastard."

Co-workers, be damned. He leaned in close and kissed her, leaving her sitting there, cheeks beet red, glancing around to see if anyone had noticed, while he made his way to Ben's office.

A few moments later, he was out the door.

Ellie slumped back against her chair and watched him stride out of the squad room. Suddenly, everything seemed duller, dimmer, flatter without him. She couldn't believe how quickly he'd come to matter.

It wasn't just that they'd slept together, although that fact certainly accounted for some of the nervous excitement that had been jumping around in her belly since she'd woken that morning.

It was more the hope that maybe she *could* be healed, that there was a possibility, however slight, that the pain and loss which never left her would somehow become more manageable.

He had given her that. And she loved him for it. And other things.

She just plain *loved* him.

There. She'd said it. Maybe not out loud, but near enough. Fear and uncertainty warred with the nervous excitement. He'd told her he loved her. But what if he'd just mistaken good sex—no, scrap that... *Great* sex—with love? How was that possible? He still loved his wife. Didn't he?

But his wife was dead. Could she hope that his feelings for Lisa had lessened, become more manageable, like the crippling pain she felt for Jamie?

Could she be that lucky? Did she *deserve* to be that lucky?

She shook her head in annoyance. What the hell was she thinking? Not more of that psycho-babble crap. Of course she deserved to find love. It wasn't her fault Jamie had been killed. It had never been her fault. She knew that now.

On some sensible, sane level, way down inside her, she'd always known it. But the death of her child had a way of twisting her thinking, warping her outlook until she'd almost been buried beneath the guilt.

It was just another one of Clayton's gifts. He'd made her see Jamie's death as a tragic accident, made worse by the fact the perpetrator had never been caught. But it didn't make her culpable.

She didn't even blame Eva. She'd never blamed Eva. It was her, Ellie Therese Cooper, Jamie's mother, who'd taken the blame, fairly and squarely on her shoulders until she'd almost broken under the weight of it. Rational or not, it was the way she'd felt.

She took a huge lungful of air and held it for as long as she could. Exhaling slowly, she shook her head and rotated the tension from her neck and shoulders. It had been a long couple of months. Hell, it had been a long three years. She couldn't believe her baby had been gone for that long.

His cherub face swam before her and she blinked back tears when her memory of him smiled. The noisy bustle of the squad room receded. He looked different, a little older than she remembered, but that couldn't be right.

He wore a white sailor suit that she'd never seen before. It had navy trim around the edges. Goosebumps rose on her skin. She rubbed her arms with her hands, feeling a sudden chill in the air.

Jamie smiled again and waved. "Good-bye, Mommy. I love you."

Tears pricked her eyes and she scrubbed at them with the back of her hands. God, just when she'd thought she'd turned the page on her grief, now she was hallucinating. In broad daylight. At work, no less.

She shook her head in disgust. It was ridiculous. It just went to show how unstable she really was. *Or maybe it was the sleep deprivation?* It was madness. But he'd looked so real. And the faint smell of baby powder still lingered in the air.

A calmness descended upon her. In the midst of the noisy, crowded squad room, she felt at peace. As if her son had given her permission to let go. Had said good-bye.

"Ellie, Clayton saw me on his way out. Are you okay to go and door-knock on your own? With everyone doing their bit, I haven't got a spare body to partner you with."

Ben's grim visage filled her vision. She blinked and cleared her throat.

"Of course." She picked up her copy of the list and showed him the names she'd highlighted. They all lived within close proximity of the disappearance sites.

"I'm going to check these ones out. I'll let the others know so we don't double up."

"Good. Let's hope we find him."

She stood and reached for her coat. Her thoughts went fleetingly to Clayton. She felt a pang at his absence. She drew in a breath and squared her shoulders, determined to do what she could to find their killer and bring the investigation to an end. Maybe then they could concentrate on how to make a relationship between them work. It wouldn't be easy, but she was willing to try.

The icy wind tore at Clayton's cheeks. He tugged his heavy winter coat closer around his shoulders and tightened the woollen scarf around his neck. The tepid sun shone valiantly, but it wasn't a match for the bitter air. Winter in the nation's capital was not for the faint hearted, even in the middle of the day.

He'd caught a taxi straight to the hospital within minutes of the plane landing and had quickly located Janet and Olivia. Still lying on a stretcher in the emergency room, his daughter had only just been seen by the orthopaedic surgeon who had informed them an operation wouldn't be necessary.

Her arm was broken in two places, but they were simple, clean breaks and would only require manual manipulation to reset.

Clayton kissed her on the cheek and hugged her close, mindful of her injured arm. "I'm so glad you're all right, sweetheart. You scared me half to death."

Olivia turned and offered a little smile. "Daddy! I'm so glad you're here. It hurts, Daddy."

His chest tightened with emotion. He pressed his lips together and managed to nod. "I know, sweetheart. The doctor will give you something for the pain in a little while.

You're such a big brave girl. You're going to be just fine. Okay?"

She nodded and then winced against the pain. He took her hand in his and squeezed it. "I've missed you, baby. I've been so lonely without you. It feels like forever since I held you."

"I've missed you too, Daddy. Have you seen Uncle Tommy and Uncle Declan?"

"No, honey. I've been a little busy. I've been doing my best to solve the case I've been working on so I can come back home to you."

"Have you finished it now?" she asked, her eyes wide with hope.

Clayton grimaced and squeezed her hand again. "No, baby. Not yet. But we're getting close."

"Good. I can't wait for you to come back home. I like staying with Grandma and Grandpa, but it's not like being at home with you."

Clayton swallowed the lump in his throat. Leaning over, he brushed a strand of blond hair away from of her eyes.

"I know, sweetheart. I like being home with you, too. I'll be back soon; I promise."

The doctor approached and advised it was time to reset the arm. Olivia's eyes immediately widened in fear.

"Daddy, please don't go. I want you to stay."

"I'm not going anywhere, baby. I'll be right here for as long as you want me."

The doctor administered a generous dose of laughing gas and a light sedative. Clayton remained by his daughter's side. Holding tightly onto his hand with her uninjured arm, Olivia endured the ordeal without any noticeable side effects.

Clayton leaned over and kissed her. "I knew you could do it. You're such a brave, brave girl. I'm so proud of you."

Olivia smiled sleepily. The sedative was already taking affect.

"Thanks, Daddy. I'm so glad you came."

"Me too, sweetheart, but you know, I have to return to

Sydney? I need to finish the case I've been working on. I hope it won't be too much longer. I'll come back home as soon as I can."

Olivia struggled to keep her eyes open. "Promise?" she murmured.

Clayton hugged her close. "I promise," he whispered.

It was much later when he remembered about the plans he'd made with Riley. Clayton left Olivia sleeping peacefully and sporting a fresh, white cast. He found her grandmother and asked her to sit with Olivia. She was happy to oblige and he made his way outside the hospital to call his brother. With his back turned into the biting wind, he dialed Riley's number. It was answered on the second ring.

"Hey, little bro, what's happening? You wanna catch up for lunch?"

"Ah, no, I'm sorry, Riles. I'm in Canberra. Slight emergency. Olivia fell off some playground equipment and broke her arm. We thought she needed surgery, so I hopped a plane down here."

"Shit, that's no good, mate. Is everything okay?"

Clayton ran his fingers through his hair. "Yeah, everything's fine. They managed to reset it without going to theater, so we're all good. She's resting at the moment."

"Thank Christ for that. It must have nearly given you a heart attack."

"Yeah, you can say that again."

There was a moment of silence. As if he knew what Clayton was thinking, Riley spoke again, his voice low.

"It was a broken arm, Clay. That's all. You're not gonna lose her. A broken arm. Kids get 'em all the time."

Clayton choked with emotion. "I know, mate. I know. It's just that... You know..."

"Yeah, Clay, I know. You haven't been inside a hospital since Lisa died. It must have brought back memories."

Swallowing the lump in his throat, he muttered the only reply he could manage. "Yeah."

"She's okay, little brother. She's okay."

"Yeah."

Another silence ensued. On the other end of the phone, Riley took a deep breath and exhaled slowly.

"She's gone, mate. She's never coming back. It wasn't your fault. It's just one of those shitful things that happen sometimes for no goddamn reason. But you can't just stop living. Time hasn't stood still, no matter how much you wish it had. You deserve to find happiness again. Olivia deserves to have you happy again."

Tears leaked slowly out of Clayton's eyes, warm against his frozen cheeks. He knew what his brother said was right, but it hurt so much to let her go. Let *them* go.

After a moment, Riley spoke again. "When are you heading back to Sydney?"

Clayton swiped at the moisture in his eyes. "Probably later this afternoon, if I can get a flight. Ellie's holding the fort, but we need all the help we can get. We're closing in on the guy. I have to get back."

"She seems nice."

Despite the sadness that weighed down his heart, a reluctant grin tugged at Clayton's lips. He knew exactly where his twin was headed.

"Yeah, she's nice."

"I think she likes you."

A chuckle escaped him. "Really? What makes you say that?" He could almost see Riley squirming.

"I saw the way she looked at you. She barely gave me a second glance, and we both know that's not how it usually is."

This time he laughed outright. "One thing I can count on you for, big bro, is for making me feel good about myself."

"Hey," Riley replied, a little defensively. "I'm just telling it how it is."

"Whatever floats your boat, Riles. How is your latest girlfriend, anyway? Bronte...? Belinda...? I can't keep up with them."

Riley snorted. "You're not going to get out of it that easily. I know you're trying to change the subject. We're talking about you, not me. What's going on with you and the delectable Ellie? And don't tell me nothing, I'm your twin, remember? I can sense these things."

Clayton scoffed, but his heart jumped at the mention of Ellie's name. Riley was right. There was something going on. He was in love with her. If he knew how Ellie felt, it would make things a hell of a lot easier.

Last night had been magical. All that he could have dreamed of when he broke his self-imposed celibacy. And she'd seemed to have been as involved in their lovemaking as he had.

But this morning, something had changed. She'd been distant and removed and he still didn't know why. What he did know was that he wasn't prepared to let her brush it off. He wasn't the type to walk away, at least, not without a decent explanation.

Now that the drama of Olivia's accident was over, and he was reassured she was in good hands, his thoughts returned to Ellie. He didn't know how it had happened, but she'd exploded in his heart, filling the empty coldness with warmth. For the first time since Lisa died, he felt happy and content. He wasn't going to walk away from that without a fight.

"So, what is it, little brother? Do I have to drag it out of you?"

Riley's chiding tone dragged him back to the present and he smiled into the phone.

"Okay, okay. You might be sensing something." He took a deep breath. "We spent last night together."

There. He'd said it out loud. The relief he felt was instantaneous. The weight on his shoulders and in his heart seemed to lift and lighten, making him feel better than he had in three years.

"I *knew* it," Riley pounced, as Clayton had known he would. "Tell me everything. I want all the juicy details."

Clayton grinned, knowing his brother didn't mean it. As close as they were, they'd never pried into the intimacies of each other's private lives.

"Let's just say she's as delectable on the inside as she is on the outside."

Riley's voice caught. "Oh, Clay, you don't know how glad I am to finally hear you say that. After Lisa, I didn't think you'd ever feel that way again."

Emotion clogged Clayton's throat.

"Me, neither." He cleared his throat before continuing. "I might have been a bit short with you and the others over the last few years whenever you brought it up, but I do appreciate where you've been coming from. I know I haven't exactly made it easy for everyone."

"No worries, mate. We only did it because we cared. It's been tying me up in knots seeing you so unhappy. If I could have brought her back, I would have."

"I know that."

Riley broke the silence a few moments later. "If you head up here this afternoon, we might still have time to catch up for dinner."

Clayton checked his watch. It was just after one o'clock. "Yeah, if it's a late one. Once Olivia is settled back home with Janet, I'm going to head out to Woden Cemetery. Then hopefully, I'll get a seat on an afternoon flight. I'll let you know how I'm doing a bit later on."

"No worries, Clay. Brandon's still overseas, but I'll give Declan and Tom a call and see what we can arrange. Say hello to Olivia for me and tell her I can't wait to scrawl my name all over her cast."

He grinned into the phone. "Will do. And thanks," he added softly.

Not needing to be told what he was referring to, Riley replied, his voice equally soft.

"Anytime."

CHAPTER 21

The temperature felt like it had dropped at least five degrees when Clayton stepped out of his mother-in-law's car and made his way into Woden Cemetery. He headed towards Lisa's grave. The biting wind had turned into sleet. He narrowed his eyes against its sting.

It was as wet and dreary as the day he'd buried her. Olivia had been barely fourteen months old and had been left with some distant cousins during the ceremony. He'd been surrounded by his family—his parents and his brothers and sisters. Lisa's parents, Janet and Bob, had been there, of course, along with Lisa's older sisters.

He frowned. For the life of him, he couldn't remember the last time he'd seen them. Neither of them lived in Canberra, but still, distance wasn't really an excuse. He kept in contact with his family and some of them lived more than six-hours' drive away.

He had to make more of an effort to keep in contact. After all, they were Olivia's aunts and she barely knew them. The fact they weren't close was as much his fault as theirs.

He brushed at the moisture that clung to his jacket and found Lisa's headstone. It was less than two months since he'd been there, but it felt like a lifetime ago.

Kneeling down on the wet grass, he breathed in the scent of rain, wood smoke and decay. Although she'd been laid to rest in a newer part of the cemetery, he didn't have to look far to see the moss-covered, crumbling old concrete headstones and termite-ridden picket fences that surrounded some of the older graves.

He reached out and touched the cold dampness of her headstone with unsteady fingers, tracing the letters inscribed in the black granite. Tears pricked his eyes and the gold lettering blurred. He pressed his hand flat against the cold stone and waited.

Nothing.

Panic gripped him. "I can't feel you." His voice was a ragged whisper. "Oh Christ, babe. I can't feel you anymore."

His chest tightened. He leaned forward to rest his head against the granite. The sleet had turned into rain and he shuddered when icy rivulets of water trickled underneath his collar.

He didn't know how long he sat like that, but gradually he became aware that the stone had warmed beneath his skin. He sat back on his haunches and inhaled the damp, mossy, earth smell that filled the air. Closing his eyes, images of Lisa assailed him and his tension eased.

She was smiling, looking healthy and beautiful and glowing, like she had right before Olivia had been born. Her smile seemed to go right through him and touch his soul.

I'm so glad you came to see me, Clay. I've missed you. Her voice was a mere whisper of sound inside his head. He strained to hear it.

Oblivious to the tears that ran down his cheeks, his hands tightened their grip on the granite.

"I miss you, too. I miss you so much." His voice cracked on the last word and he dragged in an uneven breath.

It's time to let me go. I'm fine. I'm happy. I'm at peace. Open your heart to love again, my darling. I want to see you smile. I'm so sorry I put you through all this. It wasn't your fault. I told you I was fine. I told you it was just the lack of sleep. I told you lots of things. But I did love you, Clay. I loved you more than anything. That's why you have to let me go, Clay. Remember me, but let me go.

He was crying in earnest now. His hands were frozen on

the stone. Sobs shuddered through his body. Her voice grew fainter.

Let me go, Clay. Let me go. Her voice faded away and so did her image. He leaned heavily against her headstone, his forehead coming to rest on the cold, wet granite.

Gradually, his breathing quieted and his pulse rate returned to normal. He heard the sound of a bird singing somewhere off to his right in the bushland which surrounded the cemetery. The lightness of it sounded so odd on such a cold, dreary day.

Lisa's words reverberated in his head until they sounded like a mantra. It felt like a layer of pain was being torn away each time he heard them.

He let go of the granite and slid down to sit on the ground, unaware of the wet grass soaking into his suit pants. Slowly, tenderly, he traced her name with his fingers.

Realization filled him. She was happy. She was at peace. She'd told him so. The weight of guilt and loss slowly, inexorably lightened.

A huge sigh escaped him and with it, the pain he'd been holding onto for so many years. Reaching up, he undid the clasp of the chain around his neck and tugged it free from his shirt. The gold ring shone dully. Bringing it up to his lips, he kissed it before tucking it away inside the pocket of his coat. One day, he would give it to Olivia.

Pressing his palm flat against the cold stone for a few more minutes, he mouthed a silent thank you.

Lex Wilson was late for work. Impatience surged through him. He thought he'd left enough time, but it had taken him longer than he'd expected.

With the final piece glued into place, he stepped back and admired his handiwork. She was perfect. Her eyes, her nose, her lips. Even the tips of her pink-painted fingernails. The delicate cotton and wood sandals slipped on and off her feet with ease and matched the purple satin and tulle evening gown he'd stitched with his own hands.

Her thick, blond hair curled enticingly around her hips and was tied back with a matching satin ribbon that he'd stolen from his daughter's jewelry box. Pride surged through him and he grinned. She was sure to fetch a high price at the markets. Michelle would be pleased, which was a good thing. His wife, in a temper, was something to be feared.

Knowing he was getting later by the second, he went to the sink which was plumbed into the wall of the shed and quickly washed his hands. There was no time to scrub. He gazed over at his tools and the mess of wood shavings that lay curled across his workbench. He'd have to clean up later.

Wiping his hands on an old towel, he looked up at the corkboard above him and smiled at the newspaper clippings pinned there. It had been three years since he'd started his collection. Three years. Where had the time gone?

The earliest clipping, and probably his favorite, had yellowed and turned up at the edges, but the photo of what remained of the child's pram was as clear as the day it had been taken. A day he would never forget.

A smaller photo of the grieving mother captured his attention. Excitement stirred in his belly, like it always did when he let himself remember. The sound of the impact. The crunch of the pram beneath his wheels. The screaming. Oh, he'd never forget the screaming.

His heart thumped, but he couldn't give in to the pleasure he knew awaited him. He had to get going. His shift started in less than ten minutes.

Knowing he had no time to spare, but unable to resist, he turned away from the clippings and strode quickly over to one of the freezers on the far side of the overcrowded shed. Moving the boxes of junk and empty paint tins off the top, he lifted the lid. His heart caught in anticipation. He stared inside at each carefully preserved limb.

Adrenaline coursed through him. He was nearly there. It

wouldn't be long. Soon, very soon he'd be ready to complete his most magnificent creation yet.

Clayton sprawled across two red, vinyl-covered seats in the busy departure lounge and took a sip from the Styrofoam coffee cup he held in his hand. The usual assortment of travelers milled around, some reading newspapers or magazines, others staring blindly through the floor-to-ceiling windows at the collection of planes on the tarmac.

He inwardly sympathized with a young mother who struggled with an over-tired toddler who ran raggedly back and forth between her and a distant bank of chairs. He knew what it was like to go it alone. He'd offered to distract the child with a game, but the mother had politely declined. Not that he blamed her. Trusting a stranger didn't come as easy as it used to most people, especially young women. He only wished the female victims in Sydney had been a little more cautious. It could have saved their lives.

He sighed at the senseless loss of three young lives and tried to stem the surge of impatience. He had half an hour to wait before his flight boarded. Clouds rolled in across the hills and fog blanketed the landscape outside the windows. He hoped takeoff wouldn't be delayed by the weather.

He'd settled Olivia back into her room at her grandparents' and had left her happily drawing pictures on her fresh, white cast. She'd been thrilled when he'd drawn a huge love heart using a red permanent marker and had scrawled both their names in it. With a prescription for pain medication filled and a bowl of chocolate ice cream in her belly, she was more than content.

He'd found Janet in the kitchen, clearing away the afternoon tea things. He gave her a sincere smile of gratitude.

"Thanks for everything, Janet. I really appreciate it. I don't know what I would have done without you."

Her eyes softened on his face. "You're welcome, Clayton. You're always welcome. She's our granddaughter." She shrugged and added simply, "We love her."

He closed the short distance between them and gave her a gentle hug. "I know you do and I'm forever grateful. Without you and Bob, I don't know what I would have done. Certainly, with my work, I wouldn't have been able to do what I have. Having your support has made a difference to my life—to both our lives."

He pulled away and looked down at her. "I'm sure I don't tell you often enough how important it is to me."

She smiled softly at him, her face wrinkling around her worn brown eyes. Lisa's eyes. "We know, Clayton, we know. But it's nice to hear you say it."

"So, where's Bob? With all the drama going on, I forgot to ask."

Janet rinsed her hands under the faucet over the sink. "He's down the south coast, at Merimbula, on a golf tournament. The 'Golden Oldies' as they like to call themselves. They've arranged a three-day friendly competition with the club from down there. He left yesterday."

"Well, good for him. You ought to go with him one day."

Janet shuddered in mock horror. "Me, with a golf stick? Not in this lifetime."

Clayton laughed, feeling good as the fear and panic of Olivia's accident slowly abated. "You sound just like your daughter."

Her gaze sobered. "That's the first time in three years I've heard you mention her without pain."

She wiped her hands dry with the tea towel and took her time returning it to its hook on the cupboard near the sink. With a soft sigh, she turned around to face him.

"How *are* you, Clayton? There's something different about you. You seem more relaxed, more at peace with yourself. Even through the commotion of Olivia's injury, I noticed it." She paused. And then said, "You went and visited her, didn't you?"

He nodded. "When I borrowed your car, I ducked out while Olivia was asleep and we were waiting for the doctor to come and discharge her."

His mother-in-law's gaze didn't stray from his face. "So, how was she?"

He closed his eyes against the rush of emotions. Sadness at letting go. Relief she was happy. Determination to take his life back with both hands.

He opened them on a heartfelt sigh. "She's good, Janet. She's really, really good."

Tears pricked the older woman's eyes. She stepped forward and put her arms around his waist. Her words were muffled against the heavy cotton of his shirt. "I'm so glad to hear that."

"Yeah," he whispered. "Me, too."

A voice over the intercom announcing his flight number jolted him back to the present and he sat up straighter to listen: Due to the weather conditions, the flight would be delayed another half hour.

Disappointment coursed through him and he slumped back against the seat. Now it would be even longer before he'd be back in Sydney, back with Ellie.

His thoughts centered on her and, he pulled out his phone and dialed her number. His heart beat faster while he listened to the call ring out. He'd braced himself for her voicemail to cut in but then she answered.

"Hey, there stranger. How is everything?"

He grinned into the phone, feeling like a teenager. Suddenly, two hours felt like a lifetime. "Everything's good. Everything's great." He realized how much he meant it.

"How's Olivia? Did she have to go to theater?"

"No, we were lucky. Just a bit of nitrous oxide and some hand-holding from her daddy and we were all put back together. She's sporting a bright new cast from her wrist to her elbow that's going to make her the envy of everyone on the playground."

Ellie laughed and his heart skipped a beat.

"I'm so glad to hear it." Her voice dropped lower. "And how are you going?"

He smiled into the phone. "I'm good. I'm fine. Everything's going to be just fine."

"So, when are you coming back?"

He heard the eagerness in her voice and felt warm all over. "I'm sitting in the airport as we speak. I was booked on the four-thirty plane, but they've just announced a delay because of the weather."

"Good old Canberra winter, hey?"

He grinned. "You've got it in one."

She cleared her throat. "I'm out in Penrith doing door-knocks. We've split it up between us so we can cover more ground."

"Who's riding with you?"

"No one. We're short-staffed. I told Ben it was fine."

"Save some of them for me. I'd love to be the one to knock on the door of the bastard who's responsible for this."

"I know how you feel, believe me, but you probably won't get in until late this afternoon. I'm going to do my best to get through the names on my list today."

"Yeah, no worries. I'll see how I go. With a bit of luck, I might be back there by six. I'll call you when I land."

There was a pause before her voice dropped to a husky whisper. "I can't wait."

His stomach did a somersault in anticipation. "Um, Riley's still in town and wants to catch up for dinner. My brothers, Declan and Tom, might tag along, too. I was wondering... That is, would you like to...?"

They both knew what he meant. His invitation signaled so much more than sharing a meal. He waited with bated breath for her reply.

"I'd like that, Clayton. I'd like that very much."

———

The pale afternoon sun had made a beeline for the horizon when Ellie climbed back into the unmarked car and crossed the penultimate name off her list. The air had turned chilly. She switched on the ignition and turned up the heat. There was only one name remaining: *Lex Wilson*.

Wilson. She still couldn't remember why it sounded familiar. It was a nondescript, common Australian surname and one that shouldn't have caught her attention.

Checking the address on the paper, she leaned over and punched it into the GPS mounted on the dashboard. Pressing 'go,' she did a U-turn and headed in the direction shown on the screen. Picking up her radio, she called into headquarters and informed the operator where she was going.

She hadn't heard from Clayton. He was probably still in the air. At least, she hoped he was and that his plane hadn't been delayed any further.

Glancing at the vacant seat across from her, she felt a wave of longing. She couldn't believe how much she missed him, how quickly she'd become used to having him beside her, joking, laughing, plotting, teasing, grinning. He hadn't even been gone a full day and already she was pining. There was absolutely no hope for her.

She was doomed.

She was a goner.

She was a write-off.

She was in love. Head-over-heels, forget-about-the consequences in love, Fed-be-damned, in love. She shook her head at the incongruity of it. She'd never have believed anyone in a million years if they'd told her she'd find the man of her dreams while she was caught up in the middle of a nightmare multiple-murder investigation.

Nothing about that scenario made sense. But then, when did love ever follow the rules? No one got to choose who they fell in love with. Hadn't she read that somewhere? Read it; heard it—it didn't matter. It was the truth and that's all that did make sense.

He'd sounded so good when he called. So calm, so happy, so keen to get back. She only hoped he'd meant what he said when he told her he loved her.

She'd discounted it earlier as just words uttered at a time when most men forgot how to think with their brain. But now, she wasn't so sure. He'd seemed so serious, so earnest, so genuine. And the man she'd come to know over the past couple of months wasn't the kind of guy to throw out declarations of love without thinking about them first.

She only hoped she wasn't making their connection into more than it was—just because she wanted it to be that way.

Ellie sighed and flipped her indicator to the left to make the turn into the Cranebrook Street she'd set as her destination. She'd just have to wait until she spoke to him again. Then, she'd know for sure.

She glanced at the clock on the dashboard. Five-thirty. At least another half hour before he landed.

"This is bordering on ridiculous," she muttered, pushing thoughts of him aside. She checked the last address on the paper that sat on the passenger seat. Twenty-six Harpers Drive. Which meant it was the red brick-and-tile bungalow ahead on her left.

She pulled into the curb and shut off the ignition. The house looked like all the others on the street, with nothing to distinguish it except for the flourishing flower beds that grew along the fence line. Impressed at the display in the middle of winter, she recognized the pretty pink and yellow bell-shaped flowers of a common Correa bush, at least two different types of Grevillias, with their spiky olive foliage, a magnolia bush laden with creamy-white flowers and an early flowering native wisteria, whose bright purple flowers crept in gay abandonment along the front fence.

Climbing out of the car, she made her way up the concrete path leading to the front of the house. Though the path was old and cracked, it had been swept clean and ended at a freshly painted front door. Knocking twice, she stepped back and waited.

There was no response.

She cleared her throat and called out. "Police, is anyone home?" Silence met her once more and she knocked again.

After another couple of minutes with no response, she turned and walked along the patterned-tile porch and peered through the front window. Heavy cream curtains had been parted to let in the light and she could just make out lounge room furniture through the gauzy-white film still covering the window.

A good-sized plasma television, which was turned off, graced one wall and faced out to a newish brown-suede couch. The room was as neat as a pin. Not exactly where she imagine a psychopathic serial killer would live.

She called out again through the window, but the house remained stubbornly silent.

Retracing her steps down the worn concrete path, she crossed the front lawn and made her way down the side of the house. It was possible someone might be in one of the rooms furthest from the street and couldn't hear her.

The backyard was as tidy as the front. The grass was as green as you could expect at the end of winter and was cut short with the edges trimmed. More flower beds formed decorative borders along both side fences and between the cracked concrete driveway which led to an old, but freshly painted, empty carport.

A child's faded-green swing set stood in one corner, along with a sandpit containing toys. Two small bikes with white plastic baskets attached to the handlebars stood propped against the side of a color-bond shed that filled the back half of the garden.

Ellie pulled her coat around her shoulders in an effort to ward off the late afternoon chill and made her way over to the building. She was still a few feet away from it when she noticed there was power to it and the door was padlocked.

It wasn't surprising. This was the western suburbs, after all. In fact, she'd be surprised to find any backyard shed unlocked in this part of Sydney.

Standing on tiptoes, she put her face up to the dirty Perspex window and peered in. The light was fading fast and she could barely make out a workbench set in the middle of the room.

As her eyes adjusted to the dimness, she recognized other shapes. An old car body, a lawn mower and a three chest freezers all materialized in the gloom.

She breathed on the Perspex and rubbed it with her hand in an effort to remove some of the grime. The indistinct shapes on the workbench morphed into tools—chisels, a small mallet, a tin of paint. Wood shavings curled in small, riotous bundles at one end, almost as if they'd been brushed out of the way and had landed in a tangled heap.

Wood shavings. Her heart accelerated, but she forced herself to remain calm. Wood shavings didn't necessarily mean it was their killer. A lot of people worked with wood. Look at the professor and Rick Shadlow. Neither of them had turned out to be the perp they hunted.

All of a sudden, Ellie registered the sound of a motor vehicle approaching. She stepped away from the shed in time to see a white van come to a stop inside the carport. Making her way across the yard, she waited for the occupants to alight.

The high-pitched voices of children reached her ears as the passenger-side door swung open.

"Me, first! Me, first! You always get to go first!"

"No, me! Mama, you said I could go first today."

An older female voice intervened. "Amy! Anissa! Enough."

The voice was stern and the children fell silent immediately. Two girls about the ages of nine and seven jumped out of the car, tugging school bags out of the van as they did so. Ellie moved closer. They stopped in their tracks when they saw her, curiosity plain on their faces.

"Hi, I'm Detective Cooper. I'm looking for your dad."

"He's at work," the girls replied together, then turned to glare at each other.

"She asked me," the older one whined.

"No, she asked *me*," the younger one yelled back.

"Girls, enough."

Once again, the children fell silent, their eyes lowered. The woman Ellie assumed to be their mother rounded the back of the van. She stuck out her hand. "I'm Michelle Wilson. I'm sorry about my daughters. They know better than that. Now, what were you saying about my husband?"

Michelle Wilson's eyes were a pale blue; her face was open and kind. White-blond hair hung down her back in a casual ponytail. Ellie guessed she was in her mid-thirties.

She took the hand the woman proffered and shook it. "It's nice to meet you, Mrs Wilson." She glanced toward the children. "You have them well trained. I'm impressed."

The woman's eyes crinkled in a smile. "Not without a lot of effort."

Ellie smiled back. "I'm sure. Look, I'm making some enquires about men in your neighborhood who are employed by the Orange Cab Company. Your husband works there, doesn't he?" Ellie watched her closely, but the calm expression in the pale blue eyes didn't falter.

"Yes, yes he does. He's been there for years. He loves that job."

"I take it he's not home at the moment?"

"No, no, he's at work. He's working the late shift tonight."

Retrieving her notebook and pen from the pocket of her jacket, Ellie jotted down a few notes. "What time did he start?"

"Mm, let me think. He started at three o'clock and goes through to about three in the morning." She grinned and shook her head. "I'm usually asleep in bed. Most times I don't even hear him come in."

Ellie kept her voice casual when she posed the next question. "It looks like he does some wood working in his spare time." She inclined her head toward the shed. "I saw some tools on a workbench through the window."

Michelle smiled again. "I don't know where he finds the energy or the time. He only has the weekends off. He spends hours in that shed. He loves being in there almost as much as he loves his job."

Ellie's heart skipped a beat. "What does he do in there?"

The smile turned into an outright chuckle. "You're not going to believe it, Detective, but he makes dolls."

"Dolls?"

"Yes, wooden dolls. He carves them by hand. He paints all of their features and sews their clothes. Tiny dresses and shoes. Hair ribbons to match. They are magnificent."

Disappointment surged through her. Lex Wilson hardly sounded like a serial killer. Still, he was worth talking to. Who knew—he might have seen something.

"What time does your husband go to work tomorrow?"

"Oh, not until the afternoon again. He usually sleeps for a few hours after he gets in and then potters around in the shed until it's time to go."

Pulling a card out of her wallet, Ellie handed it to the woman. "Here are my numbers. Please, ask him to give me a call when he's free. I would like to speak with him."

Michelle's eyes clouded over. Her face turned serious. "Of course, Detective. Is there anything the matter?"

"No, no. It's nothing to worry about. We're doing some routine questioning. That's all."

The woman still looked doubtful, but slid the card into her handbag.

Ellie looked up at the darkening sky and tossed her notebook and pen back into her pocket.

"Thank you for speaking with me, Mrs Wilson. I would appreciate it if you could let your husband know I was here."

"Of course, of course."

Ellie made her way down the driveway. About half way down, she turned back as another thought occurred to her.

"What does he do with them?"

Michelle's brow furrowed in confusion.

"The dolls," Ellie added. "What does he do with them?"

A wide smile lit up the woman's face. "Why, he gives them to me, of course. And I sell them at the markets." She inclined her head toward the vehicle in the carport. "That's why I have the van."

CHAPTER 22

Ellie slumped back against the car seat and sighed in disappointment. Okay, so maybe the killer wasn't on her list. With only so much manpower available, she knew there were still at least fifteen or so names that hadn't been allocated. Maybe tomorrow they'd get lucky.

With another sigh, she switched on the ignition and pulled away from the house. She should have known just by looking at it that it wasn't the house of a madman. The neat lawns, the gaily colored flowers, the stern but friendly wife, the bickering kids. It all seemed too normal.

As she negotiated the late-afternoon traffic, her thoughts wandered to the shed. A taxi-driving doll maker. Who'd have thought? He made them; she sold them.

Then a memory hit her and her foot slammed on the brake. Michelle Wilson, the owner of the white van. The van Ronald Carter had seen in the laneway beside his house right after his freezer went missing.

A chest freezer. Like the ones she'd seen in Lex Wilson's shed. But why the hell would Michelle Wilson be stealing chest freezers? It didn't make sense. The woman didn't seem to have a deceitful bone in her body.

Could she have been lying? Ellie immediately discounted that. She considered herself to be a pretty decent judge of character and she'd have sworn Michelle was exactly what she appeared to be—a busy mother trying to raise two rambunctious children and doing her bit to support her family.

Could her husband have used the van? He worked with wood. She'd seen wood shavings piled on the end of the workbench. Wood shavings had been found in Josie Ward's hair and underneath Angelina Caruso's fingernails.

Her mind drifted to the paint tin. It was probably used to paint the dolls. In the dimness, she hadn't been able to tell what color it was, but she suddenly recalled the pink paint chips that had been found in Angelina's hair.

The impatient beep of a horn behind her reminded her she'd slowed almost to a stop. Adrenaline surged through her and she pumped the accelerator.

The peculiarities were piling up. It was all circumstantial and a good lawyer would probably explain all of it away, but still, it was a bit of a coincidence and was definitely worth further investigation.

The clock on the dashboard told her it was just after six. With her cell phone on hands-free, she dialed Clayton's number. Excitement coursed through her when he picked up.

"Hey, there gorgeous," he exclaimed. "I was just thinking about you. My plane just landed. It's good to be back up here and into some warmer weather."

Ellie grinned, glancing across at the heater she'd turned up full blast.

"So, how'd you go with your door-knocking? Any luck?" he asked.

"Well, I'm not sure. Seven out of the eight on my list were non-contenders, but the last one was interesting."

"How so?"

"Well, I don't know if it's anything, really. Just a bit of a hunch. Lex Wilson is a wood carver. He's got a shed out the back of his house where he makes wooden dolls."

Clayton's tone sharpened. "Dolls?"

"Yes, and the other thing that's interesting is that he does the late shift on Tues—"

"Dolls. Fuck, it's him. The taxi driver from the airport. Lex Wilson. *Fuck.* Did you speak to him?"

Ellie frowned at the urgency in Clayton's voice. "What do you mean, the airport?"

"Ellie, did you speak to him?" His voice was tighter.

"No, he was at work. I just told you he works the late shift—"

"On Tuesdays," he finished. "It fits. It all fits. It's him. I can't believe it. It's him. The fucking taxi driver."

Ellie's heart faltered. "How can you be so sure? Just because he's a wood worker, doesn't mean—"

His breath came harsher through the phone. "I caught his cab the first night I arrived. I remember the name. He told me about the dolls. It's him, Ellie. I'm sure of it. Please, trust me on this. Where are you now? I hope you're still not at his house."

"No, I'm heading back to the station. I was going to review the files on the missing freezers. You wouldn't believe it; I finally remembered why the name Wilson seemed familiar. It's the name of the owner of the van seen by Ronald Carter. Michelle Wilson. I received the results from the Roads and Maritime Services a few days ago.

"That's it. Ellie, that's it. The freezers. He's using them to store the bodies. The parts he's saving. They're in the fucking freezers."

Cold fear prickled her scalp. Her breathing laboured. Clayton was right. It did fit.

"Get yourself back to the station," Clayton ordered. "The traffic's banking up over here, but I'll see you as soon as I can."

Ellie shivered at the urgency in his voice. "Okay. I'm on my way."

She ended the call and returned her attention to the road. A fat drop of rain splattered against her windscreen and she frowned. She hadn't even noticed the gathering clouds. Night had settled in, along with the storm.

The first drop was followed quickly by another and another. She flicked her wipers on and soon had to turn them up high when the rain hit with a vengeance.

Early evening traffic was still heavy as people rushed home from work, eager to get inside out of the storm. Her thoughts were a jumble of fear and excitement. They had him. They *had* him!

277

She had to call Ben. They needed to put together an arrest team. Wilson was at work until late. It would be safer to arrest him at his home. She prayed he wasn't out there now trolling for another target.

A jagged arc of lightning lit up the sky in front of her and she jumped. The sound of the thunder that followed it a few moments later reverberated through the car. Ordinarily, she loved to watch the power and fury of a storm—when she was safely inside four solid walls.

It was a different matter experiencing one from inside what felt like the insignificant nothingness of the squad car.

Accelerating as much as she dared through the blinding rain, she made her way along the four-lane highway toward the heart of Penrith, and refuge.

A loud clunking sound came to her over the noise of the storm. The steering wheel tightened in her hands and the vehicle pulled to the right.

With an effort, she corrected her direction and centered the car in the lane. Again, it pulled to the right. The noise got louder and suddenly, she realized what it was.

A flat tire. Just what I need.

With a glance in her rear-view mirror, she lifted her foot off the accelerator. The car limped to the side of the road. Switching off the ignition, she turned on the hazard lights and punched the station's number into her phone. There was no way she was going to climb out into what had become a deluge to change it.

The call finally connected and she explained her predicament to the switchboard operator.

"I hate to be the one to tell you this," the woman said, "but the truck's already out on a call. I'm sorry, but you're the second officer to call in a flat tire in the last ten minutes. They've only just left for a job over at Glenbrook. It's difficult to say, but they could be gone awhile—at least an hour or so."

Her shoulders slumped on a loud groan. "An hour?"

"Or so. Could be less; you never know your luck."

"Yeah, the way mine's been going, I'll be lucky to see them before midnight."

The operator chuckled. "Well, they're not exactly known for their punctuality and in this weather, who knows?"

"Gee, thanks for your support and understanding."

"Hey, I'm not the one stuck on the side of the highway."

She ended the call on another heavy sigh and peered in the rear-view mirror at the bank of car lights behind her. She could probably catch a taxi. That would be quicker than waiting for the tow truck.

A shiver of unease trickled down her spine. Lex Wilson was somewhere out there. Right now. In his taxi.

She shook her head. She was being silly. What were the chances of coming across him? There were hundreds of cabs on duty right now. It was peak hour. She'd hail a cab and get back to the station. It would probably take her ten minutes, fifteen, max. And then she'd see Clayton again and together they'd work out how they could put Wilson away forever.

With newfound courage and resolve, she dialed the station and left details of her change of plan with the switchboard operator. The rain had eased slightly, but was still coming down. Taking another look out the back window, her heart leaped in gratitude when she spied what she was looking for.

The cab was still a fair way back, but headed in her direction. She leaned across and picked up her handbag from where it sat on the passenger seat and pulled her phone out of the car kit. Tugging the keys out of the ignition, she pushed them under the floor mat.

Glancing again through the rear-view mirror, she judged the distance about right to give the driver enough time to see her and pull over. Bracing herself against the rain, she opened the door and climbed out, dragging her handbag with her. Hailing the cab with an outstretched arm, she sighed in relief as an indicator came on and the taxi moved across the lanes of traffic toward her.

It came to a stop behind her vehicle. She hurriedly covered the short distance and went to open the rear passenger side door. It was locked.

Damn!

She tapped on the window, hoping the driver would notice. He didn't respond and she surmised he couldn't hear her over the storm. She tried the front passenger seat and the door cracked open. She thought briefly of Clayton and their conversation about riding in the front, but the rain was soaking through her clothing and the odds of stumbling into the killer's taxi were next to slim. With a sigh, she opened the door wider and collapsed onto the seat.

"Oh, thank God you came along," she breathed. "You've made my day. I thought I'd be sitting out here half the night."

The driver smiled, showing perfect, even teeth, starkly white against his dark, scruffy beard. "No problem, I'm happy to be of service. Where can I take you?"

Ellie returned his smile gratefully. "You wouldn't believe it, my car's got a flat tire. Of all the days to get a flat, I have to pick the wettest evening we've had for over a month. Is that bad luck, or what?" She relaxed against the seat, brushing at the errant raindrops that clung to her skirt and jacket.

The driver's smile was slow and thoughtful. "I think we make our own luck, good, bad or indifferent."

"I guess that's one way to look at it." She pushed her handbag onto the floor near her feet, only realizing afterward she still held her phone in her hand.

"So, where are you going?"

"Penrith Police Station. I'm on my way back to work."

The man nodded. "Of course, you're a police officer." He turned away and manoeuvred the cab into the traffic.

Ellie glanced at the clock on the dashboard and dialed Clayton's number. He answered on the second ring.

"Hi. I'm sorry, Ellie. I've been caught in traffic. The rain's a bitch. I'm probably still about fifteen minutes away."

She smiled into the phone. "Don't worry, so am I."

"Really?" His voice held a touch of concern. "You should have been there ages ago."

"Well, that was the plan, but I got a flat tire. It's pelting down out here and the tow-truck's at least an hour away."

She glanced at the driver who was pretending not to listen. "But it's all right. I caught a cab a few minutes ago. I'll probably arrive about the same time you do."

"Okay. Well, I'll see you soon."

"Looking forward to it." She ended the call and kept hold of the phone. She couldn't be bothered hunting around in the dimness of the car for her bag. With a sigh of anticipation, she settled back against the seat.

Lex Wilson couldn't believe it. The girl from the newspaper clipping was in his cab. She looked a little older and her hair was shorter, but he was sure it was her.

Excitement curled in his gut. She looked more like Snow White than Rapunzel, but if he took her, he could finish his creation tonight. He could barely sit still at the thought. It was perfect. *She* was perfect.

She'd even been okay to sit in the front seat. He wasn't a religious man, but even he could tell it was a sign. This was meant to be.

Too bad she was a police officer. He'd known that, of course. The newspapers had been full of it. The irony of the policewoman attending the scene of the accident, only to discover her son was the victim. The pleasure of it had been excruciating. Almost as excruciating as watching the horror on his mother's face when he'd switched on her hairdryer and had tossed it into the bath with her. She'd died with her face frozen in terror. He chuckled at the memory.

But something told him to proceed with caution. Killing police officers was not something he'd do lightly. He'd never once even considered tracking her down to add to his collection. But she'd found *him*. It was karma. It was fate. It was meant to be.

His wife, Michelle, knew about his mother, of course. It was the reason he'd ended up in the orphanage. He'd never known his father and after his mother's untimely accident, the poor little boy who'd discovered her dead in the bath, had been placed in temporary foster care.

His mother's family, the few who had turned up for the funeral, had patted his head and expressed their sympathy, but that was where their charity had ended. There were numerous excuses as to why none of them could possibly take the young boy in. Two weeks after he'd buried his mother, he'd arrived at the Wallsend Home for Orphans.

If he'd thought his life would improve with the death of his mother, he'd thought wrong. He was bullied and teased by the staff and other children, alike. Nothing he did earned praise. He was continuously punished for the slightest indiscretions. To his horror and shame, a few weeks after his arrival at the orphanage, he started wetting the bed again.

Life descended into hell. For six long years, he suffered in silence, vowing one day to get even. The only bright spot in the entire sorry saga was his wife, Michelle.

Right from the start, she'd been his champion. He didn't know what he'd done to deserve her support, but not a night went by that he wasn't grateful for it. If it hadn't been for Michelle, he was certain he would have died, along with the nameless others that were buried in the back garden of the orphanage.

As soon as they were able, they left the place behind them and struck out on their own. At sixteen, life on the streets was hard, but they had each other, and that's all that mattered.

It was his idea to return and end the life of Richard Weston. The dorm master had made it his mission to single Lex out for punishment as often as he could get away with it. The memory of scrubbing filthy urinals with his toothbrush whilst Weston pissed on his head would stay with him forever.

The man deserved to die and Lex had vowed he'd make it happen.

In the end, Weston had died with hardly a whimper. Procuring a handgun from a friend off the street, Lex and Michelle had snuck into the dorm master's suite in the dead of night. Weston had woken with the pistol jammed against his temple. Within seconds, it was done. They'd left as quickly and as silently as they'd come and had never returned.

They'd never spoken of it again, but Lex had never forgotten the indescribable euphoria the moment Weston's heart stopped beating. It had reminded him of his mother's death. It reminded him how much he hated people in authority and how he would never be under the control of anyone again.

As soon as he was able, he changed his name. He wanted to distance himself as far as possible from the nightmare of his childhood. A few months later, he and Michelle were married. It was the happiest day of his life.

In time, their daughters, Anissa and Amy, arrived and his life was complete. He went to work, raised a family and learned to be happy with his new life. But then there had been the accident. And it *had* been an accident. He'd been trying to change the channel on his radio. He'd looked away from the road for just an instant and it had happened. He'd hit the woman and the baby on the pedestrian crossing. He hadn't even had time to brake.

The shock of it had momentarily stunned him and then reaction had set in. He'd pushed his foot down hard on the accelerator and had gotten the hell away from there.

It was only later, when he'd watched it on the news, that he'd discovered the baby had belonged to a police officer. It was then that the pleasure had started. He'd thought of all the times he'd pleaded with the police for help and how every time they'd looked the other way. Every single time.

The joy of inflicting pain on a member of their close-knit fraternity had seeped into his veins, had reinvigorated him as he'd relived the sounds and the sensations of the accident.

He'd shared the moment with Michelle, who had cautioned against taking it any further. But, the feelings persisted.

He tried to control them, ignore them, but they wouldn't be denied. He'd started cautiously, discreetly. A girl here, a girl there. Street girls—nothing girls, with no fixed abode and no family. His hits were sporadic, with no fixed methodology.

Each time, he refined his technique. Sometimes he'd go months between killings. No one suspected a thing. No one even noticed. The tiniest of entries in the middle of the newspaper—and sometimes, not even that.

But slowly, inexorably, the beast inside him demanded more. His conquests increased and the interval between them fell away. He was out of control. It was like his mother and the dorm master and the baby all over again. He'd never been happier.

Now, the sweetest prize of all had fallen into his lap. The most glorious head sat about a foot away from him, totally under his control. He tingled at the thought of handling it.

Well, perhaps not totally. Not yet.

His gaze swept over her as the cab passed a street light. Police officers were always armed. He hadn't seen any evidence of a gun, but that didn't mean she didn't have one tucked away inside the waistband of her skirt.

What to do? He was in a quandary. If he acted on his initial impulse, he could finish his creation tonight. But what if it was a mistake? She certainly looked fitter than the others and being a police officer, she'd probably fight back. Then there was the phone call she'd just made. Somebody knew she was with him.

The only advantage he had was surprise. And the Taser gun he'd ordered off the Internet that lay concealed down the side of his seat. Already, it had been put to good use.

Her head moved and she gazed across the dashboard of the car. In the dimness, her eyes widened and her body stilled.

Lex tensed. Something had changed. He didn't know what, but she had straightened in her seat, her body now alert as she inched toward the passenger door.

Adrenaline surged through his veins. If he was going to go ahead with it, he had to act fast. It was now or never.

Ellie's heart pounded and the blood rushed to her ears, almost drowning out the noise of the rain and the passing traffic.

Lex Wilson. His name was right there on the envelope sitting on the dashboard. A pile of mail. Innocent, innocuous. Addressed to a psychopath.

Shit. She was in his cab. The man Clayton thought responsible for multiple murders. Gruesome murders. Murders she could barely think about now that she sat less than a foot away from him.

Her gaze slid to the mandatory security camera that should have been anchored on the dashboard. It was nowhere to be seen.

She looked at his hands, sure and confident on the wheel. There were stains on his fingers.

A sliver of fear moved within her belly. Her heart did a somersault. It was him. She was sure of it. She inched her breath out between tight lips, frantically trying to come up with a plan while she strove to act normal.

"So, what do you do when you're not driving taxis?"

His teeth glowed whitely in the dull light. "I'm a doll maker."

Her pulse ratcheted up another notch. "Really? Dolls? That sounds interesting."

She plastered a smile on her face while her mind continued to work with furious speed. She had to get out of there.

"It is," he replied easily, his voice betraying his pleasure. "It's my other passion. My wife's always complaining about how much time I spend in the shed with my girls."

The breath caught in her throat. Surreptitiously, she texted Clayton, praying silently that he'd understand.

In taxi. Wilson.000

She glanced down and found the send button. Pressing it, she prayed Wilson hadn't noticed anything amiss.

He looked at her curiously and she searched her memory with frantic haste to pick up the thread of their conversation.

The dolls. His wife. The girls.

She cleared her throat. "You must enjoy it, then. Making the dolls."

He turned to her, his eyes glittering in the light from the streets. "You wouldn't believe."

Oh, God, she was going to be sick. Wrenching her gaze away from his, she turned to stare out the window. They had to be almost at the station. If she was quick, she could bolt out of the car the next time he stopped for traffic lights.

Traffic lights. It suddenly dawned on her she hadn't noticed any for a while. Another glance out the window and she realized they were back in the suburbs. Leafy trees on the nature strip shrouded the soft, yellow glow that came from the windows of distant houses. He must have turned off the highway and she hadn't noticed. She'd been too busy trying to get her head around the fact she was in his car.

Fear tasted sharp and acrid in her mouth. She had to think. And fast. While she still could.

She cursed the fact she was unarmed. And in high heels. Of all the days to let vanity overrule practicality, it had to be today. She'd woken that morning with Clayton in her bed and had wanted to look sexy and feminine and desirable. All the things he'd made her feel while they'd explored each other's bodies in the hours before.

She'd never dreamed when she'd slipped on her three-inch heels that she'd be riding in a taxi with a demented killer.

The traffic had thinned. She cast a furtive glance at him and saw that he was grinning. Fear tightened in her belly.

Slowly, carefully, she undid the clasp of her seatbelt and held it by her side. At the same time, she used her toes to slip off her sandals, preparing herself for flight.

He turned into a driveway. She looked up and saw the white van. Terror constricted her breathing. Screaming, she made a dive for the door.

"Oh no, you don't."

A dark fist flew toward her and connected with the side of her head. She gasped and cried out, her ears ringing from the impact. Her eyes blurred with tears. Frantically trying to work the door open, she caught a movement out of the corner of her eye.

He held a Taser gun inches from her face. Her scream of horror was cut short when pain exploded in her chest.

He'd hit her.

Within seconds, she was immobilized.

Clayton checked the clock on the squad room wall and frowned. Ellie should have been there by now. She'd said she was only fifteen minutes away. They should have arrived together and yet he'd managed to bring Ben up to date and get the ball rolling on the Tactical Response Group who would make the arrest—and still, she hadn't appeared.

The beep of a new text message sounded on his phone. He tugged it out of his pocket and opened the message.

Then he froze.

Fear, hot and choking, clogged his throat. "Luke, Cheryl, Bill, Jacko. Whoever else is around," he rasped.

Heads looked up from desks and peered around partitions at the urgency in his voice.

Luke strode over. "What is it, Clayton? What's wrong?"

Clayton swallowed against the lump of terror in his throat. "It's Ellie. He's got her. The bastard's got her."

Luke blanched. "Jesus Christ, are you sure?"

The question set Clayton's feet in motion. He crossed the length of the squad room with frantic strides, searching for a Kevlar vest and a weapon. Coming up empty, he rounded on Luke.

"Yes, I'm, fucking sure. She just sent me a text. Read it and see for yourself." He shoved the phone into Luke's hand and continued his futile search.

The panic in his voice finally seemed to register. People swarmed around him. He could barely hear over the questions that were hurled from all directions.

"Where the fuck do you keep the gear around here?" he

shouted. "I need a vest and a piece. And I need them *now*."

Luke looked up, his face ashen. "In the cupboard down the back. The boss has the key." He pointed to a steel, two-door upright cabinet. Clayton strode toward it.

"*Ben!* I need to get into this cupboard." He banged on it with his fist. Dread continued to course through him. "And where the fuck is that suspect list? I need the address of Lex Wilson."

Ben appeared in the doorway of his office, his face lined with age and fatigue. "What are you going on about, Clayton? What's happened?"

Clayton rounded on him. "It's Ellie. She's in the fucking cab with him."

Ben raised his arms. "Whoa, slow down. What the hell are you talking about?"

Luke handed Ben the phone. "She needs help, boss," he said quietly.

Ben looked at the text and his face turned grim. "Oh, Christ."

Clayton snatched the phone out of his hand and shoved it into his pocket.

"I need a vest, Ben, and I need a gun. Now open the fucking door before I break it down." He glared at his old friend. Panic and fear surged through him. Ben held his stare, his features implacable.

"I'm not sure you should go with—"

"The hell I'm not." Clayton spat the words at him and pushed his way into the office. "Now, where the fuck are the keys?"

Ben grimly followed him and pulled out a set of keys from the top drawer of his desk. Shooting Clayton another look of concern, he hurried to the cabinet and unlocked it.

Clayton was beside him in an instant. Reaching in, Clayton removed a bulletproof vest and holster and strapped them on.

In silence, Ben took a gun and magazine out of another locked steel box and handed it to him.

Their eyes met.

Clayton nodded his thanks.

Chapter 23

Ellie frantically sucked in what air she could around the tight gag jammed inside her mouth. In desperation, she tried to keep the fear at bay. Her nostrils quivered with the effort. The shock at being tasered gradually subsided and she cautiously turned her head to one side in an effort to orientate herself.

Spying a sink and a chest freezer, her gaze dropped to the floor. It widened as she recognized a pile of pale wood shavings. She was in Lex Wilson's shed. She was sure of it. The smell of paint burned her nostrils.

She lay on the workbench in the middle of the room. Her hands were pinned to her sides and something heavy pressed across her chest, holding her captive. She lifted her head as far as she could and saw that a thick rope had been tied around her middle, the pressure so immense, it felt like she was suffocating.

The tightness of the rope, combined with the impenetrable rag in her mouth nearly severed all contact with oxygen and her desperate lungs fought to breathe.

A shadow fell across her field of vision. Wilson appeared at her side. His eyes held a wild glint of anticipation and a fresh wave of terror washed over her.

"So, Detective Cooper. Welcome to my workshop. How are you feeling?"

How the hell did he know who she was? A shiver of terror arced through her. She twisted her head from side to side, groaning against the gag—her only weapon, the scorching heat of her gaze.

"Now, now, now. That's not the way to greet me. I feel like I've known you for so long. I feel like we've been friends forever."

She stared at him in confusion.

He leaned down close beside her head and caressed her cheek with the back of his hand. "I was going to keep Angelina's head, you know. All that honey-blond hair. I even sawed it off her in anticipation of adding it to my collection. But something held me back. There was something not quite right about it. I decided to wait for something special." His fingers caressed her cheek again. "Something *very* special."

Moaning in horror, she turned her face away.

And saw it.

The wall of newspaper clippings.

The picture of Angelina Caruso's head.

The photo of her jewelry.

The story about Josie Ward, picturing her grieving parents.

Sally Batten's mother, desolate in her huge armchair.

So many others Ellie didn't recognize...

A close-up photo of Jamie's mangled pram.

She gasped and blinked her eyes to clear them, certain she'd got it wrong, but the article was still there. The one that showed her being held back by a paramedic, her face bleak with agony and despair.

Oh, God, it was him. He was the one who'd killed Jamie.

Bile rose in her throat, threatening to choke her. She coughed and gasped and tried to dislodge the revulsion that blocked her airways. Her head spun and lights sparkled behind her closed eyelids. She was suffocating.

And then she was exploding with pain.

Lex's fist connected with her rib cage, snapping bone beneath his knuckles.

"Breathe, Detective. I don't want you dying too early and missing out on all the fun."

Despite the agony, she struggled against the ropes that bound her, knowing her time was running out. A knife appeared in Lex's hand, the blade glinting in the light. He moved closer and cold steel pressed against her neck.

She gasped in ice-cold fear. White-hot heat seared her neck and blood trickled down the side of her throat. Shivering with panic, she tried not to choke on the rag in her mouth. He grabbed hold of her head and ran the knife lightly across her throat, from one side to the other.

"I guess I could do it right now. Make it quick and easy, like I was with the others. But then, they weren't quite as special as you."

There was a wildness in his eyes that drove terror straight through her heart. Fear got the better of her and she felt her bladder give way.

"Fuck! You pissed on my table! You fucking pissed on my table!"

This time, his fist connected with her stomach. Pain crashed through her, setting her nerve endings on fire.

"You're going to fucking pay for that, bitch."

The door to the shed opened. Relief poured through her. Wilson looked up in surprise.

Clayton!

No, not him. Someone else.

A moment later, her captor sighed in pleasure and a wide grin stretched across his bearded face.

"Michelle, my sweet. What a lovely surprise. I've often wondered if you missed it as much as I did."

The woman Ellie had spoken to earlier—spoken to and had entirely discounted—appeared in front of Ellie, a frown of concern marring her face.

As if oblivious to her unease, Wilson smiled at his wife. "I've saved the best till last, my sweet wife. Isn't she the most magnificent creation you've ever seen?"

He indicated Ellie on the workbench and Michelle stepped closer. Her eyes widened in recognition, replaced quickly by fear.

"Lex! How could you? This one's with the police. Why did you have to bring her home?"

He shrugged. "I know, my sweet, but what was I to do?

She climbed into my car, right when I needed her." He shrugged again. "What was I to do?"

Michelle didn't look convinced and Ellie prayed fervently with what little strength she had left that the woman would intervene.

"It's too risky, Lex. You need to let her go. She was here earlier, asking about you. Someone will know she was here. They will come looking."

Wilson appeared to weigh up the wisdom of her words. Ellie held her breath, desperate for anything that would delay the inevitable. At last, Lex let out a sigh and nodded.

"You're right. It's too risky. But I can't just let her go. She knows too much." He looked around the shed. "She's seen too much."

"Please Lex, let her go. Think of me. Think of our girls. You need to stop."

"Yes, you're right. Of course, you're right. I'll take her to the theme park. No one will think to look for her there."

Ellie frowned, her mind in a turmoil. *The theme park?* What were they talking about?"

Michelle's shoulders slumped on a loud sigh. "This is it, Lex. This is the last time. It must stop." Her gaze burned with determination. "We'll go and see someone—a doctor—someone who can help you."

Ellie held her breath. Lex moved closer to his wife. He wrapped his arms around her and pulled her close. "Okay," he whispered. "It's over. I promise. Just as soon as I get rid of this one. It's for the best. For everyone."

Michelle nodded, her expression one of sad resignation. "All right. Go, but hurry home. I'll stay here, in case the police come calling. Can you handle her on your own?"

"Of course."

"What are you going to do with her?"

"I only want her head. After that, I will get rid of her."

Michelle gave a short nod of agreement. "So be it."

The woman turned and left the shed as silently as she'd entered. Working quickly now, Lex loosened the rope that held Ellie bound to the workbench and eased her into a sitting position. Her arms remained tied behind her back.

Lex pulled the Taser gun out of his pocket and pressed it against her heart.

"We're going for another ride. One false move and I'll shoot you. At this close range, there's no guarantee you'll survive. Do you understand?"

Ellie drew in a breath to speak and choked on the filthy rag. Giving up the effort to communicate verbally, she nodded.

Lex's eyes glittered in anticipation. "You're going to love where I'm taking you. It's so much better this way. What better way to celebrate my finest achievement than from the top of the old rollercoaster?"

Clayton checked the magazine of his gun for the third time and drew in a deep breath in an effort to steady his trembling fingers. He knew Ben's concern about his involvement in the search for Ellie was well founded and he would have probably reacted the same way. But he couldn't sit at the station waiting, wondering what was happening while the woman he loved was in the hands of a psychopathic murderer.

Not a sound could be heard from inside the shed that sat non-threateningly in the darkness that surrounded Wilson's backyard. They only had Ellie's ambiguous text to point them in this direction, but everyone at the station, including Clayton, agreed it was the place the made the most sense.

Wilson needed a place to take his victims. The other girls had been butchered someplace other than the location where they'd been found. It had always been Clayton's premise that the killer they hunted had a house of his own.

He caught the eye of Harry Turner, the head of their hastily assembled TRG squad. A single nod. It was time.

In silence, the other squad members took their positions. Clayton watched while Harry counted them down. Moments later, the yard was filled with noise.

"Go! Go! Go!"

The door to the shed burst open and the room was filled with TRG officers, shouting and yelling and pointing guns. Clayton's gaze zeroed in on the workbench in the middle of the room. Apart from a rope as thick as his arm, the table was empty.

Moving closer, he smelled the acrid odor of urine mixed with the smell of paint fumes. A wet patch marked the wooden bench. Small, dark stains that looked suspiciously like blood also marred the surface.

He looked around, spotting three chest freezers and various tools that had been left out on the bench that ran along the opposite side of the shed. A tin of pink paint sat amongst a pile of wood shavings.

They'd found him. But where was Ellie?

With a feeling of foreboding, Clayton strode over to one of the freezers. Gritting his teeth, he lifted the lid.

"Holy fuck!" The expletive was muttered by Turner, his tone thick with shock and disbelief as he peered around Clayton at the contents of the freezer. "Are they...?" His voice faded off.

Clayton stared at what he presumed were the legs of Sally Batten and nodded grimly. "I'm afraid so."

Wishing he could find relief in the fact that they'd at last identified their killer, Clayton turned away from the sad display before him. Ellie was missing. As far as he knew, she was with the monster who took pleasure carving up women while they were still alive.

Fear cramped his belly. He glanced over at Turner and saw the newspaper clippings.

The blood drained from his face.

Ellie stared out the window of the taxi and prayed for a miracle. Hopes of Clayton finding her were fading fast. She'd prayed that he'd decode the text she'd sent him and head over to Wilson's house, but now that they'd left the property, she knew he'd never locate her in time.

There was no way he'd even think to look for her at the derelict theme park that used to house Australia's Wonderland. Not being from Sydney, he probably wasn't even aware it existed.

The park had been closed for years. It had been inhabited by homeless wanderers from time to time and went through cycles of being a hangout for drug dealers, but by and large, it was considered abandoned and would never find its way onto most peoples' radar.

Moving slightly on the seat, Ellie struggled to find a more comfortable position. Her arms were still bound, but Wilson had retied them in front of her, explaining that he would need her to help him by pulling herself up into the carriage of the roller coaster.

"You can see for miles up there," he'd smiled. "It's the best view in Sydney. What better way to complete my creation?"

She'd shuddered at the madness that gleamed in his eyes and had turned away from him, refusing to allow him the satisfaction of seeing the desolation and despair that threatened to overwhelm her.

She shifted her weight again and frowned at the lump beneath her bottom. Working her hands closer toward the offending object, she realized her phone was still in the pocket of her jacket.

Her heart clenched with elation and was immediately followed by disappointment. She couldn't possibly get it out and use it with her hands bound the way they were... *Or could she?*

Her life was at stake. She refused to give up without a fight. She snuck a glance at Wilson. His attention was fixed on the road in front of him. He hummed a tune she didn't recognize. A slight smile played around his lips. He appeared lost in his thoughts, like he didn't have a care in the world.

She inched her hands in the direction of her jacket pocket and walked her fingers beneath her until she finally came into contact with her phone. Her heart skipped a beat. As carefully as she could, she grasped the phone between two fingers and pulled, praying desperately that her grip would hold. Inch by inch, the phone moved toward her hand. At last, she'd tugged it far enough out of her pocket that her fingers could close around it.

She wanted to collapse in relief, but retrieving the phone was only half the battle.

Peeking at Wilson from beneath her lashes, Ellie was confident his attention still remained elsewhere. With the phone now grasped firmly in her right hand, she brought it to her lap and glanced down. As quickly as she could, she opened a new message screen and typed a one-word message to Clayton.

Clayton dragged his hand through his hair for the umpteenth time and clamped his jaw shut on another curse. The officers around him gave him a wide berth, their faces reflecting his frustration and fear.

Lex Wilson had only one known place of abode. A computer search under his wife's name had come up with nothing. After examining every inch of the backyard shed, Clayton and the TRG members had pounded on the door that led to the house, demanding entry.

A confused and half-asleep woman had met them at the door. After identifying herself as Michelle Wilson, she'd denied any knowledge of her husband's whereabouts, claiming that the last time she'd seen him had been earlier in the afternoon, right before he'd left for work.

After searching the premises and finding nothing but a couple of sleeping children, the men had reluctantly withdrawn and by tacit agreement had headed back to the station to regroup.

Clayton clenched his fists in an effort to stop himself from driving one of them through the nearest wall. He needed to hit something, anything. Hard. Not knowing Ellie's whereabouts was driving him beyond the point of reason. He'd lost count of the number of times he'd stared at his phone, willing it to conjure some form of contact from her, but it had remained agonizingly silent. If it hadn't been for Ben's cautioning frown, he'd probably have lost all control.

He'd never felt so scared and helpless in all of his life. Ellie was out there somewhere with a madman and he didn't have a clue how to find her. The beep of his phone inside his shirt pocket sent his pulse skyrocketing. He fumbled in his haste to drag it out of his pocket. He glanced at the screen and his heart went into overdrive. It was a text from Ellie.

1derlnd.

Frustration surged through him. What the fuck did that mean?

"Ben!" Clayton covered the distance to Ben's office in four large strides. "Ben!"

Ben stepped out through the doorway, his face lined with fatigue. "What is it, Clayton?"

"Ellie's sent me another text."

"Oh, thank God! That means she's still alive. What did she say?"

"That's just it," Clayton growled. "It doesn't make sense." He showed the phone to Ben.

Ben looked at the screen and frowned. "Onedrlnd?"

Luke strode up. "What's happened?"

"Clayton received a text from Ellie."

"Oh, thank Christ," Luke breathed. "Let's hope it's truly from her."

"Yeah, well, she could have been a little less cryptic," Clayton said.

"What did she say?" Luke asked.

"Look, the number one dr lnd," Clayton replied.

"That's it?"

"Yeah."

Luke fell silent. A few moments later, he clicked his fingers, excitement exploding across his face. "I've got it! It's text for Wonderland, Australia's Wonderland! The theme park at Mt Druitt."

"What theme park?" Clayton asked, impatience sharpening his words.

"It was huge when I was a teenager. We used to love going there on the weekend. It was Sydney's answer to Dreamworld on the Gold Coast. Unfortunately, the owners couldn't make it pay." He shrugged. "It's been closed for nearly a decade."

"So what's there now?" Clayton asked.

"I don't know. Most of it was demolished, but I think the old roller coaster's still there."

"We get calls every now and then from people complaining of unsavory types hanging around there," Ben added. "The place is surrounded by an eight-foot fence, but you know how it is, there are ways and means."

"Is it possible Wilson could have taken Ellie there?" Though it wasn't easy, Clayton curbed his instinctive urge to jump into the nearest squad car and hightail it to the theme park. He waited.

Ben frowned in thought and then nodded. "It's possible, especially if he's been there before. He may have cut a hole in the fence. There's no security monitoring it, so breaking in is relatively easy if you have access to wire cutters."

Clayton's heart rate picked up its pace. "How far away is it?"

"About twenty minutes or so," Luke supplied. "Less if we use the sirens."

Adrenaline poured through Clayton's veins. He stared at Ben and waited for the man's approval.

"Let's do it."

Clayton spun on his heel and strode back into the squad room. Ben called to the men who lounged against various pieces of furniture and quickly brought them up to speed. The air filled with electric anticipation as officers readied for the task ahead.

Clayton checked the weapon he'd been issued and collected his Kevlar vest. With his heart hammering, his thoughts turned to Ellie. He sent a silent prayer heavenward that they weren't too late.

———————————

Lex brought the taxi to a stop outside the high wire fence that surrounded the old theme park and ordered Ellie from the car. Eyeing the Taser gun balefully, she did the best she could to exit the car without falling. The bindings cut into her wrists and she'd long since lost feeling in her fingers.

There had been a moment when Wilson had pulled into a gas station. Hope had flared in her heart. She'd thought frantically of a way to escape, or at the very least, to attract someone's attention.

But the place was deserted and Wilson had parked as far away from the console operator's window as possible. He'd locked the car on his exit and paid for his gas with a credit card at the pump. The whole episode took less than five minutes. The disappointment of not making good her escape had almost suffocated her when Wilson climbed back into the driver's seat and continued on their way.

She thought about Clayton and the text she'd sent him and hoped desperately that he understood. Otherwise, there was no way anyone would find her. He was her only hope.

With a large flashlight in one hand and the Taser gun in the other, held close to her side, Lex nudged her forward. Barefooted, Ellie stumbled on a sharp rock that bit into the soft skin of her foot. She cried out and almost fell.

"Keep moving!" Lex shouted and prodded her forward. Drawing in a quick breath, Ellie's ribs burned in protest. She bit down on a gasp of pain and continued on until the dark shadow of the old roller coaster loomed ahead of her. Like the vertebrae of a forgotten dinosaur, it was silhouetted against the night.

As they moved closer, Ellie made out a few of the individual carts that used to run on the roller coaster track. She remembered coming to the theme park with her parents when she was a kid. She'd beg them to allow her to ride on the roller coaster, but they'd always turned away, telling her it was too dangerous. The machinery had been old, even back then.

"Get in," Lex ordered, indicating the cart with a thrust of his head.

The flashlight played over the rusted metal. Cobwebs clung to its crevices. Ellie shuddered at the thought of climbing into it. The park had been closed for years. She couldn't believe the roller coaster could still be working.

"It's perfectly fine," Lex explained, sensing her reticence. "I was here only a few months ago. Wait until you see the view. Your final moments looking out on one of the most spectacular sights of Sydney. It doesn't get any better than that." He chuckled in genuine amusement.

Ellie shuddered, refusing to even contemplate it. In an effort to distract him, she questioned him about the ancient ride.

"H-how do you make it go?" she asked, knowing the electricity to the Park would have been disconnected when it closed.

"By gas-powered generator. I brought one out here a couple of years ago. It goes like a dream. With no one around for miles, it's the perfect place to come and reflect on my handiwork."

Lex prodded her again with the Taser gun. "Now, get in. We're wasting time. I've waited so long for the perfect end to my creation. Now that I have you, I'm getting impatient. The sooner we get to the top, the sooner I can end this."

Casting around in the darkness, Ellie searched frantically for a sign that Clayton was on his way. The only illumination came from the distant glow of street lights. For a moment, she thought she heard the sound of sirens, but a few seconds later, she realized she'd imagined it. The night was still and quiet.

Her heart sank. Fear renewed its grip on her mind. Lex pushed her hard from behind and she fell into the cart with a cry. Unable to use her hands to cushion her fall, she collapsed awkwardly against the hard, rusted metal. Pain shot through her hip and radiated along her spine. Her ribs and belly were engulfed in fire. She couldn't move.

"Move over," Wilson shouted. "There's hardly enough room as it is."

Tears of pain rolled down Ellie's cheeks. "I-I can't," she gasped. "It-it hurts."

"It's gonna hurt a hell of a lot more when I start with the saw." He shoved her hard with his shoulder. She gasped from the agony the movement caused. "Now, get over."

Moments later, the sound of a motor started and Wilson scrambled in behind her. The flashlight glinted off something metallic in his hand. When Ellie realized it was a hacksaw, her blood iced over.

Biting her lip against the panic that threatened to overwhelm her, she closed her eyes against the nightmare unraveling before her and prayed for the end to be quick.

Clayton broke every record known to man in his haste to get to the theme park. A couple of miles from the park, he ordered everyone to cut their sirens and lights. No use giving the bastard a heads-up that they were onto him.

Seven minutes after he left the police station, he brought the police vehicle to a sliding stop outside a high chain fence. Followed closely by Luke, he leaped out of the car, a pair of heavy wire cutters in his hand.

Within seconds, he'd cut a hole large enough to allow entry. Shouldering his way through, Clayton paused only long enough to take directions from Luke before forging onward into the dark shadows that apparently housed the roller coaster.

Tugging his revolver out of the holster, Clayton eased off the safety and crept forward on silent feet. The sudden sputter of an engine nearby startled him. He spun on his heel in the direction of the sound. Luke came to halt behind him, swearing under his breath.

"What the hell is that?" Clayton's whisper was harsh in the stillness.

"I don't know. Sounds like some kind of motor."

"It's coming from over there." Clayton indicated with his chin, hoping Luke could see him in the dimness.

"That's where the roller coaster is."

Blood pulsed heavily in Clayton's veins. Dread tightened his gut. Was Ellie even now at the roller coaster, at the mercy of a madman? Signaling to Luke, he started in the direction of the noise, the other officer close on his heels.

The cart made its slow ascent along the steep steel rail, squealing raucously in protest. Ellie clung to the side with her fingernails, even as the bindings around her wrists cut into her flesh. The cart rattled and swayed alarmingly, sending renewed shivers of fear coursing down her spine.

Behind her, Wilson cackled in glee, shouting above the sound of the generator about the wonderful evening and the magnificent view of the city lights, far in the distance.

When the cart reached the top, he fiddled with some kind of contraption on the side of it and brought it to a stop. Ellie was grateful the inky dullness of the night camouflaged the full extent of their position, high above the ground.

A flimsy, wooden maintenance platform hung precariously at the top of the rollercoaster. Wilson yelled at her above the noise of the motor and prodded her once again with the Taser.

"Get out."

With no choice but to do as she was told, Ellie stumbled awkwardly and half fell onto the platform. It creaked and swayed and she cried out in terror. The madman behind her laughed.

Joining her on the platform, he spread his arms wide.

"Does it get any better than this?"

Ellie shuddered and willed herself not to look down.

Wilson stepped closer and slid the back of his hand down her cheek in a slow caress. "I waited and waited for something special. I was always taught patience is a virtue."

Ellie tensed. Her heart thudded inside her chest. Fear, more terrifying than anything she'd felt before, paralyzed her, leaving her powerless to do anything but stare at her tormenter in horror. He turned away and moments later, swung around to face her, brandishing the hacksaw.

Sheer desperation and a realization she no longer had anything to lose, took over. Adrenaline surged through her. Despite the agony in her chest, she thrashed around in a frenzy of motion, using her bound hands to attack him.

With the gag still tightly ensconced in her mouth, she snatched tiny breaths of air through the filthy rag, throwing her head from side to side while she battled to get away. Her moans of distress and terror were little more than faint mewlings through the thick cloth, but she refused to give in.

"Easy now, easy," Wilson crooned, his hand grappling with a rope that he'd produced from his belt. "Don't fight me. It is what it is. From the moment you climbed into my cab, there was never any doubt. You're mine."

He inched closer, the rope hanging loosely from his fingers, the hacksaw discarded on the platform—for the time being.

Fear, dark and impenetrable filled Ellie's mouth. She retched and fought and tried to scream.

He flung the rope around her and pulled it taut, almost knocking her off her feet. She screamed again, the sound barely registering as the terror she'd tried so hard to hold at bay almost overwhelmed her.

With quick and efficient movements that spoke of previous experience, he secured the rope to the platform. Within moments, she was once again immobilized. Standing above her, he brandished the hacksaw, grinning maniacally. She flung her head from side to side in increasing desperation. Despite her efforts, the saw tasted her skin. She could do no more than whimper.

———

Clayton came to a halt at the foot of the roller coaster and watched in helpless fury as the cart containing Ellie and the man who sought to kill her, rattled its way to the top. Slipping the safety on his revolver, he thrust the weapon back into the holster and paced the ground while he took a few seconds to assess the situation.

Fear surged through him at the thought of climbing so high. His breath shortened, tightening his chest. He sucked air deep into his lungs in an effort to overcome his panic. Terror for the woman he loved congealed into a cold, dark mass of determination. There was nothing for it: He had to make the ascent.

Drawing in a couple more gulps of oxygen, he pushed his own fears aside, knowing he had to go up there after her, despite his own weaknesses. If Ellie died, he'd never forgive himself. He'd lived with that kind of guilt for too long. He refused to make the same mistake again. Steeling himself against his panic, he glanced at Luke who watched him with concern.

"Are you all right, Clayton?"

With his lips compressed into a rigid line and unable to form words if his life depended upon it, he gave Luke a tight nod and lifted his foot onto the first step. He would conquer his fear of heights—or he would die trying.

"What the hell are you doing? You can't go up there without a harness. You don't even know if it'll hold your weight. If it gives, you're good as dead! Wait for some of the others to arrive. They'll—"

"No." It was all Clayton could manage, but he tried to convey all that he felt as his gaze burned into Luke's. Ignoring the sputtering of protests that erupted from the other officer's lips, Clayton leaped into the next cart. It rattled and banged as it made the ascent and he clung with fierce determination to the old steel sides.

Keeping his gaze directed steadfastly on the couple above him, he was thankful the night made it impossible for him to fully register how high he was above the ground. It also meant it was unlikely Wilson had seen him and he was hopeful the noise from the generator below him would conceal the rattling of his cart.

The cart ahead of him came to a halt. He looked up as Ellie fell onto a rickety platform. He caught the glint of metal off the teeth of a saw and his heart iced in fear.

The distance between them yawned in front of him and he chafed at every second it took to close the gap. He reached for the gun in his holster and swung it in Wilson's direction.

"Drop your weapon," he shouted. "Step away from her! Now!"

Wilson stood and faced him, his eyes wide with surprise. The saw swung wildly in his hand. "Fuck off. She's mine." Turning back to Ellie, he lifted the saw and lowered it over her neck.

Clayton squeezed the trigger and fired.

EPILOGUE

Ellie's bruises had finally started to fade. From greenish-blue to purple and then to mustardy-yellow, they'd covered half the colors of the rainbow. The gash where the knife had sliced across her neck had scabbed over, but the doctors had warned her she would bear a scar.

Her back rested against the smooth trunk of an ancient fig tree in the middle of Sydney's Hyde Park. Clayton's head rested in her lap. She moved her position slightly in an effort to lessen the dull throb in her chest. The broken ribs were still healing. She was glad that was the only damage.

Drawing in a deep breath of the warm spring sunshine, heavily perfumed with an abundance of flowers, she stroked a hand over Clayton's stubbled cheeks.

"Mm, that feels nice," he murmured, his eyes remaining closed.

Her fingers moved into his hair and massaged gently over his scalp.

"Ah, I feel like I've died and gone to heaven. Don't stop, please." A grin tugged at his lips and she found her lips pulling upward in response.

"You're a man easily pleased, Munro."

His eyes opened, and he squinted up at her through the dappled sunlight. "A psychopathic murderer dead and buried. A day off to have a picnic in the park with a beautiful woman; what's not to like about that?"

She shuddered at the mention of Lex Wilson. Clayton's eyes darkened with concern.

"I'm sorry, sweetheart. I shouldn't have mentioned him."

Ellie bit her lip to keep it from wobbling and drew in a deep breath. "I can't believe he'd killed for so long. When he started talking about all those poor women he'd murdered over the past three years. He actually laughed when he told us he only chose the ones no one loved."

Clayton nodded in grim agreement. "I still can't get over how he went from making wooden dolls to creating a doll from human body parts. I mean, what kind of sick bastard does that?"

"He did have a tough childhood."

"Lots of people have tough childhoods. It doesn't turn them into homicidal maniacs."

She thought of Wilson's wife and young children. Though Ellie harbored some doubts the woman was as shocked by the discovery of her husband's actions as she'd claimed, there was simply not enough evidence to charge her as an accessory.

It was the children Ellie felt sorry for. She couldn't imagine the devastation Wilson's secret life would wreak on their lives. Still, there was nothing she could do about it. Besides, she was having enough trouble getting her head sorted.

Ellie shuddered. She was lucky to be alive. She knew that. Wilson was dead. The city was safe. *She* was safe.

As if sensing her fragility, Clayton sat up and shuffled across the picnic rug until he was close to her side. A strong arm came around her and pulled her to his chest.

She sighed. "I'm okay. It's just that...sometimes I can't bear to think about it... And Jamie..."

Clayton shook his head. "I still can't believe the bastard was the hit and run driver who killed him. It seems absolutely incredible, and yet the proof was there. We'll never know why."

"That's part of the reason I'm still not sleeping well. I'll never have those answers. Did he *mean* to kill my son? *Was* it an accident?"

Clayton hugged her tightly. "Give it time. It's only been a few weeks. And you came so close. I can't imagine how terrified you must have been. People take months, years even, to get over that kind of trauma."

Remembered fear weighed down her limbs. "I'm so glad you got there in time," she whispered.

The look in his eyes intensified. He pulled her in hard against him. "I thought I was going to lose you. The terror I felt when I got your message—my entire world came crashing down around me. I'd only just found you. I'd only just given myself permission to love again and you were snatched from me. It was happening all over again." His voice broke.

His hold on her tightened, his expression fierce. A few moments later, he drew in a deep breath and released it on a shudder. "I can barely remember what went on that night. I know I practically forced Ben to give me a gun. And when I had to go up in that damned cart, I thought *I* was going to die. But fear of heights or not, there was no way in the world I was going to sit back and let someone else do their best to save you. It mightn't have been good enough."

Ellie's voice was muffled against the soft cotton of his T-shirt. "You couldn't save Lisa, so you wanted to save me."

Another shudder went through him. It was a long moment before he responded. "I lied to you, Ellie."

Apprehension knotted in her stomach. She tried to pull away, but he wouldn't let her. He drew in a deep breath and let it out on a sad sigh.

"What is it, Clayton?"

He met her gaze. "You asked me once if I'd ever buried a child and I told you no. But the truth is, I have."

She stared at him, confused. "Why would you lie about it?"

He shrugged, his eyes willing her to understand. "You were upset with me about Jamie. I didn't want to trivialize his death with my own story."

"What happened?" she asked softly.

Clayton stared off across the park, his gaze clouded with

memories. Ellie found his hand and squeezed it, reassured when he returned the pressure.

"Dominic was the reason Lisa and I were married. Not that we weren't going to anyway, but we'd always planned to do it after we'd finished college, put some money behind us first, that sort of thing."

His gaze bounced off hers. "Lisa went into labor early. He was born premature. Way too premature." Another ragged breath. Ellie tightened her hold and remained silent.

Pain etched itself on his face. "He only lived two days."

Her stomach clenched. She felt his quiet sadness and then she felt her guilt. She'd accused him of not knowing what it meant to bury a child. She'd felt so self-righteous in her grief, as if her grief meant more than his. She'd been a selfish, self-centered bitch.

And he hadn't said a word.

"Clayton." She rasped his name. A lump of self-loathing lodged itself in her throat. "How you must have hated me."

Surprise flooded his face. "Hated you? Why would I hate you?"

She shrugged helplessly. "The things I said to you, accused you of. You never once defended yourself. I was such a bitch. I can't believe how selfish and conceited and *awful* I was. And you didn't say anything."

"I wasn't trying to score points with you, Ellie. You were hurting as much as I was. None of us can really know how someone else grieves." He leaned over to brush a loose strand of hair off her face, his touch tender and full of love. "All we can hope is to understand at least a part of their need to do it in their own way, and in their own time. And make sure they know that we'll be there waiting for them when it's over."

The breath left her body in a rush. She threw her arms around him. "What did I ever do to deserve you?" she whispered. "I love you so much."

He kissed her softly, mindful of her injuries. "I love you, too, Ellie. More than I ever dreamed possible. I can't wait for you to move in with me and start our life together."

310

Ellie pulled back as uncertainty filled her. "You want me to move to Canberra?"

He nodded, his eyes shadowed with hope. "Would you do that?"

Emotions overwhelmed her. There was a little sadness at the thought of leaving Sydney, but mostly joy at the thought of sharing a new life with Clayton. Noticing the increasing tension around his mouth, she offered him an encouraging smile. "Are you sure you want that right away? What about Olivia? What is she going to say?"

Clayton's face lit up. "I think she'll be happy that her daddy is happy. It's been a long time since she's seen me smile. *Really* smile."

"I hope she likes me."

Clayton pulled her close and pressed another kiss on her lips. "She'll love you as much as I do. There's nothing surer."

NOTE TO READERS

I do hope you have enjoyed reading about the first hunky Munro brother as much as I have enjoyed creating him. Clayton's story came to me after listening to a song by Diamond Rio called "I Believe". It's a beautiful song about love and loss and hope and it is all that I dreamed Clayton to be.

Of course, he needed Ellie to bring him through the pain of his loss and to see life was still worth living. Ellie, sharp, cantankerous, but with a heart of gold, hiding her own pain behind a wall of sarcasm and irritability. I love Ellie, with all her faults and failings. I love what she does for Clayton and I love what he does for her. They complement each other and that's what true love is all about.

In Book Two of the Munro Family Series, you will meet another Munro brother. **The Investigator** is Riley Munro's story and he's every bit as gorgeous as his twin. Here's a sneak peek:

A woman who thought she could run away from her past...

At fourteen, Kate Collins ran away from home. Ten years later, her mother has disappeared without a trace. Faced with no other choice, she returns home. Kate's convinced her stepfather's responsible, but he's a highly decorated police officer. Who will take her accusations seriously?

Banished to a small country town after reporting his city superiors for corruption, Detective Riley Munro is never going to accuse the town's recently retired Police Commander of murder. But Kate's fear and distress seem genuine and her mother does seem to have disappeared. With reluctance, he agrees to investigate.

After making rudimentary enquires, he's told Kate's mother is on a cruise. The information pans out. On the verge of closing the case, Riley is taken by surprise when he receives a subtle threat from his boss, the new Police Commander, to leave Kate's stepfather alone.

Why would the new Commander feel the need to warn him off? With his instincts on alert, Riley digs deeper and discovers not only is Kate's mother in a wheelchair, she also hates the water.

Is Kate telling the truth? Is her stepfather, the former Police Commander, guilty of murder? Or is Riley allowing the sad vulnerability in Kate's beautiful eyes to cloud his judgement?

The Investigator will be available in April, 2014. If you would like to receive news on upcoming Munro Family stories, release dates, book launches and other snippets, please feel free to subscribe to my newsletter at www.christaylorauthor.com.au. I love to hear from my readers. You can contact me at christaylor@antmail.com.au Let me know who your favorite Munro family member is.

THE MUNRO FAMILY SERIES

THE PROFILER
(Book One—Clayton and Ellie)

THE INVESTIGATOR
(Book Two—Riley and Kate)

THE PREDATOR
(Book Three—Brandon and Alex)

THE BETRAYAL
(Book Four—Declan and Chloe)

THE DECEPTION
(Book Five—Will and Savannah)

THE NEGOTIATOR
(Book Six—Andy and Cally)

THE RANSOM
(Book Seven—Lane and Zara)

THE DEFENDANT
(Book Eight—Chase and Josie)

THE SHOOTING
(Book Nine—Tom and Lily)

THE SCANDAL
(Book Ten—Bryce and Chanel

About The Author

Chris Taylor grew up on a farm in north-west New South Wales, Australia. She always had a thirst for stories and recalls writing her first book at the ripe old age of eight. Always a lover of romance and happily-ever-afters, a career in criminal law sparked her interest in intrigue and suspense. For Chris to be able to combine romance with suspense in her books is a dream come true.

Chris is married to Linden and is the mother of five children. If not behind her computer, you can find her doing the school run, taxiing children to swimming lessons, football, ballet and cricket. In her spare time, Chris loves to read her favorite authors who include Richard North Patterson, Sandra Brown, Kathleen E Woodiwiss and Jude Devereaux.